BOURBON RUNAWAY

A Bourbon Canyon Novel

WALKER ROSE

LE Publishing

Copyright © 2024 by Walker Rose

Editing by Razor Sharp Editing

Proofreading by Fairy Proofmother Proofreading, Deaton Author Services, and Judy's Proofreading

Cover art by Okay Creations

All rights reserved.

No part of this book may be reproduced in any form or by any electronic or mechanical means, including information storage and retrieval systems, without written permission from the author, except for the use of brief quotations in a book review.

The characters, places, and events in this story are fictional. Any similarities to real people, places, or events are coincidental and unintentional.

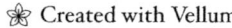 Created with Vellum

I've been a recluse since the accident, but there was a wedding I refused to miss. I just never expected to come home with the bride.

Now, I have a runaway bride in my Montana cabin who needs time to lick her wounds. Summer Kerrigan is as bright as her name, even on her worst of days. Too bad she's been off-limits since she dated my brother in high school. It doesn't matter that fifteen years have passed since we lost him. She was his. She'll never be mine.

When she goes back down the mountain, I can't forget her.

Turns out I don't have to.

When she surprises me with another visit just before a blizzard snows us in together, staying away from her becomes impossible. It's tempting to let her all the way in, except every time she's come into my life, the bourbon empire heiress has left again to return to her own. One I'm not a part of. One I can never be a part of. Unless this damaged mountain man can find a way to keep up with his pretty bourbon runaway.

CHAPTER ONE

Summer

Today was a beautiful day to get married, but I willed the clock to slow down.

"Look at it all come together." My youngest sister, Wynter, leaned over me, fluffing my veil in the mirror. Her blond hair was curled into ringlets and bound back so the corkscrew strands could cascade down her back. The silver dress she wore washed her skin out, making her light tan pale. I should've insisted on letting my sisters choose their own color.

She spread the sides of my veil out. With the light over our heads in the church room I was holed up in with my attendants, the fabric gave me a halo.

Wynter feathered her fingers over the lace at my shoulders. "Such lovely material."

She'd been making comments all day. About the nice church that Boyd and his family had chosen. The nice dress. The nice vacation in Bali.

Everything was so *nice*.

A bride wanted more than nice for her wedding day.

A bride wanted more than her sisters trying to make it seem like everything was okay.

My stomach roiled and I pressed my fingers to my lips.

"Oh my god," Wynter whispered. Her wide gaze darted to Junie, our more worldly and second-youngest sister, as if Autumn wouldn't understand what she was worried about. Autumn wasn't as naive as everyone thought.

I rolled my eyes. "God, no, Wynter. I'm not pregnant."

Fear speared right through my heart at the thought. Shouldn't that be disappointment? I was in my mid-thirties, and I was finally getting married. I wanted a family, yet the thought of getting pregnant now left me almost as sick as the idea of loading into a tin can with wings afterward.

A goddamn plane. Boyd knew how I felt about flying.

Yet he'd surprised me with the tickets to Bali like my claustrophobic ass should jump up and down. Tomorrow morning, I'd be sitting in first class, as if that made it better to be stuck in a coffin with a hundred other people. My chest squeezed and tears pricked the backs of my eyes.

I blinked rapidly and smeared my mascara. "Shit."

"Let me get a wipe." Autumn jumped off the stool. Her dress swished, not at all the summer dress I'd pictured when I'd fantasized about a wedding as a kid.

Her red hair was done similarly to Wynter. A nice, elegant style. To keep the tears at bay, I glanced around the room in the mirror. Plush couches. Gallery-worthy artwork. Crown molding. This wasn't the church I'd grown up in, the one I'd thought I'd be married in, but the room was nice.

So. Nice.

"Got it!" Autumn brandished a makeup wipe like it'd solve all my problems.

Wynter stopped her by putting a hand in front of my face. "That'll take all the foundation off."

"Oh, right." Autumn narrowed her eyes on me and contemplated the issue with Wynter.

Junie stood and joined them, her doe-brown eyes contemplative. The three stood in a half circle in front of me, focused on goddamn makeup like it was their lifeline. Anything to ignore how melancholy I'd been today.

"It's fine." I held my hand out for the wipe. "I don't care if the dark bags show through."

The three blinked at me. More tears threatened to well. My hand shook.

"Summer," Wynter said quietly. "Whatever you want to do, we've got your back."

She wasn't talking about the makeup. Hope surged inside me but I tamped it down. What was I thinking? Boyd was a good man. A nice guy.

Nice. Fuck me. Which he also did, in his methodical, predictable way.

He also bulldozed over me at the most inconvenient times. Like with this wedding. "He was so excited about getting married after being at your wedding, Wynter," I said in a near whisper. I'd been enchanted too. Wynter and my new brother-in-law, Myles, had radiated happiness on their big day. They were meant to be together, and I'd wanted that for myself. So when Boyd had proposed the day after—so as not to impose on the happy couple's special day, and that was considerate, dammit—I had thought it was an indication of what I should do.

Like Mama sometimes said, "Piss or get off the pot."

When I'd said yes, I'd ignored the small voice in my head chiding me about how a sudden wedding wasn't what I wanted. Boyd had said four months was plenty of time. A Valentine's Day wedding would be perfect. He'd never forget our anniversary, haha. I'd laughed at that, when inside, I'd felt let down in some small way.

But my baby sister had gotten married. I was so much older than her, had always looked out for her, yet she'd found the love of her life.

I had Boyd.

The insistent voice in my head was back, listing Boyd's shortcomings. I'd shut her up for so long, it was second nature, but today that bitch refused to be quiet.

He asked me to dress *extra nice* when we were meeting his fellow associates. Did he think I was a frump otherwise?

He'd tossed some of my favorite old shirts, and I'd had to hide a blanket an old boyfriend's mother had crocheted me so he wouldn't throw it out too.

He dominated all the nights that used to be girls' nights, planning festive and fun dates instead until all my friends had moved on without me.

That voice was getting loud now, echoing through my head and blowing the blinders off.

Junie squeezed my shoulder. Her hair was streaked with red, which I'd heard about from Boyd and his mother. I told my sister the color didn't matter. I wanted Junie at my side, and if she had neon-yellow or ink-black hair, I didn't care. Her style differed from Wynter's and Autumn's. She'd covered the red by tying her hair in a knot at the base of her neck.

"Are you trying to hide the red in your hair, June?" I didn't use her nickname, so she'd know I wanted a straight answer.

Guilt and fear flashed across her face.

I narrowed my eyes. "Did Boyd talk to you?"

She chewed the inside of her cheek. In her was a war —tell me the truth or lie. "Mrs. Harrington did," she finally said.

Corinne Harrington. Boyd's mom and a downright witch. Was she the reason Boyd had urged me to add more and more blond highlights to my strawberry-blond strands? Why was hair color an issue anyway?

Why was I doing everything he asked?

Boyd's mother was also on that voice's list. Corinne had casually mentioned that we had to limit our numbers to somehow exclude the fosters my adoptive mom had taken in. Mae Bailey loved all her foster children, and while Lane and Cruz had only started working with her this summer, and while they were adults, they were already engraved on her heart as *hers*. Not only were they Myles's brothers, they were decent men. Guests I had refused to let her leave off the invites.

But the crowding, Summer, Corinne had said. *The church should not be bursting at the seams.*

Boyd had given me the silent treatment for two days after I'd told his mother that if my family and friends weren't here, I wouldn't be either.

Now they were present, and I didn't want to be.

"Summer?" Wynter asked, grabbing a stool and dragging it over, heedless of the train of her dress or her eight-month baby belly. I had wanted to wait to get married until Wynter had the baby. I didn't want her to be uncomfortable on my happy day, and I didn't want her to stand in heels when she was ready to deliver any day.

Mrs. Harrington thought Wynter's baby belly would be a disgrace. A blemish in all the pictures. Her aghast reaction was the only reason I'd sided with Boyd to have the wedding earlier.

Why wait for spring when we can be expecting our own child by then? he'd asked.

I'd looked forward to having kids, but when he'd continued to ask when I'd get my IUD taken out, I had said after the wedding. I'd made the excuse that I didn't want my hormones in turmoil during the ceremony. No clue if that was a thing, but he'd quit pressuring me.

How many times had I formed workarounds for his personality?

My heart stammered again. I pressed my palm against my chest. What was going on?

"Summer," Wynter said again. I didn't realize I'd taken my gaze off her and was staring at the perfectly polished hardwood floor.

"Yeah?"

"Do you want to get married?"

I nodded, but tears welled and spilled onto my cheeks. "No," I whispered. I shook my head, blinking and getting mascara on my cheeks. Waterproof my ass. "No, I'm just stressing."

Junie gripped my shoulders and leaned down so we were eye to eye. "What would you tell me if I was in your position?"

The answer came easily. I'd tell Junie it wasn't too

late. I would tell her she didn't have to go through with it, and I'd have her back. I'd tell her to leave now, and I'd take care of it.

More hot tears flooded my eyes. "I can't cancel. It's too late."

"Do you love Boyd?" Autumn asked.

I licked my lips, the saltiness of my tears stinging my tongue. "Yeah?"

Wynter exchanged a *knew it* look with the other two. "If he loves you, he'll understand."

"It's not a question you have to answer right now either," Autumn said. My three sisters once again surrounded me like a tripod. "I think you have to tell him to call this off, that you're not ready, and then later, you figure out if you love him and whether you want to stay with him."

Tell Boyd the wedding was off. A tremor passed through me. He'd be so upset. I'd be on the end of that coldness he developed when he was angry. "It's just so rushed."

I didn't specify what was rushed, but they all nodded, their expressions solemn.

"Want me to get him?" Junie asked.

I shook my head and carefully took the veil off. Autumn snagged it from my hands like she was afraid I'd put it back on and forge ahead. She hung the beautiful headpiece up across the room, far out of my reach.

I'd made the first, tiny step. I could take another. Then another. I wouldn't face him in this room, the one that had my veil hanging on a garment stand or my luggage for the Bali honeymoon he wanted to take.

"I'll have him meet me by the back exit, by the storage room." The door was closest to the parking lot, but the main entrance was around the corner and would be the one all the guests entered. "Don't tell the guys yet, okay?"

The last thing I needed was my pushy brothers starting a scene with Boyd and his uptight mom and his dad, who was probably half wasted already.

I rose and my elegant white satin gown draped into perfect place. The lace around my neck and over my chest and arms itched like crazy. I had wanted a simple gown, like what Wynter had worn, but I'd copied her already by fast-tracking a wedding mere months after she'd gotten married.

I was the oldest. I was supposed to lead by example, but my baby sister had found love and settled down. She was expecting her first kid. That was supposed to be me.

Today wasn't the day to be competitive. I shouldn't have let Boyd carry me away and hurry a life event I'd been dreaming about since I was a little girl.

My skirts billowed around my legs as I walked to the far door that connected to a different room that my sisters had used to change in. I kept my slippers on, leaving my heels by the veil. I stopped in the hallway and messaged Boyd.

I need to talk to you. Meet me by the exit at the south corner of the church where the big storage room is.

He'd know. His groomsmen had bitched all night about hiding all the church decorations per Corinne's request so they didn't contaminate photos.

Someone would have to put them all back and I doubted it'd be Boyd's friends. My brothers would. In a heartbeat.

I put my phone in a hidden pocket deep in my skirts.

My heart rate calmed, having something that was mine, that I'd picked out, on my person. As I ventured into the empty hallway, I liked that my family could reach me. I wasn't forging ahead alone.

Tate had called me three times in the last month. He rarely called. Since I'd announced the impending nuptials, Teller and Tenor had both made more stops at the family's distillery in Bozeman to see me.

So, yeah. My family would have my back. Boyd would understand, and if he loved me, he'd want me to be happy. He'd feel bad for pressuring me.

I scurried to the meeting spot, only the sound of my dress rustling to accompany me. Boyd didn't reply. I waited, shifting my weight from foot to foot, my nerves making me fidgety the longer I stood there. I didn't look down. I didn't want to see the silver *BRIDE* stitched across the tops of my slippers.

Soft piano music filtered down the hall from the chapel. The entrance was down another hallway. My sisters and I had been put in the room the farthest away. The church was large and already filled with murmurs. How many people were in attendance?

Mama would be greeting everyone who arrived. Mrs. Harrington had insisted Mama stay with me, like Mama was too unrefined to greet any of Boyd's side. My mama might seem meek and subservient, but she did what she damn well pleased. I should've taken notes.

"What's going on?" Boyd's commanding tone cut through the quiet.

I spun, a gasp escaping my lips. Had he been in the chapel greeting folks? Or was the plan to keep me and my family locked up until it was time to perform?

The clarity I was experiencing today should've

happened much sooner, but at least it hadn't waited longer. "I'm—uh . . ." Turned out, canceling a wedding was hard to announce to the groom.

"Summer," he snapped. "We have ten minutes and you look—" He made a tsking sound. He gripped the sides of my face and smoothed his thumbs under my eyes. The smeared mascara. "You're a mess."

"Thanks," I said sarcastically.

He scowled and tried to rub the black off his thumbs with his fingers. "You know what I mean." He closed his eyes and seemed to collect himself. "You're beautiful, but I know you want to be radiant on your wedding day."

He did that a lot, didn't he? Reframed a situation to be about what I wanted so I'd look foolish if I disagreed. He was saying what *he* wanted. He got me to do what *he* wanted.

I lifted my chin. "I wanted a summer wedding."

He got a dumbfounded expression. "Okay? You're telling me now?"

"I told you before. I wanted to wait." I was dancing around the topic and that was unlike me. Summer Kerrigan did not pussyfoot. "I'm not going through with the wedding." I blew out a hard breath. There. I'd done it. A spark of pride lit in my chest.

He barked out a laugh. "Good one. How did you know I was getting tense and that I needed to lighten up?" His eyes twinkled, but there was an aura around him, an accumulation of ominous energy.

The feeling wasn't new. I usually acquiesced when I sensed he was displeased. Boyd was a catch—on paper. In person, I was no longer sure. "I'm not kidding, Boyd. I don't want to get married right now." I squared my shoulders. I wasn't just canceling a wedding. The last few minutes had been more than enlightening. I was ending the whole thing. "I don't want to marry you."

His features went deathly still and that vibe grew stifling. I didn't see him move his arm until the slap rang through the hallway. My head snapped to the side, but even then, I needed an extra second to figure out why.

He'd *slapped* me. I put my hand to my face. Stinging heat spread through my cheek, and he crowded close.

"We're not playing this game today," he said in a low, threatening voice.

"You hit me."

"That was not a hit. Now, go back to your room. Clean that shit off your face and don't come out until you're my gorgeous bride."

Thoughts tumbled through my head. He was pressing me against the wall and looming over me. Menace dripped from his voice while he talked to me like I was a child. Like I was a lifelike doll that was his to position the way he wanted.

I'd been letting him do just that all this time.

Humiliation spread through my body where shock had just been. How had I not seen it?

"You're not embarrassing me like this." He snapped the lapels of his tux jacket. "I'll buy some extra time while you get presentable."

A shard of steel lined my spine. "I'm in a wedding dress with pretty ringlets cascading from my head like an icy waterfall. Isn't that presentable enough for you?"

He shoved my shoulders and the back of my head thunked against the wall. "I'll deal with that mouth tonight."

"I don't want what you have planned for it."

He pulled his arm back and too late I saw the fist

aiming for my gut. My lungs turned to ice. I couldn't breathe.

Then, he was yanked away from me and slammed into the wall across from me. A pair of wide, familiar shoulders blocked my vision, longish dark brown hair with a slight curl touching the collar. The curved wooden handle of a cane stuck out from between the men, horizontal to the floor.

Boyd was pinned to the wall by a cane.

I straightened. He'd almost punched me, and I had cowered.

I had cowered in front of the man I was supposed to marry. The man who had just slapped me. How could I have not seen Boyd for what he was? His parents were awful. Why'd I think he'd be different?

"You keep your goddamn hands off her," the new arrival snarled in a deep voice that wiped away cobwebs from memories I'd rather forget forever.

It couldn't be him.

I'd invited him because Mama had put his and his parents' names on the list, and I'd been too busy to protest.

I crept around to see his face. Boyd was struggling, but he was no match for the man with the cane who had his knee to Boyd's groin. One swift shift upward, and Boyd would be swallowing his balls.

I caught sight of the enraged face of my protector and my pulse fluttered. Jonah Dunn. The older brother of the boy I'd dated in high school, the one whose mom had crocheted my favorite blanket.

The boy who'd been killed in a car crash.

The scar bisecting his face was more prominent thanks to the angry flush. His dark eyes were no less deadly than Boyd's, and Jonah had his polished walking cane pressed across Boyd's chest. Yet I didn't fear Jonah.

"Stay out of this, asshole." Boyd's handsome but plain face was turning red.

I inspected my now ex-fiancé like he was an ant. There was nothing exemplary about him and the effect wasn't from his looks. He had to work hard not to be ordinary, and he stepped on other people to get to the next level, be it through perceived charm or his manipulative personality.

What had I seen in him? Why had I stayed?

I was so stupid.

My sisters had been so ready to help me ditch my nuptials. They'd seen it.

Had everyone been able to discern the dim future I was sprinting into but me?

I'd seen what Boyd wanted me to see. A nice smile, a good job, and a mellow attitude. All false but the smile, thanks to Invisalign.

Boyd tried smacking Jonah, but Jonah batted his hands away while keeping Boyd pinned to the wall like a bug in a display. Accurate.

Boyd bared his teeth. He tried to kick, but Jonah's knee twitched and Boyd was so damn proud of his freshly shaven balls he instantly went still.

"I'll call the cops," Boyd huffed.

I stiffened. Boyd had connections. He had power. Jonah wasn't known in Bozeman. He was barely known in Bourbon Canyon anymore.

I couldn't let Boyd walk away from hitting me. I couldn't let more than me be humiliated by this man. "Boyd, you're going to go into the chapel and announce that today is canceled. You're not going to trash my name or I'll march right out and tell them how I got the red spot on my cheek."

I didn't have to look in the mirror to know that my left cheek was blazing.

Jonah jerked and smacked Boyd's head against the wall, like the reminder infuriated him. I . . . didn't mind.

"My family isn't dealing with the fallout," I continued, secure in Jonah's hold on him. I'd let Boyd bulldoze me enough. "If you give them any shit whatsoever, I will tell my brothers—*all* of them," I stressed so he'd know I meant Myles and, by extension, his brothers too. "And I'll be their alibi."

Boyd's face was now magenta.

"What is going on here?" Corinne's scandalized voice rang down the hall. She was storming in our direction. An angry monarch in a shiny pewter dress and three-inch matching heels.

Jonah didn't let go. He stroked his dark gaze down my body, leaving a hot flush behind. "You okay?"

His deep growl sent shivers across my skin, cooling the heat he'd caused. His scruff-lined jaw was hard enough to be carved from stone, but I could only make out concern in the black depths of his eyes.

I nodded. A lie.

His eyes narrowed, pinching the scar that ran near the corner of his left eye.

"Get your hands off him before I call the police!" Corinne's volume would draw attention. I didn't want to be on display, stared at. Pitied.

I didn't want to be a spectacle. It would be my parents' funeral all over again. I had to shut her up. "I didn't realize your son made a habit of hitting women."

Her steps stuttered, and her righteous expression

faltered. Then she lifted her chin, back to commanding mother of the groom. "I didn't realize you made a habit of lying."

"Keep telling yourself that while you announce the wedding's off." I pointed at my smarting cheek. My heart was hammering against my sternum. The anger was dying and the desperation was growing. I didn't want everyone to see how deluded I'd been. They'd known he wasn't good for me, but they couldn't have known he was this bad. Calling off the wedding was exposing enough. "Boyd knows what'll happen if he shit-talks me." I lifted my chin toward Jonah. "You can let him go."

Jonah's eyes were still narrowed. He hadn't looked at Corinne once. He turned his hard stare on Boyd. "Get out of my goddamn sight, and I won't hit you the way you hit her."

Shame burned along my skin. I dropped my gaze to the floor as Jonah stepped back, keeping between me and Boyd as much as he could, and jerked his cane from Boyd's chest.

Boyd took a full inhale, trying to make himself bigger, but Jonah spun the mahogany cane in his hand.

I knew what it was like facing Jonah's anger. I'd been on the receiving end. And like Boyd, I'd deserved it. But Jonah would never hit a woman.

I forced myself to meet Boyd's glare. Hatred shone in his eyes.

He snarled, baring his teeth. "I regret the years I wasted on your hillbilly ass."

Jonah growled and stepped forward. Boyd scurried away. My ex put an arm around his mom to comfort her. I got a clear vision of how my marriage would've been. Me, alone, against them.

She stopped, nearly tripping both of them. "Get the ring," she cried and clutched his arm.

Boyd's glare skipped off Jonah and landed on me.

The stupid, obnoxious emerald-cut ring he'd claimed was a family heirloom and was adamant that we couldn't resize. I'd been terrified for four months the damn thing would land in the toilet and Corinne would roast me in hell.

I yanked it off and chucked it down the hall. "Be a good boy and fetch that for your mother."

"She always was crass and unrefined," Corinne told Boyd as she hauled him in the direction the ring had bounced. "I told you."

Acid sloshed into the back of my throat. That woman didn't know me. Yet I couldn't escape the sense that she did see me and that was why I'd tried so hard to please her and Boyd. I wasn't crass and unrefined, but I was a scared and selfish girl at the worst of times.

Jonah ignored them again. His dark focus was on me. "Summer?" he said quietly.

The tears were back and spilling over. I'd made a mess of this day. I would have to face my family, Jonah's parents, other family friends, and tell them I'd fucked up. People had spent money and time to get to this damn wedding, and it was my fault they were getting nothing out of it.

My skin crawled. My lack of action had cost people I cared about everything before. And now it was happening again.

"I don't want to face them." I didn't want to see anyone. I was supposed to be the role model, yet I'd been snowed.

I was a fool. A scared and selfish little girl.

"I can't let my sisters see me like this." Could I leave before they heard what had happened? Could I just leave? "I don't want to go home."

If I went to my condo in Bozeman, I might have an encounter with Boyd. He didn't have a key, but he could come pounding. If I went home, to the house that always felt like home, Mama's house on the Bailey ranch, then I'd be witnessed in all my failure. I'd have to face my brothers' questions and stay strong for my sisters and I just wanted to *be*.

Jonah's steely gaze went to the exit door. His eyes were a deep indigo blue. I hadn't remembered until he glanced toward the glow of the exit sign. There'd been a lot of things about Jonah Dunn I'd tried to forget.

The muscles in his jaw clenched. "All right. Get your stuff."

I shook my head. A walk of shame. A spectacle. I'd be the center of attention for all the wrong reasons. "My stuff is in the changing room. I just can't . . ." The tears continued to roll. "I was so stupid." My voice was ragged, barely a whisper. "So stupid. I don't want them to see."

His sigh was barely audible. He put an arm around me and led me to the exit. "I'll get you out of here."

His steps were uneven and his cane hit the ground erratically. When we barreled out the door, a cold wind hit me in the face. Another detail I hadn't wanted for my wedding. Frigid weather and snowpack on my happy day. Forecasted snow and dark gray clouds in the distance. More snow was coming.

Happy Valentine's Day.

I sank into Jonah's side, not caring where he steered me, only that it was away. The steel of his body shouldn't be comforting but it was. I'd known Jonah for a long time, but this was the closest I'd ever been to him.

"Summer!" Wynter called.

I tensed and almost stopped but was helpless against Jonah's strength. "She can't be running out here. She's too pregnant."

He finally halted and looked over his shoulder. "I'll get her home."

I snuck a peek. My sisters were charging outside. Myles already had an arm around Wynter's waist to keep her from chasing me. Junie's eyes widened when her gaze landed on Jonah. He didn't get out much, and Junie no longer lived in our hometown. She probably hadn't seen him for years. Did she know who he was? Jonah had once been close to my brothers, especially Teller, but the guys were all older than us.

My brothers crowded in the doorway. Tate, Teller, and Tenor, all in suits, all with severe concern etched into their faces.

My stomach sank. They'd get involved and they'd want to run Boyd out of town—or run him over. I didn't want to be in the center of the mess I'd caused.

"What'd he do?" Tate asked Jonah like he knew I wouldn't tell him.

Tate tried to step around Junie, but Autumn nudged in front of him. She pushed my suitcase toward me, the wheels bumping on the pavement. I didn't know how she'd known I'd need it, but Autumn was more observant than the others.

One roller hit an ice chunk and the bag tipped. Teller tried to shove through my sisters. He'd probably grab the luggage and me too. He'd rightfully want an explanation and then want to kick Boyd's ass.

I cringed. I wanted to forget how stupid I was. I wanted to slink away and nurse my pride.

Jonah put a hand up. "She wants privacy." He cleared his throat like he wasn't used to talking this much or this loud. "Take care of that piece of shit inside of there." He tipped his forehead toward the church. "Make sure that asshole can't get near her again." He limped forward and bent his big body to pick my suitcase up. His left leg didn't bend as much as the right.

"Summer?" Tenor was my mellowest brother, but anger and worry gleamed in his eyes. "You good?"

"I will be," I said quietly. "I just need some time to process what happened. Please tell Mama not to worry."

We all knew she was going to.

Jonah passed me and tossed my bag in the rear passenger seat. His old red-and-silver pickup was a balm to my nerves. He didn't drive a flashy car like Boyd. Jonah's old truck was covered in dust with thicker dirt caked around the wheel wells.

When he opened the door for me, I noticed *him*. I'd never seen him out of jeans and a flannel, but he was in black slacks and a dark blue dress shirt. He looked good, ruggedly handsome in a dark and mysterious way, but I'd rather he was in denim.

He opened the passenger door. "Get in."

I faced my family. "I'm sorry," I said, barely loud enough to carry on the cold wind toward them. Then I gave a little wave that was supposed to be reassuring, but my hand trembled. I got into a truck with a man I hadn't spoken to in years, but it was better to leave my wedding with a near stranger than with the groom.

CHAPTER TWO

Jonah

I had a bride in my passenger seat, but I was a thirty-nine-year-old bachelor.

I maneuvered out of Bozeman and headed toward Bourbon Canyon. Summer was curled up with her head on her hand, staring out the window. Snow had fallen last week and then Montana had had a couple of days of above-freezing weather. The streets were a mix of brown and grungy white. The closer to the edge of city limits I got, the thinner the snow piles were, covering the landscape more evenly. The brown wasn't from dirt but dormant grasses, and from green fir trees farther up the hills. The ground disappeared again under the white of the mountain peaks.

She was so quiet. I'd never seen Summer quiet. She fit her name. Bold. Bright. Sunshine. The embodiment of confidence and happiness. As a kid, she'd been bossy, opinionated, and stubborn. Time might've polished her, but her edges couldn't be dulled.

If she didn't want to be around anyone, that made me her guy.

Not her man. Never her man.

An old, familiar ache burned behind my sternum. I wanted to go home. I hadn't wanted to leave, but I had owed my mom an appearance at the wedding. Summer's wedding would make her more emotional than most. The thoughts of what-could-have-been haunted her. I owed my brother to see that Summer married someone who deserved her. I owed it to myself to see her happily wed to another man.

Now my mom wouldn't have to sit through the nuptials, and I would make sure that pompous, abusive jackass of a groom couldn't find Summer. I had a cabin in the mountains outside of Bourbon Canyon. No one would bother her there. Her disgusting fiancé likely wouldn't get over himself enough to go looking for her.

I glanced at the gray sky. Another snowfall was in the forecast, regular weather that townsfolk wouldn't notice, but Summer might have to camp out with me a few more days than planned.

"Why were you there?" she asked, her voice tiny.

Shit, I'd almost forgotten I wasn't alone. No. Her strawberries-and-sugar smell wouldn't let me. She was infusing the cab of my truck, her scent curling around me and amping up the ache in my chest. How long before I quit smelling her when I climbed in?

"My family got an invite and insisted I go." I'd balked. I'd argued with Mom. I didn't like making trips to town, much less to Bozeman.

She'd reminded me I'd been holed up in the cabin

most of the winter—again. I hated when Mom worried, and I couldn't tell her I went to town more often than she thought. She'd ask why and things would get awkward.

A guy got tired of his hand.

Eventually, Mom had pulled the brother card. *Can you do it for Eli?*

Summer's laugh was dry and sad. "So I wasn't the only one who didn't want to be there?" She let out a weary sigh. "No, I meant why were you in the hallway? Did you see us arguing?"

They hadn't argued. She'd told him she didn't want to get married, and her oaf of a fiancé had hit her. "I was looking for a bathroom."

Her lower lip pouted out, pink and swollen from getting chewed on. She might look ready to drop but that sharp mind of hers was whirring. "Do you need to stop somewhere?"

"Why?" I maneuvered around a curve.

"You didn't get to a bathroom."

"I didn't need to take a piss." My hand tightened on the wheel. "I needed to get away from the crowd." Away from the thought of seeing Summer walk down the aisle.

She twisted toward me in her seat as much as her seat belt would allow. "Were there a lot of people?"

"Not many I recognized."

She let out a relieved breath. "Corinne invited half the town and wanted to restrict my guest list."

Corinne must be the woman who'd been ready to fuck me up. Good thing Summer had known the exact threats needed to get her ex and his family to behave. I wasn't sure my reputation would survive fighting a wealthy woman off me and Summer.

"Has he hit you before?" I had to know if I should regret my restraint.

"No." She rested her head on the headrest. "But now I can't quit thinking of the signs. He isolated me. Made me question my own mind. He was controlling. I can't believe I fell for it all. I was just so busy with work."

I slid my gaze in her direction for a second, then focused on the road.

"What?" she asked, defensive.

Summer wasn't the type to let her boyfriend bulldoze her. My brother had trailed behind her like a lovesick puppy. Summer had done what she wanted, and if Eli had wanted to be with her, he'd had to keep up. "Why are you taking responsibility for his actions?"

"I was minutes away from marrying him." Another long exhale. "Where are you taking me?"

There was an edge to her question. If she didn't like my answer, she'd tuck and roll out the door, highway speeds be damned. This was the Summer I knew. "My cabin. You wanted privacy. You can't get more private." Except I'd be there.

She studied me. "Are you sure?"

No. She'd needed help, and I'd jumped to serve, just like all the men in her life, except that dickweed ex. "You can have the guest room. I'll leave you alone."

"It's just . . ." She shook her head. "The last time we talked—"

"People change." I didn't want to remember her last visit to the hospital after the accident that had taken my brother's life. She'd come to see me a few times. Probably more than I remembered since I'd been out of it for so long. She'd quit coming because I'd told her to.

"They do." She went back to staring out the

passenger window. "They change sometimes right before your eyes."

And we were back on her ex. Safe ground. "Is what's-his-name going to be a problem?"

"I don't think so. He hit me and you saw. They can call me a liar, but the seed would be planted in people's heads. Add in that I didn't go through with the wedding and I'd look more truthful than him."

"Do you live with him?"

She shook her head. "Thankfully, no. Daddy—" She sniffled. "Daddy, uh, told me once that he didn't want his girls living with men before marriage."

"I didn't realize he was that old-fashioned." Darin Bailey had been a good man, but he hadn't seemed like he'd deny his girls much of anything.

"He encouraged independence—emotional, mental, and financial. And . . . he didn't care for Boyd." Her admission came out on a wave of shame.

Darin Bailey wasn't Summer's birth dad, but she was still her daddy's girl. All the Kerrigan sisters were. "You stayed with the one guy Darin Bailey didn't like?"

"Don't judge." She turned toward me and those lips formed a mutinous line. "Daddy didn't like any of my boyfriends." She went back to window gazing. "Except Eli, of course."

Everyone had liked Eli. He'd been the likable brother.

Darin had hated Boyd Harrington. The thought gave me a boost. When I'd been better friends with Teller, I'd enjoyed chatting with Darin. He'd been an easy guy to get along with and had been aware of his family's contributions to the town. He'd gone out of his way to be affable instead of entitled.

I could understand why he'd disliked Boyd. Boyd's and Summer's names in fancy script on the invitation had irritated the shit out of me. The entire invite had. Cream-colored paper. Lace overlay. I had to break through three envelopes to get to it. Even the wrinkles were fancy, like it was antique papyrus or some shit. But her name in complicated calligraphy had just been *wrong*.

Summer wasn't a complicated name and it shouldn't be made into something it wasn't.

"I'm going to judge," I said to goad her.

Her anger flowed over me when she turned toward me. "Is that what you do? Sit in that boring cabin and get all judgmental?"

I kept driving, but satisfaction settled deep in my gut. There was the fire that fueled the woman. She'd lost it when that asshole had slapped her. "No, Summer. *We're* going to sit in the boring cabin and get all judgmental."

She paused. "How bad is it that I'm looking forward to it?"

For her? This was nothing but a blip on her radar. Sunny Summer Kerrigan would continue to bulldoze through life, doing things her way.

For me? Once she was gone, I'd be left thinking about everything I'd lost.

Summer

Ages ago, I'd been to Jonah's cabin. He lived on the edge of Bailey land, on the farthest reaches of the Dunns' land, so close that if our families didn't get along, there could be issues. But Jonah kept to himself, respected his property and ours, and was overall a dream neighbor.

According to Teller, and from what I'd seen, Jonah was as much of a recluse as he could be. The thought made the "dream neighbor" label sad.

When Jonah was a kid, he used to help Tate and Teller on the ranch. The three of them, along with Tenor, would race four-wheelers and snowmobiles, pull out the tractors they got stuck in the mud, and hunt and fish until we thought they weren't coming home. They didn't stop as they entered their adult years. During my brothers' college breaks, either Jonah was back at the house or Teller was at his.

Then Jonah's brother was killed. Eli Dunn. My high school boyfriend. Jonah had withdrawn into himself, become a hermit, and made it clear he didn't want to see or speak to me again.

I must've looked extra pathetic in my puffy wedding dress if he was letting me hide at his place.

Memories surged as we got closer to the cabin. Eli and I stopping in when Eli's mom couldn't get ahold of Jonah and sent Eli to check on him. Eli grabbing camping equipment for the weekends out with friends I refused to go on. I'd never told Eli the real reason why. He'd been my friend before he'd been my boyfriend, but there was so much I hadn't told him.

Until he'd figured out part of it. And things had ended horribly.

Jonah drove up the base of the mountain, the wipers on the pickup swiping at the flurries coming down.

"We were supposed to fly out tomorrow morning." I didn't know why I was telling him. The honeymoon should've been another red flag, and I was tired of feeling like a fool, but I also didn't wish to spend time in the past. "Before the worst of the snow hit."

"Where were you going?"

"Bali."

He let out a low whistle. "Nice." His profile was harsh in the dash lights. All ridges and angles. His face was narrower than his brother's had been. A sharp line of a nose. Dark slashes for brows and thick lashes. His hair had been shaggy the few times I'd caught a glimpse of him in town, but today he'd neatly brushed it with a smart part on the side. I preferred the shaggy look. "Do you want me to take you to the airport?"

God, no. I was almost more relieved to skip the honeymoon than the wedding. "He's probably going or has canceled everything." I continued scrutinizing my passenger window. The familiar landscape eased my nerves. I'd quit shivering a few miles out of Bourbon Canyon. "I didn't want to go anyway."

"You didn't?" He did the quick-glance thing. The lick of heat from his attention was hard to ignore. The man was focused on driving, but he didn't miss much.

How long had it been since one of the guys I dated had focused on me and what I felt? When they weren't thinking about what I could do to them or for them? Was that why I'd stayed with Boyd?

His nitpicky and controlling behavior came off as personal concern and I was attention starved? "Bali, right? Should be a dream vacation." I shuddered. "I hate planes."

"Did the jackass know that?"

"Yes." What a stupid little girl I'd been. "He said he'd

help me relax. Told me it'd be fine, and I . . . let him steamroll right over me."

"Don't do that," he growled, so deep, almost menacing, but the shivers that traced over my body weren't from fear.

I was all mixed up inside. "Don't do what?"

"It's not unreasonable to expect to trust your partner. You didn't let him bulldoze you. You trusted him and he abused it."

I turned from the window. His jaw was tense and his knuckles were white on the wheel. Jonah was upset. On my behalf.

Today wasn't the worst day of my life, but I needed the reassurance.

I never thought I'd find comfort in Jonah Dunn.

The tangle of emotions inside my chest added a few more knots. To take my mind away from my destroyed wedding and my unlikely rescuer, I hunted for a view of his cabin through the flurries. The peak of a building I hadn't seen before poked through the fir trees.

"What's that place?" His cabin should be tucked farther in, but he'd either moved it, which was absurd, or he'd had a few trees removed since I'd been here last.

"My shop."

"You have a shop?" How long had it been since I'd been to Jonah's barren cabin? Over fifteen years had gone by since I'd last ventured up this mountain.

"I have a shop," he echoed.

The area overall hadn't changed, but the scenery was different with the giant metal-sided shop with one large garage door on the side and a smaller one on the end. A regular door was beside it, facing the cabin across a short expanse.

The view was still stunning. Jonah had built the cabin halfway up the small, sprawling mountain, overlooking a valley that had a stream cutting through it. He used to hunt waterfowl with Eli, and I'd been invited to their parents' house for pheasant stew or roast duck.

The water was mostly frozen with a few wet-looking spots from the recent unseasonably warm days, but the grasses along the back were brown and much of the growth was covered with snow. Trails laid down by the wildlife tracked from the tree line to the water's edge. The other side of the valley was Bailey land.

No matter the season, the area was pretty.

Jonah turned into the driveway and—whoa. The shop was nicer than I'd first thought, with timber accents the same color as his house and a brown tin roof. There was a rocking chair sitting outside by a side door.

Did Jonah watch the sun rise over the lush stream in the summers?

I shouldn't dwell on Jonah's habits, but thinking about him was easier than dwelling on how my family was handling the Harringtons. Or how disappointed the guests were that they'd made the trip to Bozeman for nothing. Did the drama make the trip worth it?

Nope. Not dwelling on today. I focused on Jonah's house.

The cabin was an A-frame structure made out of thick round logs with a brownish-red tin roof. It was just as simple and stunning as it had always been. Large windows took up the wall, and with the sparse trees, the view of the valley would be breathtaking. I could enjoy my favorite winter drink, a spiced coffee with a splash of bourbon, and admire the view.

A garage had been added using the same materials.

Jonah pulled inside. He hit the button for the garage door and we were enclosed in darkness.

"Are you sure you want to stay here?" he asked. He'd killed the engine, but neither of us made a move to leave. "The snow's getting heavier and you know what it's like. Doesn't take much to block you in."

I nodded. Where Mama lived, it was easier to get in and out when the weather was bad. We had the equipment to move snow if needed, as long as the visibility was there.

"I can take you to your mom's," he offered.

He'd have to go close to town to get to Mama's, and then he'd have to get back before the snow got too deep or the wind kicked up too strong. "What if you get stranded in town?"

"I can stay with my parents."

From his tone, I could tell bunking with Adam and Vera Dunn wasn't ideal. I didn't want to inconvenience him more than I had, but also, I didn't want to leave his side. He'd stepped in when I'd been too stunned to move. I'd been a rabbit before a hawk.

Why was Jonah so willing to help me? I thought he hated me.

My siblings would do the same for me, but they were family. They'd feel like they had to. They would know not to berate me for impulsive weddings or last-minute cancellations. Jonah didn't have to. He didn't owe me. He *should* hate me.

When I fucked up in life, I did it big.

"I'd like to stay." I picked at a nail. My pretty manicure was a soft wild-rose color, the same shade I would've made the bridesmaid dresses without Corinne's pushy influence. Her lips had thinned when she'd seen my fingertips.

She'd said black and white with a touch of silver was the perfect winter look. Maybe the next bride Boyd manipulated would have the same style as her.

"I just need quiet, and I wouldn't get that with my family." Fatigue overwhelmed me. My adrenaline was crashing. Weeks of late nights following days of running between appointments for cake tastings and with photographers and the church staff were calling in their debts now. I rubbed my eyes, letting out a long sigh.

"Take the guest room upstairs. Go get some rest."

The guest room had been his bedroom, once upon a time. Before the accident that had claimed his brother's life and left Jonah with lifelong injuries. If Jonah knew the role I'd played that day, he'd kick me out and make me walk home.

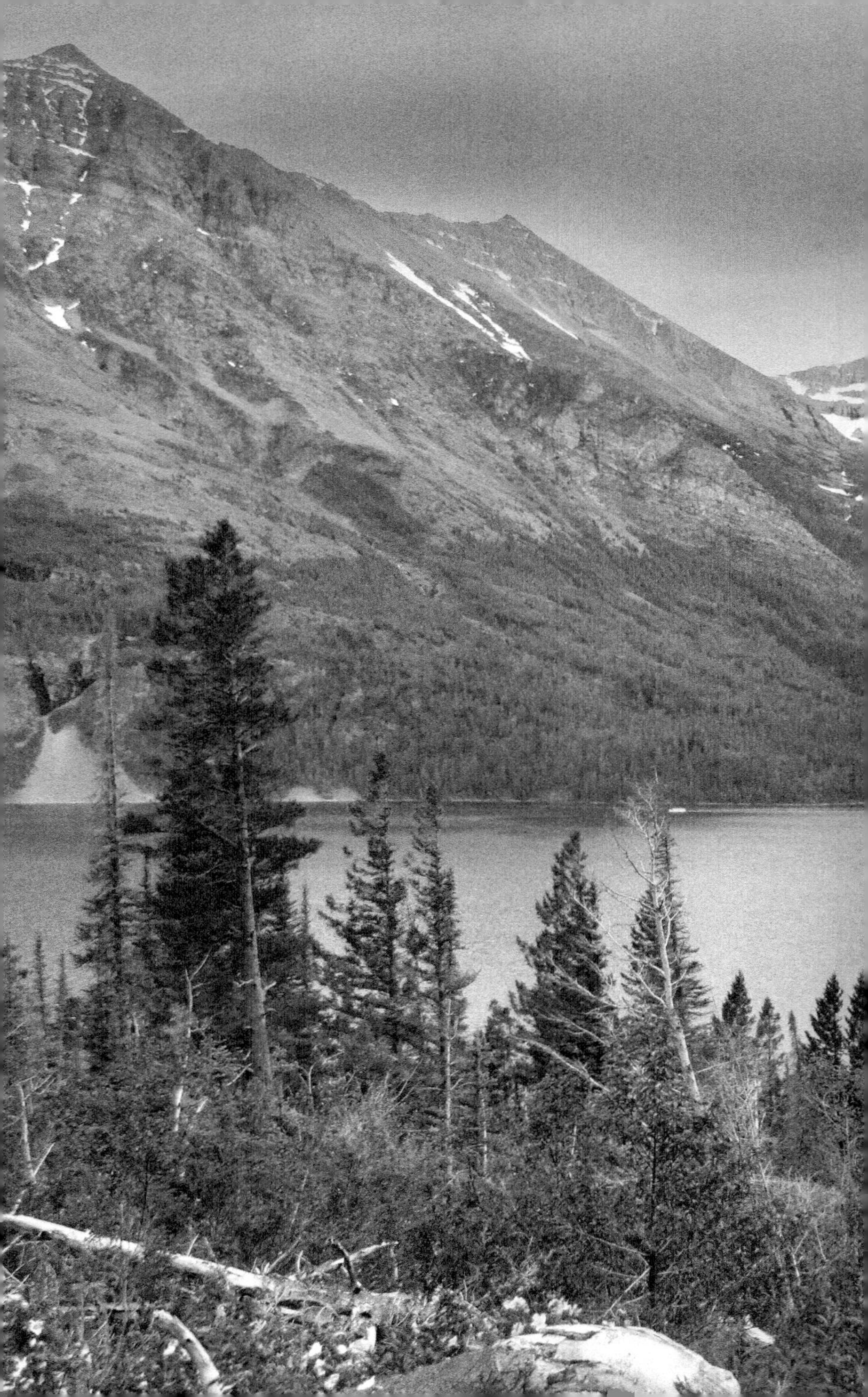

CHAPTER THREE

Jonah

I wasn't used to having someone under my roof—not as a guest and definitely not overnight. I wasn't accustomed to noticing my cabin and wondering what Summer would think of it. Would she think I should decorate better? I had few pictures up. No knickknacks. I let the wood and the view through the windows showcase the beauty.

Would she notice all the canes I had propped against walls? I didn't rely on them in the house as much as walking outside and in town, but they were handy if I was stiff or especially sore after working in the yard or in my shop.

The shop was calling my name. I'd taken yesterday off, taking way too fucking long to find a pair of slacks and a shirt that would work for today, and I had plenty of projects to catch up on. My productivity always took a shit this time of year. I didn't mind being plugged in by snow or storms, but then delivery trucks couldn't get up or down the mountain.

I roamed the kitchen, my limp echoing louder than ever. I had on my boots. I'd been determined to keep my day normal, but last night, Summer had disappeared upstairs in her elaborate wedding gown after we had arrived and I hadn't seen her since. Now, it was midmorning. Should I check on her?

My left knee fucking hated stairs. My left foot wasn't far behind.

I went back out to the living room and gazed up the stairs, as if I could ascertain how she was doing through her closed bedroom door. Everything was quiet. She'd left the light off in the library nook I had made when I first moved in. Nothing of hers littered the landing from what I could spy between the slats of the carved wooden railing.

She must still be sleeping.

My phone rang. I didn't have to look to know it was my mom. She was the only one who called, but she'd been trying to get ahold of me since I'd left the wedding yesterday. I'd sent her a message, but she wouldn't quit until she heard my voice.

I answered on the way back to the kitchen so I wouldn't wake my guest. "You don't have to worry."

"Of course I do," she said without hesitation. "How is she?"

I had no fucking clue. "Sleeping." Maybe.

"Poor thing. You know, I saw them together once and you just get that sense. I didn't like him." The corner of my mouth tipped up. Mom said it like her feelings were a secret and a warning. She didn't like him, so he must be a miserable person. Most of the time, she was correct. "Her brothers were so upset after you left. And the rest of us were . . . well, confused. I know I was."

Mom was baiting me and I knew it, but there wasn't much I wouldn't give her. Except a daughter-in-law and grandkids. I'd failed miserably on that account. Sometimes I was angry with Eli that he wasn't here to give her the dream grandchildren she desired.

"How did you get involved?" Mom didn't beat around the bush. I wasn't answering and she'd continue to rain questions down on me.

"Right place, right time." Wrong place, right time? I wasn't sure. I hated being dragged into drama, but I wouldn't change stopping that asshole from hitting her again. He'd slapped her knowing it likely wouldn't bruise before the ceremony was done and he'd been about to hit her again where no one would have seen the mark he'd leave behind. My blood boiled.

Something Mom said sank in. *And the rest of us were . . . well, confused.*

How many in attendance other than family knew Summer had left with me? Goddammit, how had it looked? "Is there speculation?"

"Oh, you know, there'll always be speculation, but don't worry. Tate told me that she'd left with you and asked me to keep it to ourselves. There weren't many others from Bourbon Canyon there. Anyway, I didn't realize you two had kept in touch."

Mom and Dad wouldn't talk. They were more aware than most. After Eli's death, talk about how nineteen-year-old Eli was a closet drunk and that we might've known had run rampant through town. People had speculated that his crash had been inevitable. He had partied and made stupid decisions like a lot of small-town teens, but his accident had been in the middle of the damn day, with no one else around but me.

I pinched the bridge of my nose. My brother had been on my mind heavily lately, but with Summer under my roof, he was a constant presence. He and Summer could've given Mom those grandkids. Summer was the daughter Mom always wanted. I could've been the cranky uncle who taught them how to hunt and fish and camp.

"She just needs space," I answered, "and when shit happens, family is sometimes the last to give you room." Didn't I know it. "I just happened to be around with my pickup keys. Nothing more."

"Right. Yes. She knows you, and I'm glad that you were willing to help."

The level of willing I'd been—to drop everything and bring Summer to the safety of my house—burrowed into my conscience. "Couldn't exactly feed her to the wolves."

Mom snorted. "Well-dressed wolves. That mom of the groom. She was intimidating. You should've seen the way she looked at my dress. And I think . . ." She dropped her voice to whisper, "I think the groom's father was already drunk."

"He was." Loud and boisterous and flashing a flask. He came off as charming and suave but a little too tipsy for moments before his son's wedding. His boasting about the cost of the whole event had been part of the sensory overwhelm that had prompted me to find a bathroom.

"She dodged a bullet. Poor thing," she said again. "Take care of her."

"Will do." I hung up.

Summer Kerrigan took care of herself. It was why I'd needed a couple of seconds after seeing her get slapped. No one crossed Summer without knowing what they were in for. Touch one Kerrigan, you riled the whole sister nest. A guy in town had multiple slashed tires to show for it.

But then she'd just stood there, staring at her ex, her eyes wide, while he'd crowded her. I'd never regret stepping in.

I might regret bringing her to my place.

I'd slept fitfully in case she started roaming around, looking for food or for the bathroom. Silly, since there was a bathroom in her fucking room. Who was I fooling? I'd stayed awake in case she wanted company in an unfamiliar house.

I had a beautiful woman in my house and I was on high alert. But of all women, Summer was the last one I should be thinking about in that way. She had been my brother's true love.

She wouldn't consider me in that regard either. I'd been deluded enough to think so once, hopped up on pain meds I hadn't wanted but had needed, and I'd chewed into her for even talking to me. I'd been an idiot then, and I wouldn't make the same mistake now. I was no Boyd Harrington.

Before the accident and the scar and the limp and my downgrade in attitude, I'd dated enough women, but they'd been the opposite of Summer. Women who hung out in bars instead of running them. Women who wanted a good time, not a long time. I hadn't had time outside of my hobbies to make room for a relationship. Now? The type hadn't changed, but it was them who didn't want a relationship with me. I was the guy women bragged about sleeping with—once. The oldest Dunn brother who looked like he'd murder you in your sleep after he fucked you senseless.

That was a direct quote. And people wondered why I only went to town out of necessity.

I went to the sink and gazed out the kitchen window. Only about three inches of snow had fallen so far. Every so often, the wind would pick up, send the flakes swirling, then back off, making the weather unpredictable enough to stay off the roads. Not bad enough to be stranded for long. The front would pass, the roads would get cleared, and I could get Summer to her mom's place.

This weekend would've been perfect to work. My parents wouldn't have worried that I wasn't getting out much because I'd have been snowed in, and I could have worked around Mom's daily check-ins.

The floor creaked above my head. Then came the sound of water running through the pipes. She was using the bathroom upstairs.

While she was busy, I made a fresh pot of coffee. I knew she drank the stuff. I'd seen her leaving Mountain Perks a few times over the years. Would my black tar be too plain for her? Too strong? Not strong enough? Fuck it. I had creamer in the fridge. It wasn't like I'd had a chance to prepare for company.

The water shut off and I waited, the smell of fresh coffee filling the house. Another squeak came, from the stairs this time. The staircase was on the other side of the kitchen wall. The rest of the house opened up into the living room and eating area. My bedroom was under the guest room upstairs. I had planned an addition if needed, but my youthful foresight had been unnecessary.

The whisper of stockinged feet.

Summer crossed the living room while staring out the windows. Her damp blond hair tumbled down her back, and she wore a short-sleeved sundress that hung past her knees, but she had on gray fluffy socks that were familiar.

My socks. I must've missed a drawer of belongings when I'd moved out of the room upstairs. I wouldn't have noticed jack or shit missing when I had switched bedrooms. Resentment and fury had filled me in those days, along with bitterness that the move had been needed in the first place and pain exacerbated by the multiple trips up and down the stairs.

I leaned against the counter, taking the weight off my left foot and knee. She went to the glass and gazed outside.

When she turned, I took a drink from my mug. Yesterday, she'd had a face polished with makeup she didn't need, but it had enhanced the golden brown of her eyes and the natural blush on her cheeks. Freshly scrubbed, she was radiant. Her lashes were still thick, but lighter, and the light from the window made the gold in her eyes glow. Her dress was too fancy for a mountain cabin, and not heavy enough for winter, but she looked like she belonged here anyway.

Shame burned behind my chest.

She was Eli's girlfriend, asshole. If he hadn't died, she might've been my sister-in-law. Fate had had a different future in store for her, but she'd just broken off a wedding. I shouldn't be thinking about her belonging to anything related to me.

"Morning," she finally said.

For less than an hour, it'd still be considered morning. "Want some coffee?"

Relief filled her eyes. "Yes."

Did she think I was going to tell her to load up her belongings into the truck as soon as she opened her eyes? Was that why she'd stuck to her room until now?

She padded across the wooden floor. I liked a cool environment. Those socks would keep the chill from leaching into her feet, but I could also turn the furnace up.

I didn't move as she peeked in the cupboard above the coffee pot. A small triumphant sound left her when she spotted the two other mugs I had.

She filled her cup three quarters full and glanced around.

"Creamer's in the fridge," I said gruffly. The sight of a woman making herself at home resonated deep inside me, but that it was *this* woman was wrong.

Another relieved smile. The "ooh" she made when she found my chocolate mint creamer went straight to my dick. I made it reverse direction. Nothing about my privates needed to pay attention to the sounds Summer made.

She topped her mug with creamer, making the coffee a light brown.

I grunted. "Little coffee with your creamer?"

She smirked. "Do you have whipped cream?"

"No."

"Eh, well." She inhaled over the top of her mug and took a drink. A small sigh left her. "This'll do."

"The roads are covered and the wind is strong enough to decrease visibility. The snow should stop soon, but the plows won't be out in force until Monday." The crews worked weekends, but they'd be clearing emergency routes and town roads. The route to my place was neither.

"You mind?"

"Wouldn't matter if I did." I didn't mind, but at the same time, I wanted her gone.

Her stomach grumbled. She put her hand to her abdomen and took another drink. She cupped her mug in both hands and wandered back to the window. "I love the windows in the guest bedroom."

I dropped my gaze from her, focusing on the swirling brown at the bottom of my cup. I used to adore that view too. I had built that room to be mine. Spacious, with a gorgeous overlook. Simple.

My room now was in the back of the house. The picture out the window was pretty, full of fir trees and the road that wound up the valley, but not like upstairs.

I waited for her to ask about food, but she never did. Unless she'd packed snacks in her suitcase, she hadn't eaten since before I'd intervened between her and Boyd. "You hungry?"

"No." Another long exhale. "My stomach disagrees, but I have no appetite."

She had to eat. I couldn't have her collapsing on me in the middle of nowhere. Then the wrath of her family would be aimed at me instead of her shitty ex.

I pulled out bacon and eggs. I was pulling a skillet out of the cupboard when she appeared next to me.

"Need help?" she asked.

Her sweet-strawberry-sunshine scent wafted over me. I'd smell her everywhere if she stayed in my house too long. "No."

"Do you have any . . ."

I straightened from my bend, wincing at the pinch in my hip. I hadn't done my stretches this morning. Or yesterday morning. This whole month had been shit for taking care of myself with that damn invitation staring at me. "Have any what?"

"Produce?"

"Bananas."

She waited like she thought I'd rattle off a list. The tips of my ears burned. I had nothing else.

Her mouth quirked when I didn't continue. "The banana's fine."

A spark of irritation heated the back of my neck. I didn't have whipped cream or basic fruits and vegetables beyond a few bananas that were close to what Mom called the *banana bread stage*.

I spun on a heel and pain laced up my leg. "Fuck."

Summer got closer, her scent growing impossibly stronger. "What? What's wrong?"

Embarrassment wiped out my restraint. "Goddammit, Summer. Back off a little, will ya?"

Her eyes widened and her mouth dropped open.

Shame swamped me from head to toe. She meant well. My pain wasn't her fault. I pressed my hands on the countertop and let my head hang. "It's my leg." And her. I was forgetting myself around her in the home where I could usually be myself. Where I didn't have to pretend I was doing fine for the few people in my life who gave a fuck.

"And I'm in the way. I'm sorry."

She was sorry? Fuck. "No, Summer. I don't like . . ." I pinched the bridge of my nose. The throb in my leg dulled, concentrating around my knee. ". . . people," I finished, lamely, realizing too late she'd think I meant her.

There was a moment of silence. Had I offended her? How could I have not?

"Do you have internet out here?" she asked.

I wasn't prepared for the subject change, but I grabbed on to it. "Haven't you tried your phone?"

"Battery's dead. I left the charger at the church." She leaned against the counter while I started opening the package of bacon. "Hopefully, one of my sisters found it."

"I have Wi-Fi." For a small rural town, Bourbon Canyon and the surrounding area got good coverage. "I don't stream much of anything. See if your phone works with my charger."

"Where is it?"

Shit. Her scent was bad enough in my living room, kitchen, and probably in my bathroom. I couldn't have strawberry sunshine invading my bedroom. "I'll grab it. Start the bacon?"

She nodded and glanced away. "I don't mean to be trouble."

"Since when do you care if you stir up some trouble?" My question wasn't teasing.

A furrow formed between her brows. "Being a bother and stirring up trouble is different."

"Mom told me once it's okay to be a bother sometimes."

She arched a reddish-blond brow. "Did you listen to her?"

I limped past her. She'd know the answer.

Summer

Jonah's charger didn't work for my phone. He left me with his phone and went outside. I had heard the telltale scrapes of metal on concrete, but when I went outside to see if he could use help shoveling snow, he'd growled at me to get inside. I wasn't dressed for shoveling.

He was right. I was dressed for a Bali honeymoon. Instead of being across the ocean in a private villa, I wasn't far from home in a mountain cabin.

And I was glad.

The constant stomach pain from worrying about the flight was gone. The anxiety smoldering in my gut? Vanished. I could finally be hungry again, and after the generous portion of crispy bacon and scrambled eggs Jonah had fed me, I was ready to eat again. Months of nibbling here and there, worried I was going to end up becoming one giant ulcer before I stepped on the plane, was over with one slap. I was ravenous.

I got up from my movie marathon and went to the kitchen.

He'd left his phone on the table so I could call who I needed, and I hadn't touched the thing. Last night, before my phone had died, I'd sent them all messages thanking them for dealing with the fallout and also letting them know I needed some time, and when I knew more about the roads, I'd update them.

I wasn't due back to work for over three weeks. I couldn't very well stay at Jonah's for that long. Could I?

No. I couldn't.

The way he'd barked at me this morning should've sent me running, but I'd recognized the outburst for what it was. Sick of someone hovering. Sick of being checked on and people thinking you weren't strong enough to handle the basics. My memories of those feelings were old, but I knew them well.

His cupboards were full of canned goods—beans, stews, soups. His fridge was a repository of processed meat and his freezer was stocked with beef and some pork and chicken. I found canned vegetables that'd go well with a roast. Did he have plans for supper or was he going to dive into one of the many packs of bacon again?

Fuck it. I was throwing something in the oven for supper. When I was looking for a roasting pan, I found a small door around the corner, opposite the one that led to the garage. A storage space under the stairs with onions, potatoes, garlic, and squash.

Produce that wasn't brined. Perfect.

I set about cleaning and cutting potatoes. They'd been pulled from the ground and stored. I couldn't see Jonah crawling through the dirt with his leg, but his mom used to have an impressive garden. She must've kept it going. Without her, Jonah might not touch a veggie.

My gaze kept straying to the phone. I should call Mama. Her number had been the same since I'd first memorized it as a kid. I might be able to recall my sisters' numbers, but Mama should hear from me.

I tossed a seasoned frozen roast with cut potatoes and onions in the oven. Then I called Mama.

"Hello, Jonah. How is she?"

Of course, Mama had Jonah as a contact. She let people go when they wanted to be released, but she was always ready to let them back in. "No, Mama, it's me, and I'm fine."

"Summer, oh my god. I'm so glad to hear your voice."

"I didn't mean to worry you." I had so many apologies to make.

"Don't ever regret doing what you need to do."

"I shouldn't have—"

"Boyd hit you."

My throat closed up. I hated to confirm her suspicions, but she also sounded certain. "Yes," I whispered.

"Autumn went to make sure you were okay and she heard you cock off to Corinne. Good job on that."

Jonah wasn't the only witness, but at least Autumn hadn't seen the slap. That moment had made me feel as powerless as when our parents had crashed when we were kids. Scared. Helpless. Unsure what to do. I never wanted to be in that place again.

"I'm sorry I didn't go home," I blurted. Mama had been there for everything after the worst time of my life. She'd been there for all of us. And I'd run from her.

"Honey, I know how you are. Can't let your sisters see you crumble. But I am surprised you went with Jonah. I didn't think you two got along."

We'd bickered when we were younger. First, I'd been his friends' annoying little sister. Then I'd been a cocky senior dating his brother, and finally an arrogant college freshman who refused to be told what to do. Jonah had been the uptight older brother who didn't go to college and thought I was annoying. At that age, I'd had complicated feelings I'd been trying to sort out. Then after the accident . . . Well, I'd thought Jonah hated me too. "We didn't talk much, but he saw what Boyd did and stopped him from doing worse. I guess after that, I felt comfortable with him."

"I don't see Jonah tolerating behavior like that."

"He didn't."

"Good."

Mama's righteousness soothed me. "With the snow and wind, I don't know when I'll be home."

"You're safe there. Jonah will make sure of it."

"He has coffee and internet or I would walk home," I joked.

Mama chuckled. A moment later she went quiet. "How are you really doing?"

"I'm . . ." I should brush off her concerns and insist I was fine. But I wasn't, and I didn't want to lie to her. She *knew*. I also didn't want to get into the way I felt. I wanted to pull the blankets over my head. I'd give Mama a little of the truth. "I feel like a fool. I feel depressed, and I get these weird moments where I want to panic, and then I'm ashamed because you all had to deal with the fallout, and then I'm embarrassed I even got that far. I should've seen Boyd for what he was—and I know. I *know*." Jonah's comment about Boyd abusing my trust flittered through my head. I knew I shouldn't be ashamed. But I was. "So for a few days, I'd like to watch movies and not have to face reality."

"You do that. I'll talk to your siblings."

"Thanks, Mama."

I was setting the phone down when Jonah walked in from the garage on a swirl of cold air. The rumble of the garage door shutting cut off when he closed the door to the house.

He stepped out of his boots and shrugged out of his coat. When he plucked the black stocking hat off his head, his dark hair stuck up in a million different directions. He should look silly, not sexier and more approachable than when every strand was combed into place. This was the Jonah I was used to seeing. The older boy who used to hang out with my brothers.

Shoving a hand through his hair, he caught my eye. Then he sniffed. "Are you cooking?"

"I hope you don't mind. I even found vegetables."

He narrowed his eyes. "Where?"

"Under the stairs."

He relaxed. "Oh. I thought you meant like lettuce and apples when you asked."

"I did, but potatoes and onions are nice too. I cut some up with the roast."

He brushed snow off the bottom of his jeans and crossed through the kitchen. I had quit hearing shoveling, but he hadn't been in the garage.

My curiosity got the better of me. I'd always been in Jonah's business when I'd been younger. "What were you doing?"

"Working."

I got that he was closed off and private, but it'd be a long weekend if he didn't converse more. "What do you do for work?"

He glanced over his shoulder before he rounded out of the kitchen to the hallway that ran on the other side of the stairs. "I make things."

I got up and followed him, stopping at the foot of

the stairs. "Top-secret things? If you told me you'd have to kill me?"

He stopped outside the door across from what must be his bedroom and gave me a flat look. "What do you think I do all day out here?"

I lifted a shoulder. "Mountain-man stuff?"

His expression remained unreadable. "Yep."

He disappeared into his room.

What had I said wrong? And why did his reaction kick up my stomach acid again?

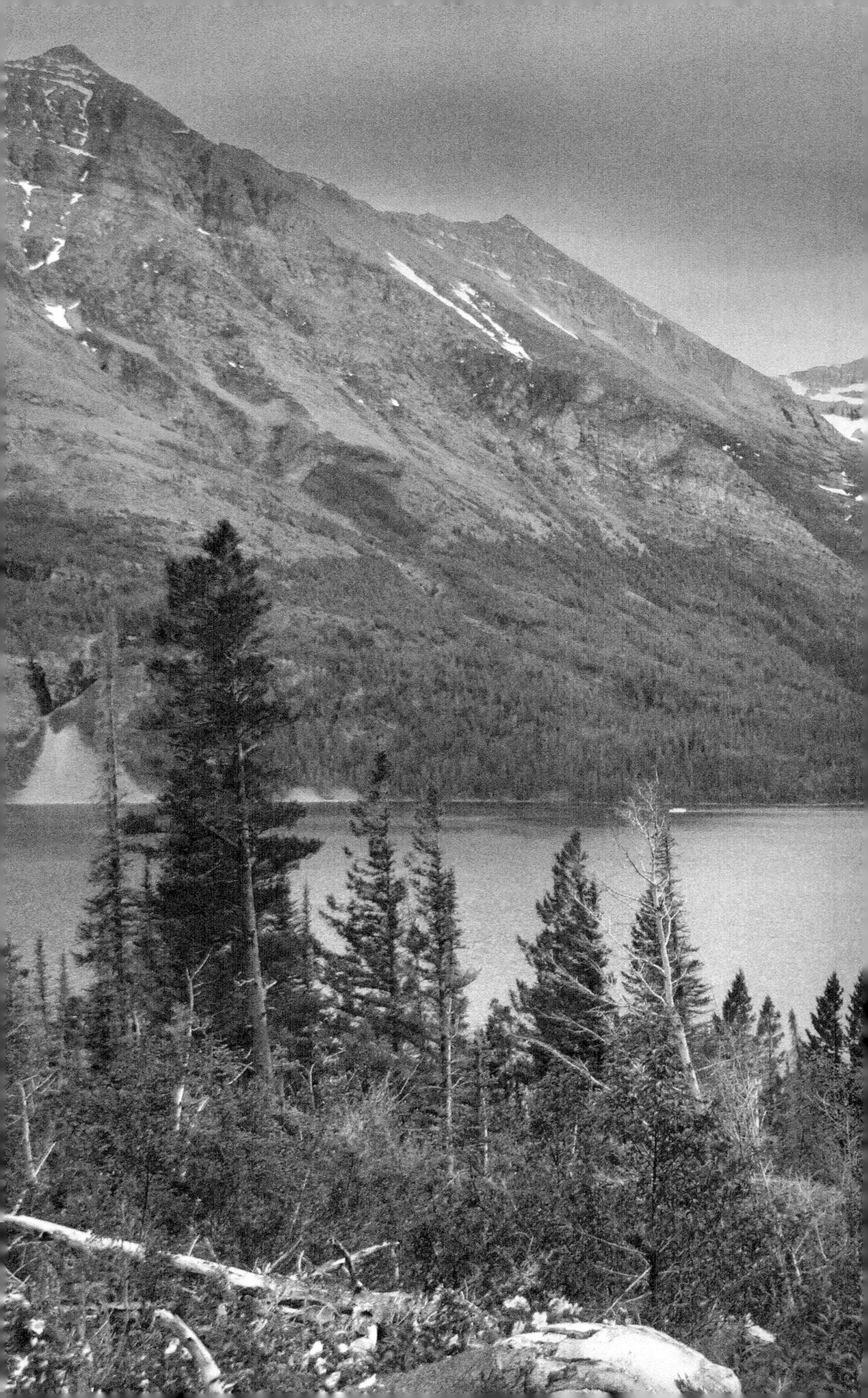

CHAPTER FOUR

Summer

The delicious smell of dinner cooking didn't pick up my spirits like I'd thought it would. I hoped a show would. I found the one free streaming service he was subscribed to. I went to the movie options.

Bride Wars was featured. I looked for another option. *Made of Honor*. Nope. I picked another. *Bridesmaids*.

Damn. The universe had a horrible sense of humor.

I shut the TV off and went to the window.

The snow wasn't as heavy as before. Every few minutes the wind would settle and the blanket of white took away the definition of the landscape. I squinted. I couldn't tell where the driveway turned into the lawn or dropped off into the ditch.

We weren't having a blizzard, but on rural mountain roads, it didn't matter.

The bedroom door opened, but I didn't turn around. I was already intruding in his home. The guy should be able to go into the bathroom without me watching. A squeak of the door was followed by the shower kicking on.

What did he do for work? I could ask Teller, but my phone was dead.

Although Jonah and Teller didn't hang out anymore. I'd overheard Teller talking to Tate and Tenor once. He'd tried dragging Jonah out, but Jonah's attitude was hard to put up with. Sounded like Jonah had chased my brother off, much like he had me. Although there was one part of that conversation that must have been different.

For so many years, I'd tried not to think about Jonah. But I'd worried about him. I'd discreetly kept tabs on him. Then, eventually, I'd had to move on. I lived and worked in Bozeman and tried to leave that time in my life behind.

After the heartbreak of losing Eli, Jonah's outburst had wrecked me. As if I hadn't felt guilty enough. As if I still didn't.

The shower turned off. I continued staring out the window. The sun was setting, but in the reflection of the glass I caught a flash of skin. I zeroed in on the spot, and in the two seconds it took for Jonah to go from the bathroom across the hall to his bedroom, I got a wavering look at his wide, muscled shoulders and the way his back tapered to his waist. His midnight-blue towel was wrapped around his waist. He had the same kind of towels in the bathroom upstairs.

My pulse hummed, the rate higher than moments ago. Great. Now, I was being creepy.

I had no business being attracted to him. None. I never had.

Yet it had never stopped me.

I might've ended my engagement a day ago, but I was still a red-blooded woman in her prime. Jonah was the exact opposite of Boyd.

Jonah looked like he could rend me limb from limb, and Boyd hated when his fingers were sticky. Yet Boyd was the more dangerous of the two.

"Doesn't the TV work?"

I yelped and slammed my hand to my heart. "Oh my god, Jonah. How are you so quiet?"

When I spun, I caught a flash of embarrassment. His damp hair was slicked off his face, revealing dark scruff. The ends of his long strands brushed the top of his collar. He was in a loose green flannel shirt and blue jeans. He leaned on a cane I'd seen propped against the wall by the stairs.

"Rubber bottom," he said gruffly.

I was a creepy intrusion, and now I could add insulting to the description. "That's not what I meant." His expression remained neutral. He didn't believe me and explaining I'd been dwelling on the quick glimpse I'd caught of him in a towel wasn't an option. "The TV's fine. But everything kept coming up wedding themed."

"That sucks."

"Tell me about it." My ten-thousand-dollar wedding dress was sitting in a heap in the corner of the guest bedroom. I had plenty of reminders I'd been a bride the day before.

He went to the couch and grabbed the remote. Gray socks were on his feet like the ones I'd found upstairs. He propped his cane against the cushions and guilt wound inside me. Autumn had said she thought he rarely came to town because of his injuries. She'd seen him in the grocery store once and a kid had loudly asked his mom *How did that guy get his scars?*

Jonah was flying through the options, subscribing to the most popular services.

"What are you— You don't have to do that. How much will all that cost?" He'd already put himself out enough for me.

The air in the room grew frosty, and he slid his icy gaze toward me. "A guy doesn't have to be an investment banker to be able to afford a few things."

"And a guy doesn't have to think that just because I dated a guy with money means I'm superficial," I snapped, then stiffened. There I went again.

He reclined against the back of the couch, a small flicker of satisfaction in his eyes. "There she is."

"Who?" I looked outside. Was someone taking chances on the blanketed roads in the dark?

"The annoying girl I used to know."

A large part of me sparked alive. A smaller but significant part of me cringed. "You've called me worse."

He sat forward, his expression stricken. His right leg was bent more than his left, but he rested his arms on his knees. "When?"

"At the hospital. After the funeral."

His face paled under his scruff and the scar stood out even more. With a sinking stomach, I realized why he'd kept the scruff. His facial hair hid the worst of his scarring along his jaw.

When he'd been rehospitalized for an infection in his knee and the doctors had been worried they couldn't save his leg, the jagged scar on the left side of his face had been hard to look at. Still fresh and not completely healed, the pink and red puckered flesh had been as furious as the rest of him.

I didn't know what I had thought, visiting him. Perhaps I did know and that was even worse. I'd deserved to be driven off.

"I, uh . . ." He clenched his teeth together.

"You were in pain. Angry and grieving." We'd all been, and that was why my last interaction with him had sat so poorly for so long. And because I'd believed him. His words rang clear. I still remembered what he'd said perfectly.

I don't have the fucking time to deal with you, Summer. Eli spent every damn day worshipping the ground your arrogant ass struts on and yet he's dead because of the poison your family makes. He got a taste for it because you taught him all about bourbon, Little Miss Know It All. What'd you think coming here? I'd want to steal my brother's girl? If you want a guy to follow you like a lovesick puppy, I ain't it. We aren't friends, and we aren't family. Now we never will be. Get out of my goddamn face and don't ever let me see you again.

Jonah cleared his throat. "What I said . . ." He clenched his jaw.

"It's fine." I regretted saying anything. That day topped one of the more horrible ones of my existence, but at least no one had lost their life. I'd eaten some humble pie, and then I'd gone back to college. I'd moved on and tried not to think about how right Jonah had been. I'd forced myself to continue on and never look back. "I didn't think about how it would look and I should've."

There were so many things I should've done differently then. So damn many.

"I don't know what I was thinking," he said roughly,

his denim eyes on mine. "I wasn't in my right mind, and I shouldn't have spoken to you like that." His gaze dropped to the floor. "I knew better. I knew you weren't there out of more than concern, but I was mad at the world. I'm sorry."

The oven beeped. Words locked in my throat. He shouldn't be apologizing, yet I was caught in the past.

I scurried into the kitchen, leaving him to stare at his clasped hands.

Jonah

She ate primly, cutting her roast, sliding the piece of meat through her steak sauce. Then she leaned forward ever so slightly and slipped the food between her pink lips.

The reminder of our last significant conversation had killed the awkward but comfortable air between us. I'd pulled up a bunch of channels for her to watch, many with a free trial period, not that I needed to pinch my pennies, and then I'd taken her comment and lashed out at her.

I speared a piece of medium-done roast and stuffed it in my mouth. The savory flavor bloomed over my tongue. "This is Dunn beef."

She sawed another chunk off. "I thought so."

Was I trying to impress her? To show her I wasn't a useless mountain man? Everyone thought I did nothing up in my shack in the boondocks. I didn't, but I was also no longer able to help Dad as much as he needed. My horseback days were done thanks to my left leg, but also, I had my own work.

These days, Dad hired out, preferring to take more of an office and oversight role. Mom had done the same and I sat out more ranch events every year. I was tired of Dad scrambling to make accommodations, and I was busy with my own job, so it hadn't mattered.

Did Summer even remember when I had crossed paths with her and Boyd the Slapper? Two years ago, I'd made a stop at the hardware store. I'd been waiting for my order to get brought out. Summer had walked in, said a surprised and tense hi to me, and I'd nodded. She'd kept walking. The jackass hadn't waited until I was out of earshot before snidely asking if she knew all the homeless men in town.

I hadn't heard her reply, but now I was dying to know how she'd responded.

We ate in silence. Darkness cloaked the house.

She picked up her plate, but stopped, holding the dishes off the tabletop.

Heat prickled my body. When she set her items down and ran her hand over the polished wood, I could've groaned. The surface became an extension of me.

"This table is amazing. Reminds me of the north entrance of Yellowstone in the spring after the melt."

My ears heated. Good thing my hair was long enough to hide the red tips. Goddammit, of course she'd nail the exact effect I'd gone for. She traced a finger along the river of blue epoxy poured between the slabs of black walnut. The path between the wooden frame wove like a river and the color reached the top of the wood before fading like water along a shore.

She feathered her fingertips along the edges. "So smooth. I've always loved these tables. There was one I wanted last year. I saw it in Kendra's Eats and Seats, but Boyd . . ." Her shoulders slumped. "Just another time I listened to him when I shouldn't've."

Kendra's Eats and Seats was a small sandwich shop and furniture store. Customers could buy the items they ate off and sat on. Local crafters used Kendra's place to sell a lot of their wares without having to worry about the sales part of the deal. Kendra took care of it all and loved showcasing local talent.

"Was it the coffee table with a half-barrel stand and a wood and resin top?"

She tapped her finger. "That's the one. You saw that too?"

"I made it."

She blinked at me. Blinked again. "You *made* that?"

"The barrel is from Copper Summit."

Her lips parted and she continued to stare at me.

"Carrie Kloss bought the table for the dentist's office. Pretty good work for a homeless guy, huh?" Why had I tacked on the last part? She didn't need to deal with asshole Jonah this weekend.

The shame from yesterday returned to her eyes. I was a son of a bitch.

"I'm sorry you heard that. Boyd was insecure and I told him he was being rude." Her lips pursed. "He pouted for a week." She shook her head like she was coming out of a fog. "I'm surprised you work with oak barrels. Or Copper Summit."

"Like you said, I was upset. I know Copper Summit Distillery isn't responsible for Eli's death. And neither are you," I tacked on quietly.

Her eyes grew haunted. "Right," she murmured. "Does Teller deliver the barrels?"

I frowned. "Why would he? He's got better things to do."

"He'd make time."

He probably would. Teller was another tenacious Bailey, but even he'd given up on me. "We don't have much in common anymore. It's not like I can haul a canoe anywhere."

"Why can't you canoe?"

Because I'd gotten tired of how many accommodations I needed to do what used to come so easy. "Same reason as hunting. Uneven ground and a bulky canoe make my knee upset." My whole left side.

Sadness filled her eyes, and instead of my ire rising toward her, I was upset with myself. I had the strongest urge to earn so much more than sadness from her. I could canoe if I wanted. I might need to book another massage afterward, or take a few more over-the-counter pain meds, but I could do it. If it was a short trip from car to shore. And if the shore wasn't terribly rocky.

I missed the fun. I missed laughing with my friends. I missed trekking anywhere I wanted. As always, thoughts of Eli crowded around my wants and guilt took over. My mood wasn't the only one that changed.

Summer's demeanor had shifted to melancholy. Did something about our conversation remind her of her wedding? She shook her head. "I need to take a bath."

"Leave the dishes. You cooked. I'll clean up." It was the least I could do for letting my resentment show when she'd stuck with me for support.

She kept her head down and nodded. Then she scurried from the room, the hem of her beachy dress fluttering.

I tipped my head back. I was the asshole brother. I shouldn't have brought up that day I'd seen her and Boyd. Eli hadn't been a saint but he'd never made her feel bad about herself or her circumstances.

I put away the leftovers and loaded the dishwasher. I was about to go sit on the couch but changed course to my bedroom. She might want to watch TV, and she didn't need to be afraid of another outburst from me.

When I passed the bathroom, the water was running but I caught an unmistakable sound. Quiet weeping.

My chest was flayed open. She was crying. I'd made the broken bride *cry*.

Goddammit, the sooner the roads were cleared, the better she'd be getting off my land and back to her family. I'd never lay a hand on her, but making her cry didn't make me much better than her crappy ex.

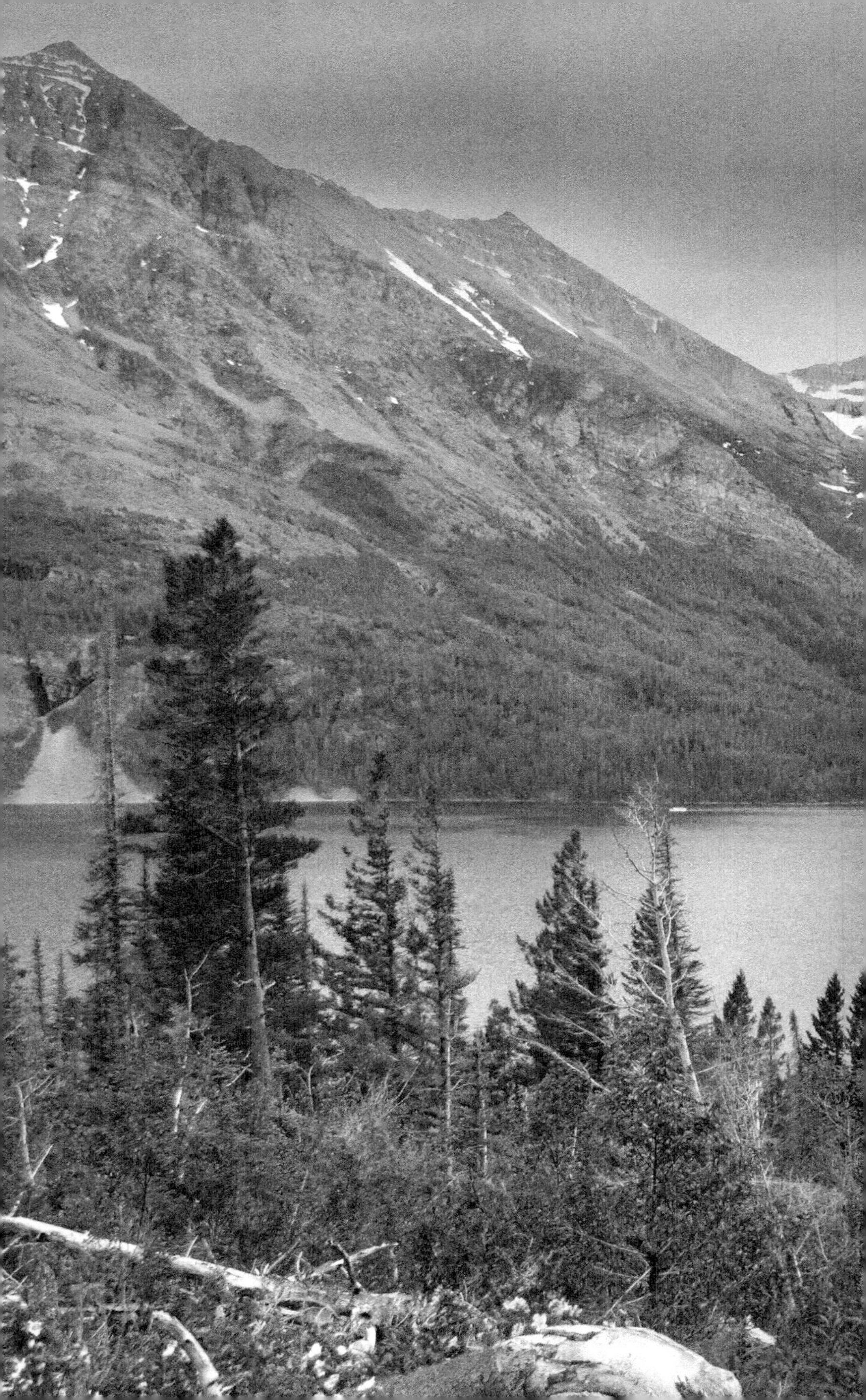

CHAPTER FIVE

Jonah

I came in from the shop to make a sandwich out of the roast Summer had cooked two nights ago. My stomach had been rumbling for the stuff all morning. I didn't usually bother with breakfast. I preferred to get lost in my work, but staying in the shop all day made me antsy when Summer was in my house.

The snow was cleaned off the concrete pads in front of the garage and the shop. My driveway was clear. The wind had diminished to a light breeze. All we were waiting on was the roads to get cleared. I took my gear off and found Summer on the couch. Again. Just like yesterday.

She'd gone from *Die Hard* to *Final Destination* to *Twister*. An eclectic mix. Now she was on *Legally Blonde*, curled up in the same corner of my couch, wrapped in a throw quilt Mom had made me when I'd first moved in.

Her blond hair was sticking out, too pale from what

I was used to. Her hair was like her shampoo. A hint of strawberry. Not that I'd paid attention, but the rare times I'd caught a glimpse of her roaming through town, she'd looked different. She'd been more polished with each sighting. Her hair was lighter, her nails always done instead of plain, and her clothing looked more and more city and less like the jeans and T-shirts she used to run around in.

A younger Summer had always appeared ready to run the distillery or jump on the back of a horse. Present-day Summer was a step away from the investment banking world of her douche ex.

A younger Summer had come to my hospital room, dressed like an angel in a loose white top, skin-hugging blue jeans, and well-worn cowboy boots. She'd sat on the edge of my bed and put her hand over mine. At the time, I'd been going through brutal physical therapy on that arm. She'd sat on my left side, and she hadn't been afraid to touch me or look me in the eye. She'd been properly sympathetic and absolutely gorgeous. The grief and anguish in her eyes had matched my own. Her skin had slid against mine, a slice of heaven in my fog of pain. I had only wanted her to keep touching me. My fingertips had tingled with the urge to stroke her. The guilt and shame had staggered me. So I'd turned into an absolute prick and run her off.

The movie finished and she scrolled through a list for more.

"Find anything good?" I asked to fill the silence between us. After our dinner together the other night and her cry in the bathroom, she'd been subdued.

I did not like a subdued Summer.

She lifted a shoulder. "Do you want to watch something?"

I wanted to see her smile. I wanted to hear her laugh. It'd been so damn long since I'd heard her laugh.

I wasn't exactly a comedy connoisseur. I played all kinds of music in my shop and sometimes I listened to podcasts and the news. "Know any funny shows?"

Her blank stare stayed on the TV. "No."

If I was the one who'd put out her fire, I'd never forgive myself. "Douchebag didn't believe in comedy, so you gave it up too?"

She frowned, but a spark of light flamed deep in her eyes. "What's that supposed to mean?"

"It means you're a sad sack, and I can't stand it."

Her mouth dropped open. "My wedding—"

"Turned into a shit show. I was there."

"I don't know how bad of a shit show—"

"Does it matter?"

"Jonah—"

"Summer."

She narrowed her eyes on me. "You're interrupting me."

"I learned it from this annoying girlfriend of my brother's."

Her lips twitched. "I did not interrupt you."

"Please. I couldn't finish one thought before you were telling me how I should be doing something differently."

She gave her head a small shake, but a small smile appeared. "You're being a dick on purpose."

"As opposed to . . ."

A faint giggle left her. "There's something to be said for self-awareness."

"I'm very aware of myself, sunshine." The endearment slipped out, and I couldn't take it back. I also didn't care to.

Astonishment flickered over her face. "I got in my head."

Grateful she'd ignored the pet name, I kept the humor going. "Scary place to be."

That earned me a scowl.

I crossed the expanse of the living room. My leg was achy from the snow removal and my knee was especially threatening. I should've grabbed a cane, but I wasn't making a U-turn.

Dropping onto the couch, I let out a breath. Fire laced through my hip. I needed to stretch and get a massage. Neither would be happening soon. Summer wouldn't be here much longer, and now that she was opening up, I didn't want to miss the show.

"The roads should be clear tomorrow," she said.

"Yup." I changed my weight to my good hip. "Pick a movie."

"What if I don't know any funny ones?"

"Then watch one of the bridal shows you didn't want to touch the other night. See if you're ready to return home."

She was in the middle of lifting the remote when she paused. "You know what? I think you're onto something."

Screens flashed as she scrolled through different menus. "Here. Maybe it'll make me feel better."

"Runaway Bride is a little on the nose, isn't it?"

She rolled her eyes and cuddled into the corner of the couch, drawing the throw up to her chin. "If I can't take it, I can't go home." Her eyes widened. "Oh, I mean, I'll go. I don't need to keep crashing—"

"I know what you mean. If you need longer, you can stay. I'll try to figure out how to get everything done around you."

The corner of her mouth hooked up. "You interrupted me again."

"I learned from the best."

She laughed. "I wonder who it was." A wistful sigh left her. "Do you have popcorn?"

"Nope." The same food had been in my cupboards for years.

"A sweet wine or maybe a Summer's Summit?" She lifted her brow. Summer's Summit was the line made for her. Darin Bailey had made all his kids a special blend.

Cold shrank my good humor. "I don't have alcohol in the house."

"Oh." She made herself tinier in her corner. "I'm sorry. I should've . . ." Squeezing her eyes shut. "I'm so sorry."

Me and my big damn mouth. "Like I said, I know Copper Summit isn't to blame. I used to be on meds that I couldn't have alcohol with. Now, I can't tamper with my balance."

She gave me a placating smile and turned her attention to the TV, but her expression was introspective. She wasn't seeing the show.

I reached over and snatched the remote out of her hand. After pausing the movie, I leaned over. "You're going to stay out of that cunning brain of yours, quit second-guessing everything you do, and we're going to enjoy the movie."

She studied me for several long heartbeats. She

sucked her lower lip between her teeth and pulled it back out. "And you said I was bossy."

Summer

I set my bag by the door to the garage and stepped into my slippers. They were stained gray from sprinting through the parking lot.

Jonah crowded into the nook by the back door and stuffed his feet into his boots. "Is that all you have to wear?"

I straightened. I was in my fourth flirty floral dress. At least I had leggings for this one. My other dresses were dirty and all I had left clean were my bikinis and beach wraps.

I shrugged. "I'm Bali ready. It's fine." The trip to Mama's house would only take twenty minutes.

"It's cold out."

"I came here in a wedding dress." Admittedly, the wedding dress had more fabric, but I wasn't putting that thing on again.

His eyes darkened. "Wait here." He disappeared into the garage.

Several minutes ticked by. I had no phone to scroll through, only the silence I'd appreciated during my stay. My condo in Bozeman was quiet. Sort of. My neighbors were mostly working professionals who kept to themselves, but it wasn't like living in the country. Sounds of traffic and people talking invaded the space. There were no sounds of nature unless a storm rolled through.

When Jonah returned, he had a pile of winter clothing in his hands. He handed me a pair of blue ski pants. "Everything's cold. I don't keep the garage heated. A waste of money when I have the shop to work in."

I eyed the pants. "I could wear these as overalls."

He grunted and hung a black winter coat up on the wall next to me. "Try them on." Underneath the clothing was a pair of mud boots. "These were for turkey season."

I would swim in it all, but the gust of cold air that had come in from just the garage was enough to spur me into action. "You must have a lot of extra winter clothing." I had my fun winter wear and my winter work gear. I didn't throw away old coats. They were rotated into the ranch clothing.

"These were for my . . . old hobbies."

Old hobbies. He had let it all go. He spoke like he had to, yet he'd been outside doing manual labor half the time I'd been here. Building furniture wasn't an office job. Why'd he given everything else up?

The snow pants swamped me, but I tugged them all the way to my chest and cinched them. He handed me the coat. My fingers were lost inside the sleeves, but he zipped the front for me.

"Guess I won't need gloves," I said, holding a droopy sleeve up.

"And it has a hood. Now try the boots."

I stepped out of my sandals and into the boots. They were cool, like the rest of the gear. Lifting a foot, I giggled. I had to keep my toes tense to take a step without walking right out of them.

His lips quirked and he grabbed my suitcase and the garbage bag I'd bundled my wedding dress in. "They'll do. You have something if we get stranded."

Grateful he was thinking about winter survival while I was low-key wishing I could stay for longer, I went into the garage.

I walked like I was one of Autumn's students making a path through two feet of snow on the playground. My boots dragged on the floor and I snickered, then waddled like a penguin.

He came around from behind me and opened the door. The corner of his mouth lifted when I shuffled the rest of the way. "You gonna balance an egg on your feet?"

My laughter grew. So fucking silly, but Jonah had gone with it. Boyd would've had a comment that made me feel uncouth and embarrassed.

I climbed in, struggling to keep the boots on. "Where's your coat?"

He bent to guide my foot in and hold the dangling boot so it didn't fall on the ice-cold floor. "In the back seat."

I glanced back as he loaded my belongings. The tan material of a work coat was on the back seat. A hat and gloves were probably under the jacket. He'd have a true winter survival kit under the seat.

When he got behind the wheel, the cab shrank around us. His fresh-cut-pine smell wrapped around me. So different from Boyd.

I was returning to the real world. This respite wasn't my life. Mama's house was welcoming and cozy, and I could have private time, but not like the cabin. I didn't have to hide in a room to get peace. Jonah could be on the couch with me, watching a show with a stoic expression that didn't reveal if he was enjoying the movie or not, and I didn't feel crowded. I didn't feel like everyone was in my business.

He backed out of the garage and I squinted. With the sun high in the sky, the snow glare was blinding. I put the shade down but my eyes started to water. Had I been in Bozeman so long I'd forgotten how piercingly white the country got after a snowfall?

How was Jonah driving? Lines winged out from the corners of his narrowed eyes. No sunglasses for him. My pair was in my car, which was at Mama's, thanks to my brothers.

I wouldn't have to go back to Bozeman until it was time to return to work. "It's going to be weird."

He concentrated on the freshly cleared road. "What is?"

"Going back to an empty condo." I lived alone, but for the first time in a long time, there was no one to make plans with. No friends. No fiancé. And most of my family was in Bourbon Canyon. "I was with Boyd for two years but it feels like so much longer."

"One he can't get into?" This time, he spared me a glance, menace in his eyes.

"No. He never had a key. And he never wanted to hang out there when he had an obnoxious milk box house."

"Milk box house?"

"A new-age build that looks like he cut a flap in the middle of a milk box and stuffed a smaller milk box inside." I'd never told Boyd I thought his place was ugly. The regret was strong. I had pushed to sell and buy a different house after the honeymoon. "Anyway, I keep expecting things to be different but they won't be, really. He hardly came to Bourbon Canyon with me to visit my family. He worked long hours. Our dates were mostly his work dinners and they were so boring."

"What would you have rather done?"

I stared out the window, closing my left eye because it was still fucking bright. "Talked. You know how you sit at a bar and just get to know each other?" I turned my head in time to see a muscle flex in the corner of his jaw. Shit. Right. "Sorry."

"Don't be. I'm not a bar guy."

He used to be. He hadn't been a barfly, but he and Teller, and sometimes Tenor and Tate, would be out at night as much as they had been during the day. Jonah used to do tastings with Daddy and my brothers. I'd been jealous when they'd become a guys' night. Mostly, they'd been outdoorsy guys, but Teller and Jonah used to be seen around town all the time.

"You and Boyd didn't *talk*?" He lifted a brow, but that pop in his jaw was still there.

"We didn't—I mean—it wasn't— The sex was boring." Oh my god. I'd said that. Those words had gone out of my mouth into Jonah's ears. I hadn't even confessed to my sisters that Boyd was lackluster.

Jonah stopped by a larger county road that would skim the edges of town before heading back out of city limits to Bailey land. "A milk box house and boring sex? Jesus, sunshine. You know you deserve better than that."

The nickname rolled off his tongue again. He'd never had a pet name for me when we were younger. It would've been inappropriate, considering I'd been dating his brother, but whenever he said it, I preened. We were different than we had been. Maybe things between us could be different too.

"I think I just wanted to be married. To get on with the family life. Wynter's doing it and she's six years younger than me."

The brow ticked up again, but he remained quiet.

Why did all my embarrassing admissions slip out around him? He already thought me annoying and had spoken as if he hated me. We were at rock bottom. Maybe that was why I'd left with him. I had nowhere to go but up.

I didn't have to be the oldest and wisest sister. I didn't need to be the perfect girlfriend. I wasn't the nepotism baby trying to prove she was a boss bitch at work. With Jonah, I was just flawed Summer Kerrigan.

We were still sitting at the intersection, so I kept talking. "So, anyway, after Daddy's illness and death, Wynter's wedding and the baby, and then my wedding, I'm going to return to Bozeman and just . . . be." Did I know how?

His narrowed stare was directed at the windshield. "Promise me one thing, Summer."

I owed him so much the answer was easy. "What?"

"Take every day of your honeymoon. Stay with your mom and learn how to just *be* so you don't let any more Boyds into your life."

I smiled, warmed inside that he was thinking of my well-being. Except staying at Mama's with nothing to do but chores while people sidestepped around me was like a cheese grater to the skin. "I'll make you a deal."

Humor lit his gaze, but the hardness didn't soften. "You can try."

"I'll stay with Mama for the duration of my honeymoon *and* work remotely. I need to preserve my sanity, and I really do enjoy my job."

"Good enough." He didn't make a move to turn and continue driving to Mama's. "Eli would've wanted you happy." He sounded like he was trying to convince himself.

My throat grew thick. Eli would've wanted me happy if he'd known he was going to die. If he hadn't gotten drunk that day, who knew where life would've taken us. "I had to move on."

"I know." He nodded and his Adam's apple worked up and down. "I know he was just really happy with you. It'd have gutted him to see you with a guy like Boyd."

My mouth went dry. I tried licking my lips. "Yeah. It'd have gutted him," I said hoarsely. "But we were just kids. People grow and change. It was young love. Puppy love."

Jonah's brows crashed together. "He was head over heels for you."

Eli had been. He'd been fun in high school, but he'd gotten smothering when we'd started college. "Didn't mean I was his happily ever after."

Jonah shook his head. "Good thing he died not knowing different."

I made a choking sound.

Jonah grimaced. "Shit, I'm getting all morbid. I just . . . think about him a lot."

"He idolized you." Eli had one major flaw and that was basing his identity on others.

"Yeah, he did. That's why he was in my cabin, drinking my bourbon. He'd seen me and Teller solve all of life's problems over a glass and he thought he'd do the same. I just wish I'd known what was bothering him."

I bit the inside of my cheek. I hadn't told anyone about that day. The outcome was bad enough. The details would make a hard time even harder. "I know it's easier said than done, but don't be too hard on yourself.

Eli had his own mind. He had his own feelings and his own reactions. We can't . . . We can't take responsibility for what he did." My chest tightened and my breathing turned shallow.

Easier said than done was right.

Jonah was shaking his head, his jaw cut from granite.

I put my hand on his arm, only my fingers sticking out of the long sleeve of the coat. "I know. Just try not to be too hard on yourself. He wouldn't have wanted that." When I pulled my arm away, my hand disappeared in the material.

His gaze flicked down to where I had touched him through his sweatshirt. "If anyone knows what he would have wanted, it's you."

My nod was shaky. I had known what Eli wanted, and I'd known what I wanted. Neither of us had gotten it.

I lifted my sleeve, striving to change the subject. Once again, I was a chicken and taking an out when I saw it. "When we get to Mama's, I'll change and give these back to you before you leave."

"Don't worry about it. I'm not skiing anytime soon." The echo of loss was louder than any humor in his voice.

He let off the brake and pulled onto the highway. I was tempted to tell him to turn back. I'd run away from my wedding, but I wasn't ready to return to my life. But after the last few minutes, if I stayed with Jonah, I'd only be reminded of another time I'd fled my problems and let more than myself down.

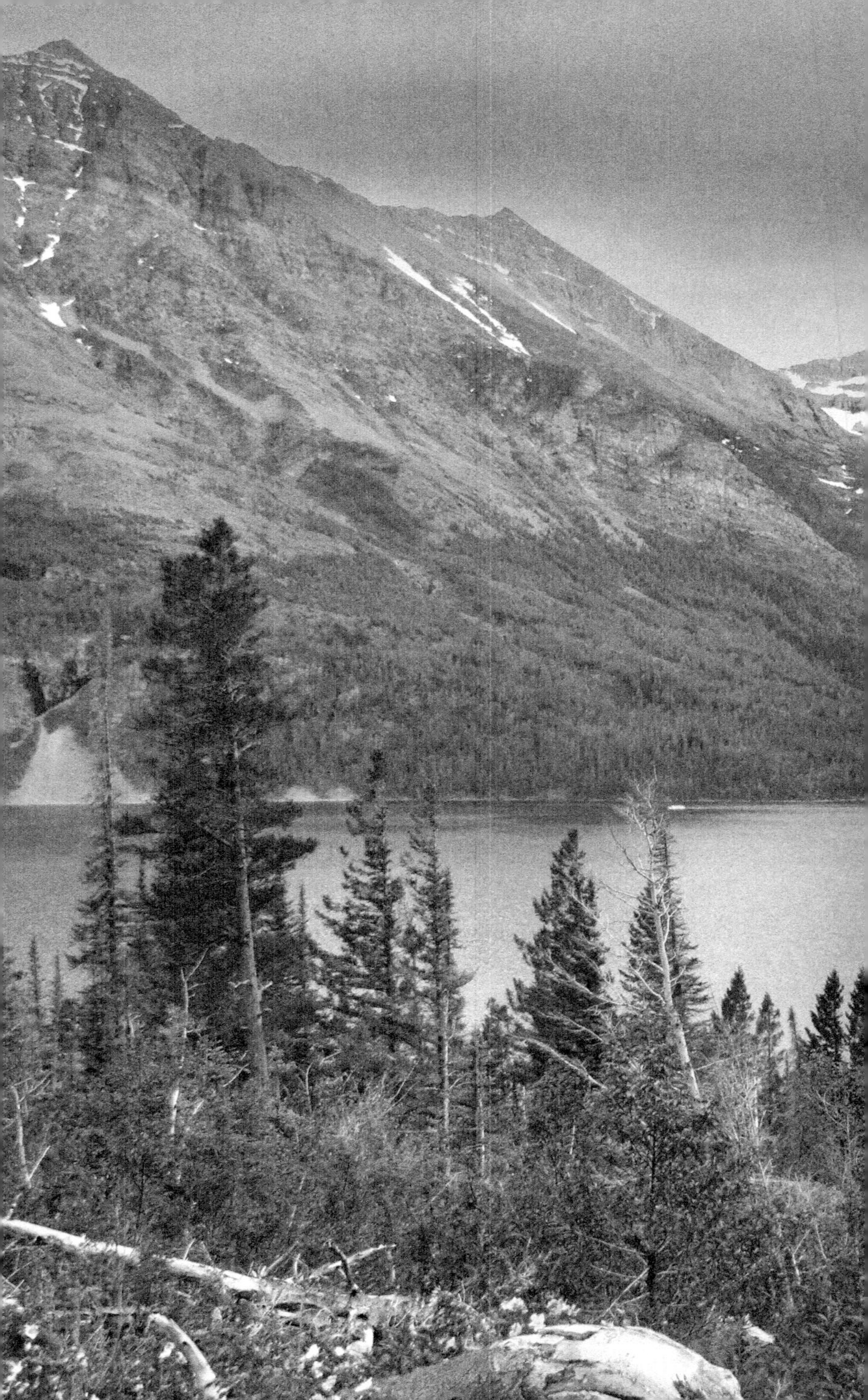

CHAPTER SIX

Summer

The day after Jonah dropped me off, Tate drove me to Bozeman to grab some clothing that would work better for a Montana winter instead of a Bali honeymoon. He acted like a lookout until I was all packed into his pickup. Then he also interrogated me on who had the keys to my place.

I'd never been so grateful for Boyd's elitist personality. Our break was fairly clean, and his need for maintaining a certain status would keep him away from me or I would be loud about how he'd hit me.

Tate parked by the back door of Mama's house. "You call if you need anything."

"Got it." I went to open the door.

"No, Summer."

I stopped with my hand on the handle. He was using his bossy-big-brother voice. "I *know*, Tate. I'm fine."

"You're the girl who bought me for Scarlett at a bachelor's auction as a way to get us together."

"Would you have asked her out otherwise?"

"Maybe, but that's not what I mean." He rested his elbow on the steering wheel and twisted his torso toward me. "You butt in. You interfere. You tell us what to do."

I frowned and picked at my plaid pajama bottoms. I'd been tempted to keep Jonah's snow pants on. Only a day had gone by and I wished I was at the quiet cabin, hiding from life. "You make me sound awful."

"That's not what I mean either," he said, exasperated. "You care about us, but what makes you think you're the only one of us who can help? You got snowed in with Dunn instead."

"What do you mean? He hasn't done anything bad."

"*I* know that. How would you know that?"

"I've known him most of my life, Tate."

He let out a sigh. "My point isn't whether or not Jonah is a decent guy. I wouldn't have let you leave with him if I hadn't thought you'd be safe. I'm trying to point out that you avoided everyone who's invested in your happiness and went with someone who's been tucked into his mountain cabin since he left the hospital for the last time."

For the last time. The ache behind my sternum returned. Jonah had had such a rocky road to recovery and then he'd secluded himself. "He's punishing himself."

"No kidding."

I rolled my eyes at his sarcasm, then dropped my gaze to my hands. "I was ashamed."

"We weren't ashamed of you."

I gave him a small smile. "Thank you. I kind of needed to hear that."

"I thought I was a failure when I got divorced."

I tipped my head and considered him. Tate was the oldest of us all—of his brothers, of me and my sisters, of all the fosters who'd been through Mama's house. He was infallible. I often forgot he was just a guy going through life wondering if he was making the right decisions.

Only he had. Maybe he and his ex hadn't been meant to be, but they were amicable. They co-parented around his ex's heavy travel schedule. His wife, Scarlett, glowed each time I saw her, and not just when she was pregnant. My friend was happy in a way she never had been when she'd been single and would shyly drop her gaze when Autumn and I talked about Tate.

"You succeeded even in divorce," I pointed out. He hadn't broken her heart and she hadn't lashed out and done something stupid.

"Divorce has a way of making everything feel like the opposite of success." He scowled at me. "How did we end up talking about me again?"

I smiled. "Busted."

"You're the most stubborn of us all."

"Take that back! I cannot out-stubborn Junie."

He rocked his head from side to side. "You're right. But we're not talking about her. You can come to me if you need anything. I'm not my wife or Autumn, or Junie or Wynter, but you can talk to me. I won't fly off the handle. I'd like to think I've matured in my old age."

"I guess I just wanted an escape. I had to figure out how I felt first."

He nodded. "I can see that. Jonah would definitely give you the space."

A string tugged at my heart. Jonah had given me space, yet he'd been close when I'd needed someone to understand. We weren't friends, but we also weren't *not* friends. "He doesn't go to town very much, does he?"

Tate's lips pressed together, like he was deciding what to say. "Teller said he leaves more than we think. I mean, he has to get groceries and get supplies for his business."

"Right, the business. I had no idea he built furniture."

"Everyone knows. His pieces disappear as soon as there's a sales tag on them. So he's going to town for drop-offs, and, uh . . . Plus, I mean . . ." He cleared his throat.

"What?" I narrowed my eyes on my brother. Was he blushing?

"He's a guy." He glanced at me, but I had no idea what he was getting at. Jonah being a man was the first thing I'd noticed about him. Tate sighed. "He has, you know, *needs*."

I gasped, my primordial brain registering what Tate meant before I could mull it over like an adult. "He goes to town to get laid?"

"I don't know if he and Jackie Weller have a thing or—"

"Jackie Weller?"

"I don't think it's serious."

I'd disliked her before, and when I crossed paths with her, I preferred to pretend she didn't exist. She had been Jonah's on-again, off-again high school girlfriend. Then after school, she'd married a guy who'd come through town to work for the oil fields and Eli had said she'd left Jonah without a word. Made him feel like crap.

I'd known she'd gotten a divorce and taken her maiden name back, but that she was hooking up with Jonah? Or more? That was news.

He would've mentioned a girlfriend, right? I hadn't fucked up a relationship, had I?

A relationship. "How serious are they?"

"Can't be too serious since she's at the bar every weekend. I've seen her hopping in other guys' trucks."

A booty call. My relief wasn't acute. The tightness remained in my shoulders and the anger hadn't subsided. Why would Jonah keep seeing Jackie? She treated him like dirt. "I don't like her."

Tate's gaze intensified. "Not many people do."

My skin itched from his scrutiny. "He deserves better." I wasn't jealous. I was surprised. That was all.

"Preaching to the choir, sis."

Sis. Another nickname. Like Mama's honey, sweet pea, and my precious girls, I had shared that nickname with others. Generic. Some would argue that sunshine was as generic of an endearment as you could get, but I held it to me as something Jonah had called only *me*.

Tate was still watching me. I had to get inside and sort my thoughts. Like why I glowed inside like sunshine when Jonah called me that. I needed to rest and process the last few days. "Thanks for the ride."

"Remember what I said."

I definitely would, but we likely weren't thinking about the same statements. I got out and grabbed one of my suitcases. Tate retrieved the other.

Mama was already opening the door.

"Hey, Mama." I entered and set my bag down.

Tate came in, toed his boots off, gave Mama a peck on the cheek, and took the luggage I'd carried in. He went into the house and downstairs to the bedroom I'd be staying in.

I hung my winter coat up next to the one I had to return to Jonah. I had been tempted to wear it, but the fit was way too large to justify it to Mama or Tate.

She gave me a hug, squeezing almost as hard as she had yesterday. Tears pricked the backs of my eyes, but that was where they stayed. Was it abnormal that I hadn't cried over Boyd?

She stepped back. "Wynter and Autumn are coming over tonight. Is that okay?"

Yesterday, she'd been busy outside, taking care of the chickens and checking on the horses and cattle with Tenor and Myles's brothers. Mostly, I thought she'd been giving me space. I didn't deserve Mama. "I'm sorry I left so suddenly." I'd already said it, but it needed repeating. She wouldn't bring up the wedding until I did. Did she worry I'd go hide in another mountain cabin?

"Don't ever be sorry for taking care of yourself."

If taking care of myself meant barely dressing, that was what I was doing. I wore an old pair of red flannel pajama pants and a fluffy Montana State sweater. My hair was limp and I was makeup-free. Boyd would be disgusted if he could see me. I was comfortable.

"I am surprised who you sought refuge with." Mama could be nosy when she wanted, but she was the queen of leading sentences.

"You and me both." I shuffled to the kitchen table. Two steaming mugs were on the table, and she had a bottle of french vanilla creamer sitting by one. Tate must've texted her before we left Bozeman to let her know when we'd arrive.

I sank into the chair. She took a seat while I was topping off my coffee with International Delight.

"Jonah was there when I needed him," I said, needing to explain why I hadn't turned to her. She wouldn't take it personally, but I had to let her know my choice wasn't personal. Leaving with Jonah of all people was most definitely a personal choice, but I was already mixed up enough. I let the thought go.

"I heard what Jonah did." When I looked at her, I caught the smile playing over her lips. She'd known the whole story when I'd called her from the cabin and she'd kept most of the knowledge to herself. "Corinne Harrington wasn't as quiet as she hoped when she cornered Boyd in his dressing room and chewed him out. She yelled at him for not being able to overpower, I quote, 'that horribly scarred man with the cane.' "

"I'm surprised that's the worst of what she said." I dug my teeth into my lower lip. "I should've seen it coming."

"Aw, Summer. You take on too much responsibility. It's his duty to be a good person, and hitting his fiancée ain't it."

"Jonah said the same thing." Despite the curiosity in her eyes, I didn't care to talk about my time with Jonah. It had been cathartic, restful, and short, but long enough to bridge the gap that had formed between us since I'd last seen him in the hospital. "Is it all right if I stay a few days before I return to work?"

She frowned. "I thought you were staying the whole time."

Jonah had encouraged me to take all my time off, but

I'd invited myself over to Mama's without asking if she had room for me. I knew she did. She'd make room even if she didn't, but I didn't want to assume. I also didn't care to dwell on how I wished I was in a quiet mountain cabin with unusually strong Wi-Fi and almost no fresh produce. "If you don't mind, I'd like to stay here, but I also want to work."

"Are you sure you're ready?"

She meant, could I face everyone? My story was out there. Boyd Harrington's wedding getting canceled at the last minute might make a splash in Bozeman. Summer Kerrigan running out on her fiancé to stay in a cabin with Jonah Dunn would burn through Bourbon Canyon like a *brushfire*. My next trip to the grocery store or the coffee shop would likely stop conversation when I walked by. Inevitable. I'd experienced it before, I could do it again.

"Everyone knows what happened. I might as well face the chatter, and really, I'd rather be busy."

"I'm sure Teller and Tenor would arrange a way for you to work from Bourbon Canyon's location if you want out of the house."

So tempting. But also exposing. My family worked at Copper Summit, but everyone at Copper Summit was considered my inner circle. Out of everyone, they'd know the real details.

She patted my hand. "Think about it for a while. Do what you need to here. If you have to take over the kitchen table, do it."

I stared at the wood grain of the table. A standard wood table. Jonah's work was functional art.

I had to quit thinking about him. I could work at home until it was time for me to return to the office with no Balinese tan. I could help the guys and Mama with chores and soak up my daily dose of fresh air and sunshine.

But if I used Bourbon Canyon's headquarters to get some work done, I'd be out and about. I could run to town and get some coffee. After my first trip, my stops would get less awkward and I would be less self-conscious. I would be out and about more. And maybe I would see Jonah again.

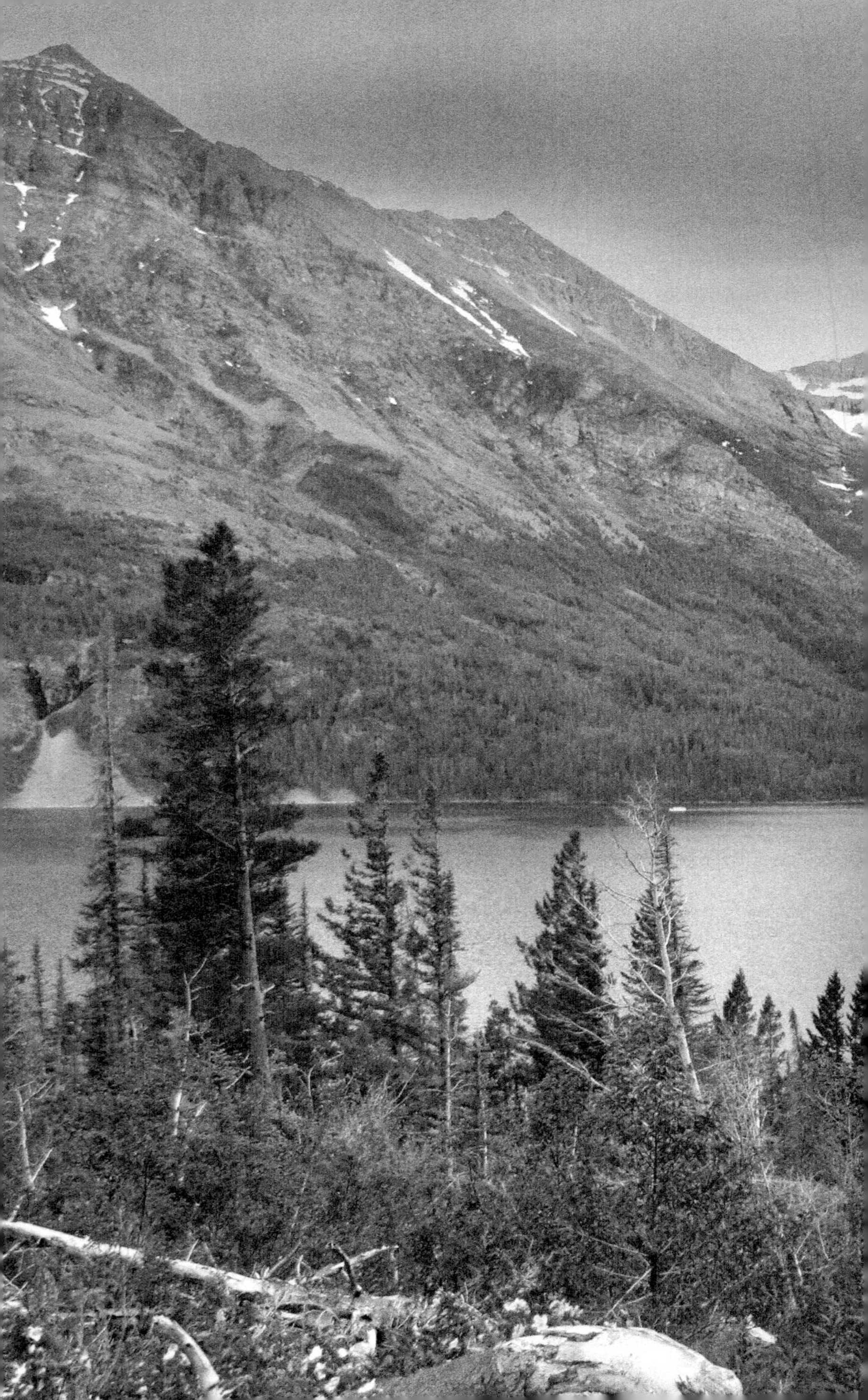

CHAPTER SEVEN

Summer

Autumn was in the bar area of Copper Summit when I was done working. When I'd asked Tenor if I could use some space to work remotely, he and Teller had made it happen. If they hadn't, Wynter would've made me share her desk, but there was an empty office on the top floor where I could look over the mountains that were once mined for copper. Our view was pristine. On the other side, off of Bailey land, half the mountain had been carved away.

"Hey." I slid onto a barstool. "Are we drinking here?"

Autumn frowned as she tapped through her tablet. She was doing inventory and her auburn hair was piled on top of her head. She was dressed in loose slacks, a white turtleneck, and a cranberry cardigan. Since it was a Thursday, she'd probably come straight from her classroom. Wynter hadn't been tending bar as much now that she was so pregnant, and Autumn had taken over. Teller insisted she was working too much, but Autumn ignored him like usual. "We can. There'd be somewhere to sleep when we got shitfaced."

"It's no fun to get plastered where family can see us."

She smirked and closed the cover on the tablet. "You sound very Junie right now."

"I'm not on stage, getting panties thrown at me."

"I thought some dude threw his jock strap."

"That was at last month's show." My country-star sister was making her way up the fame ladder, but she still had some very small-town-bar experiences.

"Let's go to Curly's." She went to the safe to lock the tablet in.

My stomach rumbled at the thought of homemade buns and cinnamon butter at Curly's Canyon Grill. "Are you taking over inventory for Wynter?"

"Yep," she answered, popping the p. "Can't have me doing man's work."

I frowned. Our parents weren't like that. Neither were my brothers. Daddy had taught all of us ranch work and distillery duties. We'd settled into our preferences. Autumn taught third grade and sometimes worked the bar we kept to showcase the spirits via cocktails. "What work do you want to do?"

She shook her head and puffed a lock of hair out of her face. "It's nothing. I'm just cranky today. Ready?"

The older sister in me wanted to keep pushing, but I was in a period of my life where I didn't want to be prodded either. My sisters could poke me right back. So I left off. "Curly's it is. We can complete the circle of feminism and disappoint Curly that we aren't our brothers."

She laughed. "You noticed he prefers them too?"

My sisters and I got booths in the back. We were Kerrigans. He put the Baileys front and center so the town could see its most influential family was visiting his establishment. Curly was a dick, but his restaurant served good food and there were few choices in a town as small as Bourbon Canyon.

Fifteen minutes later, we were getting seated at the second-to-last booth from the back. "Did you see the jumbo muffins he has at the counter?"

She nodded. "I might have to buy a couple of the strawberry-cream-cheese ones."

We'd joked about drinking but both of us ordered our Coke with nothing but ice. The server dropped the sodas off and took our order.

I stirred my drink with my straw after she left. "We should've asked Scarlett to join us. I worry she'll think I don't want to include her anymore, but she's been so busy with the littles." And Chance had taken to her so thoroughly, with his own mom on the road so often.

A forlorn expression crossed Autumn's features. "I'm sure she's enjoying her new wife-and-mother role," she said wistfully.

My heart went out to my sister. Autumn loved kids, but staying in Bourbon Canyon to work was like trading a work life for a love life. She'd used dating apps, but the options in town weren't for her and no one else wanted to downshift from a bigger city to Bourbon Canyon.

She straightened and flashed me a forced smile. "Anyway, I got the impression that you wanted to talk, and that you didn't want anything getting back to Tate."

"Thank you." Despite what Tate had said, he was the brother version of me. Sometimes a little too pushy and full of advice. I wanted a shoulder right now. I needed someone to help me be myself. I'd succumbed to being Boyd's girlfriend and then his fiancée. A future bride.

Always labels. The girl with the homeless parents. A Kerrigan, not a Bailey. Eli Dunn's girlfriend. Then other guys' girlfriend, followed by *You know, the one from the Copper Summit family?* Then all things attached to Boyd.

Sunshine was a label I didn't mind. It was more personal. I'd like to think it was me.

Autumn leaned her elbows on the table. "Besides, I can't get all the dirt on Jonah with them around. Spill it."

I gave her a flat look. Protectiveness toward him formed a wall. I hadn't come to gossip about Jonah. "There's nothing to spill."

Her look was dubious. My brothers often treated Autumn like a sweet summer child, isolated from the worst of life, and thankfully, she was, but she was sharp. She sniffed out my bullshit before most people. "Boyd is such a pretentious prick, and I love how he got served some piping-hot humble pie."

I gawked at her. "You didn't like Boyd?"

"None of us did. But we wanted to support you."

I opened my mouth. Slammed it shut. None of them? They hadn't told me what they thought of him. Humiliation flared hot and bright, scorching the back of my neck. "Why wouldn't you say anything? I would've if it was you."

Her gaze turned knowing. "Yeah, you would've. Which is why we know how it feels." Touché. "I also didn't think you'd actually marry the guy. And then—boom—wedding. By then, I think we all thought it was too late and you just needed our support."

Ultimately, it'd been their encouragement that had gotten me to cancel the wedding. They didn't act like I would've, but the outcome was the same. "Jonah was looking for the bathroom." I wouldn't share why. I liked how he'd entrusted me with the reason. "He saw Boyd slap me."

Her disgusted snort turned heads, but we ignored everyone. The trick in a small town was to act like we had nothing to hide. "We should've gutted him."

"Jonah pinned Boyd against the wall with his cane." The image would forever be imprinted in my mind.

"He should have bitch-slapped that cocksucker with his cane." She shook her head, the green in her eyes sparking.

A couple glanced our way, and Autumn shot them a syrupy smile as an apology for swearing. I returned their stare with a militant glare that said *mind your own business and you won't hear her swear*.

She nudged my shin under the table. Fair. She had to live here while I could leave, which I'd do as soon as my "honeymoon" was done.

She pushed an errant curl behind her ear. "What'd you do at his place?"

"Slept. Watched TV." Talked. That part was my favorite. "He worked. Did you know he builds furniture?"

She cocked her head. "You didn't?"

Why did everyone act like his job was something I should know? "He said he gets old barrels from Copper Summit and I hoped he and Teller were talking again."

Sadness entered her eyes. "They aren't close like before." She took a long drink of her soda. "I think Teller worries about him when he's not seen in town for a while. I hear him grilling the delivery drivers. Jonah changed after the accident and he's never reverted back, but who can blame him."

"Jonah blames himself for Eli." He shouldn't. The burden rested fully on my shoulders. Only I knew why Eli had gone to Jonah's place that day and drunk too much.

Our food arrived and Autumn moved on from all things Jonah. She told me about her third graders' antics, how she felt so much older than some of the new teachers ten years younger than her, and if it weren't for Scarlett, she might've quit. I loved our incredibly normal conversation.

When it was time to go, Autumn scooted out of the booth. "I'm running to the restroom before I load up on muffins."

"I'll buy mine while waiting."

The same server who'd helped us met me at the bakery counter. I ordered two strawberry cream cheese and two pumpkin cream cheese. Mama would have at least one. Oh wait, Myles's brothers, Lane and Cruz, would be around too.

"Can you add one more of each?" I recalled the guys' appetites. "Wait, two more. You know what? Do a half dozen of each."

Autumn's muffins would be my treat.

The server smiled and busied herself with boxing my order.

"Summer? Surprised to see you here."

I turned, my stomach dropping as my brain registered whose voice I'd heard.

Jackie Weller.

The jealous punch to my gut was staggering. I pulled

my coat around myself and didn't bother faking a smile. "Jackie, hi."

"Aren't you supposed to be on a honeymoon?" she asked innocently.

She'd always been snide and snotty when she'd come around the Dunns' place and I'd been over there with Eli.

She was going low, and I didn't have the energy to go high. "I'm sure you've heard I didn't get married," I said flatly.

"Right." She narrowed her eyes on me. "You were staying at Jonah's?"

My family wouldn't have talked, but I hadn't been inconspicuous in my wedding dress crawling into Jonah's truck. Word got around. "Is that what they're saying?"

Humor danced in her blue eyes, but I hadn't known how to take her when I was younger, and I wasn't sure now. Was she laughing at me? At the situation? At the irony that we'd run into each other now of all times? "They're always saying a lot, but I'm sure it's because people remember how it used to be."

I hated to ask. *Don't ask*, I screamed at myself, but the question left my lips regardless. "How what used to be?"

"How you used to have a thing for Jonah."

My heart skipped a beat. "I did not."

She lifted a dark brow. "I felt so sorry for Eli. You never looked at him the way you did at Jonah."

I stiffened. It had *not* been like that.

Had it?

The server plopped my muffin boxes on the counter. "Here you are, ma'am."

I could've done without getting called ma'am by a

teenager in front of Jackie, but I was thankful for the reprieve in the conversation.

"It's a good thing you didn't end up with the wrong guy though, isn't it?" Jackie brushed her long, dark hair off her shoulder. "Enjoy your dessert."

She sauntered away. The temptation to open one of my boxes and lob a muffin at her head was strong. She'd gotten under my skin years ago, but the problem tonight was that I wasn't sure who Jackie had meant.

Jonah

I was not people-watching in the hardware store's parking lot. I was not making extra trips into town because Teller had mentioned Summer was still staying with Mae Bailey and working at Copper Summit. So I wasn't hoping to catch a glimpse of sunshine-colored hair and flashing amber eyes.

At some point, I should go into the hardware store. I doubted I'd see Summer there, but there was a chance. A possibility she'd run an errand for Mae or for the ranch. She might've sat around my place, but she wouldn't sit still at her mother's house. She wouldn't be content to watch her brothers and their hired guys do all the work.

I got out of my pickup. It was the end of February and cold air stabbed through my sweater, but I left my coat in the cab and pulled out my cane. With a new delivery of empty barrels came some more work as I moved them around my shop. After shoveling last week, my entire leg was on fire, and I was a month overdue for a session with my massage therapist. Icy parking lots and bum legs didn't go well together, so today was a cane day.

I picked my footing until I got inside. I needed brackets and small screws and nails for a few tables. I had a special order of custom metal for the decorative features of two end tables and a coffee table I was making. The owners of Kenwood's Hardware Store also stocked some epoxy and coloring for me.

"Hey, Dunn." Macy Kenwood, one of the owners, greeted me. She adjusted a red apron with giant pockets around her neck. "I'll run and get your order. You doing more shopping?"

"Yeah, I have a few things to grab."

She rushed toward the back of the store.

Macy and Buddy, her husband, loved my business, and I appreciated their nothing-but-the-facts approach to visiting. We talked about our respective fields and that was it. They didn't pry, and best of all, once I'd started woodworking, I didn't catch them staring at me with morbid fascination or eyes full of sympathy.

And people wondered why I didn't venture into town much after the accident.

Their looks weren't the only reason.

I gathered extra epoxy, sanding paper, and a new blade for my table saw. Along with the new Copper Summit barrels a day ago, I'd been given some planks of wood for custom orders. The local weather station was forecasting a storm next week and I didn't want to be caught without enough supplies. If my internet went out, I'd be stuck with my generator and books.

It'd happened enough that even a recluse like me got bored silly.

"I'll getcha over here." Macy waved me to an open

till. She and Buddy handled me themselves after one of their young cashiers wouldn't quit gawking at my scar. I wasn't self-conscious about it like I used to be, and not in the way most people assumed, but Macy had noticed and intervened. "I saw your last piece at Mountain Perks. You do such good work, but I think you're undercharging."

The barrel barstools she was talking about hadn't been my last work. Since I'd finished those stools, I'd also shipped two tables and a pair of decorative chairs with the backs made out of oak barrels. "I price down the local pieces. People who special order a custom epoxy table from a guy in the middle of Montana and have it shipped to Boston can afford a little more."

She chortled. "Be careful with that info. I might start thinking you're a softie," she whispered conspiratorially.

"I need to swear you to secrecy, or I'm going to start getting trick-or-treaters."

"Can't have that." She chuckled as she finished ringing up my order.

Her teasing was another reason I'd made an extra trip today. I was used to being on my own, but the days could get long, and lately, they'd been longer. Winter still had a hold on the state, and if a storm was coming, I needed to socialize before getting snowed in again. I'd learned the hard way that being left in my head for weeks on end wasn't good for me.

"If you can't make it in," she said, "just shoot me a message or email if you need another order."

I preferred to order face-to-face. Mostly to keep myself from becoming feral. "Will do."

I put my can in the cart and wheeled it through the parking lot. The smell of greasy burgers teased my nose and my stomach growled. I didn't eat as fully or regularly as when Summer had stayed with me, and since she'd left I'd had little more than scrambled eggs. My shop had been my refuge. A place where I didn't look around and see her.

Across the table when I ate, there was nothing but emptiness. I hadn't canceled a single streaming service subscription. And the smell of strawberries grew fainter each day she was gone.

She was my brother's goddamn girlfriend. But the reminder failed to wipe her from my mind like it used to. A nineteen-year-old Summer was a pale replica of the woman she'd grown into. A nineteen-year-old Summer was the past.

Too bad my attraction to her wouldn't stay in the past.

My stomach rumbled, loudly, insistent that more scrambled eggs wouldn't cut it.

I should go home, start a custom table for the Boston guy tomorrow. Once I was absorbed in a project, I wouldn't come up for air until it was done. Then the storm would hit and I'd cook another roast to gnaw on for a few days.

The smell of burgers filled the air. My stomach cramped. Fuck it.

I loaded my items and drove to the bar a block down the road. Curly's would serve a good meal, and I could even order one to go like I usually did when I splurged, but a hot bar burger sounded good.

When I entered, I went to the side of the counter that flanked three large monitors, one playing a basketball game, another with old UFC footage, and the third playing CHIVE TV. I climbed on a stool and carefully bent my left leg to prop my foot on the metal rail close to the floor. Then I leaned my cane under the bar top.

"Dunn," the bartender greeted, only slight surprise in his voice. His gaze was stunned, but he was trying to rein in his shock. Mike had been a few years ahead of me in school. I used to come to this place all the time with Teller. "What can I get you?"

"A burger, medium, and fries. I'll take a Sprite."

He nodded and disappeared around the bar.

I scrolled through my phone and answered email queries about my pricing and timeline. People arrived, stopping midsentence when they spotted me. I kept my hair hanging over my face. I hated being stared at. My clothing was clean and I'd trimmed my beard before the wedding. There was no reason to stare. Yet their gazes burned into me.

When the food arrived, I watched the basketball game playing on the TV in front of me and steadily ate my food so I could leave. I was about to stuff the last fry into my mouth when the familiar smell of floral perfume surrounded me.

Jackie slid onto a stool two down from me. It was rare I saw her around town. Our meetings were usually prearranged. She no longer hung on me like she had in high school. She saved that for the bedroom.

"Dunn." She ran her hand over the silky strands lying over one shoulder, her gaze on the TV monitors. She was in a long-sleeved shirt as tight as her jeans.

"Weller." My typical response when she called me by my last name.

"I heard you had some company." She tapped the bar and lifted her chin toward Mike as if to say she was having her usual. She still didn't meet my gaze.

The wedding chatter had begun. Did Summer know? I was tired of being a popular topic. I stuffed my fry in ketchup and popped it in my mouth.

"No reply? Interesting." This time, she spared me a glance. Her cunning gaze burned into my cheek.

"I don't need to explain myself."

Her dark brows lifted and she turned her attention back to the Chive channel. "Nope. You never do."

I wasn't bringing up old times. Our new times were nothing significant. Two lonely people hooking up. I might even lose her number after this. After having Summer talk to me like I was a full person and not just the post-accident remnants of Jonah Dunn, I would delete Jackie's number.

I wanted more.

Jackie didn't talk to me if she saw me in a store. She didn't sit right next to me when we were both at the bar. And she didn't acknowledge me if she was talking to another man.

Was she embarrassed to be linked with me? I didn't care.

But maybe . . . I was starting to.

I slid off my stool. I didn't bend my left leg enough and knocked into my cane. It clattered to the floor. Mike glanced over and looked away quickly. I was so fucking sick of the quick look away, as if I might rampage like Bourbon Canyon's very own Frankenstein's monster.

Jackie's gaze dropped to my cane, then went back to the insurance commercial on one of the TVs.

Any attraction I had ever felt for her shriveled. I should've quit sleeping with her months ago. I shouldn't have restarted when she'd moved back to town. Hell, things should've been severed in high school. Definitely before she left me to run off with another man.

Tonight, I learned my lesson.

I gingerly bent to retrieve my cane. When it was back in my left hand, I gave it a good thump on the floor. My limp was extra loud as I made my way to the door. Stares branded into my back.

What would be said about me? Would people brush off the rumors of Summer staying with me after the wedding? How could a radiant woman like her tolerate a bitter recluse like me?

The burger in my stomach turned to lead as I drove to my cabin. When I got inside, there was no sweet-strawberry-sunshine scent hanging in the air.

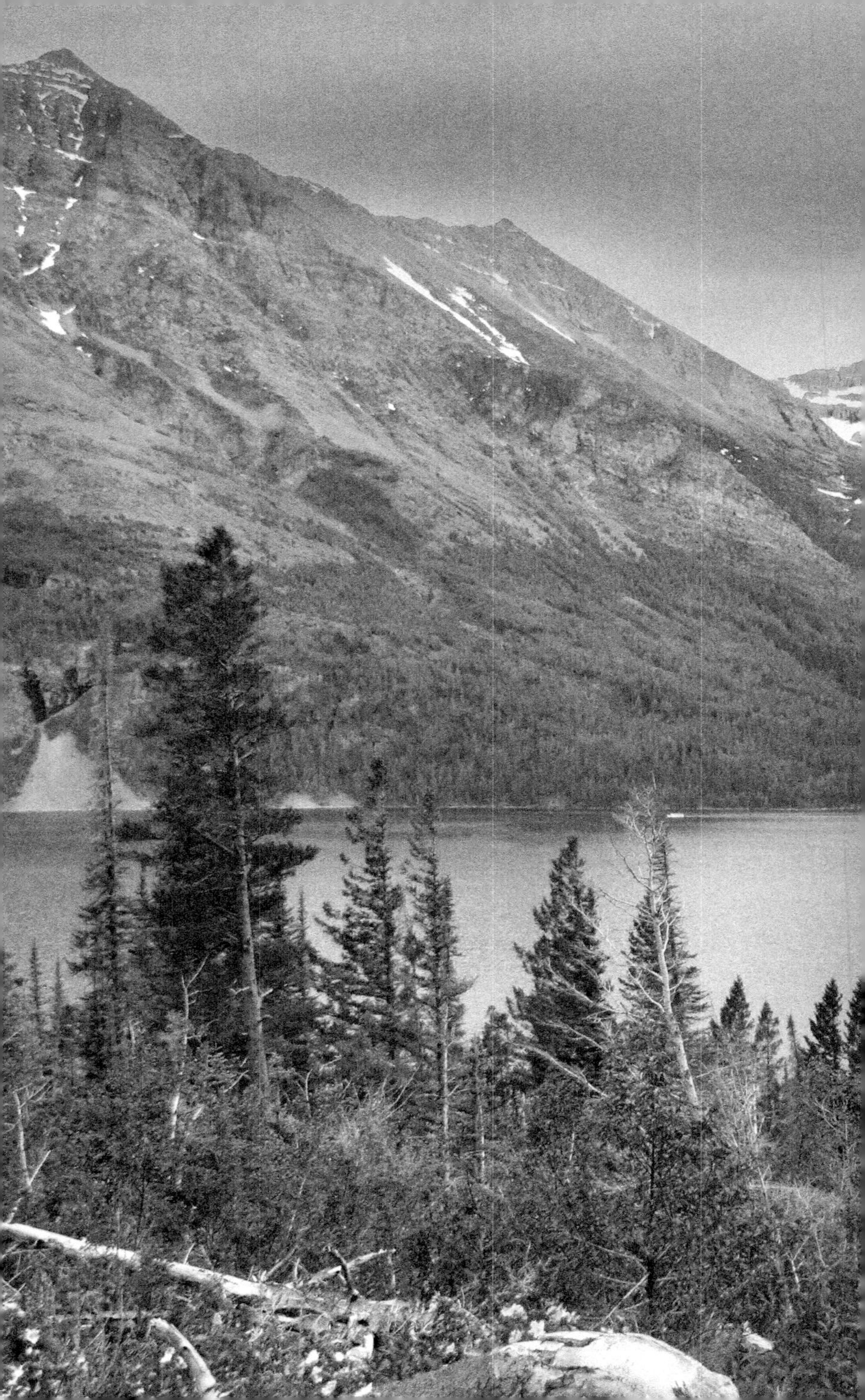

CHAPTER EIGHT

Summer

I tapped through the weather app. I'd looked at it a million times, as if the trajectory of the storm the weather center had forecasted would change despite days of warnings. Phrases like *unprecedented levels* and *stock up with provisions* were getting thrown around.

I sat cross-legged on the living room couch at Mama's house in thick flannel sweats and a heavy Copper Summit sweater. Teller had run me out of the distillery and told me to help Mama get ready for the storm. Mama could be stuck in the house for months and still be able to feed the entire family. She wasn't the one I worried about.

Jonah was old enough to know what had to be done. He'd been living in his cabin for almost twenty years, and he'd endured terrible thunderstorms and snowstorms and wind events. I'd thought about him out there all alone through the years.

I clicked out of the app. If the tracker was correct, we had a couple hours before the first flurries started.

Hell with it. I got up and grabbed my coat hanging by the back door. I shrugged into it as I stuffed my feet inside my Ugg Adirondack boots. The bottoms of my sweats piled up around the fluffy wool liner at the tops. I should change, but now that I'd decided, I was committed.

Mama shuffled into the kitchen. "Going somewhere?"

She was in mother-hen mode. She was calling Tenor, telling him to give Cruz plenty of time to grab what he wanted from town. Lane was almost back from running errands in Bozeman. She wanted all her duckies under her roof when the first flake dropped.

"I'm going to bring Jonah some supplies." I took his winter coat and ski pants off the hooks by the back door. "I need to return his clothing too."

She paused and pulled her maroon cardigan around her. Since Daddy had died, she could look startlingly older, but moments like now, I was transported back to high school when she was tasting my words for a lie. "You think he doesn't have enough?"

"I'm not sure if he's made it to town since I was there and I ate some of his supplies."

There was that steady gaze again, her expression laying down valid points like what I'd just been thinking. He'd been surviving in that cabin—and expanding—for almost two decades. She was silently tallying how much of Jonah's winter stores I could've possibly eaten in three days. She might think four, but I hadn't eaten that first evening after he'd rescued me. The question of *Why are you really going there?* lingered in her eyes.

She brushed the salt-and-pepper curls out of her face. "Better get going, then. You have your kit in your car?"

"Always." She and Daddy hadn't raised any of us to travel without survival gear. I could make a fire, shoot a flare, and feed myself if I got stranded. I could shovel a trench, bed myself down, or write HELP in the snow or grass—with flames or a bottle of dye, whatever the situation called for.

"You got a change of clothes?"

"I'll be back by then." I opened the back door.

"Summer, these storms don't watch our apps. They do what they damn well please. Pack a bag."

"I don't have time, Mama." I left the door and rushed across the kitchen to give her a kiss on her soft, warm cheek. "I'll be fast. He's got plenty of canned goods, but if he wants to stay scurvy-free, he needs some orange juice."

She gave me a flat look. "Get some oranges, then," she said dryly.

I was using Daddy's argument as an excuse. His dad had had scurvy as a kid in the middle of Montana, and Daddy and his brothers had gone around talking like a pirate when they'd heard the story as kids. For International Talk Like a Pirate Day, they'd made a cake in the shape of a parrot. And we'd grown up with orange juice and fresh produce always stocked in the house because of it.

I rushed out to my car. The chill in the air bit deeper, but the wind was nonexistent. When the snow started, it'd free-fall like the day of my wedding.

I drove to town, pushing the speed as much as my conscience would allow. I'd be no good to Jonah if I skidded off the highway. In the grocery store, I picked through the remnants. Much of town had already been through, buying food and toiletries like we were in Florida and there'd been a Jim Cantore sighting.

I picked out oranges, the validity of my excuse taking hold. Jonah didn't eat the variety he should, and he'd be stuck for days, maybe even a week without a way to replenish.

I needed to do this. For his own good.

After checking out, I was in my car and taking a different road out of town, a small county road that turned to gravel and skirted around the back edge of my family's land. Jonah had driven this route with me after my non-wedding, and I'd been assaulted by memories of taking the same route with his brother, going to pester Jonah because Eli had hero-worshipped him.

He hadn't been the only one.

Now, it was just me. I passed the area of the accident. I'd seen pictures of the wreckage. I wasn't supposed to have, but small town and confidentiality didn't always go hand in hand.

Eli's old pickup had tipped into the shallow ditch. Any farther and he might've rammed a tree, not that it mattered. The outcome had been the same. He hadn't buckled up, and he hadn't survived the impact with the steering wheel.

Jonah's pickup had been T-boned on the driver's side by Eli. His vehicle had slammed into the ditch, rolling at least once and landing on its side—keeping Jonah from getting out. The frame had held up, but the driver's door had crumpled into Jonah's side.

The sight had pierced my heart. People blamed Eli. The alcohol. Some even got after Jonah for having alcohol in his house, the stash his brother had raided. But I'd been the motivator. Eli wouldn't have felt the need to drink if it hadn't been for me.

Going to Jonah's was a bad idea.

I almost stopped and turned around. I still had time to get home. The heavy gray clouds were starting to let loose their cargo. A few flurries landed on my windshield.

I wasn't in an area where I could turn around. A snowflake landed in my line of vision, stark against the glass. I could make out its points if I dared take my eyes off the road for more than a second. More flakes fell. I could drop off the food and turn and burn. If I got stranded, I'd have to explain myself to my brothers, and to my sisters, which would be worse.

I pulled into the long driveway and wound around the trees. To anyone else, it'd look like he wasn't home. I knew his pickup was in the garage, and he'd probably been in the shop so long the snow that was falling remained untouched. I parked behind the second stall that was full of lawn equipment.

Instead of going to the house, I went to the shop. If he wasn't in there, I'd take his absence personally. It'd mean he'd been avoiding me when he'd spent so much time out there while I had been under his roof.

Cold snow dotted my hair and ears, falling into my eyelashes. I hefted the two grocery bags I'd gotten him when I reached the shop door and knocked.

I waited.
Nothing.
I knocked again.
I waited.
Nothing.

He *had* been avoiding me. Hurt heated my face and melted the snow faster than usual.

I trudged across the driveway to his house. Should I just leave the groceries and his winter clothing and text him? I hadn't gotten his number when I'd used his phone, but my family would have it. No, I didn't want the inquiries that would come if I asked them for it.

Embarrassed and second-guessing myself, I climbed the porch that encompassed the width of his cabin and knocked on his front door.

I waited.

Nothing.

Was he hiding?

I knocked again. And again I got no answer. Great. Now for the entire storm, I'd sit at Mama's house and bathe in self-recrimination.

I was about to turn when another thought occurred to me. What if he was hurt? What if he couldn't answer?

My heart rate sped up and the idea blossomed into dread. Was Jonah okay? I couldn't leave until I knew. I tried the handle, and surprisingly, it turned. He'd locked all the doors when I'd been here, but he was leaving them open when he was alone. He was a thoughtful man.

Warmth sparked in my chest, but the anxiety grew. Was something wrong?

I stepped into the living room and listened. He wasn't watching TV and the kitchen light was off. Both rooms were open in front of me and I could see down the hallway to the bathroom and his bedroom. The hallway was dim as well, along with the upstairs, but a sliver of light filtered through from under the bathroom door. I heard water running.

Relief poured through me, crisper and more refreshing than the outside air. He was taking a shower.

I could leave the groceries, hang his gear up by the back door, find something to write a note on, and get going. He had no idea he had company, and now that I could be mostly sure he was okay, I could go with a clear conscience.

Stuffing my disappointment away, I toed out of my boots. I'd miss him but he'd have the groceries and wasn't that the point of my trip? I needed to get home. The snow was falling heavier, forming a curtain outside the big picture windows.

I padded to the kitchen and placed the bags on the table. I looked around for paper, but couldn't find anything. The water shut off. Maybe I should call to him from the hallway?

Then I'd scare the shit out of him and he could slip and fall. No, it'd be better if I was gone completely. I scurried to the front door and was stuffing my foot into a boot when the bathroom door opened and Jonah emerged.

Air evacuated my lungs. He had a towel draped across his shoulders and was rubbing it against his damp hair. The rest of him? Bare. So many muscled inches. The towel covered his wide shoulders, but his strong pecs were only dusted with dark hair thinning down to his rippled abs. His legs were long and his thighs thick, his right more so than his left. The scars on his left side stuck out stark and jagged, but I wasn't paying attention to those. My gaze zeroed in on his privates.

Look away!

I couldn't tear my focus off his groin. His heavy ball

sack would've been impressive if it weren't for a cock that was thick and long even while flaccid.

"Jesus, Summer!" he barked and snapped his towel off his shoulders. He tried to jump for his bedroom, but his foot slipped.

He skidded and banged a shoulder against the wall. "Fuck."

"Jonah!" I ditched my boots and ran toward him.

He tried to stabilize himself, but he was whipping his towel around to cover his genitals and it unbalanced him more. He teetered on one leg, hit the wall again, and slid down, grunting the entire way.

Shit, shit, shit. I got to his side and knelt by him. His knees were bent, the left side at a sharper angle than I'd seen before.

"Fuck!" He straightened his left leg with a wince. Pain twisted his features and he was breathing heavily.

"What can I do?" I took inventory of him. No blood. Only lots of hot skin and—my gaze skated away.

His incredulous dark eyes cut into me. "What the hell are you doing here?"

I batted away the irritation his tone caused. He had every right to be upset. "Are you okay?"

He grunted and dropped the towel over his lap. The back of his head thudded against the wall. "I will be."

His eyes were pinched and his breathing was shallow. "Where do you hurt?"

"My pride," he muttered and rolled to sit squarely on his bare ass.

"I'm sorry." I'd messed up. He would've been fine without me, but I'd gotten into my head. I'd jacked things up again. "I brought you some groceries. I wasn't sure how much you've been able to make it to town."

His stare turned disbelieving once again. "You brought me groceries?"

"Produce mostly. So you don't get scurvy." Oh, god. Listen to me. Had Mama heard what I'd just heard? Lame excuses to see a man I might have an eternal flame for?

"Christ, Summer." He closed his eyes and seemed to concentrate on his breathing. "I'm not a pirate."

"That's the thing. Did you know that rural folks used to get scurvy if they didn't get the right nutrients? It makes sense though, right? Like, we're in the middle of nowhere and can be isolated for long periods of time. My grandpa Bailey had scurvy as a kid."

He cracked an eye open, stark disbelief shimmering in the dark depths of his iris. "You brought me groceries because your grandpa had scurvy like eighty years ago?"

My cheeks smoldered while I did the calculations. "Well, it would've been more like ninety years ago."

We held each other's gaze for a moment, then he shook his head. "Can you give me a moment? I want to stand up without mooning you."

I hadn't gotten a good view of his ass yet. Based on the rest of this body, I bet the view was spectacular.

"Summer?"

Oh. I hadn't moved. I was still crouched next to him, my hand on his blistering hot shoulder. "Sorry," I squeaked and popped up. I ran to the kitchen and stood by the table. I pressed my fingertips into my forehead. Outside, past the living room windows, the snow was falling heavier than before, large clumps of flakes hitting the ground and piling deep.

If I didn't leave now, I'd be stuck here, but I couldn't

bring myself to go. I had to make sure he was okay. I was the reason he was hurt. Again.

Jonah

I sat on my bed, my head hanging and my forearms pressed into my thighs. My left leg throbbed after getting jackknifed. The slam into the wall had reignited the pain I sometimes got in my shoulder.

Was Summer still here? I wanted her gone as much as I didn't want her to leave.

She'd brought me groceries.

Her reason was wild but it was also all her. She was always looking out for others, but why would she risk the weather to make sure I got some well-rounded meals? I'd bought groceries yesterday. I'd even gotten some fresh fruit and veggies.

Mom had been after me to keep my doors locked, but no one visited who wasn't expected. I never would've guessed I'd be caught stark naked by Summer Kerrigan.

She'd seen everything. Including when my leg gave out and how utterly painful it was when it happened.

I blew out a breath and inhaled slowly. Exhaled. The sharp thudding was turning dull. I rose, testing the stability of the knee. My foot wasn't happy either, but it'd hold me up. I rolled my shoulder and tested all my joints so I wouldn't fall on my ass again.

I shrugged into a loose red flannel and pulled on my jeans. I left the socks off so I wouldn't slip. As long as the floor wasn't wet, I should be fine.

Before I entered the hallway, I took another steady breath. I could face her. She'd seen everything but so had other women. I couldn't remember their names right now. Summer had a way of blowing into my world and taking up all the space.

I snagged a cane, hating the damn thing when I was usually grateful for it, and trudged into the living room. She wasn't there, so I rounded into the kitchen.

Her back was to me and her shoulders were slumped. Her hair hung loose and was piled around the hood of her sweater.

"Doing all right?"

She spun, her bright gaze stroking down my body and back up. "You're dressed."

"Disappointed?" I meant it as a joke, striving for some way to lighten her mood, but goddammit, I really wanted to know.

Her already pink cheeks flushed a deeper red. "I'm so sorry I startled you."

She'd done more than startle me. She'd given me a moment when I'd thought I'd conjured her. The way my excitement had risen . . . Then reality had hit—jacking off to her saucy smile and bossy mouth *hadn't* manifested her in the flesh—and the situation had become clear. She'd gotten a full frontal of the scars I hated revealing. Then all hell had broken loose.

I wanted to move on from all that. I'd remember the way her gaze lingered on my dick later. "Thank you for the groceries."

She lifted her chin. I wasn't the only one who wanted to leave the last ten minutes behind. "You're welcome."

"Have you seen outside?"

She rolled her lips in and her gaze strayed to the window. "I knew I was pushing it."

"But you came anyway?"

She nodded.

Summer was going to get snowed in with me. Again. The flood of delight was wrong. I quashed it. "Who knows you're here?"

"Mama. I'm sure she's told my brothers and Lane and Cruz—Myles's brothers."

"Want them to come and get you in their pickup?"

"I don't want them to risk getting stuck."

My brain was telling me to shut up, to quit troubleshooting the situation. "Do you want me to take you home? I can stay with my parents." My mom would be delighted and I'd be smothered and forced to play board games for hours.

"I can't inconvenience you more than I already have."

I'd worked more when she was here in my attempts to avoid her. Now I spent too much time trying to forget what it was like to have Summer Kerrigan under my roof. "It's fine."

She crossed to the sink and peered out the window. The gentle rise of the base of the mountain and the trees wouldn't show her much except that the snow was coming fast and heavy. "How bad is it for you to be stuck with me for a few days?"

Staying with her for days would be torture, but that was my problem, not hers. "Dig into those groceries and see what scurvy-preventive meal we can make."

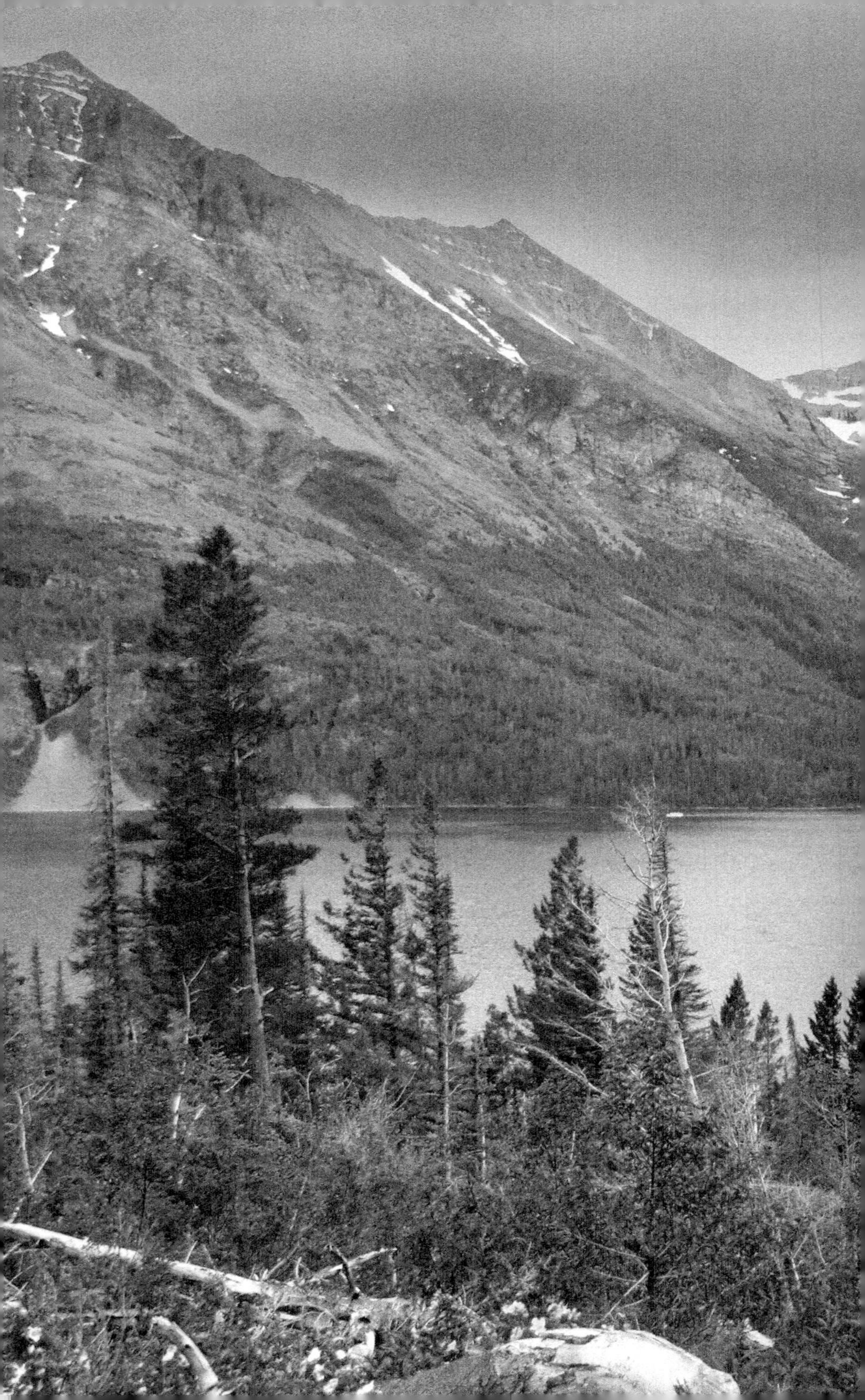

CHAPTER NINE

Summer

I couldn't believe I'd gotten myself stranded with Jonah again. I'd called Mama—I'd had a charger in my car this time. She hadn't been surprised. Then Jonah and I had made hamburgers with tomatoes, pickles, onions, and lettuce. I might've heaped on the veggies to make a good show of it.

After dinner, he'd worked on his computer at the kitchen table while I'd watched a show. I'd answered a few work emails on my phone and then abandoned it for *Sweet Home Alabama*. I wasn't used to quiet nights like this. Boyd had always had to be doing something. I might be working remotely, but I'd had a more restful two weeks than when I'd been with Boyd.

Jonah shuffled to the couch and gingerly sat down. He'd been moving slower and using his cane, but he hadn't said anything.

"Do you want to watch something?" I asked.

"No. I can space out and think of designs."

"Is that how it works?"

He changed position, and I swore he smothered a wince. "Yes. I'll look at what's for sale in stores and on popular sites, even look at some influencers in the field, but mostly I get inspiration when I can let my mind wander."

"Your lifestyle fits it."

"Yep." He changed his position again.

"Are you in pain?" Would he answer honestly?

"It's fine."

So, sort of. "How bad was the fall?"

"Nothing I haven't been through before."

He wasn't shutting me down like I'd thought he would. He wasn't being open either, but he was talking. "What usually helps?"

"Rest."

How could he rest when he was uncomfortable? "For real now, what helps?"

He rolled his eyes to me, his lips tight. The scruff along his jaw had grown into a trimmed beard. My palms itched to run along the strands. Were they wiry or soft? Did he use product? The longer the season went, did he turn more mountain man-y?

"It's fine, Summer."

I was tempted to threaten to call his mom, but that wouldn't earn his trust. Breaking into his house was enough for one day. "I'm not asking if you're fine. I'm asking what usually works."

His mouth tightened more. "Hot baths, but I don't want to bend in and out of the tub. Massage is usually good, but that's out until the storm is done."

"I can give you a massage."

He went still and the air crackled between us. My offer was genuine and I'd made it without a second thought, but now the possibility was on my mind. My hands on his strong body. My mouth went dry.

"No," he said tightly.

He'd named two things that worked and he was ruling out both. "The Wi-Fi's still working. I can search some videos. Anything's better than nothing, right? It's not like I'm strong enough to hurt you."

The corners of his jaw flexed. "You're not massaging me."

He was so definitive, it was insulting. "I only want to help." When he shook his head and twisted away, I caught his wince. Enough of this. "Go lie down, Jonah."

"Summer—"

"You're in pain. It's because of me. Let me help."

His eyes softened at my plea. "Fine." He got up as carefully as he'd sat down. His knuckles were white on his cane.

"Tell me when I can come in," I called after him. "Do what you do when you have a massage—everything off and cover yourself with a sheet."

Otherwise, I'd rub him once, and he'd say he was much better.

A flush crept over my body while waiting. I was doing this. I was putting my hands on his bare skin.

I could be professional.

God, I wasn't even an amateur.

"Ready," came his muffled voice.

Okay. I could do this and not let my hormones rage. I was newly single. I was an uninvited guest. I was stepping over the line. But he was in pain and I was certain I could help him.

My pulse thundered between my ears when I entered his room. Instead of a dark cave, I found a spacious bedroom with photographs of the valley on its walls. It was like the view from his front windows right in his room. The window had no shades, but faced the trees. What kind of wildlife did he see roaming by?

Only the lamp on his nightstand was on, casting a warm glow around the cozy, manly room with his solid cedar furniture and sleigh-style bed frame.

Finally, I looked at the bed. His blankets were tossed to the side and his big body was sprawled on his belly. I stopped beside him. I didn't know what side was his usual one, but he'd lain so his left side was close to the edge.

"Did you make the dresser and bed frame?" I asked, pushing my sleeves up. My hands shook. The massage was supposed to be clinical but the intimacy was undeniable.

"No." His head was turned in my direction and his eyes were closed like he was blocking out the discomfort. "They're inspiration pieces. I got them before I opened my shop."

His deep voice did wicked things to my belly. The electric energy between us swirled lower.

Be. Professional.

I rubbed my hands together to warm them up. "Where do you need it the most?"

He cracked an eye open.

Could I have made it sound more sexual?

"Around my knee, and my shoulder's flared up."

Both were my fault. "Okay. I'll start at the shoulder." I could figure out how to position the blanket while I worked on the less revealing body part.

I pulled the sheet down. He'd chosen a solid pewter color. So fitting with the rest of the room. I touched my fingertips lightly to his fevered skin and yanked my hands away. "Uh, do you have lotion?"

His eye was back to being a slit. "I have lube."

A giggle sputtered out of me. I was rewarded with a chuckle from him. I laughed harder. "God, this is awkward. I only want to help. I swear."

"I believe you," he said, seriously. "Check the drawer."

In the nightstand was a plain bottle of lube. I couldn't resist looking around. He had a few magazines, too many pocketknives to be useful, and little else. "No condoms?"

I bit my lip. *Intrusive much, Summer?*

"I don't bring women here."

The confession pleased me more than I could imagine. I was in his home, but no one else had been. Also, no other woman had walked in and caused him to have an accident. Regardless, he must buy condoms when he was meeting Jackie or he must keep a box somewhere to load his wallet when needed.

Not that it was my business.

"I won't use much." I squeezed the cool gel on my hand, closed the cap, and faced his big body. Time to bare some skin. "Your left shoulder, right?"

He bent his right arm and rested his face on it so his head wasn't twisted to the side. "Yep."

The flutters in my belly grew stronger as I pinched the sheet to keep from touching him before I was mentally ready. Drawing the fabric down to his waist, I took in the view. I had no reason to go lower until I started on his leg, and then I would be moving the sheet from the bottom up.

Did he work outside without his shirt all summer? His bronzed skin was tan line–free. The only lighter marks were neat scars. I traced one and his muscles bunched.

"How many surgeries did you have?" Guess I wasn't done being intrusive. I had similar lines on my abdomen from my own crash.

"On my shoulder or in total?"

"From the accident."

"Too damn many."

If he didn't want to talk about it, I wouldn't push him. I rubbed the lube on the general area of his shoulder blade.

"Eight," he said, and I continued to stroke softly, testing how much pressure he wanted, watching for him to tense. "Two on my face, two on my shoulder, and four on my leg—one foot surgery, one hip surgery, and two knee surgeries."

I ran my palm over his shoulder and down his arm. He twitched like he wasn't expecting me to roam so far away from his back. The strength radiating from him was tangible, rippling under my fingers as I floated my hands over his skin. "I had three when I was a kid."

His biceps flexed under my hands. "How bad were you hurt?"

I rarely talked about the crash that had killed my parents. Memories would come and I'd get that smothering sensation again. The tightness in my chest and the struggle to breathe. "I had a punctured lung and abdominal bleeding. I don't count getting stitches for all the lacerations."

He let out a breath. "Me either. If I wasn't under, it wasn't a surgery."

"Weird how we form arbitrary limits."

"I spent half a day figuring out what I would call a surgery versus a procedure. If I was awake, it didn't go in the surgery category."

I rubbed small circles in the muscles between his spine and armpit. A low groan left him.

"I didn't cause more damage, did I?" I couldn't get the horror of watching him crumple out of my head.

"It wasn't your fault, Summer."

It was though. All of it. Instead of doing the responsible thing and telling Jonah exactly what had happened that day, I'd avoided him. I'd stayed away and I'd used his outburst at the hospital as an excuse. But Jonah didn't realize what I was talking about. I was a coward, so I kept it that way. "I walked right into your house without announcing myself."

"You take on too much, sunshine."

I dug into the muscles at the base of his neck and he grunted. I eased up.

I didn't take on too much. I hadn't done enough.

My fingertips skated over several tiny bumps. More jagged scars from glass shards that had come from the bigger piece that had sliced his face. I didn't have the large scars he did, but I had similar ones covered by my hair and scattered down my neck.

A few more minutes went by. He wasn't bunching and tensing like he had been. A sign that what I was doing was helping.

"I was an adult," he said, his words muffled like he'd melted into the mattress. "I can't imagine what something like that is like for a kid."

I swallowed hard and my fingers stalled. "I should start on your leg." I had a lot more area to cover and the logistics would keep my mind occupied. He'd had hip surgery and the fall had likely jammed that joint too. If he'd let me, I owed him a toe-to-hip rubdown.

My breaths turned shallow as I covered his back with the sheet and moved to the foot of the bed. I rolled up the sheet, trying to keep his other leg covered for maximum privacy.

Now that my brain was full of logistics, I could answer him without trembling. "It was a nightmare. Mama Starr and Daddy Bjorn—that's what I call my birth parents—they weren't . . ." A shiver ran through me and the rest caught in my throat.

He pushed up to his elbows and looked solemnly over his shoulder. "You don't have to talk about it."

Some of the guys I'd dated had gotten really pushy. Others hadn't wanted to hear a downer of a story. Eli had listened like I was telling him the plot of a movie, then he'd tried to cheer me up, not realizing the day my parents died wasn't a topic I could move on from after a few laughs.

I squeezed more lube into my hands and rubbed them together. "Mama and Daddy weren't answering," I said, stronger this time, and he laid his head back down. "I knew something was wrong, and I knew it was bad." I kneaded my fingers into his calf and earned another groan. "I think I even knew they were dead." I swallowed hard. Almost twenty-five years had passed, and I'd had a damn good life since, but the pain of the day resurfaced as fresh as if I were in the hospital again getting told that yes, everything I had feared was true.

"That's awful."

I nodded even though he couldn't see me. I worked my fingertips into the hard tendons around his knee, following the grooves and bumping over scars. "I tried to keep my sisters from panicking while we waited for help, and then I was alone in the hospital and they were all in their own rooms and it just sucked."

"That part was almost as bad as the accident. Losing Eli will always be the worst, but the helplessness of not being able to leave a bed to do anything about it? That was torture."

He understood. I opened up in a way I hadn't around anyone. "I wanted my sisters so bad. I felt like I had failed them. Then we got to the Baileys, and I didn't have to be so strong and I felt worthless. But not for long."

"There's plenty to do at the Baileys' to give you a sense of purpose."

Again, he got it. "Mama Mae knew to throw us into ranch duties. Daddy was there with everything bourbon and whiskey. And my brothers . . ." I sank my teeth into my bottom lip. I'd never told anyone about my first impression of my brothers. "They, uh, were a lot like my birth parents. A little wild. They didn't end up homeless or cart four girls all over the wilderness because they were careless or anything, but—"

"You were homeless?" He propped himself on his elbows again.

"Yeah, I never really told anyone. Neither did Mama Mae." The social workers had known, but four girls starting with a new family in a new school didn't need salacious gossip following them. "We went from campsite to campsite for months. Sometimes they'd take day work and we could afford a hotel. The nights were getting so damn cold, and I'd hear them arguing about what to do for winter. Then the storm hit and we crashed and that was that."

"Shit." He was still watching me as much as he could from his crooked angle. "Is that why you hate planes?"

"I think so. Being closed in like that?" I shuddered. "I don't care for dark spaces. I'm not fond of storms, but I handle them better than Wynter."

"Autumn and Junie?"

Another thing with Jonah that no one else had done. He asked about the rest of my family. He knew them and perhaps that was why he was different from the pompous investment banker I'd met through work connections. "We all have our thing. Junie sings, but she also runs, know what I mean?"

He nodded. I didn't want to spell it out and feel like I was tossing my nomadic sister under the bus.

"Autumn is cautious to the point it stifles her. I guess the silver lining for Wynter is that she couldn't stand to watch Daddy Darin die slowly from cancer, so she tracked down Myles."

If I couldn't find my own happily ever after, I was grateful my sisters could have them. Although it didn't seem like Autumn or Junie was rushing to any altar like I had.

Several quiet minutes ticked by while I worked on his knee.

"The whole town seems to think they know what the accident did to me," he said.

I thought about what he said, worked it over in my head. He'd listened and understood, and I wanted to do the same. Was I just another person who assumed I knew what Jonah had gone through?

I moved north of his knee, nudging the sheet up, praying I didn't expose a butt cheek and turn the air between us uncomfortable. His muscles there were tight in a way the rest hadn't been. The massage was starting to be like molding steel with the heat of my hand.

"People call you a recluse," I said. "You don't agree with them?"

"People are annoying."

I grinned and continued to stroke around his lower thigh. His skin heated under my touch. "You never had patience for stupid shit. I thought that was why you couldn't stand me."

He rested his head back in his arms. "My brother was stupid in love with you and that was annoying enough."

My smile died. "Yeah. I cringe when I think of how we were." I'd been in love with the idea of love. Eli had been a good guy to explore those emotions with. "Puppy love can steal common sense."

He half turned instead of twisting to look over his shoulder.

I was presented again with the scarred side of his face. I recalled what he used to look like. A guy who could've walked out of the pages of an outdoor catalogue. He could've modeled the clothing, but he hadn't acted like he knew he was ruggedly attractive. That his grin was everything a young girl lived and breathed for. The scar didn't change that beauty, but it acted like a visual block for the shallow minded. People thought the jagged scar and the network of lines it turned to under his beard detracted from his looks. Instead, it just made him a different version of a handsome man.

I'd heard the comments over the years. The older crowd wondering if there was nothing a plastic surgeon couldn't do. Kids pointing his looks out in public. Then there were the younger women. Those who thought the scars and the way he avoided much of town gave him a bad-boy edge. The ladies who wanted a rough ride.

How many found out what sex was like with Jonah?

"Puppy love?" he asked, dragging me back to the conversation about Jonah.

"We were teenagers. Didn't you have that with someone? Jackie?" I kept my gaze on my task. Had I sounded jealous?

Jonah had been one of those older boys. The type of guy girls wanted attention from and rarely received. He'd been in his own world, but that place had included high school sports like football and baseball. He'd driven a big truck and had even been on the homecoming court.

He snorted. "No."

I scooted his leg out to get better access to his full thigh. He moved without much prodding, whether it was more comfortable or because he didn't want me to jerk his limb in a direction it couldn't go easily. "You two were hot and heavy."

"We were teenagers."

"I heard you were seeing her again," I murmured. Was I digging for information? Absolutely.

"We were, but we're done."

My heart skipped a beat. "Oh?"

"Sometimes you just gotta let something go that should've stayed in the past." His gruff words steadied my pulse. If he thought like that, maybe I could talk to him—about everything.

I continued to work the flesh around his thigh. He was so dang tight. That couldn't be good. I shifted the blanket higher. "I can do your hip while you're like this."

He tensed. "It's fine."

"There's that word again." I halted my upward progress. "I've learned, Jonah, that when you say it's fine, it's not. I can help."

"No."

I held his gaze. I couldn't cross my arms when my hands were slippery with lube. I'd get the gel on my sweater, and while it was water-based lubricant, I had no other clothes. "Does your shoulder feel better?"

A muscle ticced in his jaw. "Yes."

"Your knee?"

"The ache isn't as bad." Stubbornness resounded in his voice.

"Then I can help your hip."

He held my attention, his pupils dilating. He worked his jaw like he was chewing over the words. "My dick isn't by my shoulder or my knee."

Oh.

Oh. I was rubbing him down with lube. I'd heard once that erections were a common occurrence for men getting massages. Surely, he wasn't having problems getting a massage from me. Delight pushed through my shock. Would his reaction be from me?

He tugged the sheet, and if he kept straining his shoulder at that angle, he'd undo all the work I'd done. "I'm a lot more comfortable than I was. I think I can sleep now."

Disappointment was a loud gong in my ears. It didn't matter that my palms tingled from the warmth of his skin and the slide of his silky body hair under my fingers. He was dismissing me. After barging into his home and pushing him into a massage, the least I could do was leave him alone.

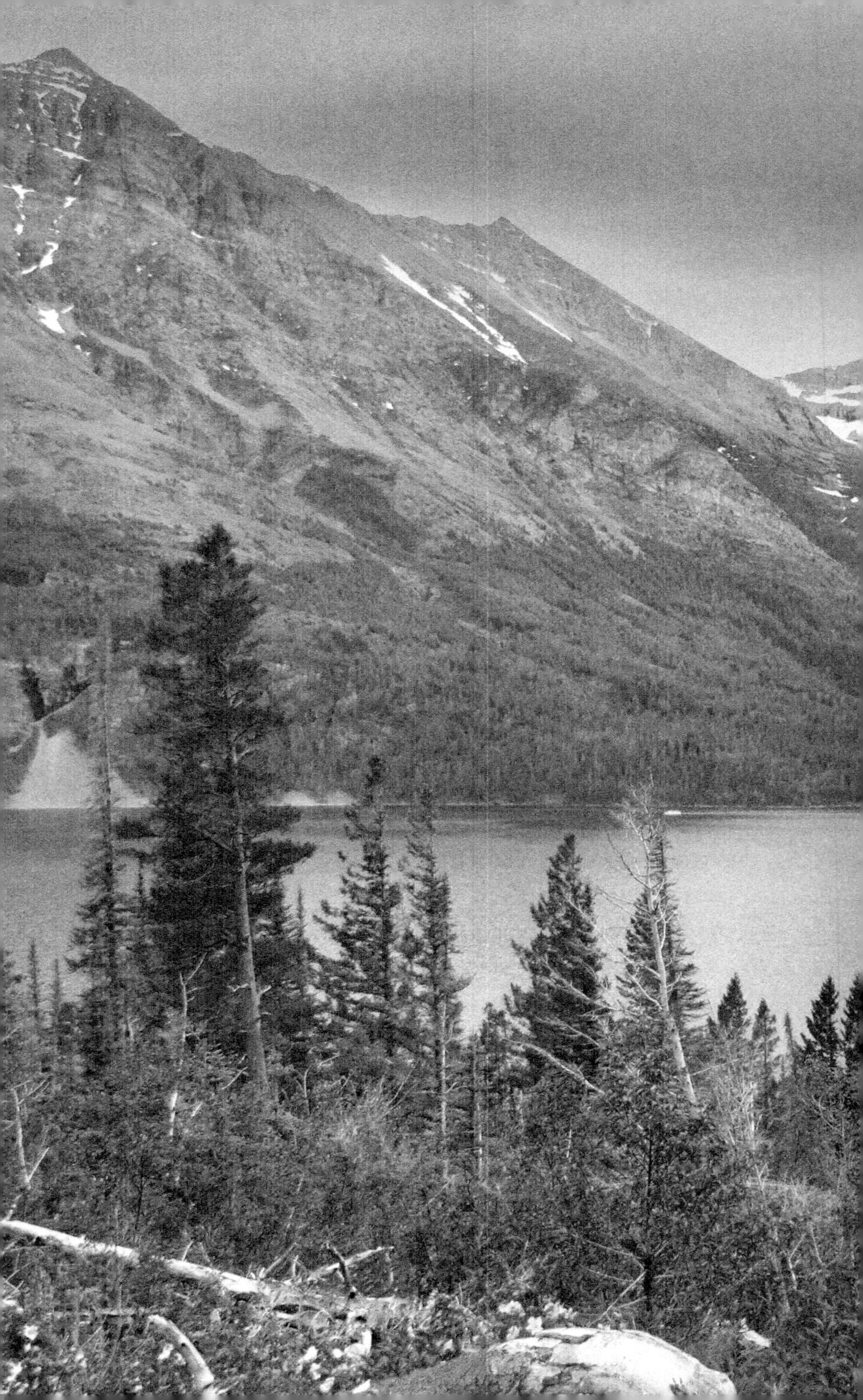

CHAPTER TEN

Jonah

I stared at my dark bedroom ceiling. The wind had picked up, howling outside. There was little ambient light, but I could picture the snow swirling and gusting, clouding the view in every direction.

The weather wasn't keeping me awake.

The inhuman restraint I'd had to use to keep from sporting an erection around Summer was obscene. I was a pervert. Smelling her while she had leaned over me, enveloping me in her strawberry-sugar scent while she rubbed me down with the same stuff I'd used to stroke myself off with the night after she'd left . . .

I'd almost let her work on my hip only to keep her in my room longer. To have her hands on me for another twenty minutes. But each time I looked at her, blood rerouted to my dick. Each time my brain dwelled on the fact that she was the one touching me and not Hannah, my fifty-five-year-old surrogate grandmother of a massage therapist, my cock swelled. Inconveniently and rampantly.

Each glimpse I'd stolen of her, she'd been bathed in weak lamplight, and now I knew what she looked like in my bedroom. I knew what she looked like in comfy clothes, like this was her home. Like we did this on our Saturday nights.

A creak sounded and I frowned. The house was sturdy, but the noise wasn't one of the normal sounds that happened during a storm. Another squeak. This one I recognized. The bottom step. The damn thing had made noise for years, and while I didn't traverse the stairs often, I knew the sound.

Summer was awake.

Was she having trouble sleeping because of the weather? Because of me? When she'd stayed with her mom, she hadn't gotten hung up on her ex, had she?

No. She hadn't brought that cocksucker groceries.

I rolled out of bed. I should let her roam and do whatever she needed to do, but after she'd told me about her parents' accident, I couldn't let her be alone.

I got up and shrugged into a shirt. I had on pajama bottoms and she'd seen almost everything, but I couldn't risk another flashing. My dick was a delinquent around her.

Before I left my bedroom, I grabbed a cane. My shoulder wasn't complaining and my knee was stronger. Summer wasn't a professional massage therapist, but she'd helped. Imagine the wonders if I'd let her work on my hip.

I found her in the dark living room, highlighted by residual light from the kitchen appliances and the flickers from the modem by the TV. She wore the same clothing she'd had on when she'd arrived—shit. She didn't have anything else.

"Do you want to borrow a shirt?"

She gasped and jumped, spinning around and then losing her balance. She caught herself on the window.

"Don't fall," I said wryly.

She flashed a quick smile. "Then it'd be my turn for a massage."

"Anytime, sunshine." My goddamn mouth.

Her eyes widened, and she let out a nervous laugh. "Right. Fair play." She folded her arms around herself and turned to stare back outside.

"Is it the storm?"

"The wind." She sighed, her shoulders falling. "The damn wind. When I hear it, I can't stand to be closed in anywhere. Sometimes my condo is too small."

Slowly, I made my way across the living room. My eyes were adjusted, but I wasn't falling down again around her. At least I was dressed this time. "Is that why you don't like to fly?"

A shiver ran across her slim shoulders. "The entire flight makes it sound like the wind is right in your ears. And you have nowhere to go."

I stopped next to her. "Is the bedroom too closed in?"

"It's not that." She glanced at me, the reflection of the blue modem light in the window in her eyes. "At Mama's house, my room's in the basement. Up there, I can hear the wind rush over the house, pulling and pushing and demanding." She shook her head. "It's silly."

"Never say that." I stared at the darkness on the other side of the window. Nature's chaos. Inside, man-made calm. "I couldn't drive for two years after I left the hospital."

She pivoted toward me and her hand landed on my arm. She didn't say anything, like she knew I needed silence to continue.

"At first, it was why I didn't go to town for so long. I have to go past that—" Words tangled in my throat, cutting off air. I couldn't go back to that isolated space, so I continued to tell my story. "Now, I've gotten used to driving past the accident site. The guilt still gets to me. I was the idiot who left his liquor unlocked. I was the idiot who never thought my underage brother would sneak into the house." I scoffed. "Afterward, I used to lock my doors up tight. All day, every day, the doors were locked." I had secured the house when Summer was staying here too. But otherwise, keeping my place unlocked was a small action I took to keep from retreating into a shell I almost hadn't broken out of.

"I'm so sorry." Her sympathy bordered on pity.

"I'm not like that anymore."

Her lips quirked. "If you were, you wouldn't have an unwanted guest in your house waking you up in the middle of the night."

"I never said you were unwanted."

The silence fell between us, expectant and heavy. I couldn't look away. We were close. I just had to reach out. I could take her in my arms and press my mouth against hers and find out if she was as sweet as I thought. Then I'd press her against the window and lift her. She'd wrap her legs around my waist, and if she worried whether I'd be able to bear her weight, I'd growl about proving I could—

Christ. I was getting hard.

"What'll help you sleep?" I owed her. I owed her as a man to not be a creep. I owed her for the rubdown. Usually when I tweaked one of the joints on my left side, I slept fitfully for a few nights until I broke down and took a muscle relaxer and slept for two days straight or made an appointment with Hannah. I was able to rest tonight. My mind was the one keeping me awake. And my dick.

"I'll get too tired to stay awake." She waved a hand and shifted her gaze to the window.

"But there's something."

She took a moment to answer. "When I was a kid, I'd crawl into bed with Autumn and we'd . . ." She grimaced but her lips twitched like she was struggling not to smile. "We'd talk shit about our brothers. 'They think they know everything,' " she ended in a high-pitched voice. " 'They're so bossy and treat us like wimps.' "

I grinned. "I know that didn't last long. Teller used to tell me about the extra work they tricked you and Autumn into doing."

She whipped her head toward me, her gaze righteous. "He was so bad. Tate could be worse. If it weren't for Tenor and his soft heart, we'd have probably continued doing everything while they"—she threw up air quotes—" 'swept the barn.' "

Laughter vibrated out of me. I could picture Tate and Teller, young and broody and cocky, thinking their sisters got it easy and making sure they righted the world.

Her grin was better than the haunted look she'd had when I'd first found her. "Good thing Montana winters are long. My sisters and I needed that therapy time complaining about them." Her smile faded. "As an adult,

I just roam my place until I can't stay awake. Sometimes, I pull all-nighters, but you know the wind is never as bad in town."

"No Boyd?"

She shook her head. "I tried to talk to him once. He said, 'Baby, it's just a breeze.'"

"What a dickwad."

"So many red flags marched past me." She shuddered. "So I'm back to wandering and waiting."

I'd made it through her massage. I could be a gentleman. "I have a big bed. You can shit-talk your brothers, and I'll stick to my side of the bed." She blinked at me, stunned. I could take back my offer and pretend I had said nothing, or I could forge ahead. "No funny business, I promise."

She softened. "I know you won't try anything," she said with a hint of resignation, but that was probably just me thinking about things better left alone. "I can be a bed hog."

"Do you steal blankets?"

The corner of her mouth lifted. "I've been told I do but I think it's all lies."

"Go on, sunshine. I just did laundry the other day, so all bedding is clean."

"Mama is a laundry maniac before blizzards too."

"Can't be stranded with no power and racing stripes."

A giggle burst out of her. "I don't know if Mama would admit that, but I'm sure that was her reason with my brothers."

"Save the shit-talking for the sheets, sunshine."

Laughing, she walked away and straight to my bedroom. I took a few seconds to gather myself.

I'd smiled more around her in the last week than in

the entire year put together. Unfortunately, I'd also gotten more erections.

"We got it stuck." I was on my third story of the hijinks Teller and I had been up to as teens, lying on my bed like I had been when I'd heard her wandering. She was on her side, on the edge, with an expanse between us. The faint glow of a night-light emanated from the hallway. My eyelids were heavy but there was no way I was falling asleep before Summer did. There'd be no one to make sure she got some rest.

"You did not. Daddy's new pickup?" Fatigue was entering her voice.

"Right down in that very valley. I had to sneak my dad's tractor out of the yard to tow it."

She yawned. "How do you sneak a tractor?"

"Bribed my brother to fake breaking an ankle."

"No way!" She perked up, and I grinned. The few times I'd mentioned Eli, the old pain wasn't there. I liked talking about the fun we'd had. I rarely thought of those memories without the weight of sadness.

"He did. Dad wouldn't call him on it after the X-ray came back clear and there was no swelling or bruising. The youngest, you know. Spoiled."

"Wynter would disagree, but totally the youngest." Sleepiness was back in her voice. "Eli never told me that story."

"I'm surprised."

"I'm not. He idolized you, but he was also jealous of you."

Acid flushed into my throat. "Why?"

"All the girls were hot for you. We were freshmen, and you were a senior. Then you became a mountain man. So many girls only talked to Eli to get close to you."

My brother hadn't told me. "Shit."

"It's not your fault how others react." The bed shifted as she propped herself on her elbow. "You know that, right? You can't take responsibility for his actions."

I had shared good memories about Eli, but that was as far as I was getting into his death. "You need to get some sleep."

Her gaze held an earnestness I couldn't decipher. She licked her lower lip like she was readying herself to say something hard, but she ended up sucking that puffy lip between her teeth and lying back down. "You have a hard time talking about the accident."

"I have a hard time talking about everything."

The corner of her mouth tipped up, but there was a sadness to her smile. "Me too. There are some very difficult things to talk about."

Did she mean with her parents who had died, or with Eli? Had she gotten to talk about losing Eli with anyone or had she powered through life and suppressed all her feelings?

Her eyelids fell shut and I let mine do the same, more content than I had been in a long time. Other than camping with buddies, which hadn't happened for years, I'd gone to sleep alone. Going to sleep with a beautiful woman in my bed was something I could get dangerously used to. I'd have been better off not knowing what I'd been missing my entire life.

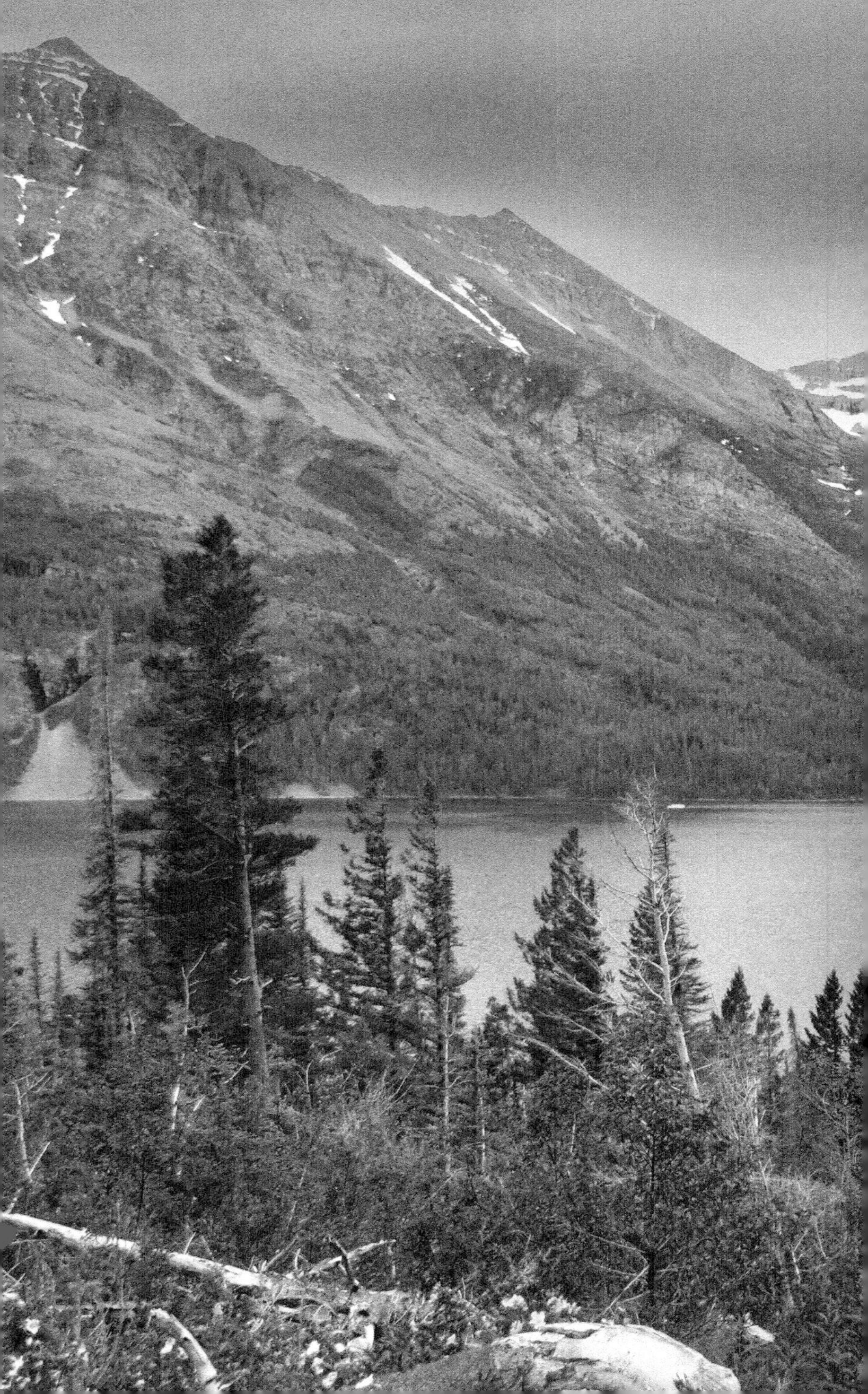

CHAPTER ELEVEN

Summer

I was toasty warm and still tired, but I hummed and burrowed into the cocoon of heat around me. A hard body met mine and a nose burrowed in my hair.

I let out a soft moan. When was the last time I'd woken up so cozy? When I'd woken up feeling so safe?

The wind raged outside, but the restless energy that plagued me during this type of weather was missing. I didn't need to get up and leave. I wasn't alone, in the dark, with the sounds of a storm over my head.

A strong arm wrapped around my middle and a large hand scooped under my sweater to splay over my belly.

God, that felt good. Warm skin and calloused fingertips—divine. I wiggled against my wall of comfort.

A very male groan sounded behind me and he stroked downward.

My lips curved upward and the events from last night played through my head. The blizzard and how it had propelled me back in time. My guilt over Jonah and how he'd been hurt. The pleasure of going to sleep hearing his stories. And then a heartbeat of regret before I'd drifted off to sleep.

My eyelids flew open. The glow from the night-light was the only light. It was still dark out, and I wasn't in the guest room.

Jonah.

His fingers danced around the waistband of my underwear. A hard, impressive erection pressed into my backside through our sweats.

"Jonah," I whispered, afraid to break the spell, but knowing I had to. I wanted this. I wanted Jonah's hands on me, and I wanted to explore the pleasure he could give. But . . . I wouldn't do it until we had a talk.

"Mm." The rumble went through his chest and into my back. Such a masculine sound. Auditory pleasure. I wanted more of that too.

He worked his fingertips underneath my underwear. Need swamped me, igniting an ache between my thighs he was so close to resolving.

"Jonah," I whined, hating to put a stop to us.

He hadn't reached my clit yet, but he was *close*. "Mm."

I frowned. Was he awake? "Jonah," I said louder this time.

His hand twitched.

"Jonah." I gripped his wrist. This could not happen when he wasn't fully awake and when he hadn't heard what I had to tell him.

He stiffened. Yep. He was awake now. His muscles twitched and he jerked his hand away. "Shit. I'm sorry."

I let out a sigh and rolled back to my side of the bed,

which happened to be a longer distance than I'd anticipated. I had been like a heatseeking missile, locking on to Jonah as soon as we were both asleep.

I rolled to my side and straightened my twisted sweatshirt. I'd almost wiggled my sweats down my ass. Thankfully, the covers hid the worst of it.

"Jesus, Summer. I'm so sorry."

"I'm not."

He snapped his mouth shut. His brows crashed together. "What?"

"I'm not, but we need to talk first."

"No, of course. I mean . . ." He worked his jaw like he was tasting words and none of them were the right flavor. "You're getting out of a relationship."

"Boyd is absurdly easy to get over. It's not him."

His expression turned neutral. The creases on his cheek from the pillow made him more approachable, along with the sleep haze clearing from his eyes. But I didn't care for the way he seemed to be bracing himself for a personal insult.

"It's not you either. It's me. And Eli."

Understanding lit his dark gaze. "You've never gotten over him."

I could've howled in frustration. On top of being ashamed of myself, I was flubbing this conversation before I'd even started, and I was fifteen years too late already. "That's what I need to talk to you about. I miss Eli. I really do. He was a good friend and a good person. But you've been blaming yourself for his death when it's not your fault at all."

He scowled and punched at his pillow to prop his head up more. "You can say that until you're blue in the face, but it doesn't make it true. He didn't just drink anyone's alcohol. He didn't T-bone some stranger. Both were me. I wasn't there for him when he was clearly bothered by something. I was there at the worst possible time." He held a hand up. "And don't say that he might've killed or injured someone else. I know all the facts."

"Not all of them." My heartbeats turned sluggish, like I was pumping sludge instead of blood. *Here I go*. What I should've confirmed before he ran me out of the hospital room. "I broke up with him. That's why he was drinking."

Jonah

I couldn't have possibly heard right. My dick was still hogging my blood supply and my brain was functioning on an insufficient supply. "Say again?"

"He was angry and hurt. He was mad at you and upset with me."

The events of that day ran through my head. I'd seen Eli at breakfast when I'd stopped in to help with ranch chores. My parents had asked what I was up to. I'd said I was bumming around with Teller. He had a couple of old bourbon barrels they couldn't sell and we were going to fuck around in his shop. That day was my introduction to repurposing barrels. Eli had been excited. Summer was home for the weekend and he'd had plans with her for the whole day.

She had broken up with him? He must've been devastated. A new, fresh guilt welled inside me. I'd known he was hurting, and now I knew why. I hadn't been there for him.

Was that why he'd been upset with me? And how would Summer have known? "Why would he have felt that way?"

The air grew thick between us. Pain filled her eyes, but the fear in them as well gutted me. She shouldn't be scared to talk to me, but I was also to blame for that too.

"I . . ."

"*Why*, Summer?" I said, her name a whiplash. My patience was thinning. I'd gone from waking up in a state of bliss I'd never known to having a boulder poised over my head, ready to drop. "Why would he hate me over your breakup?"

"I . . ." She squeezed her eyes shut.

The anxiety inside me built like thunderstorm clouds. She'd known Eli the best. She'd come to my hospital room for a reason and put her hand so comfortingly on mine. Fifteen goddamn years ago. "Tell me. What did I do that made my brother hate me enough to drink my liquor and speed down the mountain? Why didn't you tell anyone? Do my parents know?"

Her eyes were still closed tight. "No," she whispered. "I couldn't do that to them."

I relaxed only slightly. I respected her for sparing them more heartache. Losing Eli had changed them. Irrevocably.

Her swallow was loud. "I broke up with him. I was at college and he took a year off and I thought we'd grown apart, and he thought . . ." This was the part I was going to hate. I sensed it. Summer always said what was on her mind, but she'd kept this to herself for a decade and a half. "He suspected I had a thing for you."

Shock propelled me to a sitting position. A twinge fired in my hip and shoulder, but I ignored the pain. "What? You told him you didn't, right?"

Her conflicted gaze stayed on me.

"You told him you didn't," I said through clenched teeth.

A quiet sob left her. "I never lied to Eli."

I rolled out of bed and stood so fast it was a miracle my leg didn't give out. My chest was heaving. I'd driven myself out of my mind because I hadn't been there for Eli, but to think that he'd hated me too? That he'd been jealous and resentful? And worse—that a small part of me was lighting up inside, ready to celebrate that perfect Summer Kerrigan had been into me. "What the fuck, Summer? *What the fuck?* You broke his heart over me?"

"Over the fact that I wasn't in love with Eli like he was with me." She'd stood up too. Her Copper Summit sweater taunted me. The girl and the alcohol that had driven Eli to the end. "Leaving for college made our differences obvious, and I couldn't lie to myself anymore."

"Why didn't you say that then?"

"I did. He accused me of lying." Anguish twisted her face. "Then he asked me about you. No matter what, I didn't like him the way he liked me, but . . . I never lied to him. He'd know. So I told him it was a silly crush, that it meant nothing."

I recoiled and my hip complained. A silly crush? "You dated Eli in high school. What the hell were you doing noticing me?"

"Eli and I were genuine friends. You were older. I was just a little girl to you, and I wanted to date someone who treated me well." She pushed her hands through her hair. To think I'd wanted to know how the strands felt fisted in my hands while I pushed into her. "It was a mistake, and I thought I'd go back to college and forget about the hurt I'd caused him and . . . and forget about you. Then the accident happened."

For fucking years, she'd let me believe . . . "And when you came to me in the hospital that day? Were you going to declare your undying love?"

"I'd thought you should know I'd been the reason he was drinking," she whispered. "That I had broken up with him. But you were in so much pain, and you already hated me just for caring about you. I could tell it made you feel guilty. So I left. Then the more time that went by, the harder it got."

"So you left. That's what you do, isn't it?"

She hugged her arms around herself. "What do you mean?"

"You left my hospital room. You fucking left Bourbon Canyon. You left your goddamn wedding. Or do you only leave when I get involved?"

"That isn't fair."

"It's accurate."

"Look, Jonah—"

"How do you not let the guilt eat you alive? How do you go to the city and date shitty guys and work in your fancy distillery without getting chewed up by guilt like me?"

Her bottom lip quivered, and her eyes watered. "What am I supposed to do?"

"Tell the goddamn truth!"

She flinched.

I shoved a hand through my hair. My skin crawled,

hot with emotion and prickly with rage and loss and . . . regret. "Get out."

She shrank in on herself, her arms cradled around her like she was her only source of support.

She'd moved on without flinching.

I'd been so angry for so damn long. Nothing had made sense. Why my brother who never drank had overindulged. Why he hadn't talked to me first. Why he'd been so tormented in the first place.

"I'm sorry," she whispered.

The shine of her tears was more than I could take. I turned away. No matter how betrayed and furious I was, I couldn't withstand a crying Summer. "For once, do what I fucking ask you to and get out."

I heard her footsteps and her sniffles fade. I waited for the steps to creak as she went upstairs but there was nothing. Then I heard movement by the front door. I didn't know what prompted me, but I hobbled out of the bedroom. The irony that I could keep my balance because of her massage wasn't lost on me.

I rounded into the hallway. She had her coat and boots on and her hand was on the doorknob.

"What the hell are you doing?" I yelled.

She froze and looked over her shoulder. Her skin was paler in the light from the windows. "You said to leave."

"Not in a fucking blizzard! I meant leave my room."

Her mouth formed an O. Even as I raged, my attention was on her ripe lips and her tousled hair, messy from being in my bed.

Goddammit. My brother had died over this.

I stomped back into my bedroom and slammed the door.

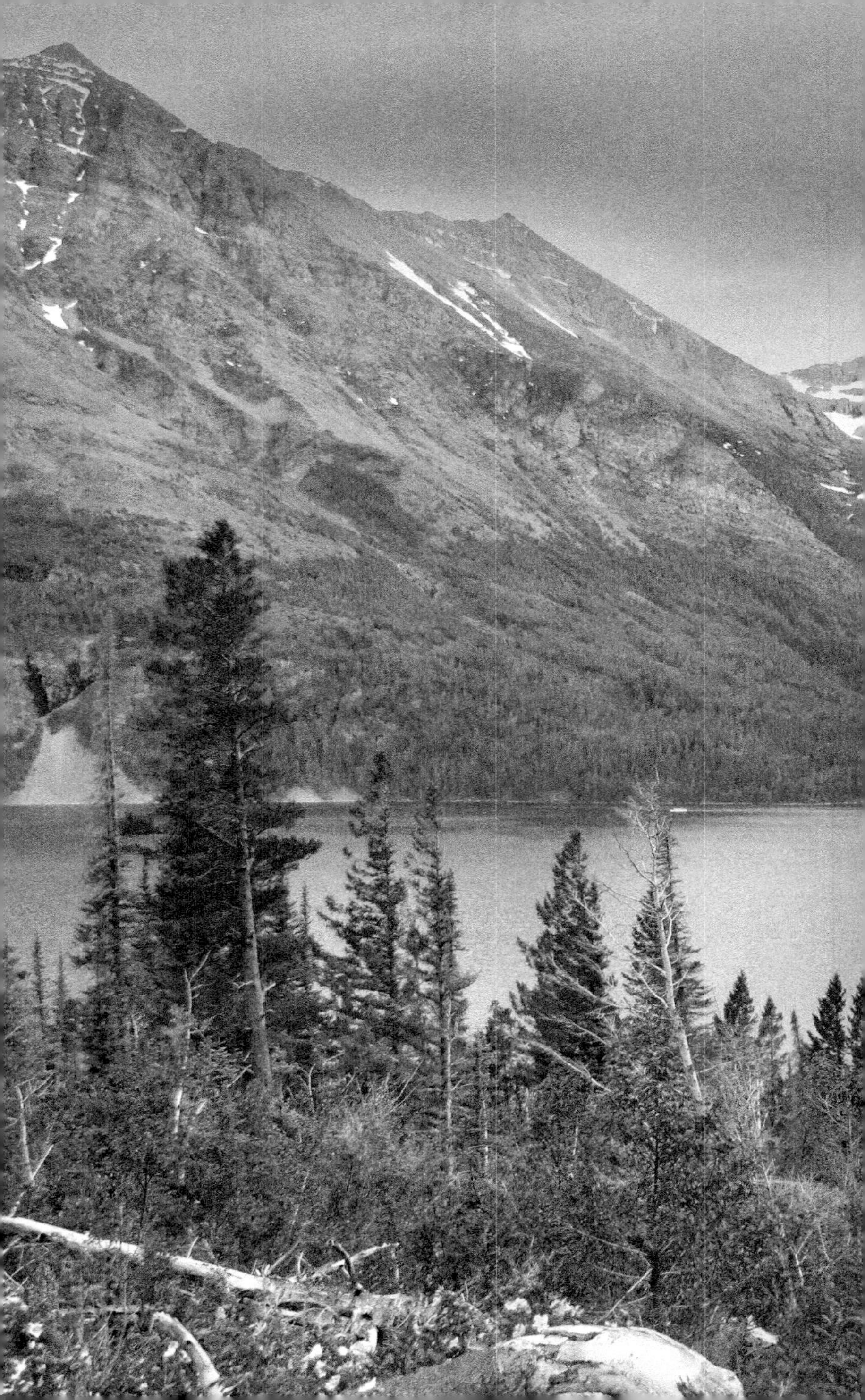

CHAPTER TWELVE

Summer

I blinked awake. I must've fallen asleep after hiding in the guest room. I'd cried myself to sleep a few times over the years when the wind howled outside. An effective sleep tactic. My eyes were crusty and I had a dull headache.

How late was it?

Noon.

Crap.

My pounding head was likely from the exertion to keep from wailing, and dehydration. If Jonah kept alcohol in the house, I would've dived into the bottles last night.

No, I wouldn't have. Too similar to what Eli had done. I wouldn't do that to either of us even if I weren't planning to drive anywhere.

I rolled up and hung my legs over the side of the bed.

My phone lit with a message from Autumn. **Was it planned this time?**

I scowled at her question. She had no idea the flame I'd held for Jonah all these years. No one did. I'd been moderately successful at forgetting him until he'd shown up to my wedding.

I lay back, letting my feet dangle. The thudding in my skull grew stronger. Things between me and Jonah had been going so well, but at the base of our talks, and every time we smiled, I'd had a jolt of guilt. True remorse. He blamed himself, and there was no way I could spin the story to make it okay not to tell him what had really happened that day. His parents didn't even know.

I was a horrible person.

I dialed Autumn.

She answered. "Are you calling because it's so good you can't type the words because they'll steam off the screen?"

Tears welled in my eyes. "No."

"Tell me what happened," she said sharply.

"I messed up so bad."

Then I told her what I'd told Jonah. Every horrid detail.

"I'm such an awful person. He hates me and now he's stuck with me."

"Oh, honey."

I wept, staying silent like last night, my face screwed up and my cheeks hurting.

"I know you're not going to listen to me," she started and I recalled saying similar things to my siblings when I gave them advice. "But this is neither your nor Jonah's fault."

I shook my head, my hair flying and my head pounding. "No, it's—"

"Eli's feelings were his feelings. His actions were his actions. You can't know he wouldn't have done it anyway. You can't know he wouldn't have gotten into his parents' stash and driven into town. You can't know whether he would've gotten hurt or hurt someone else, or both."

"I shouldn't have answered Eli."

"He asked because he knew, Summer."

"I hurt him so bad," I whispered, squeezing my eyes shut.

"A breakup does that to people. You and Eli were barely more than kids, and you knew he'd take it hard, that's why you waited so long."

I might've hoped that being gone for college would dampen his neediness. That Eli would branch out and make other friends, but instead, the longer we were together, the more his life was about ranching and me. It wasn't healthy, and it wasn't what I had wanted out of a relationship.

"This is going to sound callous," Autumn said gently, "but Eli's in the past. He's gone, and he left a mess for you and Jonah."

"I'm making Jonah feel worse, and I'm stuck here for days."

"You are stuck together. So do what Mama used to make us do when we were arguing—put our chairs back-to-back and take turns saying ten nice things to each other."

The giggle the memory inspired was out of place but much needed. I sighed. "He's so angry."

"I bet he is. It's gotta be harder to be furious at his dead brother than at himself."

And I made an even better target. A deserving target. He hadn't had the last fifteen years to get over the revelation. I'd taken that from him.

Jonah was outside. The wind continued to rage and throw snow in whatever direction it wanted. Things close to the house were still visible, but beyond, where a valley should stretch across to the mountains sloping up on the other side, there was nothing but an angry snow globe. He'd gone into the elements to avoid me.

I went into the kitchen and pushed up the sleeves of my sweater. The power was still on. I could put food in the oven to cook and hope we had electricity until it was done.

I'd made a roast the last time I was here and he'd liked it. I'd do the same, using his onions and potatoes. Closer to lunch time, I could make a salad. Would he eat? Would I have to retreat upstairs for him to come inside and live like a normal person instead of an angry mountain man?

The scrape of metal on concrete told me the answer. Daddy used to say that shoveling before the storm was done was excellent practice in wasting effort. He used to love storms and his enthusiasm had eased my own fear. His thrill had helped me and all my sisters. We would drink hot chocolate and play games all day. The only stress was worrying about the animals, but Daddy had hidden much of the burden from us when it came time for chores, if chores could even be done.

Once I had lunch going, I pressed a hand to my

stomach. I hadn't eaten breakfast, but I'd wait, too mentally fatigued to eat while Jonah was making himself suffer.

I peered down at myself. I was in the same clothes as yesterday. The sweater and pajama pants would be okay, but I should wash my underclothes. I could roam around with no bra or underwear. Jonah wasn't inside to look.

I retrieved any clothing of his I thought was dirty. The task had included going through his room to get the laundry basket and into the bathroom he used. Once I had enough to feel like I wasn't wasting a load, I threw everything in.

Rolling my shoulders, I looked down. How obvious was it? I wasn't a large-chested woman, but I'd always been happy with what I had. So had my partners. Still, it was weird to walk around his place, free-balling it.

What now?

He was out shoveling a drift that would be blown back in place and bigger than it had been before sunset. I couldn't sit and watch a show. The talk with Autumn ran through my head. He was angry at Eli. Himself. And me.

I couldn't sit inside while he was toiling away. I put on my coat, slipped my feet into my boots, and stuffed my hat on my head. I tugged my gloves on before walking through the house to the door that led into the garage.

Wind swirled through the garage. The big overhead doors were closed, but the door that led outside was open. Flakes swirled inside, and in the time Jonah had been out, a small drift had formed over the threshold.

"Stubborn damn man." As I stepped into the wind

and got smacked in the face with a hundred prickles of snow, I couldn't recall what I had planned to do when I got outside.

What was my goal? For Jonah not to hate me? I didn't care for myself, or for what I'd done to Eli. My parents had always said honesty was the best policy, but being honest that day had cost me. The entire Dunn family had paid. Jonah had stopped living while I hadn't.

"What are you doing?"

I spun and blinked against the onslaught of wind and snow. When my vision cleared, I was faced with a flat mouth. His cold, red-chapped cheeks made his pinkish-white scar stand out more than ever. The black hat was pulled down to his brows and snow had crusted over the scruff on his face. He'd flipped the collar of his heavy, navy-blue winter coat up until only his cheeks and nose were visible.

"I'd like to help." The bridge of my nose stung from the attack of the frigid air on my skin.

"You've done enough." He turned away, shovel in hand. "Get inside."

I clamped my hand on his arm. I didn't yank him around or he might fall. I'd get taken out with him, and while I'd like to know what his weight felt like on top of me, I didn't want him hurt. And I'd rather be in a warm bed. I'd rather he didn't hate me.

The hidden fantasy I hadn't revisited until recently had been shredded last night. "We need to talk."

"You've said enough."

All moisture had been sucked from my lips, but I smacked them together, frustrated. "Jonah, please." He stopped and I didn't know what to say. I looked around as if the snow-pelted surroundings and my crusted-over car would tell me what to say.

My car had been freshly wiped off and baby drifts were forming around the driver's side. Shovel marks from where he'd cleared around the tires were still visible. "What are you doing?"

"Trying to get your car inside the garage."

Oh. Just like last night, he was taking care of me. I had been terrified, leaving the house during a blizzard, but he'd sounded so tortured. He'd caught me in time and ordered me to be safe. Now he was getting my car into a shelter.

Don't delude yourself yet again. He wanted something to do and his options were limited in a storm. "I can help."

"Get inside."

My temper snapped. I threw my hands out, the material of my jacket crackling and punctuating the move. "Let me help. I keep messing up, and I never know how to fix it. Just let me do something!"

He blinked at me. The crust in his near-beard had accumulated more snow since he'd been standing still. If he rejected me again, I'd go inside and try not to cry while watching a movie. I'd be useless, like usual.

"You don't have snow pants. Go in the garage and move shit around until we can fit your car inside."

I could barely hear him over the wind, but I nodded, grateful he wasn't chasing me away again, and also glad I would be out of the wind. Flannel did nothing to block the onslaught and the skin of my legs was growing numb.

When I entered the garage, I turned on the lights, but my eyes needed minutes to adjust before I saw more than dark shapes. I took a step and my boot skated across the concrete floor. I flailed my arms but caught my balance. Good thing. I doubted I'd get TLC tonight if I hurt myself in a fall.

For the next several minutes, I rearranged small motor equipment. A lawn mower. He had three different sizes of chainsaws. Two were electric. Everything he had was neatly ordered, but since no one else ever used the other stall, he'd made a spot for them on the floor.

I found his old fishing rods and tackle boxes, moving them to make room for the weed whacker that wasn't caked in dust from disuse. A kayak and canoe were hung on the back wall. I hadn't noticed them when I was caught up in my ruined wedding. How long since he'd used either one?

His hunting rifles and shotguns were probably in the gun safe I also hadn't noticed last time, stuffed in the far corner. There was a small door toward the back.

I clomped toward it. My boots weren't slick with snow anymore, but I couldn't be too careful. I peeked inside. Too dark. Hell, I was being nosy anyway, and it was his garage. I'd find no secrets here, so I flipped on the light.

All his camping gear was arranged neatly on shelves. In a case on one shelf was a blue-and-gray tent he used to use when he'd camped with Teller all the time. Along the wall were extra paddles for the kayak. Coolers for when he used to throw pasture parties with my brothers were piled together.

Jonah had practically lived outdoors and now he kept his memories shut away, as he did himself.

"Did you lose something?"

I yelped and spun, smacking into a hard, icy chest.

His arms wrapped around me like he couldn't help himself. The cold of his coat seeped through my cheeks but his arms were banded around me and he wasn't letting go.

"Christ, watch where you're going."

I tipped my head back to look at him. "I never used to be like this."

He'd wiped the snow from his scruff before he'd reached me. Drops of melted flakes clung to his dark eyelashes and his gaze was indecipherable. "Yes, you did. You used to get yourself in trouble all the time."

I puffed out a breath. That Summer was so long ago. Adult Summer had finished her education, watched over her siblings, worked for the family company, and kept her head down. Adult Summer didn't pull pranks on boys who'd wronged her or her siblings. She didn't race cars on back roads and she didn't take bets on who could shoot the *E* out of a can of Mtn Dew at fifty yards.

"I can't risk someone else suffering because of what I did."

His jaw worked, and he carefully stepped away. His gloves remained on my shoulders a beat longer before he pulled his hands back. "Do you have your keys? There should be enough room now to get your car in."

"I can do—"

"Jesus, Summer."

Okay, then. I took my keys out of my coat pocket and dropped them in his hand. "I put another roast in. It should be done soon. Are you going to eat with me?"

He stared at me. A drop of melted snow rolled over his beard. "No."

"I'll leave it out for you, then."

He nodded and stomped out of the garage. I rolled

my eyes to the ceiling, then turned to take one last look at a life stuffed into a closet. I hadn't expected any of us who'd loved Eli to be the same after he'd died, but perhaps I'd been wrong to think such a big part of us hadn't passed away with him.

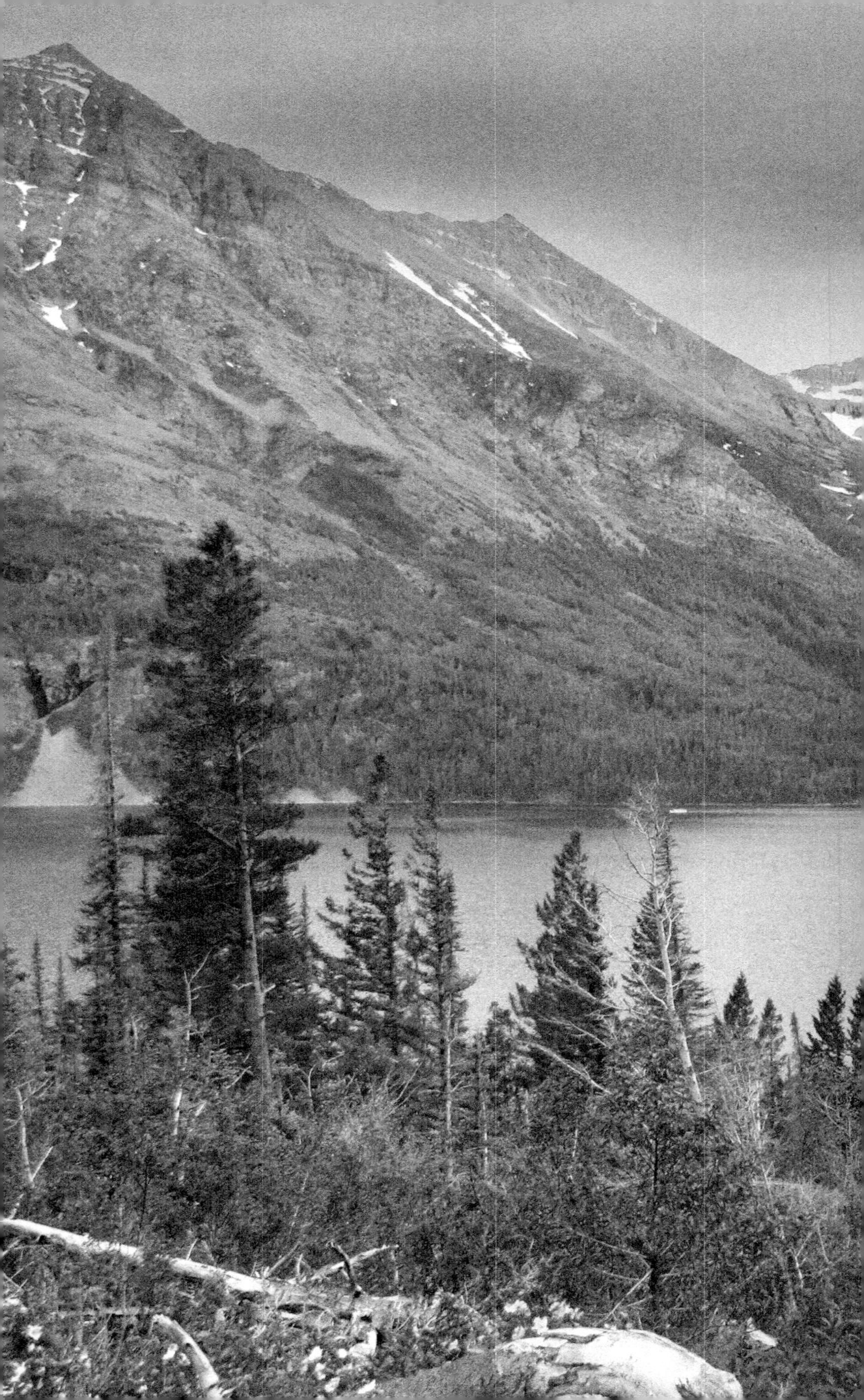

CHAPTER THIRTEEN

Jonah

I'd never inspected my ceiling so much in my life, but I was doing a lot of lying in bed, wondering. My new goddamn pastime with Summer under my roof. I threaded my hands behind my head. My shoulder was back to aching, thanks to the shoveling. My hip was fine, but my knee wasn't happy and my foot was threatening to cause problems too.

I needed a long soak in hot water with my Epsom salt mixture.

But first, I'd have to leave this room. I'd have to find out if Summer had had problems sleeping last night. I'd thought I'd stay awake to listen for creaking stairs, but working outside in a blizzard had taxed me.

Every flake of the snow I'd moved, and a ton more, was back where I had shoveled it, but her car was safe inside. Why seeing the damn thing in my driveway had bothered me, I didn't know. But now I didn't have to picture her wiping mounds of snow off and scraping windows. When the weather cleared and the roads were plowed, she could get in and leave.

Several days from now.

The wind was supposed to be a problem through tomorrow. Then more snow was on the horizon. After that, it was wait until the plows could get to us.

Summer and I would be together for days yet.

I got out of bed and let my knee take its time straightening. I rolled my shoulder and went through some gentle warmups and stretches my physical therapist thought I had ignored her about. Years later, I continued to do them if only to stay away from clinics and hospitals and therapists.

I'd take a bath and do some laundry. The power was holding firm, but I didn't want to let dirty clothing stack up just in case. I left on my sweatpants and grabbed my work clothes from yesterday on the way out the door.

In the hallway, I stopped and listened. No movement. But the sound of deep, steady breathing reached me. I padded to the living room and peered over the back of the couch. My heart twisted.

I hadn't seen a lot of fairy tales, but *Beauty and the Beast* had been my mom's favorite. I had a shit library, but I felt every inch the Beast. Summer had been in her room when I'd eaten a late lunch. She'd stayed up there the entire time, giving me the space I hated her for.

Now she was slumbering on the couch. She'd probably come down when she couldn't sleep because of the wind. I was in a warm, cozy bed, and she was on the couch with an old gray-and-blue throw Mom had given me for Christmas.

Her pink lips were squashed from half her face

being smashed into the pillow she'd brought down from the room. Her sweater was bunched up around her chest but the throw covered any skin that was bared.

I hated the blanket too.

The palm of my hand tingled. The skin of her belly had been so damn soft. Hot in all the right places.

I shook the memory away.

Her feet were bare and sticking out past her one cover. I should grab a bigger blanket—

She was fine. Resolutely, I spun and took my armload to the washroom on the other side of the bathroom. When I turned on the light, I was struck still as lust pounded into my belly.

A lacy bra hung above the dryer and a pair of matching panties were next to it. My mouth went dry, and I got tunnel vision. She wasn't wearing a bra or underwear?

No, idiot. She'd been stranded with only what she was wearing. Of course she'd had to do laundry.

How had the woman who'd ruined my life and that of my brother managed to burrow under my skin and nestle in a spot my hate could hardly reach? How had she managed to never leave my thoughts after I'd driven her out of the hospital room? Had I known what she was going to tell me?

My chest burned. I needed to take that damn bath, but I also couldn't relax after seeing the generous cup size of her bra.

I left my laundry on top of the washer and went to my bedroom. I dug out an Omaha Zoo sweater my parents had gotten me from a trip over the summer and a pair of black sweats I hadn't thrown away from when I was first discharged from the hospital. I'd filled out since then, but I hadn't trashed the sweats.

I laid them on the back of the couch and stood there like a fucking creep watching her sleep. Then, I went into the bathroom to take my bath, and as much as I swore to myself that I wouldn't, I jacked off to the thought of her not wearing underwear.

Summer

I'd found a game cabinet in the small upstairs library between the top of the stairs and the guest room. A small cupboard held some of the board games my family used to play during storms. I'd left Monopoly alone, because fuck that game. I could run a distillery, but I could barely get around the board to collect my cash once.

I'd bypassed Connect 4, Scrabble, and checkers for the single deck of cards. Now I was playing solitaire on the floor of my room. Yesterday, Jonah had been heading outside, but I'd bitten his head off. *Don't you dare spend another day in a storm avoiding me. I'll go upstairs.* And I'd pounded up the stairs like I'd gotten busted sneaking extra cookies after bedtime.

My outburst had worked. Jonah had stayed inside yesterday.

The wind had died down. I was swimming in his sweater and black sweats, but my original clothing was clean. I just had to change into them. And wash my underwear again. We didn't accumulate a ton of dirty clothes between us, but I'd wash all the bedding while I was here to stay in clean underwear.

I found a spot for my five of spades. I'd been playing cards and listening to true crime podcasts for three hours. If the power went out, I was screwed.

My phone rang, and the jolt of excitement it caused was shameful. I was so bored.

Yet did I regret bringing groceries and getting stranded? No. Jonah had needed to know everything.

Wynter's name lit up my screen. My heart stuttered while I rushed to answer. She never called if she could help it. I usually rang her if she ignored too many texts. "Oh my god, if you're calling to tell me you're in labor, I'm going to march through the snow and straight to the hospital."

Her laughter tinkled through the line. "No baby yet." Her sigh was full of disappointment. "I really wanted to spare this child a winter birthday."

"You're not due for two more weeks. You could go long enough until it's technically spring."

"Too long," she groaned. "I'm uncomfortable and bored and I need to talk to a calm voice. Myles is uptight and climbing the walls."

"Anxious he's going to be delivering his firstborn?"

"Yes. I love him, but he doesn't need to be seeing my insides." She dropped her voice. "Do you know how many moms poop when giving birth?"

I giggled. "It's natural."

"Ugh. Scarlett's talked me down once this week."

Tate's wife was the only one of us to have had kids. We weren't close to Tate's first wife, so my nephew Chance's birth announcement had been little more than a text with a photo. Scarlett had ordered Tate to blow up our phones with pictures and updates of Brinley and Darin.

"Help me take my mind off giving birth in a blizzard," Wynter said.

"One, you are not a cow. You don't need to calve during a storm."

She laughed. "It's the rancher's kid in me, that's why I'm due in the spring."

"Not my fault you followed the insemination schedule," I said primly, smiling. I cleaned up my cards. I'd lost the game. "Did you talk to Autumn?"

"Yes, but you know she wouldn't spill anything you told her."

I rolled my eyes. "But she told you there was something."

"I have my ways. Does Jonah really hate you?"

"Maybe." I couldn't give her a resounding no, and that broke my heart. "He can't help but take care of me, but he doesn't like me, that's for sure."

"It's not for sure. Emotions are complicated, and you're still recovering from the breakup."

It took me a moment to realize she wasn't talking about Eli. Cool humiliation washed through me. I'd been about to marry Boyd mere weeks ago and now thinking about him was a nuisance.

"Well, I guess your silence says a lot about how hung up on Boyd you are." She snorted. "Boyd who? That's the way it should be."

"I wish it were that easy. I broke up with Eli because I had a thing for Jonah and he knew it, and now Jonah knows it too."

"Shit." Shuffling came from the other end, like she

was getting comfortable for a long talk. "It's not your fau—"

"Everyone can say that but it doesn't make it true." If it were true, then I would've gotten over it and Jonah would be talking to me. "It doesn't make Jonah dislike me less."

"You think the man who barely leaves his house but went to your wedding and then rescued you from said wedding dislikes you?"

"Maybe he wanted to see me married off."

"Maybe he's a fan of torturing himself."

Well, that was likely true, but this was different.

"Myles was a lot like Jonah," she said thoughtfully.

She'd hidden the fact that she'd been working for Myles. Then he'd come to Bourbon Canyon for Daddy's funeral, and the jig was up. I didn't know what had gone on between them in Denver, but I knew how she'd gotten him to stay. "I'm not having sex with Jonah to get him to talk to me."

She chortled. "I sucked his dick first to loosen him up."

"TMI!"

"I bet it'd work."

I summoned as much irritation as possible to combat the naughty images in my mind. Me on my knees staring up at Jonah and his jaw granite hard because my mouth was wrapped around his— "This is serious."

"It is," she said, her teasing tone gone. "But guys like Myles and Jonah don't respond to chitchat or talking about feelings, so it's going to take a hell of a shock to get him to open up to you."

"He doesn't have to though. That's the thing. We're nothing to each other. Eli was the only thing linking us."

Now his death connected us in a way that couldn't be severed. "Enough about Jonah. He's as stubborn as the mountain he lives on. What are you doing for Easter?"

"Hopefully, I'll be overtired and taking care of a newborn."

I was glad I would be close. Bozeman wasn't a long drive, but in the winter, being able to plan a trip was harder. I might be stuck at Jonah's but at least I was in Bourbon Canyon, around most of my family again.

"But I'll be at Mama's with everyone else," Wynter continued. "She didn't want Tate and Scarlett to feel pressured to host and she wants to make sure Lane and Cruz stick around."

Mama thrived on the bustle of the holidays and having her family around. This year would be the second without Daddy, and we'd let her do whatever she wanted. "I should be out of here by next week."

"Hopefully by next week he won't want to let you go."

"Enough, Wynter. Go tame your guy with that blow job you're so proud of."

"I have reason to be proud. Ten-out-of-ten skill level. He nailed a national distribution deal right after. The trick is—"

I growled out a "Goodbye" and hung up.

What I absolutely did not do was stay on long enough to find out what that trick was.

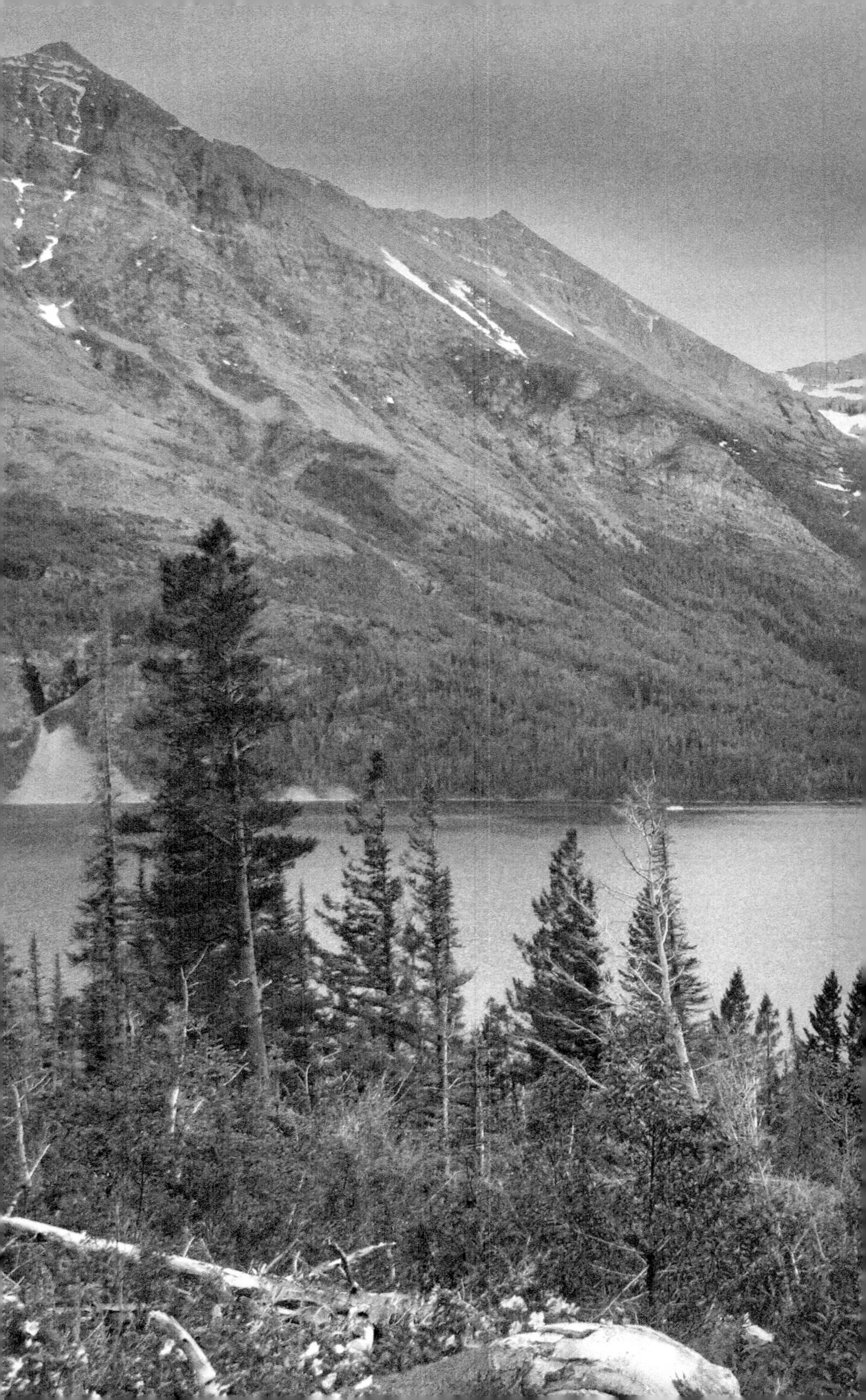

CHAPTER FOURTEEN

Jonah

I entered the house after moving half a mountain of snow. The valley was serene and beautiful and blindingly white. Stacked mounds surrounded the buildings on my property. Hopefully we'd get a warm spell to melt some of those inches before we got any heavier snowfalls in early spring.

Summer had been out helping earlier. We'd coexisted without much talking in the three days since I'd walked away from her in the garage storage closet. We took turns making meals, and we ate separately. She'd spent much of her days in the guest room. Once she'd been awake before me, and I'd caught her folding blankets on the couch.

An hour ago, she'd gone inside. From the savory smells coming from the oven, she must've thrown something in for dinner.

I took off my hat and held it up. The fabric was wet

and heavy from all the sweat of shoveling and pushing the snow into piles with my skid steer. I'd moved snow yesterday too, digging out the driveway, slowly making a path down to the country road the crews hadn't gotten to yet.

I shrugged out of my jacket. The smell of sweat rose up. I stank. After gathering all my snow gear, I went to the bathroom and dropped my load on the floor outside the door. I'd shower and add the clothes I'd been wearing.

I stripped in the bathroom, but cracked the door and dumped my dirty clothing on top of the rest. A warm shower helped unknot my muscles.

This time after I dried myself off, I wrapped the towel around my waist. I'd dress after I started the laundry. But when I opened the bathroom door, the pile was gone. Light speared the hallway from under the door of the laundry room.

She was washing my shit.

Irritated that she had to be so damn helpful, so damn compliant when I missed her fire, and so damn sexy when she was in baggy, oversized sweats, I went to the door and pushed inside.

Fuck. My breath whooshed out. Summer had on the oversized sweatshirt I'd loaned her and that was all. She was hopping on one foot, trying to pull up the baggy, black sweatpants she used when her other clothes were in the wash. Her legs were curvy and toned and bare.

Then she yelped and looked over her shoulder, her eyes wide, and the garment drew up, giving me the most sinful glimpse of rounded ass cheeks I'd ever seen.

"Jonah!" She wobbled and tried to put her foot down

to balance herself, but she was caught in all the fluffy material. She toppled.

Shit. I darted for her as she hit the side of the dryer and clambered for a hold, but her feet slid sideways.

I caught her and went down with her. My left leg went out, breaking our fall. My shoulder hit the side of the dryer and my right knee slammed into the floor. I didn't care. I had a hold of Summer's warm, slight body. So damn real. The fantasies I'd been harboring hit my brain like a nuclear bomb.

I twisted so my ass hit the floor and drew her on top of me. My pulse was jackrabbiting. "Are you okay?"

"Me? Are you okay?" She wiggled her sweet ass on my thighs as she tried to evaluate my knees. Her long legs were bent in front of her.

I couldn't think. My brain was devoid of blood. She wasn't wearing pants or underwear and she was sitting on me. The towel hadn't fallen off my hips, but it was hanging on by a whisper that was getting told to shut up.

"Summer," I gritted. My erection throbbed with growing pain. It was flaccid one second and harder than it'd ever been the next.

"Oh my god." She pressed her fingertips into the flesh around my neck, and it was like a direct line of electricity ran to my cock. "I owe you another massage. What about your shoulder?" She twisted around to inspect my front, but her gaze landed on my bare chest. Those pink lips of hers parted. She finally realized the position we were in.

A sexy flush highlighted her cheeks. Her hair was tousled and still damp. She must've taken a quick shower and waited for my stuff to start laundry. I took a silky strand in my thumb and forefinger.

Christ, she was soft everywhere. Paradise was in my lap. No barrier. "You should get off me."

Hurt flashed on her face. Next was shame. "I'm so sorry." She scrambled to get off me.

Goddammit. I wrapped my hand around the back of her neck and drew her toward me until she fully faced me. I'd put that hurt there. I'd made her feel embarrassed. I'd smothered her fire while she'd been under my roof.

I had to do something to put the passion back into her, to watch her bloom with energy, radiant and beautiful.

"Don't be sorry." I drew her closer. She was straddling me, and disbelief was in her bright eyes now. A fuck ton better than earlier.

Her gaze dropped to my mouth. I liked the way she looked at me. She hadn't asked if I was okay because she thought I couldn't take care of myself. She'd asked because she was terrified she was responsible for my pain. And she was.

But with her on my lap, I had a hard time blaming her. I had a hard time moving beyond the sheer pleasure she could produce by being herself.

"Jonah?"

"I really want to kiss you," I said gruffly.

Her gaze dipped to my mouth again. "I'm not stopping you," she murmured.

"You're naked."

"I have your sweater on."

The growl that emanated from me was more beast than man. I could devour this woman and not leave a single morsel behind. She'd be consumed.

We stayed like that. My exhales turning into her

inhales.

I closed the distance between us just a hair. "I can feel your heat seeping into my skin."

Her pupils were dilated and the heat on my leg bloomed.

Lust kicked me in the groin. My erection waved between us. It'd probably escaped the towel.

"Are you wet for me, sunshine?"

"I've been wet for you a lot over the years."

Fuck. I yanked her to me until she was flush to my chest and smothering my dick between us. My lips crashed onto hers and I dove into the warm depths of her mouth with my tongue.

She was there with me, clutching at my shoulders.

Summer Kerrigan was in my arms. She was half naked and on my lap.

Warning bells went off in my head, but I didn't fucking care. I'd convinced myself I didn't want her, and I might've succeeded had I not seen her in her wedding dress and wished she was saying her vows to me.

A low rumble left my chest and I tightened my embrace. I stroked my tongue along hers, tasting the sweet orange juice she must've had before her shower.

I shouldn't be doing this. I shouldn't be touching her. But why did it feel so right?

She wiggled on my lap, needy. Her tongue slid against mine, warm, sweet, and demanding. The rest of my towel's restraint broke. Her wet heat was against me, inciting a primal need to take her.

Yet I'd been thinking about her so long, I had to take my time. I had to savor her. As much as I wanted to revel in a woman who acted like she couldn't get enough of me—me, not the pleasure I could give—I couldn't let her go without returning the same.

I flattened my palms on her smooth thighs. Electricity ran between us, making my erection throb harder than ever.

She was so close. *Just fucking take her.*

I wouldn't. I brushed the fingers of one hand toward her center. So fucking warm and wet. Desire pounded my insides, storming between my brain and my dick. I was filled with nothing but stark need to see her get off. To feel her come on me—like she was mine.

Like she'd always been mine.

I slipped a finger through her soaked seam. She whimpered into my mouth and ground down on my hand.

I had to break the kiss. "Fuck."

She met my gaze, her lips puffy from mine, and rotated her hips on my hand. "Jonah?"

"Christ, you're close."

"Jonah," she whined again and I knew this woman hadn't been treated like she deserved—inside or outside the bedroom.

The old Jonah from twenty minutes ago might disagree, but there was no lying to myself when her pussy was in my hand and her climax was mine. My name on her lips was so damn right.

"You're going to come for me, aren't you?"

She nodded, her eyes glazed, her hips jerking erratically. "Yes."

"This orgasm is mine."

"Yes."

I slid a finger through her folds and pushed inside. Tight, hot heaven greeted me. Her walls rippled around my digit, the convulsions growing stronger as I circled her clit with my thumb.

I had to taste her, but I didn't dare break the spell. This thing between us had been simmering for too long, right or wrong.

Then she reached between us and gripped my shaft.

A groan punched out of me. I was getting jerked off, and it wasn't my hand doing the work.

I drank in her wanton features. The way her eyelids fluttered when I timed my circles with my finger thrusts. The delicate column her throat made when she tipped her head back and moaned.

I hadn't even seen her breasts. I hadn't seen the pretty pink of her pussy. The feel of her was enough.

Yet when she stroked her gaze over my face, taking in the scar, I should've thrown her off. I should've stopped what we were doing, but I could no more stop than I could lift the house off its foundation.

She grounded me. Here in this moment. The past threatened to wedge between us, but with her, I was blissfully guilt-free.

"Yes," she hissed, her hips rocking in time with the rhythm I set. "Yes, yes, yes."

Energy coiled at the base of my spine, tightening around my balls like a knot. Her fevered hand stroked me up and down while I pushed in and out of her.

"Jonah." Her eyes flew wide and her kiss-swollen lips parted.

"This is mine," I growled for no damn reason. My heels were pressed into the floor and I fought off coming. I didn't want to miss a millisecond of her release, but her grip cinched around my length, and I fucking exploded. The way she was moving, her pussy bumped against where she had a hold of me.

"Fuck! Summer!"

She shook in my arms and rode my hand while I jetted cum all over her hold. We were crushed so close together, our releases mixed.

With a final tremble, her legs gave out and she sank onto my lap, pinning my hand between us. I lacked the strength to move. I was a damn noodle, unable and unwilling to remove my touch from her body.

Was she feeling the same? Her grip was solid around me.

She tipped her forehead to mine. "Are you okay?"

Her concern brought an unwelcome dash of reality. "Don't worry about my leg."

She gingerly let my cock go and sat back to meet my gaze.

I'd ruined the moment. I withdrew my hand, slipping from her warm, encompassing body.

"No, I mean are you okay with what we did? You don't like me."

I thumped the back of my head on the dryer. I was dimly aware I'd rested both my hands on her thighs. Even with our circumstances returning, I was unwilling to let her go. "I never said I didn't like you."

Her expression turned dubious. She wiped her hand off on a corner of the towel that had survived our simultaneous climaxes. "You don't have to say it."

"I like you too fucking much, Summer. That's always been the problem."

She snapped her head up. "Always?"

"You were hot in high school, but you were my best friend's sister. Then I was out of high school. Then . . ."

"Then I was Eli's girlfriend."

I didn't bother nodding.

She ran her dry hand down my cheek. Beeping sounded from somewhere in the house. "Dinner's ready." She placed a kiss by my mouth.

I didn't turn my head to meet her. The betrayal was sinking in.

Summer

We were making progress. Simultaneous orgasms notwithstanding, Jonah was at the table with me.

My appetite should be roaring, but I picked at my pork chop. Jonah was eating like a robot. Cut a piece of meat. Swipe through gravy. Insert in mouth. Slice another chunk.

My body was humming from what we'd done earlier, but my mind was a mess. He was at the table, so he didn't hate me, right?

He wasn't looking at me. I was peeking at him from under my lashes.

Finally, I set my fork down. "I think it's safe to say we're both attracted to each other, and it's a problem because of Eli."

He quit chewing. Then he swallowed. But he continued staring at his plate. "He loved you."

"I tried to love him back." I pushed my plate away. Only a quarter of my pork chop had been consumed. "I really did. He was such a good friend, but as a boyfriend . . ." I closed my eyes and took a fortifying breath. "He was needy. Insecure. I thought when I went to college, he'd find his stride, but instead, he only waited for me. I . . . resented him."

Jonah rocked back, his utensils loose in his hands. His gaze was on me, but I couldn't decipher what was in his eyes. Was he thinking *She really said that?* Was he thinking *I should've ended the fondling as soon as it started?* Was he thinking *Callous bitch?*

I was, and I'd had a long time to come to terms with what an awful person I was. "And when he . . . did what he did . . . I was so mad at him. So damn angry, Jonah. How dare he? How dare he make me feel like that? All I wanted was freedom to be young, and he stole that from me." I licked my dry lips. His gaze tracked my tongue, his expression stricken. "He took it from you too."

"You're blaming all this on him?" he asked barely above a whisper.

My nod was shaky. "I know he didn't mean to hurt anyone or to die, but that's how it felt. Like he punished me for not loving him."

"You told him you were into me." The same dangerous edge was in his tone.

"He accused me of liking you because he could tell. I meant it when I told him it was nothing serious. Half the girls in our class were into you. I thought you were attractive and sexy and out of my league. I wasn't going to pursue you. I was in school and I really did want to be single for a while."

His brow was creased and his scar was puckered more than usual. "Then why'd you visit me in the hospital?"

"I talked to your mom, and she was worried about you. I was so exhausted."

He chuffed and his silverware clattered to the floor. "You were exhausted?"

"Emotionally," I said quietly. "What I was going through was nothing like what you and your parents went through, I know. I was going to tell you about the breakup, to ease your conscience, and just . . . have someone to share my story with. Someone who knew him." Hot tears pricked the backs of my eyes. The weight of my breakup was lifted from my chest, but the consequences were adding pressure. My conscience was not clear; it was just exposed.

"Funny how your breakups seem to crash into my life."

I flinched. He was so bitter, and it was my fault. I picked up my plate. "I'll go. You can leave the dishes for me." I pushed my chair back to stand.

"Put the damn plate down," he snapped.

I dropped my dish. The silverware clattered against it.

He scrubbed his hands over his face. "Fuuuuuck, Summer. I can't have this conversation when I can still feel you coming around my fingers." He dropped his arms. The look he gave me was bleak. "I can barely think, now that I know what it's like to come in your hand instead of mine." He dropped his head back, his Adam's apple prominent. "I feel like I betrayed him one last time."

"I'm sorry."

He tipped his head forward and speared me with a curious gaze. "You don't feel the same?"

"Not really. I feel like karma is all the shitty boyfriends I've tolerated." I had meant my comment as a joke, but had I looked for guys who were the opposite of either Dunn brother?

A crease formed between his brows. "He looked up to me."

"He really did." Eli had been insecure, and when he'd admired someone, he could get a little obsessed. His hot, popular, older brother hadn't been exempt.

"Was he at my place to talk to me?"

I'd thought about this so much over the years, but I'd been able to look at the situation from a different vantage point. "I don't know. He might've been lashing out, upset that you got all the attention. He might've needed your support and reassurance. Or maybe he'd planned to warn you off me."

"I didn't need the warning."

Ouch. "I wasn't going to pursue you. I was nineteen and single and in college." I might've lashed out too. "I also assumed that being Eli's ex would've ruined my chances for a good ten years."

A dark brow ticked up. "It's been fifteen years, and it's not much better."

We were talking in circles. I was wildly attracted to Jonah. I wanted him more than any other man I'd ever met. I'd gotten off with him quicker than any guy I'd been with. So shamefully quick. But he continued fixating on his brother, and I didn't have a good reason why he shouldn't. "I'll keep my distance. I can put a sock on the laundry room handle if I'm changing. When the roads are clear, I'll be on my way, and we don't have to cross paths for another fifteen years."

His lips formed a troubled line. I couldn't tell if he was upset that I couldn't leave right now, or that seeing me in another fifteen years would be too soon. I lifted my plate and gathered my fork and knife. "Like I said, I'll do dishes later."

"You cooked," he answered automatically.

I set my things by the kitchen sink. "It's fine. I haven't been sleeping well. It'll give me something to do."

I walked past him, taking in his strong shoulders, his messy, shaggy hair, and the way his head was tipped down like he was contemplating world peace.

"How did you move on?" he asked quietly. "How did you know everything that happened, and then just go live your life?"

I stopped before turning out of the kitchen. Overwhelming guilt crushed my lungs and constricted my throat. "When my parents crashed, I struggled to breathe for what felt like an eternity. The life I'd known was over after that accident. I know I'm selfish, but I wasn't willing to give up another life just because I'd wanted to stop being smothered."

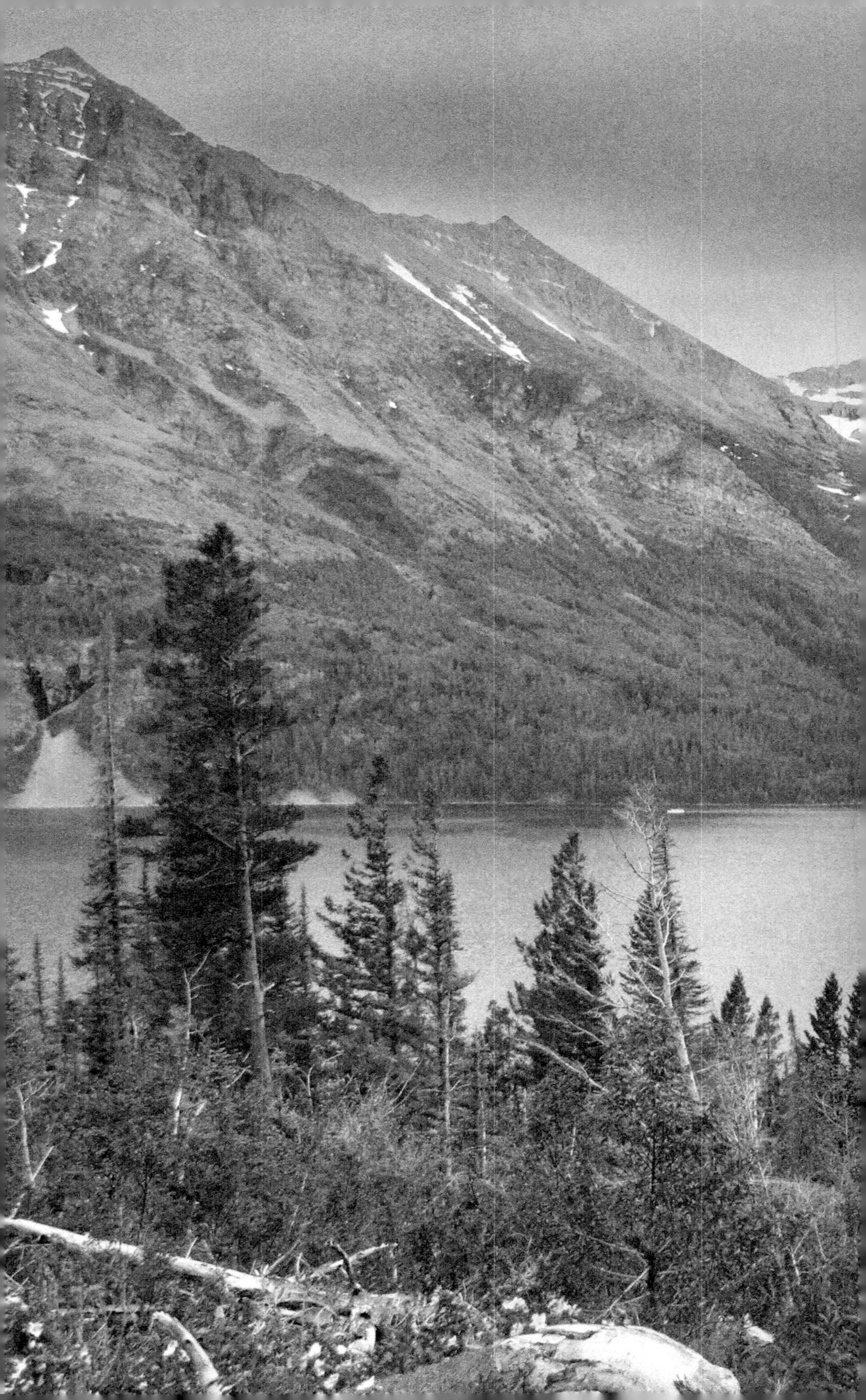

CHAPTER FIFTEEN

Jonah

I turned Summer's words over and over in my head. I was parked on the couch and it was well after midnight. I'd have a shit time returning to my normal hours if I stayed up late and slept in late.

I wasn't willing to give up another life just because I'd wanted to stop being smothered.

The fury I felt toward her was shifting, changing direction like the wind outside. My brother was the next target.

How terrible was I?

Eli was gone. I was his older brother. I should've taught him better. I should've talked to him, asked him how things were going.

I had, but casually, like most brothers did. A random announcement. *Hey, I'm here if you need me.* Eli had never needed me. He'd been private about Summer. He'd claimed that he didn't kiss and tell, and I'd never asked. I hadn't wanted to hear how magical kissing Summer was.

Now that I knew, I was in a special hell.

She'd retreated to the guest room. She'd said she'd give me space, then leave. She'd done it before.

Fifteen years had gone by.

Then four days earlier, she'd walked in on me.

Did I want to risk another fifteen years before she came into my orbit again?

I was a shitty brother.

Yet . . . I couldn't deny Summer's experience. She'd been unhappy with Eli. She shouldn't have had to stay with him to protect his feelings. Getting over a breakup had been his responsibility.

She'd tried to do the right thing by not leading Eli on. Then again, when I'd been in the hospital and she'd known I was blaming myself. But I'd insulted her, assuming she was there to hit on me after I'd been gawked at for months in my hometown. After I'd hobbled through town, getting averted stares from women I'd dated.

Jackie still didn't associate with me in public. I was her worst-kept dirty secret.

I frowned at the TV. What the fuck was playing? I had let the predictive option go wild and choose my next viewing, and now I was in the middle of a rom-com that I hadn't paid one second of attention to. I let it play.

Stretching my legs in front of me, I groaned. My joints had a general ache that was more from the barometric pressure than working outside. Exhaustion swamped me. Pure mental exhaustion. I'd been in a world of not knowing why for so long, taking on the burden of the accident and the outcome, and I'd been fucking terrified of being angry with Eli.

Now that I was? It wasn't bad. Just a general yawning chasm that would never be filled because he was gone. I stood on the edge and hollered *What were you thinking?* and I didn't get an answer. I never would and that was okay. Because I'd been taken out of the equation.

If Summer's infatuation had been just that, maybe I would've raged for longer, but fuck, I was tired. She had squirmed on my lap and moaned my name. I wasn't fucking twenty-four. I would be forty next year. And she still wanted me.

What would I do about it?

My dick stirred, wanting more of the laundry room action.

"Down, boy," I murmured. I couldn't fall on her after I'd accused her of being coldhearted at the table.

She might not want me after how I'd acted.

But I could apologize. I could tell her I understood. I could give her that. The comment she'd made about karma might've been flippant, but there was some validity there. Teenaged Summer would've never put up with someone like Boyd.

I heaved myself upright. I turned the TV off and dumped the remote on the couch. The only light was from the hallway night-light. I left my cane by the base of the stairs and stepped on the side of the first step so it didn't creak. I wasn't sneaking up on her, but I also didn't want my halting footsteps to herald my arrival, for her to open the door and wait and wait while I ascended.

Going up was better than going down, but I braced myself on the railing and wall. When I was at the top, I faced the dark brown wood of the door.

Was this a mistake?

It didn't matter. She'd tried to be open with me once, and I'd snapped my fangs at her like a wounded animal.

I was a man. She'd made me feel like one earlier tonight.

I knocked on the door and waited. The fist that had knocked was still clenched at my side.

A lamp clicked seconds before the door opened.

Christ, she was an angel in an old Dunn Beef T-shirt she must've found in the guest room dresser. She blinked, her pretty lips turned down and her hair a jumbled mess around her shoulders. She let me see her disheveled, and I knew without asking not many people saw Summer unkempt.

"Jonah? What's wrong?" Her gaze swept behind me, taking in the dark landing.

"Do you know why I was at the wedding?"

Her frown deepened. She wasn't blinking, like I'd woken her up. She'd been wide awake. Was she as miserable as me? "Your mom made you go?"

"No. I had to make sure you were happy. I told myself it was for Eli, and maybe it was, but your past with him wasn't the only reason. I had to see you. I had to see if you were really going to be someone else's woman forever."

"Why?" One word that was full of so much confusion.

"I don't know. When I go to town, I look for you. You know that? I fucking peer around every corner like a goddamn stalker." Why was I telling her this? She'd just told me how stifling Eli had been.

"You do?" She sank against the doorframe, a dreamy smile on her face. "Really?"

"Always. There was never a right time for us, and it was like I had to show myself that . . . you weren't meant for me once and for all."

Her smile dimmed. "And then the wedding got canceled."

"Yeah, it did." I crowded closer to her. This wasn't what I'd come for. I should back off.

"So what does that mean?" She didn't move away. "I guess it's not once and for all yet?" She feathered her fingers down a fold in my sweatshirt.

"No. It's not." I wrapped a hand around her neck and an arm around her waist and drew her flush with me. I crushed her mouth with mine.

When her arms snaked around my neck, I was done. I wanted her and she wanted me.

Our past was tangled. Our present was complicated. Our future was unknown, but for tonight, I'd get the only woman I'd ever wanted.

Summer

I was surrounded by him. Consumed by him. He slid his tongue along mine in a sensual dance that could make me climax while fully clothed.

Well, I didn't have a bra or underwear on.

I met his tongue stroke for stroke. His minty toothpaste flavor mingled with mine. His arms banded me to him, and his hard body was pliant compared to the rigid length pressed between us.

When he slid both hands to cup my ass cheeks and

bent, I wasn't ready. He lifted me. I yelped and automatically wrapped my legs around his waist.

"Jonah, don't you dare hurt yourself before you're inside me."

"This is the furthest from pain I feel." He took sure strides across the room. The lamp's soft glow was hopefully enough light to make the trek safely. I didn't want to see him hurt regardless, and I didn't want to be the reason for it, but I wanted to keep my legs wrapped around him.

"Are you wearing nothing but this shirt, sunshine?"

"Yes. I was going to take this shirt with me when I left." I had to have something of his to torture myself with.

He growled and nibbled my neck as he crossed the room. His long scruff scraped and tickled my skin, sending delicious shivers down my body.

He set me on the bed and captured my mouth again. With his hands planted next to me, I scooted back to make room for him to crawl on the bed, to get on top of me.

But he didn't follow. Instead, he kissed his way down my neck while lifting my shirt. Then he backed off enough to draw the top over my head.

An exhale gusted out of him as he dropped the shirt and gawked at my body.

"Fuck me, sunshine. You've been covered in sweats the whole time when I could've been seeing your perfect tits?" He leaned forward, pressing a strong hand into the comforter, the veins on his forearm prominent.

Tilting his head, he eyed a small white scar at the side of a breast. He traced over the white line with a fingertip. Then another scar on my abdomen. And a third.

"What's this from?" he murmured.

"They tried to find the bleeding after the accident." My breathing was shallow and my nipples were pebbled so tight I could feel every exhale waft over them. Was this what he'd felt like when I'd massaged him? My fingers twitched to touch him. "You're, um, entirely overdressed."

"As long as you're naked, I don't care what I'm wearing." He lifted his gaze to mine while trailing his fingers down my torso, stroking over my belly button and then lower.

I widened my legs like it was a reflex.

His expression turned contemplative, reverent, as he gazed at the junction between my thighs. He bent and hooked my knees over his shoulders.

I gasped and scooted farther up to make room for him.

"Stay right where you're at. I'm about to find out what sunshine tastes like."

"Oh, god, Jonah. Don't tell me you have a mouth as wicked as your fingers."

His heated look was so full of promise my legs trembled. "I've been dreaming about this for a long fucking time." He dropped a kiss at the base of my abdomen. "You're right here and spread for me. I must be fucking dreaming."

"Jonah," I whimpered.

He dipped his head again and flicked his tongue out, taking a little sample while holding my gaze. A satisfied rumble left him just as he buried his face in my pussy. He found my clit and played, licking and sucking and taking what I offered.

I arched my back off the mattress, but my bottom didn't move. I was in his rock-hard hold, my legs locked in his grip. His hair brushed the sides of my thighs as I writhed beneath him.

"Jonah, oh my god. It feels so good." Better than ever. There was no hesitation. No poking and muttering. No rushing me to my end so he could seek his pleasure.

Jonah devoured me, but he also savored me. He licked through my slit and prodded inside, and when I squirmed, he did it again. I hated that he'd abandoned my clit but the sensation of him filling me was just as addicting. Then he was back to my nub, circling and teasing. I could tell he was learning—what I liked best, what made my left leg shake, what made me gasp and moan. Then he settled in and used all his newfound knowledge to drive me to the brink and back.

"You're going to kill me, mountain man."

The rumble reverberated between my legs and he attacked my clit until I soared to my peak. And then he backed off.

I growled and threaded my fingers through his hair. "You're playing."

He stopped. "I want this to last forever because I won't. Not when it comes to you."

He made me feel so damn special. The pull that had been between us since we'd been in high school was stronger than ever. For years, each of us had ignored the attraction, but this tie was so much more.

I rolled my hips against his face, still tugging at his head. I needed to come. It didn't matter that hours ago I'd climaxed against him. The pressure built inside me until I swore I hadn't had a real orgasm in my entire life.

"Jonah," I whined.

"Hang on, sunshine. I need this to be good."

The energy swelled bigger, larger. I hung on a precipice. But I finally gave in. I rocked with the rhythm of his tongue, panting, but no longer demanding. I cherished the moment between us. If my heart stopped from the powerful explosion building within me, so be it.

As if he sensed my total capitulation, he covered my clit with his mouth and sucked, flicking the damn thing with his tongue.

When I detonated, stars blasted behind my eyes. I arched my back so completely off the bed, I thought I was levitating, but Jonah grounded me.

"Jonah!" His name bounced off the walls. The storm outside was cold, but the maelstrom inside was blistering hot and seared away future worries. It was just me and Jonah and that talented mouth of his.

I shook, unconcerned about how I looked or sounded. My cries drowned out the wind. When I sagged into the mattress, depleted, he released me, easing my legs down and kissing his way up my belly.

I barely had the energy to lift my head. "I wasn't sure I'd survive."

"I could do that all goddamn night."

"I definitely wouldn't make it." But at the same time, I'd like to find out. A large part of me knew that he'd make sure I was okay. He'd give me death by ecstasy but he'd also make sure not one part of me was harmed or hurting, just like he'd done since he'd rescued me from my wedding.

My legs bracketed his big body. He was half over me,

and he sucked one of my hard nipples into his mouth. I groaned as warmth started infusing my core.

I couldn't possibly be ready to go again.

"Jonah."

He lifted his head, my nipple popping out of his mouth. His gaze was dark and hot and intent, but also extremely satisfied. The man didn't say much, but when someone knew what to look for, he said a lot with his expressions.

"I need you inside me."

Another low growl. Another light kiss, this time between my breasts. "Are you on anything?"

"I had my IUD removed last week."

He pushed away. "Wait here."

He went to the bathroom, his halting gait becoming so achingly familiar I didn't realize how much I missed it when he closed himself up in his shop. He didn't bother with the light, but he disappeared behind the door, not closing it.

I tipped my legs together and propped myself on my elbows. What was he doing?

When he appeared again, his erection fought against his sweats, and he had a string of little packets in his hand.

"You keep your condoms up here?" I'd raided the little closet in that bathroom for toothpaste, toothbrushes, and razors. I would've noticed condoms.

He tossed them on the comforter when he reached the edge of the bed. "I want to make damn sure the trouble is worth forgoing my hand."

He made himself trek up and down the stairs for condoms? A little discomfort before he could find pleasure with someone else. Didn't he think he deserved companionship?

I'd have to show him differently. I rolled up and slid to the edge of the mattress. This comforter had a date with the washing machine—and maybe I could tempt Jonah into joining me for laundry time again. "I want to undress you."

He scoffed and tugged the collar of his sweater.

"Don't you dare." I pushed his hands away as I rose. When I slipped my hands under the garment, I made sure to splay my fingers across his hard abdomen. His muscles tensed under my touch.

I pushed the sweater over his head and looked my fill. "Wow." I trailed my fingers over his defined pecs. A few small scars were visible under the dark hair on his chest that trailed down to disappear under his sweats. "You're so hard."

"Jesus, Summer. If you don't quit looking at me like that, I'm not going to make it through you taking off my pants."

"But you have, like, a really nice body." The best I'd seen. Chiseled from marble. Yet his skin was soft and warm. "What do you do in that shop all day?"

"Make furniture." He stood still for me as I continued to dance my fingers across his body. He peered at me. "You really like what you see?"

I laughed. "Yes. Why wouldn't I?"

A scowl indented his brow. "My left arm is smaller than my right."

I squinted. "Maybe a little."

"You haven't gotten to my legs."

"I've already seen them." I didn't take my time with his pants. He had insecurities, and I wanted to obliterate them like he had with me minutes ago. I shoved them down and his thick cock bobbed in front of my face.

I bent, ignoring how exposed I was, and helped him step out. Then I stood back, hands on my hips. I was naked, but it was more important to me to make him feel as comfortable with himself as possible.

He was rigid under my perusal. I took my time, letting my interest infuse my face. The warmth in my belly flared hotter, kindling a small inferno. Just from seeing him. He was tall and strong. Yes, he had scars. His left thigh had puckered and jagged scars, worse than the ones on his face. A not-so-small chunk of flesh had been excised at some point in his recovery from above his knee and his calf wasn't the same shape or size as his other one.

His left hip was also smaller, like it couldn't build the muscle his other hip could. The differences between his right and left sides weren't as noticeable in his torso, but the flares of scarring around his shoulder looked more like nasty stretch marks. Years had gone by since the accident, but the trauma his body had gone through told the tale.

Still, if he thought he was repulsive in any way, he needed to borrow my hormones and have a look for himself. He could feel the strength of the throb between my legs. "You're so hot."

His eyes narrowed, his expression dubious.

I dragged a finger from his collarbone down his sternum, over his stomach, and right to the tip of his very hard cock. "I like everything I see. I always have."

I rubbed my finger across the wet slit of his erection, spreading his precum around. He jerked under my touch.

"You're going to make me blush," he finally said.

I laughed and wrapped my hand around his length. I gave him a couple of good tugs.

Then I dropped to my knees.

"Jesus. Summer." He stuffed a hand through his hair, his biceps bulging. "What are you doing—"

I took him in my mouth, holding on to his stunned gaze. His reaction told me enough. He didn't get blow jobs. I didn't know if it was because he was self-conscious or if the women he was with weren't interested, but that changed now.

I swirled my tongue up and down his length, giving an appreciative hum to punctuate that I liked doing this.

"Fuck," he gritted out. The tendons in his neck were straining and he was tilted back, like he was trying to keep his balance.

Oh, crap— Was he off-balance?

I gripped his thighs, but his stance was solid. He wasn't shaking or quivering. He was leaning back like he was afraid to miss the show. Like I was blowing someone else and he was a Peeping Tom.

His disbelief was a heady experience. Blow jobs had been expected by a couple of my exes, and they'd never been my favorite part of sex. But that was changing. I had Jonah's rapt attention, but the thing was—I did anyway. I knew that he kept tabs on everything I was doing. He'd left me clothing when I was asleep on the couch. He'd chased me inside when he'd thought it was too stormy out. He'd come to my wedding to torture himself when there'd never been anything but distant attraction between us.

I cupped his balls as I worked him, rolling them over my palm. A heavy groan left him. I would've smiled but I was enjoying the pure power of destroying him with nothing but my mouth. His muscles vibrated under my touch and he alternated between stroking his hands down my hair, caressing my cheek, and shoving them in his hair.

"Fuck, Summer. Seeing you like that does me in."

I caught his gaze again. His jaw was granite, but I liked the reason this time. His hips would jerk, just a little, like it was taking all his effort not to buck into my mouth and choke me.

He cupped my chin and pulled out of my mouth, my lips releasing with a wet, sloppy sound. His pupils dilated, his gaze focused on my mouth. "Get up and bend over."

I rose, and by the time I was fully upright, he had a condom ripped open and was rolling it on. I was about to turn when he caught me and pressed his mouth to mine. His hair spilled forward, tickling my face. I twined my fingers through the strands.

He untangled my hand and kissed each of my wrists. The smallest things he did made me feel more precious than any time in the past.

When he spun me, he didn't just bend me over. He feathered his hands down my sides, like he was memorizing my curves. Then he moved my hair to the side and kissed every tiny scar I had.

I inhaled, each little peck igniting nerve endings I hadn't known existed. I knew each little scar. I was proud of them, but they were practically invisible where they were on my body. But I knew they were there. I still had nightmares about the night I'd gotten them. I used to trace them when I was bored in class or when I was studying.

Jonah didn't stop until he'd kissed every last one. Then he put gentle pressure on my back and bent me over. The soft glow of the lamp wouldn't hide how exposed I was in this position, my ass in the air and facing him. He'd see everything, but then . . . he already did.

Jonah

I'd never seen such a pretty sight. Summer was fucking soaked, and it was from me. She'd stared at me, and instead of making some placating comment or brushing off the injuries, she'd dropped to her goddamn knees and sucked me into her mouth.

I'd never be able to jerk off again. Not when I knew the sheer pleasure of her tongue. My hand would never compare.

Now I was about to enter her. All my past experiences had been obliterated already. Once I was in her? I'd be done.

The only thing that could stop me was her. But her round ass was in the air and with her forearms braced on the bed, she was looking at me over her shoulder, her hair swept to the side like a custom-made porn poster. My very fantasy come to life.

I kneaded her ass cheeks. She had a faint tan line, teasing me with how skimpy her swim bottoms must be. Now all I could envision was her tanning on her back deck in the summer. I had no idea what her place looked like but my brain happily filled in the blanks.

"Jonah, I really want you to fuck me."

"Patience, sunshine. I almost came like a rocket in your mouth. I need a minute so I can make this good for you."

"You've already made it the best."

Fuck, this woman. I slid my hands up her back. "I don't deserve you." In so many ways.

She wiggled her ass.

My cock was reaching the point of painful. I positioned myself at her hot pussy. She swayed back just as I pushed in.

"Fuuuck." Her heat swallowed me, nearly robbing me of strength. "So goddamn good."

"God, Jonah."

I shoved the rest of the way in. Wet, hot heat. Her walls rippled and flexed around me. I wouldn't have to thrust to come. A full-body tremor went through me.

No. I would make this last. She would come for a third time, and it wouldn't be our last. I had more condoms and every last one had her name on it.

I rocked back and thrust in.

"Yes," she hissed. A flood of heat rose between us.

I braced myself on her hips and pumped in and out. Just like when I'd been licking her clit, I changed positions, testing, studying. I would be an expert on all things Summer when we were done. I'd know how much pressure drove her crazy. I'd know her preferred angles, and I'd know where she was the most sensitive.

As she grew wetter and I grew increasingly erratic, I stuffed my good knee into the side of the mattress and bent over her. I'd never do this position with someone else. If a move required bending my knees, I wouldn't do it. But I hadn't been able to hide from Summer under my roof.

So fuck it. I bent over her back and wedged an arm between her torso and the bedding.

"I think I'm going to come again," she panted.

"It won't be the last time tonight." I found her soaked clit and made the little circles that caused her legs to quiver.

She blinked at me, her face flushed and arousal scrawled over her features. "It won't?" she echoed.

"I promise." I never made promises. I had work orders and deadlines. I told my parents *maybe* and *we'll see*. But I was getting Summer off a fourth time before dawn. Maybe even a fifth. She'd orgasm until it wasn't humanly possible to do so again.

I licked and kissed across her shoulders and she bucked under me. I rubbed her clit, struggling to slow my own catapulting climax.

"I'm going to— *Oh, god.*" Her voice grew higher in pitch.

I fucking loved the sound of her cries echoing off my walls—all because of me. Whether I was inside her, over her, fingering her, she was coming because of me and I needed to hear it.

When her walls quaked around me, fisting my cock in the demanding way I was coming to associate with her, I let go. I kicked my head back and roared her name, so damn loud, like it'd been pent up inside me for years. Lightning coursed through my veins and a cramp in my left hamstring threatened to take me down.

I would not fall.

Aftershocks wracked both of us and her body milked mine. I collapsed on top of her, keeping one arm wrapped around her and holding myself off enough I didn't crush her.

I pressed a kiss to her shoulder and she turned her head to crack an eye open. "Multiple orgasms? You know how to spoil a girl."

I glanced at the three condoms left from the strip I'd pulled out of the box. "You think we're done?"

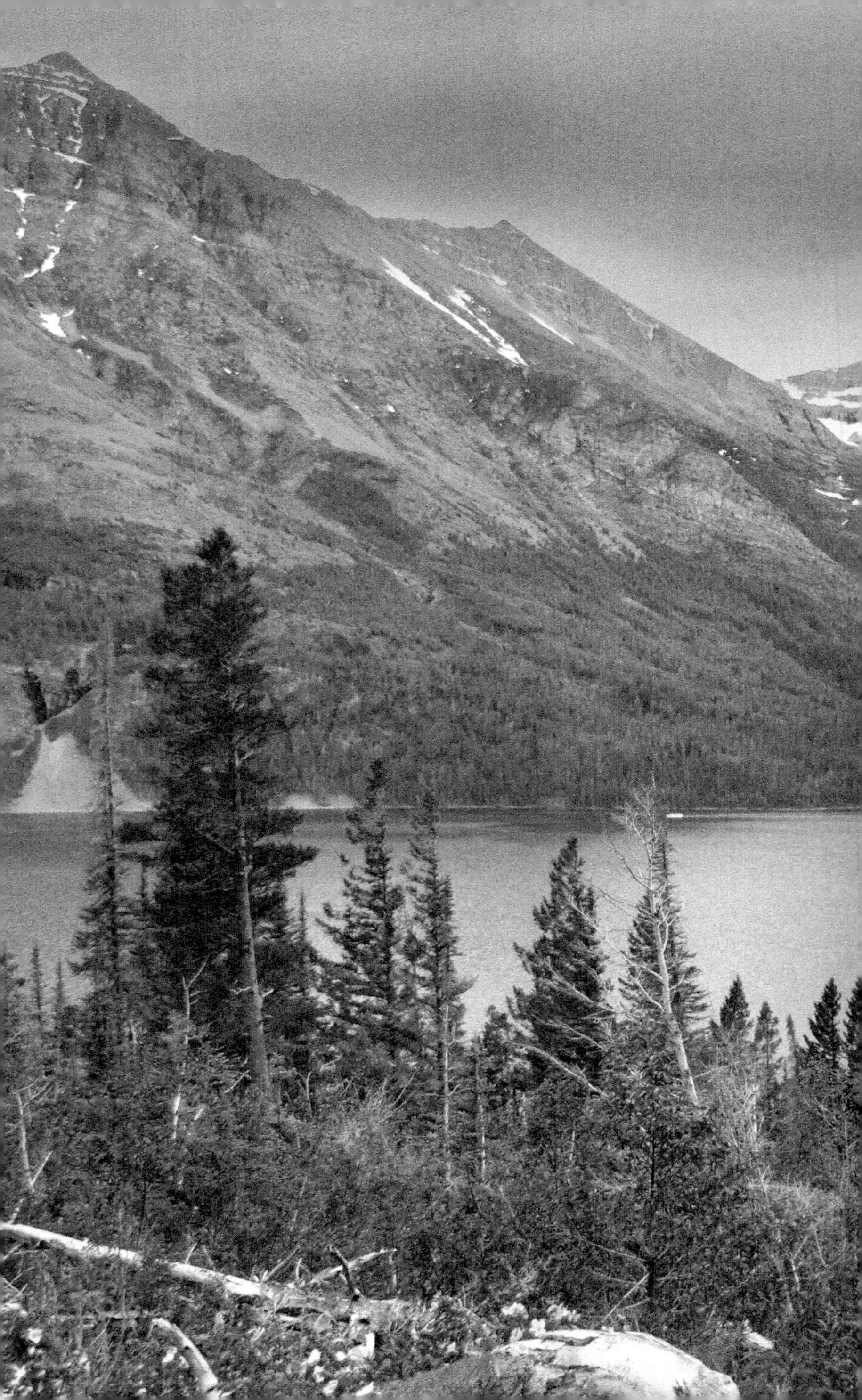

CHAPTER SIXTEEN

Summer

The wall of heat was behind me again. I'd slept better than I had in months. I curled into the warmth. A strong arm wrapped around me and hugged me closer.

"What time is it?" I murmured without opening my eyes.

"Late," he said gruffly.

"Mm." We'd had a lot of sex. The guy was powered by the moon.

I slitted my eyes open. Light poured around the blinds. Judging from the erection pressed against my back, Jonah was also powered by the sun. I wiggled against his length.

He groaned and his arm banded tighter. "You're trouble."

"I am." I was debating rolling over when my stomach growled for five seconds straight.

A laugh shuddered out of him. "Sounds like I need to feed you."

I giggled and rolled toward the edge of the bed. "I guess we need fuel."

Just as I was sitting up, not bothering to cover myself —we were both naked—my phone buzzed. I reached for it. Wynter was calling.

My stomach flipped. Was it baby time? I wouldn't get to the hospital, but I wanted to be one of the first available aunts when Wynter and Myles were ready to show off the baby.

"I've gotta take this quick," I told Jonah before I answered.

I didn't get my hello out before Wynter said, "No. No baby yet."

"Is Myles shoveling out the highway?" I pulled the sheet to my chest and wiggled to the head of the bed. Jonah draped a heavy arm over my thighs and buried his face in the side of my leg. The scratch of his scruff was pleasing.

"Almost. It's like he's never been through a Montana winter."

"Didn't Denver get snowstorms?"

"I didn't have a baby on the way," Myles grumbled from the background.

"You don't have to worry until I tell you to get the chains," she retorted.

"Don't mess with me like that, Frosty," he said.

Wynter sighed. "He's so uptight," she muttered into the phone. "I'm supposed to be the nervous one. Anyway, I've been mad nesting, and I'm going to redo the nursery for the third time if I don't distract myself. How's it going there?"

I glanced at Jonah. He was likely hearing everything. "We still have power."

"Mm-hmm. And?"

She was fishing. A part of me wanted to tell her, to be giddy that I'd broken through Jonah's armor, but a larger part said I needed to take things slowly. Jonah had a hard time with his feelings for me, and other than lust, I didn't know what else was going on inside him. He was cuddled against me, but he also had morning wood. His motivations were cloudy.

His tension was barely noticeable, but I caught it. I threaded my fingers through his hair. *Don't shut me out again.*

"We're going to watch some shows and I might even get him to play Connect 4."

"So he's at least talking to you?"

"Yes."

"Good." I could picture her rubbing her baby belly, a disgruntled look on her face. I wasn't giving her more info, but I also heard the worry in her voice. "You deserve to be treated right. If it can't be toe-curling sex, then Connect 4 is a good runner-up."

"I don't know what kind of Connect 4 you're playing."

"The kind that usually ends in toe-curling sex."

I laughed. "I won't ask about Monopoly."

"Don't." She let out a frustrated sound. "Myles is the most ruthless board game player, and he's the worst when it comes to Monopoly. He buys everything up and takes all my money. I threw the game away."

"You did not, because you think it's hot."

"It really is. I made him wear a suit last time we

played. If this storm doesn't let up soon, I'm going to get pregnant again before I have this baby."

My laughter was genuine, but the thread of envy constricting my lungs and heart was too. Wynter was living my dream. A doting husband who was a really good guy. A baby on the way. Unafraid to talk about what things were like between them. Hot and passionate, but also moody and worried.

Whenever I witnessed her and Myles together, I realized how watered down my relationships had been. How superficial. When Boyd had proposed and wanted to fast-track the wedding, I'd gone along with it, thinking we'd get there, like all the red flags would morph into a red carpet that would make my love life real and easy.

"Oh." There was rustling on the other end. "Mama's calling. If I don't answer, she's going to make Lane and Cruz plow a path to town."

"She'll call Myles first." I hoped. Little else got Mama more excited than grandkids.

"After she mobilizes his brothers. I'll talk to you later."

When we hung up, I continued stroking Jonah's hair. He hadn't moved and his breathing was even, but he wasn't asleep.

"What should I tell them?"

He rolled to his side, putting some distance between us and crossing his bare arms over his chest. "What do you mean?"

"I mean, Wynter said she got through Myles's shell by giving him a blow job. Do I tell her that a hand job works just as well?"

He blinked, then half snorted, half coughed. "I'd

prefer you didn't." He cleared his throat. "You don't have to say anything."

He was a private man. Was that his motivation? Or had he spent the time I was on the phone second-guessing what we'd done? "What is this?" I asked softly. "I don't want to get my hopes up if you're wondering how quickly you can get me out of your house."

Sleepiness was gone from his eyes and a scowl was in its place. "You want to tell your family we're messing around?"

Hurt echoed through my chest. "Is that all we're doing? Messing around?"

His brow furrowed deeper. "Summer, you stormed into my life more powerfully than the blizzard outside and I'm having a hard time keeping up. I'm still trying to figure out how I feel about you and Eli in regard to everything I did to you last night."

Tingles spread through my body. Jonah Dunn was a virile man. He was all tightly bound sexual energy, and when someone loosened the ties, he was captivating—and he'd held me captive orgasm after orgasm. I hadn't been this stiff since my high school sports days.

"I liked what you did to me last night."

"And this morning." When my mouth tipped up, he put a hand on my thigh. "I'd like to keep this to ourselves before others get involved. They're going to talk, and while it might not reach me, it'll find you."

"I don't care."

His steady, dark gaze held mine.

"Jonah, I don't care."

"You will though."

"How can you be so sure?"

"You took fifteen years to tell me you'd broken up with Eli."

Guilt punched me hard. I struggled to swallow around my thick throat. "I care what you think."

He rolled to a sitting position. "What if people in town are worse about the thought of us than I was?"

"That'd be pretty hard. You were a dick." When his eyes narrowed like he wasn't sure if I was joking or not, I giggled and held my hands up. "Kidding. Your reaction was understandable given the circumstances in all the situations involving us. But if you're more comfortable keeping our winter-storm fuckfest to ourselves, that's okay too."

He was quiet for several moments. "Fuckfest? It's been one night."

I let my gaze stray to the window. "Sounds like the weather is still awful."

The corner of his mouth tipped up. "There's still half a box of condoms left."

"How big of a box did you get?"

"You're telling me you didn't snoop once in that cabinet?"

"I peeked in and saw extra razors and shaving cream, not an industrial-sized box of protection." I'd seen a box and figured it was man-beard supplies or something. I had clearly not looked at it closely enough. "Are you telling me we're not going to have to ration how often we do it until the weather clears?"

"I'm saying you'd better grab a bite to eat so you have the stamina to keep up."

I scoffed. "I've got stamina." I hoped. I was in uncharted territory.

He flashed me a grin and we both rolled out of our

sides of the bed. I was to the dresser and pulling on the sweater I'd arrived in when I spotted him just standing at the edge of the bed.

Was he realizing this wasn't what he wanted? No. He was rolling his left shoulder and favoring his left side.

He caught me watching and pink dusted the crests of his cheeks. "It takes a minute for my knee to limber up. And I, uh, like to test my foot before I take a full step."

"Is it painful?"

He shrugged. "Depends what I did the day before."

Like carrying a woman to bed? I stooped to pick up his clothing, then tossed them on the bed.

His eyes darkened. "I could've gotten those. I'm not helpless."

Frustrated, I rolled my eyes. I should've anticipated his insecurity, and my irritation that he was feeling vulnerable in the first place took over. "Or, hear me out, you could let me do something for you since you've been doing everything for me."

His brows drew together. "You've been cooking and doing laundry."

"Which I would've done anyway. You might need a hand once in a while, Jonah. And it might be because of your injuries." I threw my hands up. "I'm still going to want to fuck you."

A gust of air escaped his lips. He wasn't fully facing me, but his dick had heard what I said loud and clear. "Point taken. I'm going to use the bathroom. You can head down."

He grabbed his shirt and flicked it right side out, avoiding looking at me. He wanted me to leave him alone. I'd done that once and it hadn't helped either of us. "Just for that, I'm going to watch you climb every step. I'm going to catalog every wince. I might even time you." His teeth ground together so hard I was afraid his teeth would crack. "And you'd better have a condom because I'm going to jump you as soon as your feet hit the floor."

His erection grew bigger. "Goddammit, woman. You're going to be unbearable, aren't you?"

"Unbearably horny. You're to blame with that tongue of yours. But I get first dibs on the bathroom. If you think you're going to sneak downstairs without me, just know—I can keep my horniness to myself. I've lived without spectacular sex since puberty right up until last night."

A laugh sputtered out of him. His smile was tight, but that could be more from the way his cock was demanding his blood supply.

A girl could get used to that reaction from a guy she was into. My hair was a mess, I hadn't brushed my teeth yet, and I needed a shower after our sexcapades, but he was hard from the idea of having me again.

He shook his head, then lifted his chin to the bathroom door. "Go on, then. I don't have all day."

"You do too." I scurried into the bathroom and closed the door behind me. I planned to rush through cleaning up, but I paused when I caught myself in the mirror.

My hair was a rat's nest. Red scruff marks etched my chest. Jonah liked my breasts. My eyes were twinkling and my grin was wider than I'd ever seen it.

I was happy. In this little cabin in the middle of a storm, I was more content than ever.

When the last flake fell, I wasn't sure what would happen. Jonah wanted to keep us a secret for a little while. My smile dimmed. No. I grabbed my toothbrush. I wasn't going to let worries of the future ruin a perfectly nice sexfest.

Jonah

She'd done exactly what she'd said she would. She'd fucking timed me going down the stairs. I'd gripped the railing with an iron fist, but despite all the acrobatics from the night before, my hip and knee were moving fine. Since I hadn't spent more than that first time standing, my foot wasn't even complaining. Chalk it up to lingering adrenaline, I didn't care. I hadn't tumbled down the stairs and taken her out like she was a bowling pin, and that was good enough for me.

Once my feet had hit the bottom, she'd pushed me back until I was sitting on the third step up and dragged my sweats down. Best reverse cowgirl ever.

Orgasms before breakfast were nice, but I could get addicted to a flushed Summer across the table from me, shoving the last piece of bacon in her mouth. She'd shamelessly stolen it and taken her time chewing. I'd almost spread her out over the table.

Now, we were playing Connect 4 just like she'd told Wynter. A box of checkers was sitting on the edge of the table.

I slid my winning tile into place. "Connect four."

Her pretty pink lips parted. "No way!" She peered closer at our game. "I didn't even notice you had three lined up."

I dumped the game pieces into the box. "I hated playing board games with Mom and Dad."

"You did a lot of that?" she asked, taking out the checkers.

"I used to hate staying inside."

"Do you now?"

Did I? I used to work through all the storms, as long as I could get through the drifts in my yard to the shop. I preferred being home rather than wandering through town. "No. Being stuck in the house for days was never fun. Having Mom and Dad pretend we were having fun when they were so worried about me or missing Eli sucked. But this . . . is nice."

A faint smile played over her lips. "It is." She pushed the black checker pieces toward me. "I'll have you know, I grew up playing with my ruthless brothers. They didn't believe in letting their sisters win."

"I'll have you know, I suck at Monopoly, so don't get your hopes up that I'm going to put on a suit and dominate you."

"Fuck that game." She pointed a finger at me. "I knew you were listening."

"Not intentionally." I'd been incapacitated, wondering if she'd talk about what we'd done. How would I have felt if she had? I'd been panicking, but also . . . really fucking proud. Summer Kerrigan was in my bed. Summer Kerrigan, the girl I'd denied myself for so long because at every point in our lives, it'd been wrong.

"Why do you have all these games, then?" She set her red game pieces on the board.

I did the same, glad to have something for my hands to do. "They're still here from when I built the place."

"For when you're snowed in?"

I lifted a shoulder. "Just to have." I couldn't tell her this cabin was supposed to have been a family home on the lower fringes of the mountains, not a lonely palace.

She made a noncommittal noise and moved a game piece.

Fifteen minutes later, I was taking out the last red tile on the board.

"Winner picks up." She pushed back. "You're such a liar. You'd probably throttle me in a game of Monopoly too."

I leered. "I have a game you can win."

Her scandalized gasp made me chuckle. "Just for that—I'm going to find the girliest chick flick possible. One that makes me cry—and you're going to watch it with me."

She grinned and went into the living room. I picked up the games and left them stacked on the table. I was looking forward to a movie, and I didn't care if it was the scariest horror film or the sappiest love story. Hanging out with Summer was becoming one of my favorite activities.

I peered out the window. A drift had built up in front of the shop door. I would have to shovel my way in, but once I reached the skid steer, the rest of the snow removal would be easy enough. I wasn't out shoveling to avoid Summer anymore.

My phone vibrated. Mom was calling.

"Hey," I answered. "You guys doing okay?" I should've checked on them earlier. Usually, they were the ones tracking me down, but I could call first. They were aging, and Dad was paring down his ranch duties, taking on fewer heads of cattle for a semiretirement.

"We're good," Mom crooned and my tension eased. I really should've checked in with them. "I've been checking the power outage notices, but they're pretty minimal, thankfully. You're doing well, then? Not getting too lonely all holed up?"

I lifted my gaze to Summer. She'd clicked the TV on and turned to see who I was talking to. Now she was scrolling through listings. "No, not lonely."

"Oh?" Interest painted Mom's voice. Who would she think I was with?

"I'm watching movies. Taking a break from building."

"Oh." Disappointment this time. "Right. I'm glad you're not tromping back and forth in this weather."

"I'm careful."

"I know, but anyone can get hurt being careful and with it just being you out there, well. I worry."

"I know you do." If there was a "shitty son" award, I was in the running. I'd been all about myself and how Summer made me feel. I hadn't thought of my isolated parents alone in a blizzard. Sure, they'd been dealing with this weather their entire life, but they were also worrying about me and I hadn't had the courtesy to be concerned about them. "I have my phone on me all the time, but I'm staying in for a while. Tell Dad to keep his ass planted on the couch."

She chuckled. "I can try, but you get your stubbornness from somewhere." There was a hitch in her breath. "You're doing good, though? You have enough food, water, and entertainment?"

"I'm not going to get scurvy anytime soon."

She laughed again, and it was good to hear the sound from her. "Aye, matey. Goodness, wait until I tell your father. Hey—did I tell you that your aunt Shawna showed one of your tables to her boss and he wants to buy a couple?"

Shawna lived in Idaho. "Give him my info."

"Oh, he snatched it up." Mom's tone was impressed awe. "He looked up your site right away and scribbled notes."

"Even better." Mom's sister Shawna got the friends and family discount—free—but if her boss was on my site, he'd seen examples of my prices.

"You sure you're doing okay? I know you're always making and shipping tables and stools and whatnot, but are you okay . . . financially?"

I could've laughed, but I hadn't realized until this moment I didn't discuss finances with my parents. I made good money. The tools and materials could be expensive, but after so many years, I had all the big equipment bought and paid for and I maintained it well. My time and expertise cost the most. I charged for packaging and delivery and my fees gave me a comfortable living. I had built the shop within three years of starting custom furniture. "I make over six figures a year, Mom. I'm fine."

"Oh. *Oh.* Well. Your expenses are probably—"

"I still make over six figures. I'm not a cheap hire."

"Well. Isn't that just . . . Mind if I tell your dad?"

I roamed the living room. I wasn't used to Mom being stunned in a good way. She could be taken aback by my curtness, and she fretted over my isolation, but proud? When was the last time she'd been proud?

When I'd walked out of the hospital, infection-free and full of resentment? No, she'd been relieved and thankful. When I'd built the shop? She'd thought I might be a prepper and start stockpiling more supplies so I'd never have to go to town. I hadn't given her any other indication, steeped in my bitterness and disappointed that she lacked faith in me. Had she been proud at any time in my adult life? I hadn't gone to college like a lot of kids. I'd planned to ranch like Dad, but it'd been an obligation and not a calling. Then I'd been one fall off a horse away from never walking again and I'd needed too many pain meds after bumping through the pastures on a four-wheeler.

I'd started selling furniture over a year after that last hospital stay. For over thirteen years, I'd been building my own business and becoming an in-demand custom table maker. Had I never shared my success with my parents?

"Go ahead and tell Dad. I'll update the gallery on my website so you guys can see more of my work. I've got a good thing going and I enjoy what I do."

"You never talk about it."

I didn't. Even the drivers that delivered old barrels or the delivery guys that brought supplies and shipped my furniture knew I wasn't a talker. I kept to myself, not wanting to prove shit to anybody. And I'd just stayed that way. "There were a lot of opinions about what I could and couldn't do after the accident."

I tried hard not to sound accusatory, but her breath hitched again. "I understand."

"I didn't mean you. Or Dad." They'd seen for themselves what I couldn't do after the accident.

"I'd love to see your shop," she said almost tentatively.

"Sure. Once the roads are clear." Hadn't they been in my shop? Once, Dad had stopped by and dropped off some old tools he never used. His way of weeding out and ramping down the ranch, but also to check on me. I might've herded him through and out.

Seemed pretty fucking immature.

"I'll call you when it's safe to come out here."

"Yes, Jonah. That'll be nice."

I ended the call before the throb in my chest could tear a vessel. My parents deserved better than me. Eli had been the type of kid they could dote on. I'd only grown worse the older I'd gotten.

Summer was quiet on the couch. I dropped to sit next to her, and she curled up next to me.

"How are your parents?" she asked.

"Worried."

She angled her head up. "Mama never quits fretting. It's a parent thing."

I gave her a knowing look. I'd seen how fast she answered the phone whenever Wynter called. "And a sister thing."

She returned the knowing look. "Yes, but we're not talking about me."

Fine. I was apparently helpless against my fresh-faced guest. "I hate that I still worry them. Mom was surprised I make a good living making furniture."

"Haven't they seen your kitchen table?"

"Yes." I smirked. "But they haven't seen how much I sell that kind of table for."

"How much?" Her expression turned almost shy. "I mean, I've snooped on your site. You had an end table for five grand?"

"Rich people like unique things."

"Rich people like custom-made products from places like Montana," she agreed. "When I first priced a small batch exclusive of holiday bourbon, I thought Daddy was crazy. I thought getting hundreds for a bottle was a pipe dream. It's just bourbon."

"Damn good bourbon." I used to enjoy having a drink once in a while with Teller. Except for a few times as a teen and a couple more after I turned twenty-one, I hadn't gotten drunk. More memories piled on. "We'd come in from a hunting or snowmobiling trip and toss one back as we unpacked and cleaned our gear."

I waited for her to tell me I could still try hunting, or even snowmobiling. And I'd tell her that even short hunting excursions made my joints ache so bad I couldn't sleep for a week. A little bird meat wasn't worth it. I could buy a goose from the butcher shop, a turkey from the grocery store. I could order venison. Then I'd be able to walk the next day.

As for snowmobiling, I couldn't risk getting in snow so deep I'd have trouble taking a step. I couldn't high-knee like I used to. I wasn't going to make myself a victim so others could put themselves in danger to come help me.

But she didn't placate me. She didn't force optimism. "I used to have a drink with Teller when we were both up late at home. The last couple of times, he asked me about Boyd. Now I can see that he was fishing, trying to get me to admit I wasn't happy."

"He's a good brother."

"They all are." She threaded her fingers through mine. "So were you."

A shock of tension rippled through me. I hadn't expected to talk about Eli. "I wasn't."

"Eli was a lot like Tenor. Quieter, more subdued, a

little nerdy, but still enough like Tate and Teller that it's clear they're brothers. Yet people are often surprised."

"I think it was the same with Eli. I kept expecting him to act like me, but he didn't. I didn't know what to do with him half the time."

"Teller and Tate are like that with Tenor."

That made me feel better. I respected the hell out of the older Bailey brothers. They had a hard time understanding a more sensitive brother? I wasn't infallible. Eli had reacted to the world differently than me. If I'd gotten dumped and the girl had told me she was into Eli, then I would've taken a trip to the mountains—hunting, fly-fishing, camping, hiking, whatever. I'd have found something to do, and I wouldn't have returned until I'd decided I was better off alone and the girl was better off with Eli. Dad would've taken over all the ranch duties like he had when I had gone where I wanted when I had wanted. Mom had worried.

Fuck.

Summer traced a pattern on my thigh. "Do I get to see some of your work too?"

Pleasure at the thought of seeing her in the place where I spent so much time radiated warmth through my chest. "When I battle the drift in front of the shop door, yes."

"You said you were updating the website?"

I nodded, but she gave me an expectant look. "You want to see some pictures?"

She snuggled closer. "Why, yes, what a good suggestion, I'd love to."

Chuckling, I pulled my phone back out of my pocket. I pulled up my album with my project images.

My chest nearly exploded from the way her eyes widened and her lips parted.

"You did all those?"

"These are from last year."

She took my phone and scrolled through. She stopped at a picture of a tree stump and flipped to the decorative end table with a winding wooden base I'd turned it into. "Seriously? You took a log and did that? We'd just make it into firewood."

"It was Bastogne walnut, and the client asked me to make a design out of it."

"Do you just make it up?"

"No, I talk with my customers. Send questionnaires. Then I give them mockups. Definitely if they're providing the resources, I spend a lot of time on each step. There are no take backs once I start cutting."

"How much did you sell this for?"

The price hovered on my tongue. I knew exactly how much I'd sold the piece for. The customer had also paid for shipping the raw materials to me and for getting the finished product to them. "Eighteen hundred dollars."

"One thousand eight hundred?" She sat up and twisted toward me. "How long did this take you?"

Having her full attention on me was unnerving. When I was naked and she was looking me over, I'd had the same sensation of wanting to run. "A week."

"No way!" She enlarged the picture and studied it. "Only a week?"

"Two days to do the physical work, and then drying times for the coatings, plus a few extra hours going back and forth in the planning stages. But it's not the only piece I'm working on during the week, and little tables like this are the smallest items I sell." And by far the cheapest.

"You're an artist."

I scoffed.

She gave me a sidelong look and flipped to another picture. A set of stools I'd made out of old barrels. The barrel staves were the backs of the seats and the steel hoops from the barrel had also been repurposed into the design.

"These were in the coffee shop," she said. "You could've charged well over twelve hundred for these but they were only marked for like four hundred dollars."

"I price lower for local. Besides, I'm just playing around with those."

"Just playing around?" She enlarged the picture and inspected every inch of the stool. "Just playing?"

"When I'm constrained to a material and to a certain design, then I charge more."

She smirked. "You charge anyone who's not from Bourbon Canyon more. I like it. Just what Daddy would've done."

"Your daddy did do it."

She snickered. The Copper Summit gift shop had cheaper bottles of their bourbon than anywhere else in the country. "Have you made your parents anything?"

I shook my head.

She glanced at me, then clicked out of the album and shut my screen off. "I heard what you told your mom about getting sick of being told what you couldn't do after the accident."

I knew she'd heard, but the knowledge didn't bother me like it should. "I know. You like to eavesdrop."

She sucked in an indignant gasp. "Do not."

"You were always spying on me and Teller."

"You guys were always up to something fun." She settled back into my side and grabbed the remote, but she didn't turn on the TV right away. "Are you sure you're okay showing me your space?"

"I wouldn't have offered if I weren't."

"You spend a lot of time out there, don't you?" When I nodded, she said, "I thought you were hiding from me."

"I was. It's not polite to lust after a runaway bride."

"And now?"

I still shouldn't be as into her as I was. Her life wasn't on this mountain. Her life wasn't even on her family's land across the valley. But we were stuck together in a storm and I wasn't strong enough to turn away someone who looked at me the way she did. "I like the idea of watching a lame-ass movie with you. What's it going to be?"

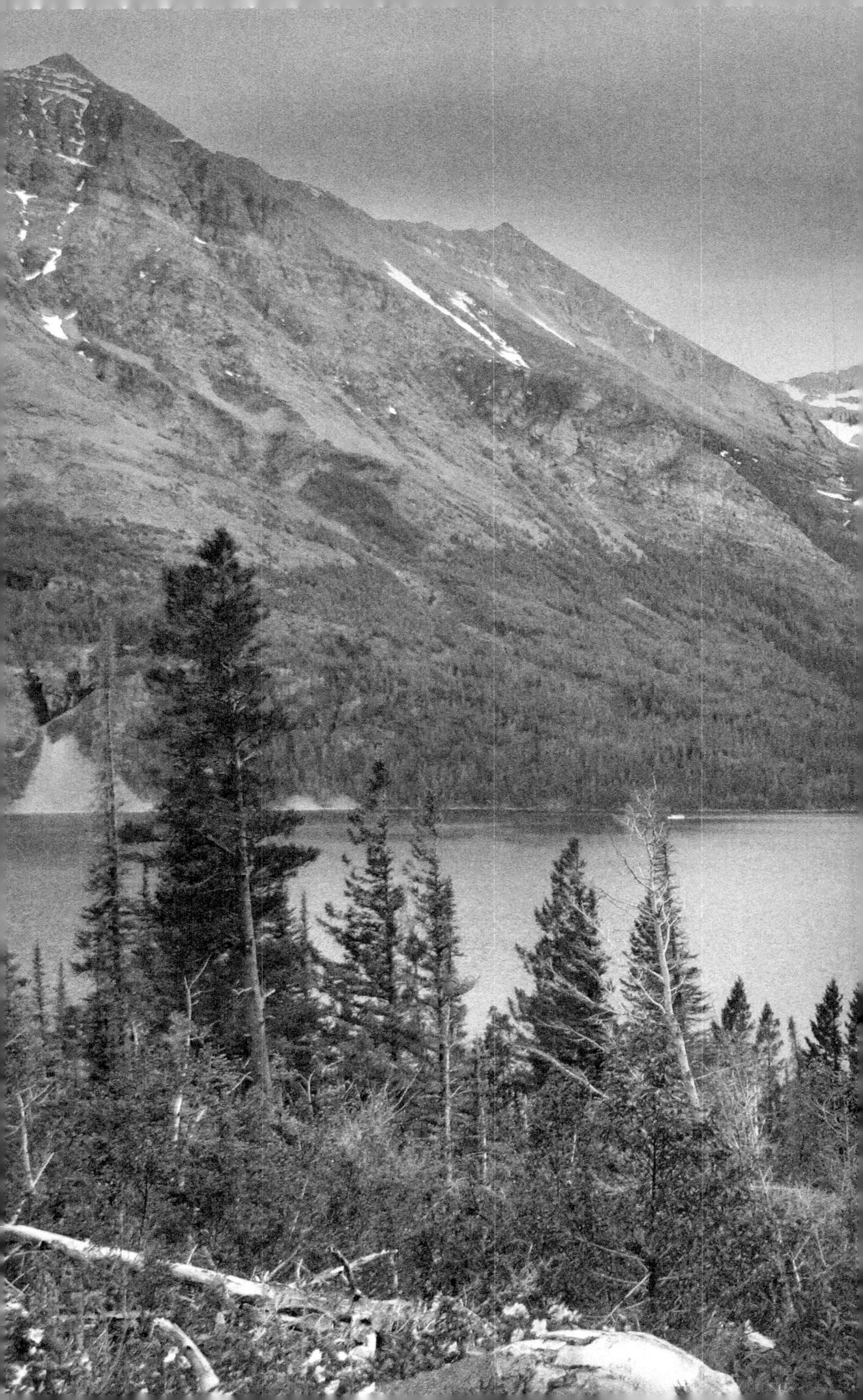

CHAPTER SEVENTEEN

Summer

Snow was still coming down, but the wind was almost nonexistent. Jonah was clearing the driveway. I'd helped shovel before he'd run me inside, then worked with the skid steer. He didn't want to chance not seeing me through the curtain of flakes while he was buzzing around the yard and driveway areas, clearing a path to the shop.

I had tried to peek into the shop when he'd opened the big garage door to drive the skid steer out. The place was well lit and full of stuff, but like the garage, everything had its place. Unlike the garage, the inside was well lit and full of life. Giant slabs of wood were leaning against the wall. There were workbenches and tables, walls full of tools, and protective gear hanging from hooks.

I'd also spied a small lounge and a door that was

probably a bathroom. How much time did Jonah spend in his shop?

Judging by those huge cuts of wood, he got his muscles from working. He might spend a lot of time on his feet, but he had an even floor and he wasn't walking long distances. I'd witnessed him doing stretches and exercises when he thought I was still sleeping.

The last two nights, I'd gone to sleep in his bed—after an orgasm or two or three—and he'd let me sleep while he made breakfast. I might not have been dozing too hard. I might've liked getting doted on.

He was a thoughtful man.

I was bursting to talk to someone about us, but he hadn't even told his parents we were a thing. To be fair, his parents might be the most complicated ones to tell. But he also hadn't said anything about continuing what we were doing beyond the storm. Once the roads were clear, was that the end of us?

I hadn't approached any of my sisters about my relationships. I hadn't wanted to worry them when I wasn't happy, and when it came to Boyd, I hadn't wanted to be told what I knew deep down inside.

This time though? The need to spill that I was sleeping with Jonah Dunn, that I was scared we were temporary, was bursting inside me until I thought I'd split apart at the seams.

I roamed the kitchen where I could see Jonah pushing loads of snow and called Autumn. There was no way I was worrying Wynter this close to her due date. I wasn't bugging Scarlett and risking Tate finding out either. Junie was on the road, and she'd tell me to hang on and enjoy the ride, to hell with the consequences.

Autumn answered. "How's this round of getting stranded with the moody mountain man?"

"Climactic."

"Oooh." Fabric rustled. I could picture her in her little house in town. She had land like the rest of us that Daddy had parceled out for her, but like me, she'd never made the commitment to build. Like me, she sometimes just took the unofficial dirt road to a little clearing and gazed at everything until life straightened itself out.

I hadn't done that in so long. But there was no point now. I could look at the snow-covered valley all day long, but I would still be as confused as before.

"Tell me all about it," she urged.

I peeked out the window one more time. I could make out the outline of him in the cabin of the skid steer. He was chiseling away at a giant drift that reached from one corner of the shop to the other. "We opened up about Eli and how I felt and how he felt. But I'm afraid once the mess of this storm is cleaned up, he's going to end things."

"Have you talked to him about it?"

"Sort of. He asked if we could not worry about it until we had to."

"Oof."

I sighed. "Right? Not exactly what a girl wants to hear."

"Maybe he's afraid that you're rebounding and don't know it."

"I'm not. I got over Boyd so fast I should've sent apology notes to everyone who bothered to come out."

She tsked. "If you hadn't done all that, you wouldn't have ended up in Jonah's bed."

And on the stairs, the couch, and last night, the

kitchen table. I stroked my fingers along the surface where he'd had me spread with his head between my legs and my heels on his shoulders. I could see her point. So many unusual circumstances had to happen to get me and Jonah in the same place and especially to get us to leave together. And stay together. "I don't think Jonah believes in fate."

"Then prove to him that there's more to it than fate, like chemistry, compatibility, and intent."

"I intend to do a lot to him."

"That might convince him more than anything."

I laughed at her seriousness. "I was joking."

"I'm not. Men respond to sex. Why do you think I'm single?"

"Autumn."

"Kidding, Summer. We're not talking about me, but I am saying if you come in hot saying you want forever and a family, that scares the shit out of a lot of men. Men you'd think would be old enough to not be led around by their dick."

I lifted my brows at the bitterness drifting through the line. Autumn wasn't shy about wanting to settle down, but thankfully, she was pickier than I had been about who she would tie herself to. Her choosiness had also led to her loneliness. I had a lot of respect for her, and a lot of sympathy. My sister had a lot of love to give.

"But seriously," she continued, "if you are clear about what you want out of a relationship with Jonah and he gets weird, then you might have to consider that you two are in different places in life. You might have to consider that he's not willing to leave his mountain cabin of safety."

"I don't want to leave it either."

"Okay, then. Say you two decide to continue the bangfest and tell everyone you're a thing—are you okay being solo at a lot of things you'd normally have your partner there with you for?"

I ran my bottom lip through my teeth. "It was kind of like that with Boyd. Jonah won't sit out my life events because he thinks he's too busy for them." I realized now Boyd had thought he was too good for the stuff going on in my life. He'd come to Daddy's funeral and left right after, citing work obligations. I'd been content to let him go.

My *daddy's* funeral. When Boyd knew what I'd gone through with my birth parents.

Jonah had been at Daddy's funeral. He'd even stopped in at the reception to give his condolences to Mama. Then he'd left as quietly as he'd come. No need to give excuses that made him look important.

"I really like it here," I confessed. "And I really like him." I'd be more devastated than any breakup if he cut things off before we were official. I also wouldn't be okay staying his little secret.

I would not be okay if I heard he was hooking back up with Jackie Weller.

"Then be honest, Summer. Tell him what you want and what you expect. Just because he's been a hermit and he's been hurt and he's been through a mind fuck about you and his brother doesn't mean you should settle for his hang-ups."

Twice in my life I'd been brutally honest. First, with Eli, and Jonah's life had been irrevocably altered, physically, mentally, and emotionally. Mine had been changed too, but I hadn't lost as much as him. The second time was before my wedding. And again, I'd tipped Jonah's existence upside down.

Yet if he didn't want to be with me, then . . . I didn't know. I didn't want to find out.

I shouldn't have called Autumn. She looked sweet and innocent, but she could cut through bullshit better than any of us.

A whisper snaked through my head. *Maybe that was why you did call her*.

Wynter and Junie would say *Get it, girl. Have that fun.* Then Wynter would tell Myles all about it.

Scarlett would tell me to take things slow. She knew enough of Jonah to know he'd been hurt, and she'd been at my wedding. She'd want both of us to be cautious.

My brothers might ask me what the hell I was thinking, then get to Jonah and tell him that if he hurt me, they'd take it out on him.

Autumn was pragmatic. She was honest. She knew me and she knew Jonah, and she knew that ripping off the bandage of truth was the best way to face this problem.

Because the storm was coming to an end. The snow was supposed to quit tonight. Then another couple of days of clearing roads and I could make my way down the mountain. How long would I be welcome back? How soon before my time pining for Jonah Dunn was over?

Jonah

. . .

Summer wandered among the various projects I had in progress. The block of black walnut was for a gamer's epoxy table. I'd sent several designs and he'd finally decided on one with a few changes.

She ran her fingers along the elm that had arrived before the storm had begun. I had ordered the wood, knowing it'd make a beautiful table I could sell online. Then she wandered to the various end tables I was almost done with. I took smaller projects to fill in the larger orders, and the end tables were easy enough to sell for a better profit margin. People could justify spending four figures on a useful piece of art better than some of my bigger tables that ran close to five figures.

I couldn't do massive dining room tables, or even meeting room tables. I was only one person, and while I was strong and used leverage to my advantage, moving giant slabs of wood and epoxy wasn't possible without help. I was a one-man show.

"Wow," she breathed as she inspected the charcoal-filled wells in the holes left behind by the knots in the wood.

She had been quiet last night. My rusty senses said she wanted to talk, but I didn't prod her. She might bring up topics I wasn't ready for.

Like, should we tell people we were a thing? Were we a thing, or did she just want to keep fucking? If she wanted more than sex, then what? I'd rarely moved beyond sex in my earlier dating. My relationships hadn't been mature or healthy, or Jackie wouldn't have left with some guy she'd just met to move to a place she'd never been before.

If that wasn't a spotlight on how little I offered, I didn't know what was.

What did being a couple entail? What would Summer want out of me?

Dating, for one.

How could I date her? She would return to Bozeman for work. Would I have to travel?

A date in Bozeman would be easier and less intrusive than going out in Bourbon Canyon, where we'd ignite the gossip tree. The rumors would flame through town. People would bring up memories of Eli dating her. Their words would make it seem like she and Eli had been a couple last year instead of over fifteen years ago.

What did people do for dates these days?

"Do you have work to catch up on?" She turned, her fingers stroking over another plank of walnut my supplier had claimed was unusable due to cracks and holes. Those were my favorite challenges.

"What you're touching, actually."

She snatched her hand away.

I chuckled. "Don't worry. I haven't started. It'll be one of the in-between pieces that I do before I start on a table order. Here."

I went to the slab, bark still on its edges. I took it from where it leaned against the wall and went to an empty shop table. I had a few. With drying times for sealant and epoxy, I had wanted a shop with enough space for me to use my time efficiently. I didn't like having nothing to do.

I laid the slab on one side and traced the long edge. "I'll have to take all this off so the epoxy doesn't only bond to the bark."

"Because then if the bark peels, the table falls apart?"

I nodded and outlined the knots. "Then I'm going to fill these, but can you see the pattern they make?"

She frowned and tilted her head one way and then the other. "Oh my god, it looks like a Labrador's face."

Grinning, I nodded. "Exactly. Can you imagine how much a custom bar-height table will go for when it looks like it has the image of a dog branded into it?"

"How much?" Her wide amber eyes were on me and so damn curious. She used to roll her eyes when Teller and I would nerd out over camping gear and hunting equipment. But this she was into. I had her attention and I liked it. "I'll fill in the cracks and holes and it'll really bring the picture to life. Usually. Sometimes a project goes sideways."

"That's art, I suppose."

No one had ever called my work "art" before. I was a self-taught woodworker. If the YouTube guys I followed ever learned about how much I'd gotten from them, they'd charge me tuition. "If the image doesn't turn out, I'll charge nine hundred." Her eyes flared and my pulse pumped. I hadn't gotten to the good part. "If there's a dog face at the end of all this, then I'll charge twenty-six hundred."

"How many days of work?"

I lifted a shoulder. "Another week. Carving the leg out of a scrap of four-by-four will take a while, but like I said, I'll be working on other projects during that week."

"Jonah. That's over five hundred dollars a day."

My chest threatened to puff out at her awe. "I work seven days a week, not five, and it might not turn out," I warned.

She rolled her eyes. "Plus the other projects you're working on and selling. That's impressive."

Now I had the strongest urge to pack the wood away and not touch it until she was gone. I was boasting. That never turned out well. "Minus cost of equipment."

Her eyes narrowed. "You're using scrap. How much was the wood?" She tapped her finger where the dog's nose would be.

"This was, uh, free. But I do buy scraps, or the buyer supplies their own."

Her head fell back and she laughed. "Can't I tell you that your work is pretty impressive?"

I swallowed hard. "Sure."

"Your products are as impressive as your dick."

I coughed. "Jesus, Summer."

"Your work ethic gets me hot."

My cheeks were flaming. She was making a point, but I was swimming in her compliments and happy to drown. "You don't need to—"

She yanked her sweater over her head and stuck her chest out as she undid her bra. "I think we need to do some exposure therapy." Her tits fell free and her bra hit the floor in my peripheral vision. "I like your wood, Jonah."

The good news was that I couldn't feel foolish from how easily she made me blush. My erection was dominating my blood supply. "Summer, what are you doing?"

"Telling you good things about yourself." She shoved down the black sweats she'd borrowed from me. "Oh, look at that? My underwear is in the wash."

I got a full view of her bare pussy. "Fuck."

She propped her hands behind her on the workbench and widened her stance. "You're an amazing artist."

My mouth went dry. Dimly, I worried about sawdust getting on her clothing from being on the floor, but mostly, I couldn't take my gaze off her body.

"Your work is the most impressive I've seen. Nothing compares to Dunn's Wood Creations."

My gaze snapped to hers. She'd said she snooped on my website, but my company's name on her lips was a new desire unlocked. I liked her saying that almost as much as the way my name spilled off her lips when I was buried deep inside her.

"I think you're dedicated and hard-working and—"

"You make me sound like a Boy Scout."

"You don't need to be a Boy Scout. You've been living those skills all your life."

"I don't tie knots." I prowled closer. Her nude body glowing under the shop lights was erotic, but it didn't compare to touching her. The shop was on the cool side and her nipples were tight and begging for attention.

"In here, you do." She trailed her fingers over her belly.

I could set her on the bench and spread her legs and devour her, but I claimed her mouth for a kiss instead. Against her lips, I murmured, "I got your point. Thank you." The last part came reluctantly. I could take compliments. I just didn't need them.

"I'm not done yet. I'd like you to use your magnificent tongue or your fantastic dick to turn me into a pile of Jell-O."

I kissed her again, plundering the hot depths of her mouth before pulling back. "It'll have to be my tongue. I don't keep condoms out here." I was cursing myself for not carrying one on me at all times. I should know after the last few days that a simple conversation could turn into sex.

Weren't all our conversations simple? Didn't I intentionally keep them that way?

I pushed the thought away. We were still stranded. I wasn't letting reality settle in.

She arched a brow, her expression haughty in a way that made my dick twitch. "Good thing I have one in the pocket of my sweats."

"Fuck." I tugged my sweater over my head and spread it out on the bench behind her. Lifting her by the ass cheeks, I placed her on the edge of the table. I kept my shop meticulous, but I wasn't out here scrubbing surfaces. Her skin would not be at risk because I was horny in my shop.

"You're really strong."

I was. I had felt weak for so long, and so often, I still did. While my mobility was limited, I could heft wooden slabs and haul heavy tools like my table saw. "Lie back and let me feast."

She tangled her hands in my hair. "I want to watch."

Lust slammed into my gut, making my abs clench. "I'll give you whatever you want."

I was afraid I might mean it.

Summer

Jonah wound his arms under my thighs and tucked himself between my legs. I propped my hands behind me. As wet as I was, he wouldn't be able to wear this sweater out of the shop. It'd freeze to him before he got to the house.

But I wouldn't worry about that now. I couldn't. He lapped his tongue through my pussy and attacked my clit like he was paying me back in pleasure for the discomfort my compliments had given him.

I hadn't realized how uncomfortable he was with accolades for all the good things he did. He heaped responsibility onto himself, along with blame, and he'd cut himself off so people couldn't tell him he was a good human.

And then he took me away from my thoughts. I couldn't concentrate on anything but the way he ate me up, looking both blissed out and determined.

"Jonah." I was also getting a hell of a view right now. Watching his tongue flick and circle my clit. He'd hold my gaze with his smoldering one for a few moments and then close his eyes like my flavor was so damn good he couldn't stand it himself.

He had on a plain white T-shirt he'd worn under the sweater, and I almost tugged it over his head. But I couldn't risk stopping my meteoric rise to my peak.

Especially when he pinned my gaze again and inserted two fingers inside me.

A shudder ran through my body and my knees fell open wider. I watched myself rock against him. He didn't have to move his hand. I was doing it for him. He kept pace with his tongue.

"I know I said it before," I panted and rolled, "but you're really good with your tongue."

A low growl resonated from him into me. I was done.

I let my head fall back. "Jonah!" Stars exploded behind my eyes and I convulsed, my legs closing on his head, but I knew he didn't care.

"Jonah!" I cried again because he didn't let up. I collapsed back and gave up any semblance of control.

Either my string of compliments was fueling an intense oral session or it was payback. I won no matter what.

Then he gently untangled himself from my legs. My feet were on the edge and I was exposed but too shook to care. I had to catch my breath before I could move.

His heat returned and he took my hand to help me sit up. As soon as I was upright, he lifted me and notched his cock at my entrance. I clung to him. My ass wasn't touching the corner of the table, like he was afraid it'd be too uncomfortable.

He thrust upward and I groaned. There was nothing like being filled with him. But . . . I also didn't want to hurt him. And I didn't want to insult him.

"Jonah?" I searched his face for any sign of pain or uncertainty. I wouldn't be offended if he dropped me.

"What was it you said about how strong I am?" His hands were a vise at my hips. He cocked his hips up as he pressed me down.

His thick length filled me, one inch at a time.

A moan left me. So damn good. "You are really fucking strong." I wrapped my arms around his neck and cinched my legs around his waist so I could ride him. "You've been throwing slabs of wood around just for this moment."

"You're damn right I have."

He fucked me standing up. Not one tremor traveled from him to me. His legs were strong and his face was carved with intent.

"You fuck as beautifully as you create your art." I kissed him and nibbled on his lower lip. His whiskers tickled my mouth, but I didn't slow the way I rode his length. His handprints would be branded on my sides. Fitting. The way we were together would forever be a part of me. After him, I couldn't have sex if I wasn't getting this.

The friction of our bodies sent my clit into overdrive and it was seconds before I was careening to a second climax. Unbelievable. The way it was between us? Unheard of. I'd never get this with anyone else.

Jonah was it for me.

As if he sensed my thought, he ground into me, igniting the impending orgasm.

"Yes! Jonah!" My voice echoed off the walls.

"Fuck! Summer!" A feral growl ripped from him and he pulsed inside me. "Fuck, fuck, fuck."

I couldn't form words as my climax peaked and crashed back down. "Oh my god," I groaned, hanging off him.

He stood strong. Unwavering. He was it for me. If only he'd say the same about me. Autumn was right. I had to talk to him. But what if that was the end of it? The end of us?

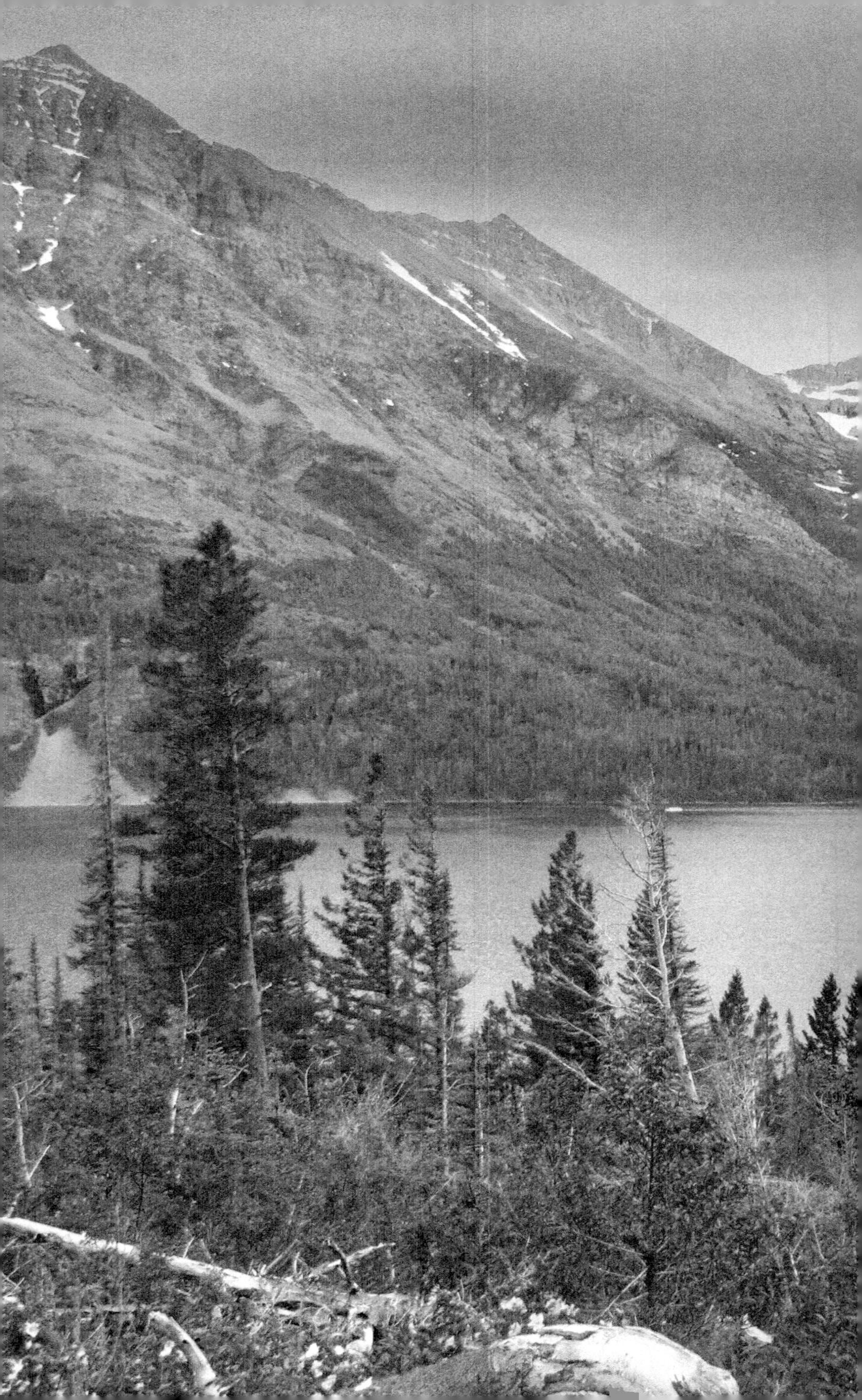

CHAPTER EIGHTEEN

Summer

The rays of the sun bounced off the piles of snow. Between the wind and the drifts, the landscape wasn't a white blanket. Green treetops stuck out and the brown tips of the tallest grasses were visible.

I shaded my eyes as I stared out the window. A winter wonderland. The road reports were good. They had been for the city and the surrounding county for a couple of days, but now the country roads were getting cleared. We were waiting on the main road, which would be cleared any minute.

My time at Jonah's was coming to an end. I'd had days to bring up *What now?* and I hadn't. I hadn't so much as asked him what he thought about us when it wasn't snowing.

The entire day before, I'd been in his shop while he worked. He'd given me a piece of wood to tinker with, like a toddler playing with pots and kettles while their parent cooked. We'd listened to music and his woodworking podcasts. There were several. I would've been bored silly, but I'd had him to watch.

His big body bunched and flexed when he heaved six-foot planks of wood around. A line of concentration creased his forehead when he was pondering his next move—to stain or not to stain, the best method to add sealant, or how heavy-handed to be with the epoxy.

I found craft work fascinating. I ran the distillery in Bozeman. So much of my job was managing people and resources, but I also knew each step. I could prepare the mash and mix additives to yield different flavors in the bourbon. I liked playing around with aging times and even sourcing new barrels for single-barrel batches to get different flavor profiles.

Jonah's work paralleled those decisions. What were the various ways to bring out the personality of the wood and how could he best enhance those qualities?

I turned grain into spirits. He turned wood into furniture. I played with the flavors to bring out the grain profiles. He changed the wood's shape to showcase the lines and grooves. Add in talent and efficiency and he brought in a lot of money, just like the distillery.

He came to a stop next to me at the glass. "What are you thinking?"

Grateful I'd let my mind wander to our similarities and not how our differences might interfere in our future, I smiled. "How alike our professions are."

A tiny frown tugged at his lips. "I never thought of what I do as a profession."

I gawked at his handsome profile. "You bring in that much money and you consider it a *hobby*?"

There was that uncomfortable shoulder lift again. "I just do it."

He had an efficient process. And while he worked, he basically did daily continuing education with his podcasts and online videos. He brought in more money than my generous wage at the distillery. How much had he socked away? The guy was a rich mountain man up here all alone.

"If everyone knew how much money you make and how good at sex you are, you'd have hordes of women climbing this mountain."

The tips of his ears burned red. "Summer."

I laughed. "I'm serious. The sex alone would sell it, with your looks."

He drew his brows together. "My looks aren't anything."

I scoffed. "You're right. It's your glowing personality that got my sweats off."

He blinked. "I'm . . . not sure how to take that."

"I like your personality. For the record."

His lips quirked. "Noted."

We stared out the window in silence. Was he having the same existential crisis about us? Or was he sexed out and counting down until I could drive my car down the road and get back to making more masterpieces and raking in the cash?

"Hey, uh . . . Would you like to go out sometime?" His voice was hoarse, as if we hadn't been conversing every day for the last week.

I bit my cheek. How carefully should I tread? Would I scare him off if I was overly enthusiastic? "If we went out, people might think we're a thing."

"We don't have to go anywhere in Bourbon Canyon. I can go to Bozeman."

"Oh." Disappointment rang through me, as clear as a choir song. "Okay."

"Bourbon Canyon is fine too. I don't want you to have to drive."

"Curly's buns are worth driving for."

"He's a dick."

I nodded, pleased I wasn't the only one who thought Curly Binstock was a good ole boy who got away with too much. But he owned the best restaurant in town and he made sure his food was good enough we all looked the other way. "Is that why you don't want to go anywhere in town?" I asked quietly.

"Yeah," he replied just as softly. "Until we decide how to proceed." He turned toward me and his gentle touch at my elbow drew me around until I faced him. "Your history with Eli"—he winced—"mine too, will make the chatter loud and opinionated. I know fifteen years have passed, but once we're seen together, it's going to feel like yesterday to those who remember."

My shoulders drooped. He was right. I didn't care, but he clearly did, and I'd respect his feelings. "Bozeman would be fine. There are some restaurants I've been wanting to try." They'd been too gauche for Boyd.

"You have to get back to work right away?"

My remote work attempts had stopped when I'd left my laptop in my loner office in Copper Summit over a week ago. Now it was Wednesday. "I should go catch up for the rest of the week." He needed to make up time too. "Saturday? We can have a sleepover."

His eyes crinkled at the corners and heat filled his

gaze. "Saturday." The heat cooled. "You have history in your place with that cocksucker, don't you?"

My heart sank. We each had separate lives, but I, too, would've had hang-ups thinking about him and other women in the cabin. "Yes, but not much. My little condo wasn't posh enough."

"No worries. Just wondering how many condoms to pack. I'm going to make you come at least twice in every spot you two did it."

I stopped at the distillery to collect my laptop before going to Mama's. The place was quiet for a Wednesday, but I'd left Jonah's when the workday was winding down. Otherwise, I might've skipped the errand. I was wearing the same sweats as when I'd brought groceries to Jonah. The roads to the distillery had been plowed a couple days before the ones to Jonah's place.

I was antsy, waiting for my siblings to pop up and interrogate me. Autumn already knew, but I didn't want to admit that I hadn't really talked to Jonah about us. She might not view the way he'd asked me on a date—out of town—as a good thing.

Going back to my condo was looking better and better. None of my family would venture there to interrogate me. After I visited with Mama, and evaded some questions she'd likely have, I could return to Bozeman.

I wrapped my charging cable and stuffed it into my computer bag, followed by the computer.

"Look who the cat dragged in."

I yelped and spun around, nearly knocking my

computer bag off the desk. "Teller! Don't sneak up on me."

He grinned and leaned against the doorframe. His beard wasn't as trimmed as it had been at my wedding, and he was in a green flannel shirt and jeans. "Didn't mean to scare you."

But he was a proper brother and had capitalized on the opportunity. I scowled. "I thought everyone was gone."

"They are, but I wanted to check on some things."

He was a workaholic. If there was nothing at the distillery that needed his attention, he was on the ranch, finding equipment to weld or animals to rescue.

I pulled the strap over my shoulder. "I'm taking off."

"How's Jonah?" he asked as if he hadn't heard me.

"Fine." My cheeks warmed. I could not blush or Teller would know.

"Weird how you got stranded with him twice."

"Yeah."

He continued blocking the doorway. I could push past him, but then he'd know I was hiding something, and he'd guess it was that I knew what Jonah looked like naked. Intimately.

"He's doing okay?" he asked again.

I softened. In all my drama about what to tell Jonah about me and Eli and when, and how Jonah would react, and when would we tell others that we were a thing now, and what did being "a thing" actually entail . . . I'd forgotten that Teller had lost his best friend.

"He is doing really well." I leaned against the desk and looked out the window at the tree-lined parking lot. The view wasn't as busy as the one out of my office in Bozeman, but it was more familiar. More comforting. I'd grown up gazing out of the distillery windows. "He won't admit how much he misses doing things like hunting and fishing and camping, but he's found woodworking and he's good. Really good."

Regret lit his eyes. "Yeah, I've seen his stuff. He's got a gift." He contemplated the floor. "You think he really can't . . . do everything he used to?"

I tilted my head and considered my brother. Growing up, Teller and I hadn't been close. He'd been a fresh teen when I'd arrived with my sisters and happy to do his own thing. Other than messing with me when it came to chores, he'd done his thing and I'd done mine. But we had Jonah in common.

"Do you blame yourself?" I asked.

Teller scowled, but scuffed the tip of his boot against the floor. "Nah." He shrugged and crossed his arms over his chest. "Maybe. I made him stick around until we caught one more fish, so I had enough to feed everyone for supper."

Eli's death had had a ripple effect on all the relationships between the people around him. My silence had only added to all the guilt. I'd told Jonah. Teller needed to know too. "I broke up with him, and he accused me of liking Jonah, and I didn't argue. What happened was definitely not your fault."

Teller's arms dropped and he regarded me, his stare incredulous. "Shit, Summer." He shoved a hand through his loose, dark curls. "Shit."

"Yeah. I should've said something years ago, but I was also—god, this sounds so bad—I was so upset with Eli for putting me in that position."

"Of course. Why wouldn't you be?" It was my turn to gawk at him. He held his hands up like he was warding off an argument, yet I wasn't sure I could argue. "He was young and a lot of young guys make stupid decisions and nothing terrible happens. But in this case, it did. We all lost Eli, but I also lost my best friend."

"He's still there," I said softly.

Teller snorted. "He was there pushing me right back out the door whenever I asked him to hang out."

"It's been hard for him since the accident. He doesn't open up easy."

"But he did. To you?"

I sensed more curiosity rather than his normal teasing, so I nodded.

"Just how close did you two get?"

I sighed and hugged the computer bag to myself. "Honestly? I don't know. I'd like to think we're very close, but I also feel like he'll cut me off any minute. I worry he still blames me, and now that he's alone again he can convince himself it's better that way."

"Did he treat you right? He's not like that douche?"

I let out a gusty exhale. "Why didn't anyone say a thing about Boyd at the time?"

"Would you have listened?"

"Yes!" I snapped, then sighed. I went back to gazing out the window. Maybe I would've listened. Or maybe I would've dug in harder and become the next Mrs. Harrington, the blond trophy wife Boyd had wanted.

"Sure." He pushed off the doorframe. "This last week, I'd like to say Mama's been worried about you, but that'd be bullshit. Every time I caught her looking out the window in the direction of the mountain, she had a little smile on her face."

The heat in my face was back. "How much should I tell her?"

After our talk, Teller would understand the privacy issue.

He let out a low whistle. "It's not going to matter. She's going to take one look at your blush when his name is brought up and know. You'd better hope Wynter goes into labor before you get to the house." He lifted his chin toward the desk. "I stopped by for another reason. Know the James place?"

"Of course." Everyone knew the James place. As landowners, we coveted the property. The Jameses had acreage that could be both farmed and ranched, and had been, but the land had fallen into disuse. The house, a once-great masterpiece of log construction, hadn't been kept since Jenni James had passed. Her husband, Henry James, was doing better than he had been, but we'd all seen his sad stock, the broken-down equipment, the neglected fields, and the pastures that were either overgrazed or underutilized, be it from lack of herd rotation or haying.

My brothers had been chatting about the place, murmuring about it going up for sale. Henry and Jenni's only son, Gideon, had moved to Las Vegas to be some big shot out there and hadn't been back to Montana once. Gideon was slightly older than Tate, and Teller thought there was a chance he wasn't interested in keeping the land in his name.

"Henry James called Tate."

"Oh my god." Henry owned as much land as the Baileys, now that Jenni was gone. He'd married into it.

The Bailey property had gotten split up between us. The main ranch area was in Mama's name. Other tracts had been signed over to each kid before Daddy had died.

The James property would be completely open. "What would we do with it?"

"Other than prevent some rich city pricks from buying it and going all *Yellowstone* on the town?"

I laughed. "It'd be a tough sell to convince the city to let them build a ski resort and airport there."

"Tough, but not impossible. Henry used to grow some of the best corn crops in the state. He used to do business with Grandpa."

"I remember Daddy saying that." Henry's wife had passed away before I'd come to live with the Baileys, but I'd heard my parents talk about him over the years. Usually past tense—used to be good to do business with, used to be reliable, used to have it all.

"We could hire someone to manage the place and grow our own grains."

I lifted my brows. Copper Summit's motto was Montana Made, Montana Proud. "Wynter would have a heyday with the marketing on that."

He nodded. "Yep. We'd have more control from field to still."

"It would be exciting." Instead of making deals, we could cut out the middleman and support more employees. The grains grown would likely go to the Bourbon Canyon location, but I might have to be involved if there was product routed to the Bozeman facility. "Keep me posted."

"Do the same."

"We aren't talking about work, are we?"

He gave me a knowing look. "Jonah's been through some shit, but he didn't show up at your wedding because he had nothing else to do. Don't let him push you away."

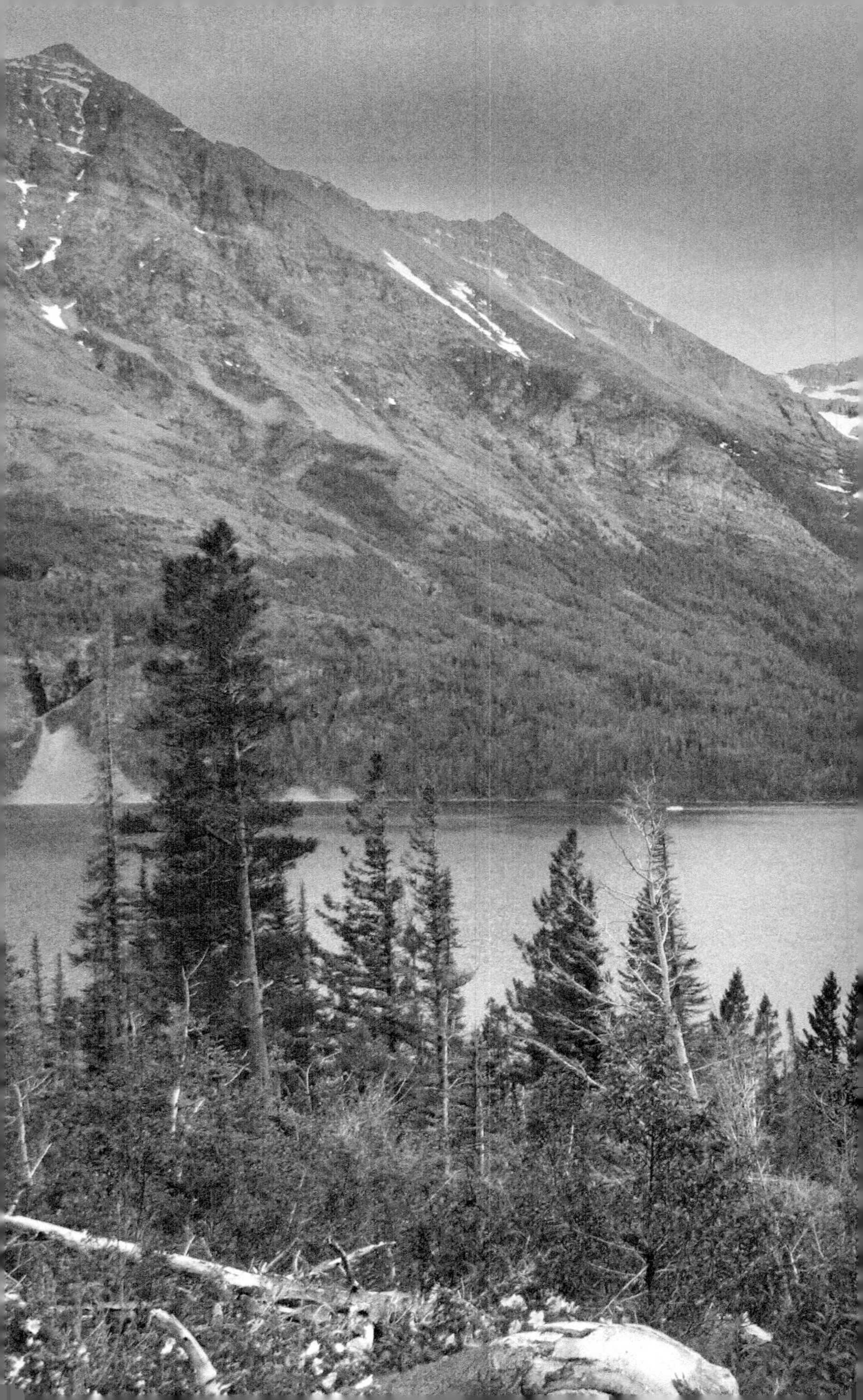

CHAPTER NINETEEN

Jonah

The weekend was taking forever to get here. Each day went by in excruciating slowness. Since Summer had left, I'd been in the shop every minute I wasn't sleeping or eating. I was already caught up.

After considering how I'd neglected my parents over the years, I'd decided to visit them. I parked in my usual spot and picked my way to the door. Mom or Dad had cleared the path to the side door, but there were enough slippery areas that I was grateful I'd brought my cane.

Mom opened the door, her expression full of shock and worry. Her salt-and-pepper hair was pulled back in a ponytail and she swam in a big fluffy gray sweater. She was nothing but wide eyes and fleece. "Jonah, is everything okay?"

"I just came to check on you."

She blinked but stepped back. "Yes, we're good. Your dad ran to town for some—well, probably to have coffee at the gas station with the guys, but he claimed to need some feed supplies for the chickens."

I entered the house and shrugged out of my coat. "Why does he bother making excuses anymore about his morning hangouts?" Everyone knew at ten a.m., several local ranchers of a certain age could be found in the booths at the gas station on the west edge of town, drinking cheap black coffee.

Mom's smile was a nice treat from her constant worry. "He truly thinks he's going to town to run errands, and that the coffee and hour-long visits are just by chance."

I went to the half-empty coffee pot on the counter. Mom would work through the entire pot by the afternoon, but she claimed the caffeine didn't keep her up.

She grabbed a Dunn Beef mug from the cupboard before I could and set it next to me. Then she retrieved her cup. I topped hers off and filled mine.

"Come. Sit." She shuffled to the small, square living room off the even smaller dining room.

Growing up, I'd known nothing but this house. It was old and cozy and compartmentalized like a lot of old farmhouses. But when I'd built the cabin, I'd wanted a big, open floor plan. A fortuitous design I couldn't have predicted.

I followed her, carefully stepping around the footrests and coffee tables that made navigating a small space more difficult when mobility was challenged. Mom had never noticed my issues getting around the house. Part of me didn't want her to change a thing, keep pretending I was fine. Another side of me was irritated as hell.

I slid between a footrest and a high-back padded chair, keeping my cane at the ready to steady myself.

"Oh my gosh, let me get that out of the way." Mom froze while bent over the stool that doubled as ranching magazine storage. Her distraught gaze went to my face.

Hell. Had she been worried about my reaction the whole time? "Appreciate it," I said gruffly and carefully sat, keeping my left leg a little straighter than my right and not bothering to hide it. I used to. I hadn't realized it until now.

She shoved the footrest out of the way. "I should probably clear some of this crap out of here." She set her cup down and shook her arms out. "I've been feeling a little claustrophobic." Sinking onto the couch, she sat forward. "How've you been? You weathered the storm okay, I see. You look good."

I might've trimmed my scruff, keeping my beard short rather than bordering on full mountain man. I didn't want to get back to that place. I liked having protection on my face in the winter, but covering the network of lines along my jaw at the base of the larger scar was no longer much of a motivation.

When a woman like Summer said she wanted to date a guy, in public, then that guy lost a few fucks about his looks. "The storm was fine. Nothing unusual. Do you guys need some help moving snow?"

Mom opened her mouth, closed it again. "Oh, uh, I don't know. Adam usually gets right on it, you know."

"He also likes his cleanup."

Fondness passed through her expression and she clasped her hands. "You and Eli would get so irritated about that." She glanced at me, all nerves, rubbing her hands together like she was cold, but she wore a giant sweater and was drinking hot coffee.

"Eli secretly enjoyed it, but he played up how much he hated getting dragged out to push snow from one pile to another because I was always bitching about it." I had wanted to get out and play, and it hadn't mattered that I was an adult. That just meant I had bigger toys to enjoy the new snow with. Making a bigger path to the shop and barn hadn't been a priority.

The idea didn't bother me so badly anymore.

"Eli did like helping your father." Her smile wavered, and this time when she looked at me, she smothered whatever she was thinking.

"What?"

"Hmm?" The hand-rubbing started again.

"You looked like you wanted to say something." When she opened her mouth, probably to brush it off again, I pushed. "It's okay. I can take it. I promise."

She blew out a breath and studied me. Her motherly concern drifted over my face, lingering on the scar, and then to my shoulders, down to where the cane rested across my thighs. She jerked, like she'd caught herself staring and lifted her gaze back up to mine.

I kept my features neutral. I had some idea what she was thinking—would she upset me and I'd never come to visit again? Had she insulted me by silently acknowledging my scars?

"When the snow melts, we're putting the house up for sale." She waved her hand around toward the picture window. "The whole ranch, actually. We'd like to sell and move into town."

Stunned, I didn't reply. My childhood home was getting sold?

When was the last time I'd thought of this place as home? But I had assumed this house would always be here. It would, just not with my parents in it.

My stomach churned. "Why?"

Anguish filled Mom's eyes. "Well . . . It's too much."

Too much. Dad was getting older, and his days of having two sons to help him were long gone. I hadn't been around. Sure, I had my injuries, but how much had I really tried? "It's a lot. But there's no way for you to keep our family home intact?"

Her expression fell. Inwardly, I winced. We'd lost so much and now the place where we had all the memories of Eli would be gone.

"It's nothing but work these days, Jonah. I'm tired. Your dad wants to slow down." She swallowed. "And Eli's gone. Our memories are ours." Her gaze turned earnest. "I'd love to see this place make good memories again. You know Rhys Kinkade?"

"I know him." He had been several years behind me in school and was now a single father in town.

"We've already talked to him. He wants to expand, and he doesn't have the acreage."

"And he can afford it?"

"He'd have to finance, but he also wouldn't need to build up his inventory. We'd include everything in the outbuildings in the sale."

My parents would have to move less equipment and they'd get a nice nest egg for a much-deserved retirement. How fucking convenient. "Sounds like a win-win."

"Yeah." Her smile was faint. "I feel like we're all overdue for that."

She got me there. I was pissy about them moving

when they just wanted to move on in life. I had. I'd used my injuries to do it.

Shame curdled in my gut. I wished there was something happier I could share with her, instead of sitting here, sulking in their living room.

I almost told her about Summer. Almost. But I kept the news to myself. I had no idea what the future held for me and Summer, and I didn't want to end up letting down my parents again.

Summer

I checked my appearance one last time. Jonah would be here any minute, but I'd been ready for hours. Weird how he'd seen me in nothing but sweats or naked the entire time I'd been in his cabin, yet today I'd been through three pairs of my best bottoms—glittery black leggings, skinny jeans that made my legs look killer with suede ankle boots, and tan pants that would go with heeled boots.

I was in the skinny jeans. I wasn't dating Boyd, thank god, and I hoped Jonah and I would like the same places. I'd told him to choose the restaurant so he could find a place he was comfortable in. I was already pushing him out of his comfort zone.

After a week of being tied to my desk, I couldn't wait for a night out. I'd been missing Jonah all week. I had it bad.

There was a knock on the door. My nerves climbed from my stomach into my throat. I did a little wiggle and tugged at the soft pink sweater I wore over a cami. It hung loose and would show more than cleavage if I let it go. Jonah might not mind.

I opened my front door and my greeting came out a squeak. Jonah had looked nice at the wedding when he'd been dressed in slacks and a blue dress shirt. His hair had been combed and his scruff had been short. I also hadn't paid a ton of attention to the details at the time and had soaked in his presence and protection and support.

Tonight, it was like Jonah had gone into the memory bank and found a younger version of himself for inspiration. His winter coat hung unzipped. He must've tossed it on when he was leaving the pickup. It was open enough to show an olive-green Henley hugging his chest. His jeans were crisp. Not exactly new, but not one of the worn pairs he used when he worked. The brown boots on his feet were a lot like my brothers' dress cowboy boots. They weren't Jonah's usual black work boots that he'd cleaned up for my wedding.

I blinked at his face. The beard was slightly shorter than when I'd left, and neatly trimmed, but his hair was combed off his forehead and to the side.

He held his arms apart and looked down at himself. "Something wrong?"

"No. Everything's so right. You look dapper, yet rugged. Like a mountain man with manners, one who can still get dirty for all the right reasons."

His smile made the corners of his eyes crinkle. "Don't ever doubt that."

"I won't." I grabbed my coat. He was staying over, so I'd give him the grand tour of my condo later.

His gaze lifted past me.

I glanced over my shoulder to see my place the way he did. I had paintings of wildflowers on the walls, but the rest was a normal condo. A big-screen TV was mounted on the living room wall. From my front door, he could see the edge of the kitchen island and the dining room off to my left. The dark living room would show the shadows of furniture similar to his. I'd gone into a furniture store and picked out a set I liked. I had a bedroom with a bathroom, a guest bathroom, and a spare room I'd made my catch-all—office, guest room, storage, library.

"It's not like your place," I said.

His chuckle was abashed. "It's not what I was expecting."

"I knew I'd be in Bourbon Canyon a lot, so I wanted a minimal-maintenance place. Yet I had Daddy's advice in my ear to build equity and all that." Plus, I hadn't planned to be in a small condo until my mid-thirties. I was supposed to have been married with kids in an idyllic house by now.

"Makes sense." He held his hand out. "Shall we?"

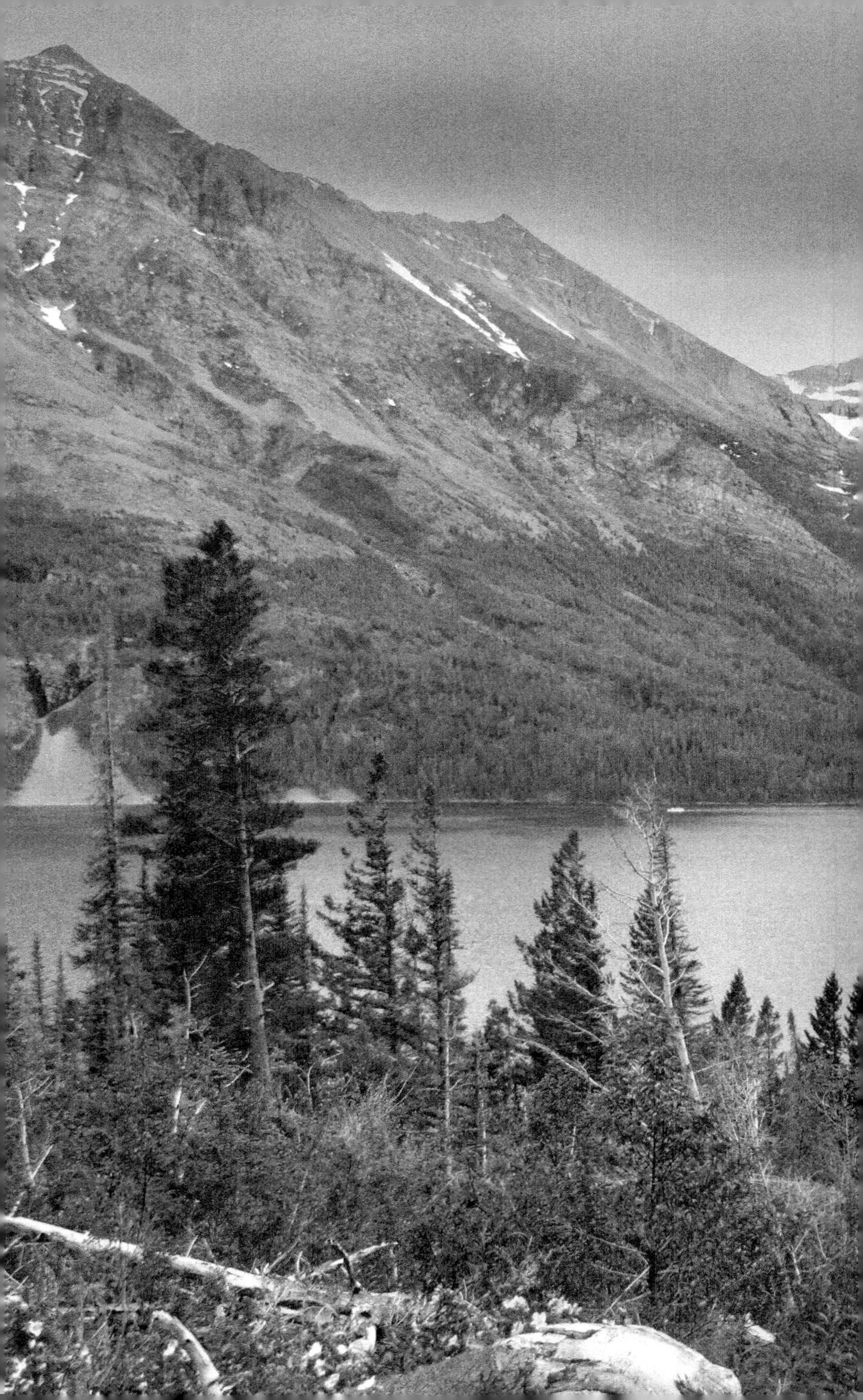

CHAPTER TWENTY

Jonah

Summer was so goddamn fine, I'd had a hard time navigating the streets of Bozeman. Those pants of her hugged her body like a second skin. Curves for miles, and I wanted those legs wrapped around my waist. I'd seen her hair in a fancy style the day of her wedding. After, she'd kept it loose or up in some sort of sloppy bun that was cute as hell. Tonight, her bright strands were sleek and hanging in large curls over one shoulder. The strawberry hue was more apparent than normal and I dug it all. She was hot.

If I hadn't wanted to prove to myself that my semi-exile hadn't turned me into a mannerless beast, I'd have pushed her backward into the condo and taken her against the door. But I could be a damn gentleman for one night.

For a few hours.

Thank fuck the place I had scoped out ahead of time

was a steakhouse. Judging from her squeal of delight when I turned into the lot, I'd picked the right place.

We were heading toward the door, and she clutched my arm. I'd left my cane in the car. The parking area was mostly clear with minimal ice. I had her anchoring me, and I'd rather hold on to her above all else.

When we got to the door, a girl swung the door open, grin plastered in place. Her gaze dipped to my legs, no doubt taking in my limp, then rose to my face, right to the scar. Her attention skittered to Summer and she smiled brighter. "Welcome!"

She glanced shyly at me but couldn't meet my gaze.

My mood darkened. I was in a different town to escape this behavior. Had Summer noticed I scared this young girl?

"Two tonight?" the hostess said in her most chipper tone. Her gaze was locked on Summer, and it was like I no longer existed.

"Yes, please."

We were led to a two-top close to the bar. Bigger tables with families and kids took up the main area.

I helped hang Summer's coat on the back of her chair and pulled her seat out. Her sweet scent washed over me, reminding me of twisted sheets and low moans. My mood wasn't so sour that I didn't notice. She sat, giving me a demure smile that went straight to my cock.

The hostess continued to talk as I limped around her and took my coat off. "Our specials are the twelve-ounce ribeye with your choice of salad and potato and a surf-and-turf plate that is our most popular item on the menu. Can I help you with anything else before your server arrives?" She spared me a quick glance and sent her focus right back to Summer.

"No, thank you," Summer replied.

I glowered at my menu. This night had barely started. Summer was fielding all the questions. Was I that hideous? I thought I'd cleaned up well. I hadn't felt as good as I did tonight in years. Yet . . . the young girl could hardly look at me.

Summer had a big heart and her reaction to me was genuine, but I'd let her down. I couldn't explain how.

The burn of her stare finally caught my attention. I lifted my gaze and she arched a brow. Her eyes twinkled under the lights of the restaurant. She was getting more gorgeous as the night progressed.

"Why'd you get all moody?" she asked.

"I'm not all moody." I hadn't read a word on the menu, but I'd kept my feelings to myself. Yet I was still turning into a shitty date.

"Spill it, Dunn."

I set my menu down. "That young girl was scared of me."

Summer peered toward the hostess station. "Why do you think that?"

"She could barely look at me after she saw the scar."

A laugh sputtered from between her lips. "Seriously?"

"Why wouldn't I be? Didn't you notice?"

Summer tapped her finger on the table as she thought. "A few things. One, she's probably in college, so she's not *young* young. Two, she's probably paying more attention to me since women are more comfortable talking to the woman over the guy. Servers do it to get tipped better. Can't have me thinking she's into you." She ticked her finger up for the last point. "You think revulsion is why she can't look at you?"

"Fear."

She snickered again. "That's not why." She dug her phone out of her coat pocket, tapped the screen, and turned it toward me.

She'd put on the camera. I was looking at myself.

"That guy look scary? Or so insanely hot you're worried your panties will combust?"

The tips of my ears flamed hot. "Summer."

She kept the camera aimed at me. "I know which one I'm leaning toward." She wiggled in her seat.

Lust kindled stronger in my gut. The only woman I cared about being into me was sitting across from me. Didn't mean Summer was right. "I don't think—"

"You don't need to. I understand her better than you." She finally tucked the damn phone away. "I'm telling you, you're hot. That scar is alluring, yes, but it doesn't take the spotlight. The rest of you does."

My face was going to be beet red. "Point taken."

She smiled, triumphant. "Good."

"It's not like that in Bourbon Canyon."

She thought for a moment, her pink lips pursed. "They know you though. They've heard stories that probably make you sound feral. People are probably afraid of how you'll react." She leaned forward. "But I bet a lot of them still think you're handsome."

I might've cared about other women's opinions before Summer's wedding. I didn't now.

She tapped a finger on the table. "I, um, should tell you that I talked to Teller and he figured there was more going on between us at the cabin than clearing snow."

Shit. Teller knew I was fucking his sister? I'd have been mortified before. I hadn't been good boyfriend material then and Teller used to tease me. He would've kicked my ass when it came to one of his sisters. "What'd he say?"

"Not much. He was surprised, but he wasn't. I'm sure he had time to get used to the idea when he heard that I was stranded at your place a second time."

"You weren't very subtle."

"And you don't have scurvy."

I laughed but then anxiety flared. "How much of your family knows?"

"Mama figured it out. And Autumn. Well, I told her, but I had to talk to someone when I thought you hated me. I don't know how much they'll talk to each other about it, but I think you can trust my family to be discreet."

Meaning it shouldn't get to my mom and dad until I was ready to tell them. They were moving and changing their life, leaving the life I'd known with them. Maybe they wouldn't think I was an even worse son than they'd thought for poaching Eli's girlfriend.

When the server arrived, she wasn't much older than the hostess. She smiled widely at Summer, then turned to me, her gaze stroking over my scar, then dipping to my chest. Appreciation sparked in her eyes.

Well, shit. I was used to morbid fascination. Not . . . this.

The change in perspective was a nice pick-me-up. Perhaps I could do with making more small talk around Bourbon Canyon, so people wouldn't worry I'd come down the mountain in a rage.

How long had I let my insecurities control my life? Had they been a handy excuse that eventually became my own reality? A way to delude myself into never leaving home and avoiding the parts of life I couldn't reclaim?

When the server turned to me, professionally aloof after the first once-over, the rest of my tension drained.

"I'll have what she's having," I said.

When we were alone again, I reached across the table. There was a part of Summer's life I had considered on the drive to Bozeman. I still wasn't interested in drinking alcohol, I had no reason to, but spirits were a huge part of her life. Bourbon was in the Baileys' blood, and Summer and her sisters weren't immune. They'd grown up learning about the distilling process, tasting the product, and working in every facet of the industry.

If I wanted Summer, then I had to accept all of her. "When we're done, can I see where you work?"

Summer

Jonah parked in front of Copper Summit. "I've never seen this place."

"Even when you and Teller were close?"

He shook his head. His dark eyes reflected the lights of the parking lot around the warehouse portion. The nicer part of the building where we sold bottles and merchandise, along with the offices, was in the front. "There's no bar?"

"No, not here. We didn't even include a tasting room. We wanted a more practical place for high levels of packaging and distribution. If Wynter had moved to

Bozeman, maybe we'd have opened a small bar. Instead, we do tours and sell single-barrel spirits."

"Darin wanted to funnel tourism to Bourbon Canyon."

"Yep." I chuckled. "That too. Daddy was clever like that. Want a personal tour?"

"I want to see what you do."

I waved toward the distillery. "I do all of it." I might have sounded a little cocky, but I could step in anywhere from finding suppliers to packaging. "I can't drive the delivery trucks though. The ones that require more than a regular license anyway."

"I was going to say—I've seen you drive plenty of delivery trucks."

"Only the small ones," I purred. Daddy had put me and my siblings in every role.

Jonah gave a disgruntled grumble and opened his door. I got out and met him in front.

After I let both of us in and rearmed the security system, I faced the open area in front of us. "Off to the right are the walkways that link to the barrel houses. When Tate was in charge, he built it attached to the building with heat cycling, but we still use the barrel house at the end of the lot. Mother Nature is in charge of the heating and cooling in that building."

"The temperature predictability must be a nice change."

"It is, especially for our more commercial lines. Most years, we get enough temperature change for the barrels to really expand and contract and pull out flavors from the wood." I gestured to the nook with the security light partway down one of the walkways. "The bottling line is on the other side. That's when the attached aging house is nice. I'll show you where all the fun is."

I slid my hand into his. This wasn't the first time I'd been in the distillery by myself. Sometimes I spooked myself being alone, but tonight excitement coursed through me. When I'd first started, I'd led a few tours, but mostly I'd settled into running the place. Just because I could jump into every part of the process didn't mean I had much opportunity to do so.

"We'll end at my office." I took him through the big double doors. The smell of warm grain surrounded us. We were closest to the mash tanks. "Want to smell some yeast?"

"It might come as a surprise, but I've smelled it before." He still followed me, a faint smile on his face.

I flipped on the lights and led him to a tank bubbling with a yellowish mash. I took a deep breath. This was the smell of my childhood.

He leaned over and sniffed. "It's all coming back to me. Teller always called it yeast farts."

"Daddy hated that term." So of course, all my siblings and I thought it was hilarious.

He got a faraway look in his eyes. "I remember the smell outside the Copper Summit at home. I haven't thought of that until now."

"Yup. It's from drying the spent grain mash Daddy would have the guys haul to the ranch." Another smell of home for me.

"There's not a quiz at the end, is there?"

"No, this is a bonus. We don't usually take an actual tour through here. That's what the big picture windows are for. It gets too crowded and the distillers prefer to work undisturbed. We used to do Saturday tours, but Tate canned those, and I haven't brought them back. This location is more about the production."

"I'm a special guest?"

I shot him a grin. "A VIP's special guest." I led him through the mash tanks to the big copper stills.

He gazed up at the condensing pipes. "I . . . missed this." The loss in his voice tore at my heart.

"Missed what?" I led him out the way we'd come in. I didn't want his words swallowed by the cavernous room.

Once we were back in the main entry, he turned to look through the windows we kept pristine so the public could see the beauty of distilling. I threaded my fingers through his.

"Hanging out at Copper Summit. Not this one, of course, but I'd bum along with Teller when he had to stop at the one in Bourbon Canyon." His throat worked when he swallowed. "It's why I had a few bottles of bourbon in the house. I liked a drink once in a while, but I admired Copper Summit. I respected the family's passion, and part of me wished . . ."

I gave his fingers a gentle squeeze. "You wished what?"

"I wished there was something I felt that way about. I helped Dad enough to build the cabin, and then I had nothing else to do. When Eli graduated, I happily let him take over more. Dad needed the help. Then when Eli was gone, Dad was left with no one. I couldn't help him, and god, the relief gutted me. I didn't want a life doing what my dad did."

I stood, frozen for a moment. Eli had commented several times that he should go to college or he'd be following in Jonah's shadow all his life. Everyone had assumed that Jonah would take over, and then he couldn't. "You didn't want to work the ranch?"

His headshake was slow and guilt stamped his features. "No. It's too much for one person. Whether I was in charge or Eli, we'd both be tied to it, and I found every excuse to get away. It was like the accident was what I got for being a selfish bastard."

"You're not selfish, Jonah."

"I am." He pivoted. It was only the two of us in this giant building, but we stood inches apart. "Mom told me she and Dad are moving. You know how fucking irritated I was? I still am. They're not supposed to move. They're supposed to stay in the place where I grew up."

His parents were selling? He hadn't mentioned a thing all through dinner. "I think that would be a normal feeling. I'd be devastated if Mama moved."

"I also feel guilty because I'm relieved. I don't have to regret not being able to help Dad anymore. And because I was kind of a dick to Mom when she told me."

"I'm sure she understands." I brushed his forearm. "And you can always apologize."

His jaw was tight when he shook his head. "I have so much to apologize for. I've never been there for them. I claimed I didn't want Dad to have to babysit me, but that's only part of it. I could've gotten over that."

"Not always. I still think my brothers look at me like I'm that injured little girl who got dropped on their doorstep one night."

He pulled me into him. "They love you."

"And your parents love you." I kissed his lips. "Would your dad really feel like he could retire if you were working the ranch? Would he always feel like he had to be around to help you because he knows how hard it is?"

His brow furrowed. "He had to downsize."

I smoothed a finger over the crease in his forehead. "Eli's death had a way of making everyone take a hard look at their life."

"Is that what you did?"

"We're not talking about me, Mr. Dunn." I pressed another kiss to the corner of his mouth. Then one to the other side.

"I'm done talking about me."

I wouldn't push him. His world was changing again. I just hoped he didn't close himself away again.

He didn't move for a moment as I nibbled along his lips, then finally he reciprocated.

I hummed, glad to have his touch on me after having to look at his sinful pecs and wide shoulders in that shirt for hours. "You know," I said between kisses, "there's no security camera in my office and I've never done it there before."

"Then I have the perfect way to end this tour."

My buzzing phone woke me. Jonah's arm was draped over my waist. He twitched when my phone didn't stop. I groaned and rolled to grab it.

When I saw it was Wynter, I gasped and sat up. "Hi!"

A tired laugh met me on the other end of the line. "Hey, big sis. Want to come meet your niece later today?"

I let out a squeal and pumped my fist. "Mom and baby are okay?"

"Tired. Both Mom and baby," she answered.

"Is Dad okay?"

"He's over-the-moon-and-stars giddy," she said with a fatigued smile in her voice. "But also terrified. And in awe."

I clutched the sheet to my chest and shot a grin at a sleepy Jonah. His eyes were slits as he watched my reaction to hearing my baby sister had had a baby. The hair that was so nicely brushed last night was all over—from sleep, and from my hands buried in the strands throughout the evening and night.

"You sure you're doing well? Are you here in Bozeman?"

"Yes." There was a yawn. "To both questions. I was in labor most of the night, so we'll get to go home in the morning."

"I want to ask you so many questions, but I'm going to be bossy and tell you to rest. When do you want me to visit?"

"Mama's going to bring some lunch around noon. Any time after. The room isn't that big."

I didn't want to overwhelm her. I was bursting with excitement, but I also knew from Scarlett and various coworkers over the years how exhausting birth and the whirlwind of visits afterward were. "I'll make a quick stop to imprint myself as the favorite aunt, then I'll back off until you and Myles are rested. I can bring some dinner."

Her soft chuckle came through the line. "Myles has arranged three months of meals already."

I grinned. "He's my favorite brother-in-law for a reason."

"I'll tell him that," Wynter said.

He was my only brother-in-law. I wished Autumn could find this kind of happiness. Junie wanted success, but the last time I'd seen her truly comfortable with herself was with her high school boyfriend. I just wanted them happy and surrounded by good people. Like I was.

I glanced at Jonah. His eyes were closed, his breathing even, but he wasn't asleep. His fingers were absentmindedly rubbing my thigh.

"I'm going to let you rest. See you this afternoon. Love you, Wynter." I hung up and sighed, a delighted gust of air.

"You like being a big sister and an aunt," Jonah commented. His eyes were still closed.

"I do." I wanted to make my sisters aunts. They already were, but I wanted to see them with *my* kids. I wanted to watch our kids run and play, bicker and argue, play pranks with each other, and be their cousins' biggest support. "I was so excited when Chance was born, but Tate and his first wife were so busy it was hard to get together—and he even lived in Bozeman. Then they got divorced, and he moved home and it's been great. Scarlett makes sure to tell us when Chance has a musical or a play. Tate's shit about passing along that kind of information."

"How many kids does Tate have now?"

"Three. Brinley's almost the perfect age for tea parties, but she's kind of shy when we all get together and there's a ton of adults. Darin's not even a year old and he's fun, but he's not all about getting squooshed by Aunt Summer. He'd rather be eating pebbles off the ground."

"You have a big family."

"Yeah." I lay back down and he curled me into him, my back to his front. "It's pretty great."

He didn't respond. I ran my fingers between his.

Questions piled up on my tongue. The one I wanted to ask most was—did he want kids? Did he think a big family was great like I did?

I'd almost lost my entire family, and I *had* lost my parents. Then I'd gained a new set of parents who'd helped me deal with the pain of losing my birth parents. My siblings had doubled. I loved my big, opinionated crew.

Jonah and Eli hadn't been as close as my brothers were, and then Eli had been gone. Did a family like mine intimidate Jonah when he'd been on the fringes until the accident?

I didn't know the answers and something kept me from asking. Jonah had reclaimed a part of himself by coming here and taking me out, but he was just starting his journey. I'd been stuck waiting in the same spot since I'd finished college and started working at the distillery.

This thing between us was new. I'd wait before we delved into discussions about the future. And maybe when I brought up the topic, I wouldn't be so worried about the answers.

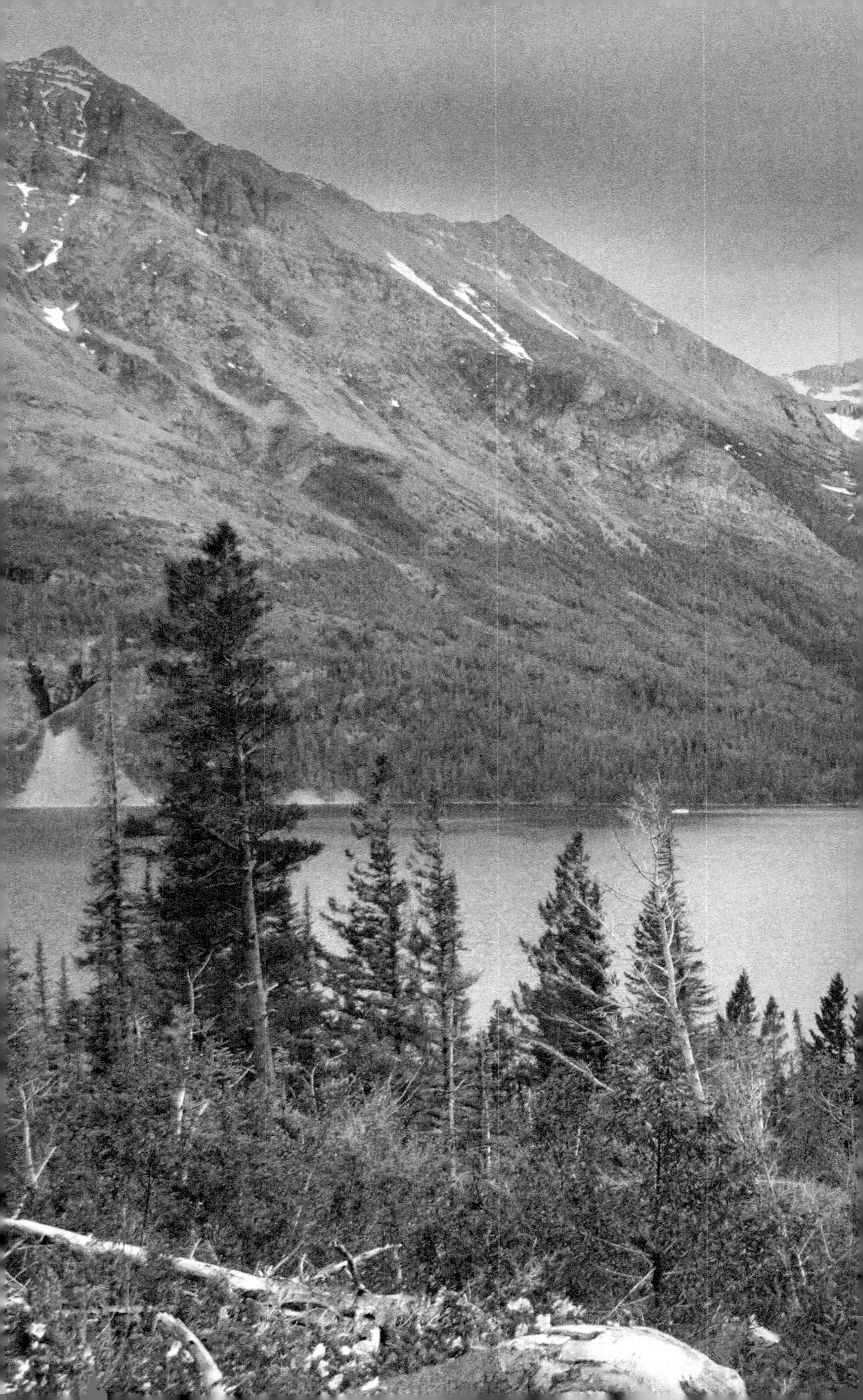

CHAPTER TWENTY-ONE

Jonah

Snow was melting and the weather forecast was clear. It would've been a good evening to travel and meet Summer after she got home from work. A month of going to Bozeman each weekend for dates and overnights had gone by. I wasn't behind on work, but I'd had to halt side projects and focus on my orders since I was gone every weekend. It had gutted me to tell Summer I had to stay home, but the bar-height table and four matching stools made from repurposed barrels wouldn't finish themselves. I needed to get them done and packaged. The delivery truck could pick them up Monday morning.

I would've had extra time, but I'd used up what cushion I had buried in Summer's sweet body on Saturdays and most Sundays. As it was, I would have to work through Saturday, barely finish Sunday morning, and spend all afternoon packaging each item. The payout was the biggest I'd commissioned. I couldn't fuck this up.

Yet I was worried about messing up what I had going with Summer. Would she think I was like her prick of an ex—too busy with work I thought was more important than her?

She had become very important to me. I couldn't let her down, but she also deserved more than a mountain bum.

I put a screw in the seat of one of the stools. The whir of the drill filled the silence. I placed another screw and the shop door opened. I jerked, the drill whirred, and the screw clattered to the floor. "Shit."

Who the hell was—

"Knock, knock." Summer pushed her sunglasses on top of her head. Her hair was back in a ponytail and more of her strawberry tint was growing out along her scalp. She smiled and sauntered toward me.

My pulse picked up and my dick came to attention. The weeks were long when she wasn't around. My podcasts weren't as interesting, and I didn't look forward to going into the house for a bite to eat.

I drank her in. I'd thought I'd have to get through the weekend and then another week before I could see her again. "Hey." I set the drill down. "You came?"

She smiled shyly and shoved her hands in her pockets, walking toward me. "I thought I could travel this time. I know you're busy and I don't have to stay in your house—"

I caught her around her elbow and tugged her toward me. "You'll be in my bed." I crushed her mouth with mine. She tasted of minty gum and heaven.

Her giggle passed right into me, and she clung to my

shoulders. She pulled away and gazed up at me with those luminous brown eyes. "So you're okay that I invited myself?"

"Since when haven't you invited yourself?"

She playfully swatted my shoulder. "Have you eaten yet?" I shook my head and she smirked. "I knew it."

When she wasn't in the house, I didn't care how often I went in to eat. If she wasn't on the other side of the table, the food was less appealing. "You don't have to cook for me."

"I want to, and I don't want to bother you. I know you're serious about getting this order done." Her gaze landed on the table. "Oh my god. Is that it?" She pulled away and I instantly missed her heat and her strawberries-and-sugar scent. She rounded the table, staring at it like she was in a museum and that damn thing was the special exhibit.

"You can touch it."

She flashed a grin my way. "I like touching your things."

I liked when her fingers were on my things.

"Wow." She clasped her hands behind her back despite my words. "*Star Wars?*"

"Yep." The client had sent collector's items of old *Star Wars* toys with specific instructions for how to place the X-wings and TIE fighters in the channel of epoxy between the slabs of walnut. Special orders were more stressful than pieces I made via my own inspiration, but this table had made me sweat a few times. My blood pressure wouldn't return to normal until I got notice that the set had arrived to the buyer unharmed.

I hadn't even taken pictures. If I put that shit on my website, then I'd get more requests. More precious objects to cover in epoxy. More stress. No, thanks. I didn't do this job to worry about epically fucking up someone's valuables.

"Impressive."

"Thanks," I said impassively. I was proud of the job, but a thousand what-ifs were running through my head and I wasn't used to the pressure. I didn't like it.

She pivoted to the chairs. I had four lined up against the wall, ready to be packaged. "Those are so cool."

I watched her swivel from one side to the other. She had to be picturing how it'd all go together.

"Seriously. That's some talent."

"I'm glad you got to see it. It's the last special order like this I'm taking."

Confusion lined her brow. "Why?"

"No more working with someone's family heirlooms." I nodded toward the table. "Those toys were the customer's dad's collectibles. He passed five years ago."

"That's such a sweet way to remember a parent's passion." She crossed to me again and tucked her arms under mine. "You made him something he'll treasure forever."

The anvil was back on my chest. "I just make furniture."

Her smirk was knowing, like she saw right through me to the way I'd cussed for eight minutes straight when I'd thought I'd fucked up an X-wing position. "Hamburgers tonight?"

"I don't have any thawed."

"That's fine. I have a salad to make while they're thawing."

I hadn't restocked the fresh veggie supply since she'd surprised me with groceries. She must've brought more like last time, this time without shocking me fresh out of the shower. "Keeping me scurvy-free, one salad at a time."

She swatted my ass. "I plan to keep those hips mobile too."

Summer

Since it was early and Jonah was spending his Saturday in the shop, I stopped at the bar inside Copper Summit to chat with Autumn. She usually arrived early to take care of the books. When I walked in, our neighbor Jason was sitting at the bar. Autumn had her head bowed over a tablet as she poked around.

When she glanced up, her lips curved. "Hey, you. Been a while."

I didn't often go more than a month without coming home, but having Jonah to myself without the town's opinions or my family hovering had been too alluring to pass up. Mama knew. Teller and Autumn. If they'd told the others, I hadn't heard about it. "I know. I'm a bad aunt and sister."

Jason craned his neck over his shoulder as I wove my way through the empty tables. By the end of the night, this place would be half full. During the summer, the bar would be packed, but early spring was only the beginning of peak tourist season.

"Look what the cat dragged in." Jason cackled.

"I made the cat work for it." I gave Jason a half hug. He smelled like fresh pine. His hat bumped my head and he chuckled and righted it. Jason made a bad first impression. A guy in grungy clothing with shaggy whiskers and a dirty hat who was having a drink minutes after the doors barely opened. He was fond of announcing it was five o'clock somewhere when he arrived.

That first impression was wrong. Jason liked to have a drink and shoot the shit with Teller or Tenor, whoever was around. He ranched all day, called it early once in a while, and came to Copper Summit to wind down. He was usually gone by six after one drink only, sometimes staying until seven if he caught one of my brothers. Jason's girls were sweet and he doted on them and his wife.

"I was just leaving." He pushed away. "Glad I could catch you. You girls are always a breath of fresh air." He strode out with strong strides that would also shock anyone who assumed he was a bar magnet, but Jason wasn't that much older than Tate.

Autumn took the cash he'd left behind and shook her head. "That guy slips me a five like he's Grandpa Bailey."

I giggled and slid onto a stool. I spun to watch Jason get into his pickup and drive away. "Who's got the fancy car? I thought for a minute Myles was escaping diaper duty to have a drink."

Autumn snorted. "I think you'll have to pry diaper duty out of his cold, dead hands."

I laughed around a spear of envy. Lucky Wynter. I caught Autumn's gaze and she smothered the same wistfulness.

I could ignore what I saw and how I felt, but I'd been away for what felt like forever and I'd been wrapped up too much in Jonah. "Someday, you'll find someone."

She shrugged and stabbed at the screen. Then she slipped the cover onto the tablet and sighed. "It's fine. I'm just . . . I don't know. Maybe I need to get another cat."

I stood and went around the bar. I dug through the bottom cupboard for one of the bottles we saved from our special batches. In this case, it was the first bottle of Summer's Summit ever produced. The line was sold everywhere, but Daddy had saved the first bottle for its namesake. I kept mine here, knowing I'd be with family if I had a drink from it.

Autumn already had two short glasses ready. When we drank together and commiserated, we had our bourbon neat. I poured a finger for each of us and tucked the bottle away, then returned to my seat.

I lifted my glass. "Here's to our future families."

"I feel like I should hand in my feminism card whenever I bemoan my single status." She returned the toast and we each took a sip. She closed her eyes. "Mm, that's good stuff."

Flavor burst over my tongue. Notes of caramel, vanilla, and smoky oak. All Copper Summit bourbon was quality, but my line was my favorite. I might be biased. "It's okay to want a family. It's okay to feel panic like it's not going to happen." It'd better be. I was feeling the same.

"I know. Logically, I do."

"I'm a boss babe, and I still want a family."

"You're also a nepo baby." She took another drink.

"True." I had walked right into my job, a position I enjoyed. If I'd had to work and compete for it, would I feel differently? Maybe, but I also knew how precious family was and I wanted my own.

"You're not exactly giving the best pep talk since you've been hot and heavy with Jonah."

I set my glass on the bar top and stared at the amber liquid. "It's only been a little over a month of actual dating. It's not like we've talked about marriage and kids."

"You talked about marriage, just not yours and his." She flashed a devious grin.

I mock glared at her. "Ha ha."

She kept looking at me as she took another sip. "Are you afraid to discuss the future with him?"

Yes. So scared. "I stormed into his life. He's gone from being a recluse to a sex god. What if he realizes what he's missed out on and wants to see others?" I took a gulp of my drink.

"Jonah was never a 'see others' type." She wrinkled her nose. "From what I remember, he was an 'if you can keep up' type. Jackie got tired of trying. He left any other dates in the dust."

I didn't think he'd return to his previous personality full force, but that didn't quell my concern. "His life is in a period of upheaval."

She polished off her bourbon, took my glass, and drained it too. That was fine. I didn't want to feel like I was drinking my worries away. "Sounds like another talk you're avoiding."

I scowled at her while she ran a small sink full of water and washed the glasses. "Another talk?"

"I think you've been neglecting to have important discussions with the men in your life. Like what you really want for a wedding."

"Boyd was different." The arch of her red brow cut me off. I'd still be in shitty relationships if I avoided hard discussions completely. Maybe I just delayed them. "I am not avoiding the talk. There's a right time to have one."

"Remember that one guy you dated before Boyd?"

I'd had a few serious boyfriends as an adult. Boyd had been the longest and the most serious, which was saying a lot since, looking back, our relationship had had as much substance as cotton balls. "Which one?"

She screwed her face up. "Um . . . Jerry? Gerald?"

"Garrett?" I said dryly.

She snapped her fingers. "Right. The guy who loved to smoke meat and drink beer."

"I like smoked meat."

"You didn't tell him that spending the weekend building DIY smokers was not your thing. And that you didn't like beer."

"I didn't like *his* beer."

Her gaze was steady. "My point is you didn't talk to him about something that might end the relationship."

"Smoked meat should not ruin a relationship." I scoffed.

"It would've with Jerry."

"Garrett."

"How convenient he moved for work, and when he hinted that you could move with him, you gave him a tour of the family distillery."

I had laid the family part on really thick. "Fine. I might be a little scared. Compared to Boyd—and *Garrett*—what I feel for Jonah is . . ." Everything. I wanted it all. If he didn't, then what?

She opened her mouth but raised voices caught our

attention. She snapped it shut and we both cocked our heads.

I couldn't make out what they were saying, but they were on the move. I swiveled in my seat to look out the window. Whoever it was hadn't left the building yet, but the guy with the nice car must be arguing with one or more of my brothers.

Finally, a guy shouted, "You cannot take advantage of an old drunk like that!"

"He's stone-cold sober when he's talking to us." That was Teller.

"You Baileys think you have the right to everything."

"If he doesn't sell to us, he'll sell to someone else." This was from Tenor.

"He'll sell to goddamn *me*." This time the stranger's voice was a low growl. "That land has been in my family for generations."

"You'll have to take that up with him," Teller said with more than a hint of defensiveness.

A door banged open. Autumn and I jumped.

A tall man's powerful strides ate up the pavement as he stormed to the sleek black car. His charcoal suit was tailored to highlight his long, lean body and wide shoulders. The fading sun glinted off his ink-black hair. He ripped the driver's side door open, and I was afraid he'd take the damn thing off. With a parting glare that should've melted glass, he slid behind the wheel and peeled away.

Teller's comments from over a month ago about buying more land ran through my head. I knew who that man was. "Gideon James."

Interest crept into Autumn's expression. "Whoa."

"Yeah." I had the hots for Jonah, but I could acknowledge when another man was fine.

"Whoa," Autumn breathed again. "I think my ovaries just packed their bags to follow him," she whispered.

I chortled. The spell of Gideon James was broken. For me at least. Autumn's starstruck gaze was still plastered to the window.

"Apparently," I said, "he has opinions about his dad selling to us."

She blinked. "What? We're doing business with that guy?" I didn't miss the interest in her voice.

"Not him. His dad must be selling without talking to him." Empathy welled for the man. If Daddy had sold it all before he'd passed, I'd have been upset. If he hadn't talked to us first, I'd have been devastated.

"That sucks." She shook her head like she was ridding herself of the last remnants of a spell. "He's going to hate each and every one of us."

Yep. Copper Summit might be buying the land, but each of my siblings and I were the owners.

Teller entered the bar, his expression tight. Tenor was behind him, pushing up his glasses. He gave me a half wave when he saw I was there.

"Looks like you two need a drink." Autumn put a mixing jar on the counter.

Teller blew out a breath and took the stool next to mine. "Make it girly. I want it so dainty that a guy like Gideon would throw a clot knowing I drank it after our talk."

Tenor sat on the other side of me. I settled in. I wouldn't have another drink, but I'd stay and let Autumn's advice filter into the recesses of my mind. Maybe she was right. But maybe it was too early to ask

Jonah what he wanted out of us. After all, he wasn't even willing to be seen on a date with me in Bourbon Canyon.

Jonah had packaged the tables and stools in protective covering and padding and hauled them to the loading door. My luggage was packed and I was ready to return to Bozeman. Mama had called while Jonah was finishing up in the shop.

He was cleaning up his workbenches and reorganizing tools. Buckets got stacked in the corners, and every once in a while, he'd stoop and pick up a stray screw or scrap of wood. He was meticulous about his workspace, but this was the most relaxed I'd seen him all weekend.

I sat on one of the stools he'd made himself with a swivel bottom and a gorgeous polished wooden seat that looked like it'd been made from stone. "You got it all done."

He nodded and grabbed the broom. Less tension rode across his shoulders, but it was still there. "Almost. When the delivery is signed off by the client, then I'm done."

I'd seen the table when it was completely finished. Stunning. Custom art. Jonah would be inundated with orders if he wanted. "You're really not doing another project like that again?"

"Nope." He shook his head and buzzed around the shop with the broom. I'd given him a massage last night after a full day of working on his feet. His limp had been more pronounced and he'd squirmed on the couch, telltale signs that he was achy. Today he was moving better. "The pressure sucks the fun out of the job."

I tried to equate his resistance with something from my world. We'd have one barrel to make a batch with and sometimes there were packaging catastrophes. Copper Summit had more barrels and could absorb a few disasters. Jonah was a one-man show and he'd take a failure personally.

But I couldn't get over how well the table had turned out, or how thrilled the customer would be when he saw it. "I think you did his dad's collectibles justice. Very few people could do that."

Instead of finding a dustpan, he grabbed a shop vac from the corner. "There are others." He sucked up the debris he'd swept together.

"What made you do this one?"

He didn't answer until he'd returned the shop vac to its spot. Everything had its place. Then he came toward me, his swagger more pronounced with his leg, but the more I was with him in the shop, the more I admired how he moved. His body was full of power and his limp was his signature swagger. I loved watching him do anything.

I had it bad.

He stopped in front of me and put his hands on the edges of the stool. "I accepted out of a moment of insanity that I blame on you."

My spine stiffened. I wasn't sure how much he was playing. "Me?"

"You're getting me out of my routine, and I decided to try something different."

Oh. That didn't sound awful. "Your customer is going

to be so happy. It's like a still shot from one of the movies."

"I know. I watched a few of those scenes over and over to make sure I got the positioning right."

I wasn't going to tell him how to do his job, but I wished he had more confidence in himself. He was an artist. But I wouldn't get anywhere pushing him, and I had come out here for a different reason. "Mama called."

"How is she?"

He always asked about my family when I told him I'd talked with someone. How were Wynter and Myles doing during their first month of parenthood? How was Autumn, since he hadn't seen her around town in a while? He'd heard Junie's song on the radio and had to tell me. He'd even asked about my brothers, but there was a thread of regret in his voice each time.

"She's good. She asked if you'd be interested in coming over for dinner next weekend."

His expression froze into a carefully neutral look, but his eyes were a storm. Surprise, uncertainty, and probably a little panic wove through his irises. "She wants me over for dinner next weekend?"

His question reminded me of when I interviewed applicants for job openings and they'd echo the question to give themselves more time to formulate a response. "Yes. Us. I can tell her to keep it small. Cruz and Lane don't even have to be there." They were the only others who lived at the house with Mama. The rest of us came and went.

Confusion wiped out the other emotions, then recognition set in.

"You've never met Lane and Cruz?" I'd talked about

them, and I'd assumed Jonah knew them aside from their names and how they pertained to the Baileys.

"Maybe I've passed them in the store."

"They were at the wedding. Probably flanking Mama. They can be a little protective."

The corner of his mouth lifted. "Good kids."

I laughed. "We all think of them as kids, but Cruz is twenty now and Lane is twenty-three. But, yeah, they've grown up a lot since working on the ranch. Anyway, we can keep it small. I can even tell Mama we'll take her to Curly's or something?"

I let my hope rise. I couldn't explain why a hometown date was important, but it was.

He wasn't jumping on the invite and my anxiety was ratcheting up with each minute. He knew Mama. He'd been willing to venture to my wedding—for his own personal reasons, but still . . . my wedding. Yet a family dinner was giving him pause.

Was the family part of it scaring him off? "We don't have to."

"No." He shook his head. "No, I'll go. It's just been years since I've been at your mama's."

Oh. He was correct. It'd be like going back in time and he'd think about how much had changed. "Should I tell her no?"

"I'm not turning down Mae Bailey."

I smiled, relieved. If he wasn't willing to disappoint Mama, then he must be willing to start telling people about us. "I can tell Mama to keep it small. To ease you in."

"Right. No, it'll be fine."

Why did he sound like he was convincing himself? I stuffed my worry away. He said he'd do it and he would.

I'd reserve any concern until after the dinner. "You mind if I stay next weekend?"

"Absolutely not."

His lack of hesitation went a long way to calming my nerves. He wanted me and I wanted him and that'd be enough. For now.

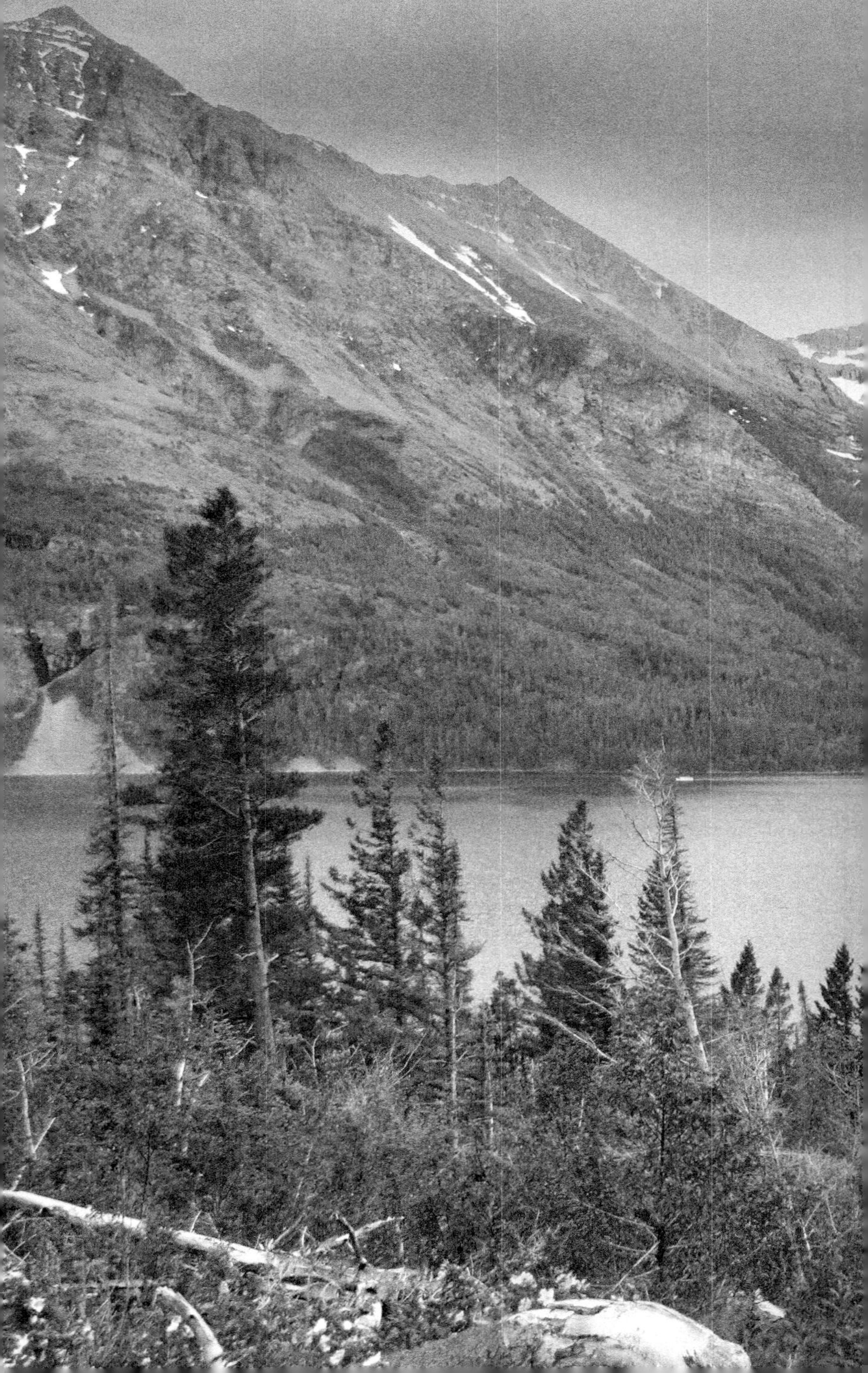

CHAPTER TWENTY-TWO

Jonah

When I pulled up in front of my parents' place, a giant Conex was sitting on the concrete pad in front of the house.

"What the hell?" I got out and stared at the giant metal box. A little over a month ago, Mom had told me they were thinking of selling to Rhys Kinkade. Were they clearing out already? We were at the beginning of April, but there was still snow on the ground.

The sight took the focus off the nerves that had been tightening my gut all the way out here, but only for a moment. I'd come for a reason that I wasn't sure they'd like, but I had to talk to them before word got out in town.

Dad came out of the house with his silver travel mug of coffee. His dark brows rose when he saw me. "Jonah? Hey."

Guilt wound through my intestines at his surprise. "Hi, Dad. You heading out?"

"Eh, I've got a few errands to run." Meaning his coffee-and-chat time at the gas station. I had hoped to catch him when he was returning, but like me, he was getting a late start. I'd had to wait for the delivery truck to arrive and, not as painstakingly as I would've liked, load the custom table and stools. "But I can stay a minute. I heard I missed your last stop."

Which was over a month ago.

Time could fly in my isolated world. "I was hoping to talk with you and Mom. Is she around?"

A line of worry etched Dad's brow. I'd stopped in out of nowhere. They were moving, and I'd been so wrapped up in Summer and work that I hadn't reached out to see what they needed help with.

They probably thought I was still upset about the house and property getting sold, but I was actually getting over it. They were aging and had to do what was right for themselves.

"She's inside. Come on in. She might've even left some coffee."

I followed Dad in. Mom was at a cupboard in the kitchen and an open box was on the floor next to her. She glanced over her shoulder and did a double take. "Oh. Jonah."

More surprise. Did I really not come over that often? I tried to think of the times I'd been here to have a meal or just to talk. There were a few times I'd come home after I was out of the hospital, mending as much as my body had been capable, but they'd jumped around to help me navigate the house, and when they hadn't been jumping, the place had been quiet. My brother hadn't been home, he'd never be home again, and the silence had gotten to me.

"Got any coffee left?" I went to the cupboard next to the one she'd been cleaning out. I paused when I opened the door. Only a few glasses and mugs remained. Everything else had presumably been packed. I took the same mug I had used last time. "I didn't realize you were moving already."

"Sort of." Mom poured what was left in my mug and set about making a fresh pot. "Rhys would like to move in before the next school year starts, so we're aiming to be out in July." She waved the empty pot around the room. "There'll be cleaning and stuff, but he said not to worry too much." She paused and her brows drew together. "I, uh, have been meaning to ask you if there was anything you wanted. I know you don't like the idea of us leaving."

I still didn't, but the thought didn't bother me like it had before. "I'm fine with your decision. Yes, it came as a shock. This place has been a constant, but we all know how things can change. I have my life and a job, and you two need to do what's best for you."

Dad slid into his standard chair at the table. "That's a relief to hear."

Mom's smile was hesitant. "I could tell the news bothered you."

"I might have to come around more so you can update me."

"I'd like that," she said softly. "I'm always afraid I'm bugging you with my calls."

"No, don't ever worry about that. I was working all weekend, so that's why I didn't answer your texts right away." I almost drew out my phone to show them pictures of the table and chairs that were en route to their owner, but I hadn't taken any. Damn. "So, how much do you have to do before Rhys is the official owner?"

Would they need my help with any of it?

"He told us not to bother with the painting or any remodeling," Dad said. "He'll do what he wants to the place."

Mom's expression turned wistful. "I get so much joy thinking about this house being filled with kids' laughter again. Can you imagine? He has two girls. Pink everywhere."

Dad leaned back in his chair and propped a hand on the back of Mom's. "Girls these days don't only like pink."

"Well." Mom shrugged but didn't lose that wistful expression. "I'll be grateful that this place can have energy within its walls again."

The sense of failure hit deep. Mom and Dad had wanted a vibrant home full of grandkids. They'd wanted both sons alive and well, and they only had one son who was alive and for so long hadn't been well.

Mom waved her hand through the air like she was scattering away the happy images she'd just painted with Rhys and his girls in the house. "Anyway, you said you wanted to talk?"

Tension cramped my stomach, making the hot coffee sear the lining. "Yeah, I did." I took another sip and embraced the burn all the way down. Ordinarily, especially after what Mom had said, this would be good news. But I didn't know how they'd interpret it. "I'm . . . seeing someone."

Both parents blinked at me. Dad set his cup down

with a thunk, a crease forming in his forehead. Mom continued to blink, her lips turning down.

"It's not Jackie, is it?" Dad asked. He held both his hands up. "I mean, I'm sure she's nice and all, it's just that—"

"It's Summer," Mom uttered quietly, her gaze dropping to the table. It wasn't a leap for her to make the connection. "You and Summer have started seeing each other."

I dipped my head down as sheer relief flashed across Dad's face, followed by a furrowed brow and a slight frown.

"Summer Kerrigan?" Dad asked, like he wanted to make damn sure he was correct before forming an opinion.

"Yes."

"You two got close when she was stranded at your place?" he asked, perplexed.

"Uh, no, not like you'd think." Grateful I had a chance to explain that I wasn't a creep who'd swooped in on a brokenhearted bride, I explained. "She came out again a few weeks later to bring me some groceries for the storm. She doesn't think I eat enough fresh produce."

Mom grunted her agreement. She'd rarely seen inside my fridge, but she also dropped off garden staples at regular intervals. I'd thought she'd been using the delivery excuses to snoop on me, but based on Summer's reaction, no, Mom'd had the same worry.

Maybe I would've gotten fucking scurvy without either of them interfering.

"She got stranded again," I continued. "I didn't know she was coming and slipped on a puddle of water, and she stayed to make sure I was okay. By the time I reassured her I was fine, the wind picked up and she was stuck. Again."

Dad's eyes narrowed, reminding me of when Eli and I were kids and the tractor that had just been fixed broke down. Dad had thought we were up to hijinks, but both me and Eli had been cutting hay and behaving, for once.

"Oh. That's . . . nice." Mom pondered her coffee. "She always was a nice girl."

"Yeah." I didn't know what else to say. "We realize that people will remember she and Eli were a thing." I wouldn't mention the breakup. My parents had been through enough. "We're taking it slow, but eventually we'll be seen together and people will know."

"That you and her are a thing?" Mom's lips pressed together. "She's only two months out from her wedding."

Barely. "I know." I had no argument. People might say horrible shit about Summer for moving on so quickly.

"Then slow is prudent." Mom's reassuring smile crinkled the corners of her eyes but didn't reach the irises. "You're happy?"

I nodded. "I've been out. With her. Bozeman, mostly. But Mae invited me to dinner at her place this weekend."

"That's nice," Mom uttered. "Eli was crazy about her." Her guilty gaze slid toward me. "But that was a long time ago."

"Sometimes, it feels like yesterday."

Dad cleared his throat. To them, bringing up Summer meant remembering Eli. To all of us, that made losing him feel like yesterday.

"You look good." Mom tipped her head, inspecting me. "She the reason for the change?"

"Sort of. She didn't ask for it." I ran my fingers over my trimmed hair. "I've been getting my hair cut in Bozeman when I'm there. The anonymity is nice." Intoxicating. Only passing glances that skipped over me.

"Once people start seeing you more," Dad said, spinning his mug in his hands, "they'll quit talking. I spent years never going inside the gas station. I finally ventured in, endured the stares, did it again, and again. Now?" He chuffed out a breath. "I'm one of them."

"I thought you were just running errands," I teased.

Both parents chuckled, and for the first time in over fifteen years, I felt like the old Jonah. The guy who hadn't let down his brother, his parents, and his best friend. I was the guy who hadn't yelled at Summer when she'd needed just as much understanding and support as I had.

I let myself soak in the joy, in the comfort for a moment, and then I caught sight of that packing box again.

I might've gotten a haircut, I might have even been out on a date, but I was still that guy who'd retreated from the world and everyone who cared about him. It was easy to be different, to think I was different wandering around Bozeman, where nobody knew me. But at home? I was trying to change, but Bourbon Canyon was changing too. And it was changing a hell of a lot faster than I was.

Summer

. . .

I was staying with Jonah again, and we drove to Mama's together. I'd asked her to keep the dinner casual and as private as possible, and true to her word, it was just us.

He parked in the spot behind the garage door that most visitors parked in. The back of the large log cabin wasn't as impressive as the rest of the house and it was hard to judge the true size of the place from this angle. Perhaps that was why I preferred to enter through the back.

When my sisters and I had been brought here the first time, the house had loomed dark and intimidating. I'd still been in pain and scared, but as soon as Mae had opened the door and appeared so joyous to meet us, a lot of the fear had left. After that, the main entrance and exit had been the back door, and the home had started feeling like ours.

I liked that the appearance never changed, only the variety and number of cars parked outside. Cruz's pickup and Lane's new truck were gone. I didn't know where Mama had run them off to, but I was grateful for the space.

Jonah had been good about being out and about in Bozeman. He actually seemed to enjoy going to places where he wasn't recognized and he blended in, instead of one of the locals everyone was poised to comment on.

We hadn't been out together yet in Bourbon Canyon, but Mama's place was closer. Tonight was a step in the right direction.

Mama opened the back door as we approached. "Come on in, kids. The roast is almost done."

I walked into the warmth of the kitchen. This room

was always hotter than the rest of the place because it was where Mama spent much of her time making coffee, preparing meals, peeking out the kitchen window that overlooked the barns and shops and pastures that were closest to the house.

"Can I help with anything?" I shrugged out of my coat and Jonah took it from me. I gestured to the hooks on the wall behind the door. He put our jackets there.

I pushed up the sleeves of my top. It might be early April, but sweater weather wasn't quite over. I'd wanted to dress up just a little. Tonight was like a date. I wasn't nervous in the same way I usually was when introducing a date to my parents. I knew Mama loved Jonah. She knew his story, and she understood his trauma. She'd worked with too many foster kids to not know the effects someone's childhood had on them. She was supportive and understanding.

I was more worried that Jonah would decide that doing anything more than dinners and casual sex in Bozeman wasn't worth it. That he'd rather have his quiet days in his shop and not be bothered. He'd rather be the mountain ghost kids murmured about—poor Eli Dunn's older brother, who kept to himself and made gorgeous furniture.

"Go ahead and grab something to drink." Mama went to the oven. "Help yourself and have a seat at the table."

I went to the fridge and pulled out two cans of Coke. Jonah nodded his thanks, and I led him to the table that Mama had shortened to fit only four to six people. With all its leaves in, the thing could seat twelve, plus more if we added a card table at the end for kids. We'd done that a few times when we had foster siblings in or when one or more of us had friends over, and we were close to doing it again now that Mama was getting grandkids.

Place settings were already in three spots, and a leafy green salad with colorful chopped veggies rested on one end. I slid onto a chair and patted the seat next to me. He caught my eye when he sat, and I snickered.

His brows drew together. "What's so funny?"

"You look like Mama's going to ask if you're defiling her daughter."

He leaned over. "I am. That's why I'm so goddamn nervous."

"Mama supports a good defiling."

The tips of his ears turned pink. "I didn't need to know that."

"All right." Mama bustled in, her floral hot pads gripping a steaming pot. She set the food on a trivet. A sliced roast with potatoes and carrots.

Jonah arched a brow at me. "Now I know where you get your recipes from."

Mama glanced between us.

The tips of his ears stayed red. "Summer has made me the same thing a few times."

Mama beamed. She was a progressive woman, but she also liked when her kids picked up their domestic talents from her. "I bet it tasted amazing. Summer's a good cook."

"Especially with fresh veggies. I heard those are critical."

It was my turn to blush.

We filled our plates. The tinkle of silverware filled the air.

"This is really good, Mae," Jonah said.

Mama's proud grin never got old. She showed her

love in many ways, but feeding others was at the top. "I hope you don't mind if I ask . . . How are your parents doing? I heard they're moving."

I glanced at Jonah. He was nodding while finishing chewing. He hadn't spoken much about the move, or about his mom and dad.

He wiped his mouth with a napkin before he spoke. "They're selling the main acreage the house is on and two pastures, maybe more. I bought the land my house is on when I built the shop."

"They have a buyer already?" Mama asked.

"Rhys Kinkade."

They were selling to Rhys, and Jonah hadn't thought to tell me? "Junie's ex?"

"They were only high school sweethearts," Mama said like she was calming me down.

Only. If people had been certain Eli and I would walk down the aisle, then they'd have bet their life's savings on Junie and Rhys. They'd been hot and heavy from middle school to their graduation year. Then Junie had left to make a career in music, and Rhys had stayed behind. He'd gotten married, and then his wife had left him and the girls. I didn't know the story behind their split—actually, I didn't know why he and Junie had broken up either, but we all assumed she'd wanted to tour and become a big name and he'd wanted to keep his roots in Bourbon Canyon.

"I didn't remember they'd dated," Jonah said.

I gawked at him. "They used to hang out with me and Eli."

Jonah's guarded gaze caught mine. "I was in my own world."

Mama's chuckle smoothed over the tension between

us. "You and Teller and the other boys were usually gone doing your own thing." Her smile was kind. "I'd say up to no good, but we all know that wasn't true. Darin and I used to joke that our income went up when you boys started hunting. We could sell more beef and eat off the wild game and birds you all caught."

The corners of Jonah's eyes pinched. "I suppose that still happens for you?"

Mama shrugged. "You know. Life happens. Tate moved, and now he's back, but with three little kids, he doesn't have time to hunt." She snorted. "Chance sure isn't interested. He knows how, but only because he claims it's an important skill if the apocalypse happens."

The corner of Jonah's mouth tipped up. He was reserved tonight, like he was afraid to open up around Mama. This had to be weird for him.

"Teller and Tenor don't get out as much as they used to," Mama continued, "but they're also more involved in the ranch and distillery than ever since Darin passed. I'm glad they had the years of freedom they did."

His jaw tightened. "Yes."

"More potatoes?" Mama asked. "I'm going to blink and it'll be time to plant more. I hope we have a good growing season like we did last year."

What had bothered Jonah? Had Mama sensed his discomfort and changed the subject?

I was worrying too much. But Jonah and I might be navigating our relationship on two different timelines, and if that was the case, I didn't know if I should slow down. If I pressured Jonah to speed up, we might only reach the end sooner.

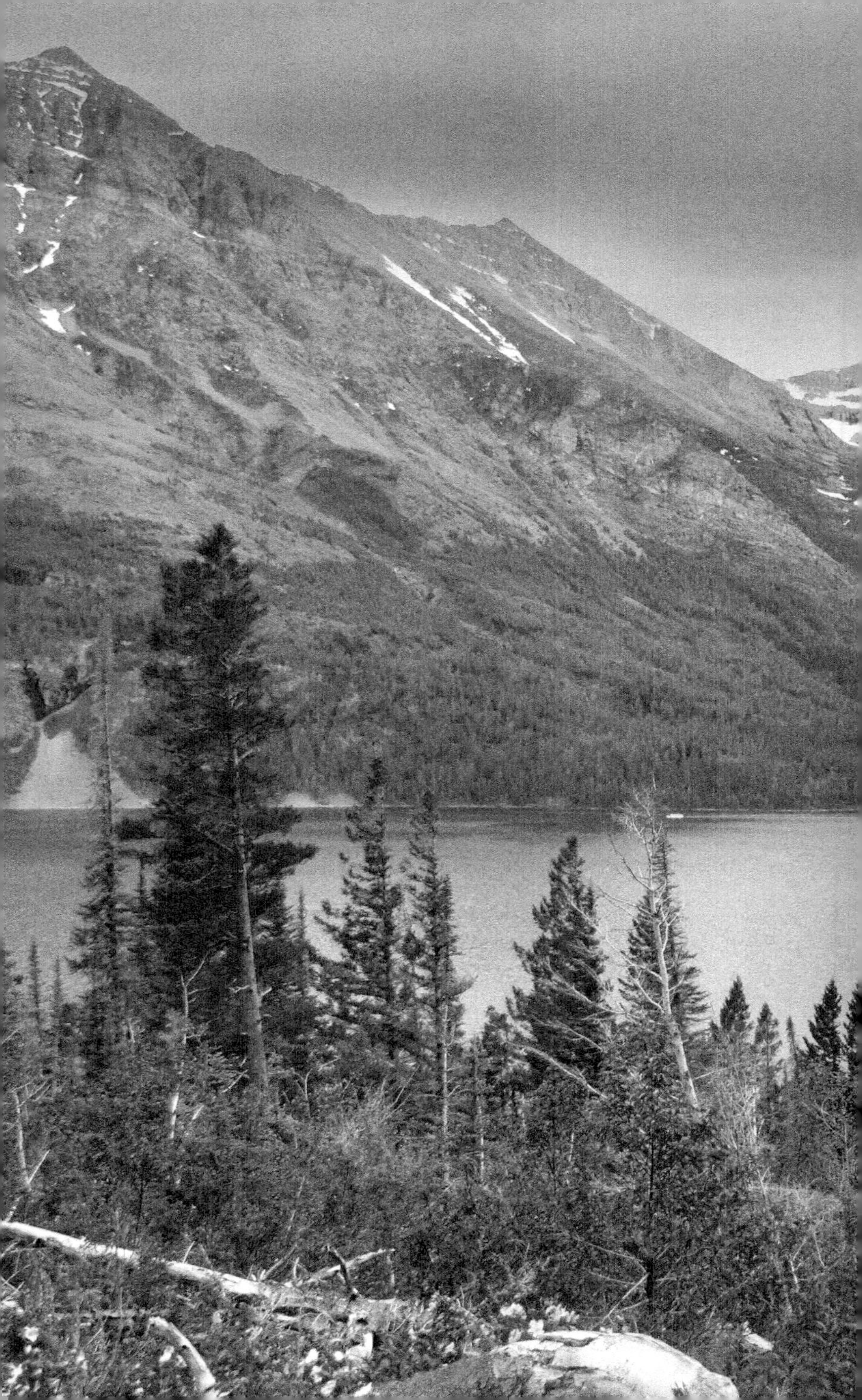

CHAPTER TWENTY-THREE

Jonah

Summer was tucked into my side in my bed. I stroked circles on her shoulder. I was drowsy in my post-orgasmic state, but I missed these moments of cuddling whenever she went back to her life in Bozeman, maybe even more than the sex.

She shifted against me and turned to face the ceiling. Usually, she cuddled into me and drifted off to sleep first. I'd succumb to sleep after listening to her even breathing and marveling that she wasn't a dream. Tonight, she was restless.

"What's on your mind?"

"Nothing," she said quickly.

"Summer."

A sigh left her. She rolled into my side and put her head on my chest. "Thank you for coming to eat with Mama tonight."

"Anytime." Oddly enough, I meant it.

"But something was bothering you."

Yeah. It was bothering me. Sure, I hated the reminder that my going off the grid had affected the Baileys. Mae might've thought she was joking about saving money with the hunting efforts of me and her boys, but she wasn't wrong. When she had a minimum of seven kids to feed, besides herself and Darin and additional foster kids coming in and out, the meat we'd hunted had been important to filling her freezer. They'd been able to take an extra head or two of cattle to the market, which translated to thousands of dollars.

Then I'd dropped off. Could I have figured out how to hunt as effectively? To contribute like I had before?

I didn't know, and everyone had moved on. The Baileys weren't hurting for money, but Teller had said once that the family fortune was tied up in the land and the distillery. Feeding all those mouths had been a challenge.

Summer was quiet, waiting for my response. I thought of how to tell her without saying I felt like a loser.

"It's different. I'm different. She's different." Teller probably was too, but I hadn't talked to him in a long time. He'd rightfully given up on me.

"We would've been anyway, accident or not. No one's the same at forty and at twenty-five."

"Thirty-nine," I said, grasping for the distraction.

She giggled and patted my chest. "What should we plan for next weekend?"

"You've been here two weekends in a row. I can go to Bozeman."

"Oh. Okay." There was still something in her voice I couldn't identify. A hint of nervousness? Of disappointment? How was I letting her down while making plans to see her?

"What if we went out tomorrow?"

My chest constricted. "What do you mean?"

"I miss Curly's buns."

"I hope you're talking about food and not that crusty man's ass."

"He is crusty, but we all agree his buns are the best in the state."

"I haven't had many other buns in the state. Maybe we need some road trips to verify the claim." I wouldn't ask her to fly anywhere, ever.

"Or we can just go have Curly's." Her words were quiet enough that this must be what she'd been worried about bringing up.

She wanted to go out. I wanted to go out, but not in Bourbon Canyon.

"I told Mom and Dad about us."

She propped her elbow on the mattress. The nightlight in the hallway outlined her features. "You did? Why didn't you tell me?"

"It was anticlimactic, and I didn't tell them about you and Eli."

She settled back into my side. "Do you think they should know?"

I thought for a moment. I had been resistant to tell them. I wanted to protect them. But in the end, that wasn't why I'd kept my mouth shut. "It's not my story to tell."

"Right." Another long exhale gusted over my chest.

The thought of confessing to my parents bothered her. Which meant she thought they should know. She thought they should have all the information, but she didn't want to hurt them either. She didn't want them to react like I had.

But she did want to go to Curly's. My gut churned at the thought. "It might not be the quiet dinner we usually get."

"I'm not a stranger to the stares, Jonah. I'm one of the Bailey girls who was in the car when their parents died. People called us the Bailey girls so much, only our teachers knew we had different last names."

"I'm sorry for what you went through, but it was a long time ago."

"Eight years."

"What?"

"My parents' accident was eight years before yours and Eli's."

Shit.

She shifted to her belly again, up on her elbows. "Eight years for the talk to die down, only to have Eli make a reckless decision that got him killed and almost killed you. Then I was the poor Bailey girl who'd lost her fiancé. You would've sworn I was halfway down the aisle when he crashed."

I winced at her blunt statement.

"And then," she continued, "there was my actual nonwedding. Might not have been the biggest news otherwise, but it made all the old shit resurface. You don't think when I bought your groceries that I got stared at? That when I went to the clinic for STD testing that the nurses gave me pitying looks? I let them think my ex-fiancé was a cheating asshole because it's easier than admitting I stayed with the wrong guy for far too long."

I couldn't wince again, but her direct hit went

through my chest wall. She was bunching Eli into that group, but her exes weren't the point she was making. She'd been talked about and stared at her whole life and she hadn't become the recluse of Bourbon Canyon. She'd retreated to the mountains to heal like I had, but then she'd gone back to her life.

I had yet to fully emerge.

The thought of letting Summer down closed off my airway. I could go to a goddamn restaurant, have some buns, and give zero fucks about the gossip.

"Tomorrow, sunshine. I'll take you out."

Summer

The parking lot at Curly's was full. Normal for a Saturday night. I shouldn't have pressured Jonah. I could see now that my request was linked to my need to determine where we were.

Jonah made me feel special, but when we only went out in Bozeman and no one in our hometown, where he still lived, knew about us, my brain wanted to tell me that what we had didn't go much further than sex.

He wasn't any of my exes who didn't really care to get to know me or what I wanted. He asked about my work, and he was interested in my family. I liked getting introduced to his woodworking passion, but we still lived very separate lives.

I could no longer use the excuse that everything was new. We'd known each other most of our lives, and we'd been sleeping together for six weeks. It was time to date. To move us forward.

Yet my guilt wasn't listening. I'd pushed him and he wasn't comfortable. I didn't want to be the cause of his stress.

"If you're really not ready for this, we can wait."

"No. You want to eat at Curly's; there's no reason we can't eat at Curly's." His shoulders were tight. He pulled into a parking spot at the edge of the lot. His cane was in the back, but I already knew he wasn't going to use it. Not for his first outing with me when there was no more ice in the parking lot.

He got out, his body as graceful as a wooden plank, stiff and unidirectional.

I rounded the back of the pickup and met him by the driver's corner of the tailgate. "You look good," I said, curling my fingers through his. I wasn't just pumping him up. He was dressed similarly to the first time we'd gone out in Bozeman. The nights could still get cool, so he was wearing the same green Henley and a nice pair of jeans with his cowboy boots. His hair was combed off his forehead and to the side, with an off-center part that was surprisingly trendy for a guy who didn't give a shit about fashion.

"You're sexy as hell," he growled. "But you always are."

I might've worn one of the honeymoon dresses I'd gotten for Bali. I had to pair this one with a lilac cardigan, and I wore ankle boots instead of sandals, but I'd caught Jonah eying my legs several times, even with as tense as he was.

A man and woman younger than us exited the restaurant, laughing and talking. I didn't recognize them, but they glanced at us and went back to chatting with each other.

Jonah relaxed only slightly.

I rubbed his forearm, and we continued to the entrance. He opened the door for me, giving me a hot, but tight once-over, his gaze dipping down to my legs like he needed to fortify himself before going in.

The hostess smiled brightly at us. She had to still be in high school.

If Curly were seating us, he might put me and Jonah up front. The mountain man had chosen Curly's establishment for one of his only eating-out experiences. But this hostess likely didn't know what the Baileys looked like and didn't care.

"Two tonight?"

"Yes," Jonah said so gruffly I was afraid he'd startle her. She didn't miss a beat. The restaurant was loud this time of night.

She led us past the muffin display—and where I'd had the run-in with Jackie. It'd been months. I had to get over this jealousy.

At the same time, I commiserated with her. Had I felt what she'd felt when Jonah wouldn't commit? That had been before the accident. Had they both just been too young, or would he have never committed?

I stuffed my questions away. Tonight wasn't the night. This was about getting Jonah used to being in public in Bourbon Canyon.

And a little bit about announcing us as a pair.

Okay, a lot.

His fingers clutched mine as we followed the hostess. We passed a retired math teacher from high school. She smiled at me, but when her gaze landed on Jonah, she *gawked*.

There was no going back.

A few booths later, I spotted Jason. His grin was broad. "Summer Kerrigan, how are y—" His eyes went wide. "Jonah?"

Jonah nodded, his fingers cinching around mine tighter until I couldn't feel my fingertips. "Jason."

"N-nice to see you out." Jason's wife and his oldest daughter stared at us. And our linked hands. "To see you both."

I smiled as we passed. "Have a good night."

Was I imagining it, or had the noise level in the place diminished? There were still people talking. Those who didn't know Jonah or me, who didn't know his past, and especially those who didn't know how Jonah and I had been connected through his brother.

Those who did? Wide-eyed gaping. Hushed murmurs and whispers. The prickle of their attention danced down my back, and I suppressed a shiver. How was it going for Jonah?

Finally, we reached a table toward the back. Only a lap through the main dining area would have taken us past more people.

Jonah pulled out a chair that would have my back toward the crowd.

"You can sit here," I said only loud enough for him to hear.

"No chance you're going to be their dinner show."

I placed a kiss on his lips. "Thank you."

His mouth quirked. "That was some fuel you added there."

I chuckled and caught the hostess's confused blink.

"Busy place," I said to keep her from standing awkwardly even longer.

Her nod was full of knowing authority. "Saturdays are always like this. What can I get you to drink?"

"Water," Jonah and I said at the same time.

When she left, his chest rose with a deep inhale. "This actually isn't so bad."

"Once she returns with the buns, it's only going to get better."

"It can't be better since I'm out with you."

I melted inside. Completely. These were the times he made me feel so damn special. And tonight, we were out where everyone could see. Anyone who wanted to gossip would know by noon tomorrow, after the church crowd had had time to talk, that Jonah and I had been out together. That I'd kissed him.

They'd know Jonah was a real man, with a real life, and he was mine. I hoped he always would be.

Jonah

We had just finished our food when Rhys Kinkade stopped at the table. He was as tall as me and his dark hair was flattened like he'd worn some sort of hat all day until he'd decided cooking dinner was too much. He had two girls in tow and they both blinked at me until Summer smiled and waved at them.

"Hey, Summer," Rhys said and turned his attention to me. "Hi, Jonah. I don't know if you know who I am—"

"I've been a hermit, but I haven't forgotten everything," I said congenially.

He chuckled. "Good to know. I just wanted to make sure everything's okay on your end with the purchase of your parents' property."

He was making sure his new neighbor wouldn't be a disgruntled recluse who held a grudge and terrorized him or his kids in his new house. I could've bristled, but he had the balls to ask me, and he was doing it thoughtfully and respectfully.

"I have no worries. Mom and Dad have made up their mind and there's nothing from their place I want that I haven't already been given."

"Good." He relaxed and his smile was less strained. "That's good. But you know, if you think of anything, just give me a call. I can give you my number. Your parents have been excellent about the whole deal, but just in case."

I dug out my phone. If Summer's kiss didn't shock the hell out of anyone paying attention, then trading numbers like I was a normal guy with friends would do the trick. I programmed his number in.

To keep a weird silence from descending, I grasped for a conversational topic. I wanted to make every part of this night good for my sexy date. "Mom's looking forward to having the house full of kids."

Rhys smiled again. He was the type of adult I should've turned into. A family guy who wanted to expand and grow with his kids. "That's what she told me. 'Who would've thought? Pink?'"

That was pretty close to the exact words she'd said to me. "She's not getting the kids or the pink from me, so I'm glad you and your girls can help her out."

The youngest girl with the ringlets in her ponytail tugged on his hand. "Daddy. I have to pee." She did a little dance in place.

Rhys must've recognized the urgency. He grimaced. "Yes, sorry." To us, he said, "Thought I could spare a couple minutes, but I pushed it. Nice to talk to you." He nodded at each of us and rushed off with his kids.

I took a pull of my water. The stress that had ridden my shoulders since Summer had asked to go out last night was gone. Tonight had been pleasant. Summer made all the difference, but it wasn't just that. I *wanted* to be out. I wanted to get to know people like Rhys. I wanted to see what he did with my childhood home. I wanted to hear how enthused Mom was about little girls filling the place.

When I met Summer's gaze, there was a line in her forehead. Her ripe lips were turned down as she considered me.

"Everything okay?"

She didn't immediately answer, but she shook herself. "Yeah, no, I'm fine."

I liked to think I knew her well enough to call bullshit. She wasn't fine. Something about the exchange had bothered her and she wasn't saying. I'd have to wait until we left.

I was riding high on nothing but steak and water—and excellent buns. I was out with my woman, and for now, all was right in the world. Finally. I wasn't going to go searching for problems.

I'd been so worried, but everything about tonight was surprising me in the best way. I couldn't wait to end it with her in my arms.

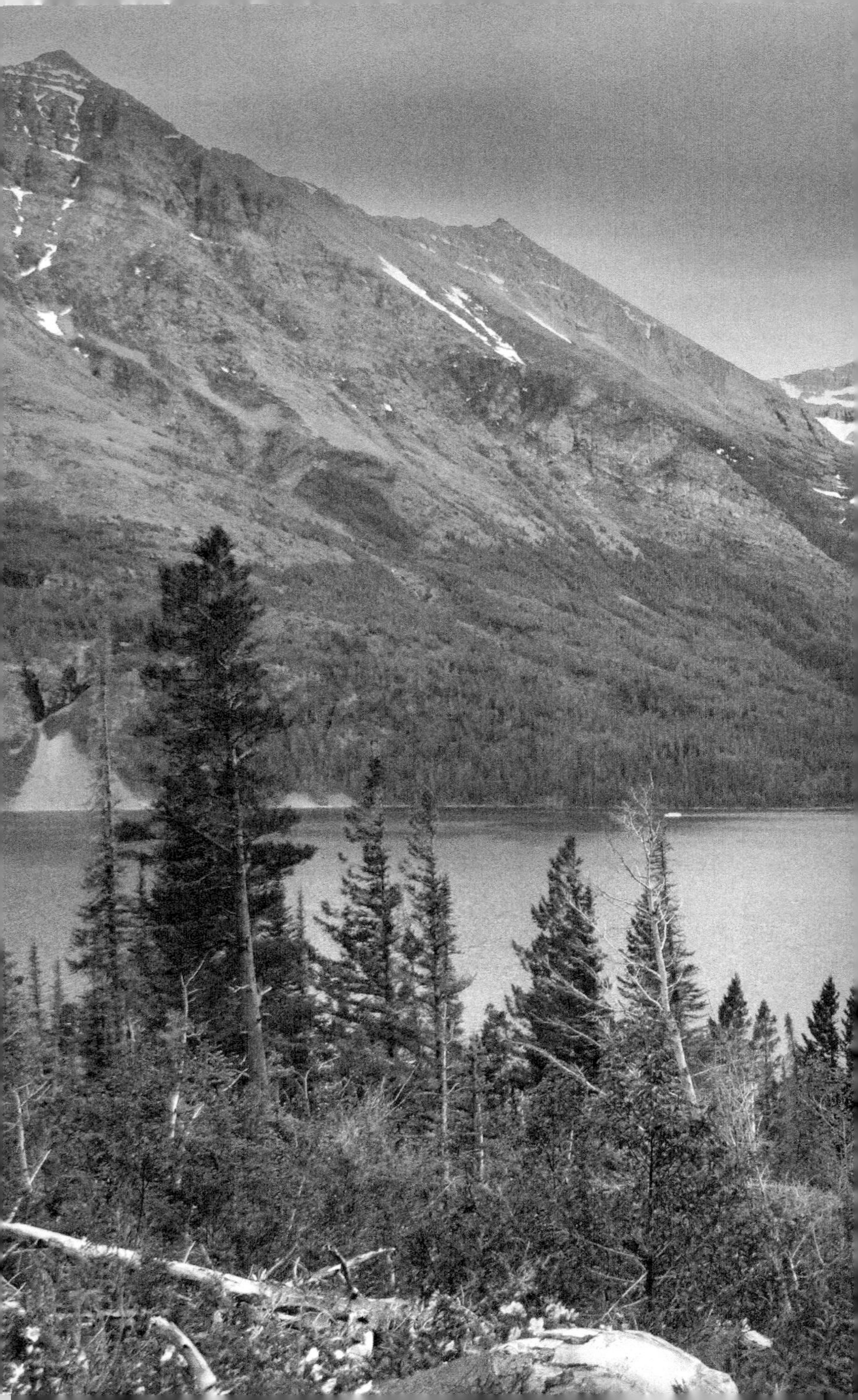

CHAPTER TWENTY-FOUR

Summer

I picked at my nails while Jonah navigated the roads home. When we drove past the place where the accident had taken place, Jonah slowed to a stop. He kept his lights on and the glow lit the ditch where Jonah's pickup must've been after the crash.

"It's different now," he said. "When I drive by."

"Easier?"

"Yeah." His eyes glittered from the dash lights and we both contemplated the area for a few moments. "It no longer feels like a penance. Instead, I remember other times I drove past here. With him, you know. When we'd go fishing and come back to hang."

"He was a good guy, and he loved his family. I think . . . I think all of this would've broken him."

"Yeah," he said roughly.

I tried to summon memories of riding with Eli to the cabin, but tonight, they weren't coming.

"You've been quiet," he said.

I had been subdued since Rhys had stopped at the table with his adorable daughters. He'd chatted with Jonah about buying Adam and Vera's house. I couldn't shake something Jonah had said.

She's not getting the kids or the pink from me, so I'm glad you and your girls can help her out.

What was I supposed to do about that? Tonight had been our start. Our official announcement to the world outside of our families that we were together. And then he'd proclaimed that he wasn't having kids.

Was he talking about at the moment? What about the future?

How long did I wait to find out?

Autumn's advice rang through my head loud and clear. I had to talk to him.

I didn't care to do it at the accident site, but perhaps it was a sign. This was the spot where our lives had been forever altered—his more than mine.

"Do you want kids?" I asked, my voice coming out small. I had to twist my fingers together or I wasn't going to leave skin around my cuticles.

"What?"

"You told Rhys you weren't giving your mom grandkids. Did you mean forever?"

A small laugh escaped him in a puff, then he caught my expression. Did I look as crestfallen as I felt? "I'm almost forty, sunshine."

"That doesn't mean you can't have kids."

"I've never had a long-term relationship, so no, I never planned on it." This time his laugh was scornful. "What kind of dad would I be? I can barely get on the floor with them."

I was cutting off my circulation like he'd done earlier in Curly's.

"I can't teach them how to hunt or fish—"

"You can."

He firmly shook his head. "Not like I would've been able to."

I studied him. He had a thriving furniture-building business. He lived alone in the mountains. Any blame on his mobility was a convenient excuse. "People with all sorts of limitations raise kids."

His jaw flexed and he punched the pickup into gear. When he pulled away, I couldn't help but feel that he'd left that spot changed again.

"What do you want from me?" His hand was tight on the wheel, his hard gaze stabbing the windshield. "We're dating. I'm getting out."

"I want to know where this is going. Where are *we* going?"

He maneuvered a turn and the headlights bounced off trees, but he kept his speed under control. "I thought we were having fun together."

"We are." I sighed. My heart ached and tears were putting hot pressure behind my eyes, but I wasn't crying. Yet. "Is this what you want?"

"I want you." He turned up his driveway. The shop glinted in the dark.

When he parked in the garage and punched the button to close the door, I knew we couldn't go into the house and pretend we hadn't had this talk.

"I want you, Jonah. But I want more too. I was ready to get married two months ago, and I was willing to overlook a less than ideal partner to have a family. You're my ideal man, but if we're not on the same page, I have to know."

Please be on the same page. Please.

The muscles in the corner of his jaw flexed. "I don't want kids, Summer."

I caught a tinge of regret, but his determination was strong. My heart broke.

I balanced on a precipice. Did I sever what we had and search for someone I was as mad about as Jonah?

I didn't want anyone else. I wanted him. It'd always been Jonah for me, and now that I had him, what did I do? What did I sacrifice to keep this guy in my life?

"Then what's our future?" Forget marriage. I didn't care to be a girl so wrapped up in nuptials that I settled for a Boyd. But what we were doing now didn't register as sincere. We lived in different towns and carried on different lives until we decided to overlap once a week. "Do I stay in my condo in Bozeman and you stay here and we just fuck around?"

"We're doing more than fucking around," he said tightly.

"No, we're not." I waved my hand between us. "If this isn't leading to anything but more of this, don't you find that . . . I don't know. Unfulfilling?"

He ground his teeth together and glowered out the window.

"Long-distance dating isn't enough for me." The words were like glass shards on my tongue, but I forged ahead. "I've kept my unhappiness in relationships to myself too many times to keep quiet with someone as important to me as you."

"So, what? I propose or this is over?"

I stiffened. "Is that what you think I'm saying?"

"Sounds like it. You dumped my brother, and now

you're dumping me. Neither of us could be what you want."

I gasped and the light from the garage door went out. "How can you throw Eli in my face?"

He shook his head, his jaw working. Then he stilled, the angles of his face hard. "Because you can stick with a douche like Boyd to the point of walking down the aisle, but if the last name's Dunn, you're ditching him. Maybe you belong in the city. Find some asshole who won't hit you this time."

His attitude didn't make sense, but I also didn't care. "Just because you haven't slapped me doesn't mean using what you know about my life to hurt me is okay. It means you're fine with being an asshole to me."

I grappled for the door handle, and after two attempts the door finally opened and I spilled out.

"Goddammit, Summer."

He scrambled to get out of the pickup, but I raced away. I might've just called him an asshole, but I guess I was one too, because I took advantage of that limp to leave him and my broken heart behind.

I sobbed the whole way home. Ugly, wrenching sobs, and I had to pull it together every time I had to pass a car. I would not crash because Jonah only wanted a fuck buddy. I would not wreck my car and miss work because Jonah was a scared dick still wrapped up in his own world. And I would not make the other drivers think I was having a medical episode and call emergency services on me.

Finally, I pulled into my garage. Only an hour ago I'd

been in a different garage with a man I'd wanted to spend my life with.

Had I done the right thing?

Was I really not okay with sleepovers and dates? We could act young and carefree. I'd be the girl who ran a distillery with the mountain-man boyfriend. We'd be a couple everyone talked about in Bourbon Canyon.

Then I'd visit Scarlett and Tate and the envy would twine around my heart. Same with Wynter. And if Autumn found the husband she so badly wanted and had the kids she'd dreamed about, would I start avoiding my family, telling myself I was too busy with dates and hot sex? God help me if Junie settled down before me.

Adults didn't need a life partner or kids to be fulfilled, but that life was what *I* wanted.

I didn't get out. It was late, but there was only one person I wanted to talk to. Two, but Jonah wasn't interested in me beyond the physical.

I called the person I knew would answer even if she'd been in a deep slumber.

Mama answered with an alert "Hello?"

"Mama, it didn't work out." The crying reignited. It'd never actually stopped, but the thought that I hadn't quit sobbing was even more pathetic. "Jonah and I . . ." *Broke up.* Were those even the right words? We'd talked about going out, but there'd been no labels beyond mountain man and brother's girlfriend.

"Aw, honey. I'm so sorry. Do you want to tell me what happened?"

I did in giant, halting gasps. I recounted the date and what he'd said to Rhys and then our argument. "Months, Mama. And I never called him my boyfriend."

"Sometimes simple words don't do justice to how we feel."

"But he didn't think of me as his girlfriend either. Eli's, yes. Boyd's fiancée, yes, but not his girlfriend."

"Maybe he just thought of you as his."

The tempo of my crying changed. Openly weeping, I put the phone on speaker, set it on the dash, and searched for a tissue.

"Summer?"

"I'm still here." I found a napkin I'd squirreled away in the glove compartment and blew my nose. "Sorry."

"Get it all out."

"I'm old enough to know better."

"We can say that all we want, but it doesn't hold water when it comes to emotions. You and Jonah are in a different place and it hurts. But you would've regretted it if you hadn't tried."

"I've only ever wanted him."

"The problem is, others aren't ours to have. They have to give themselves, and after what Jonah's been through, he's too afraid to put himself out there."

Why did Mama have to speak such sense? I should've called Autumn. She'd have at least given me one "Fuck him."

"The pain is fresh," she continued. "Old pain and new pain combined tonight for you both."

"Me?"

"Yes, Summer. You went right from Boyd to Jonah."

"But—"

"I'm not saying that's a bad thing, but I'm saying it might be affecting how you two are dealing with each other."

I couldn't see her point. I was over Boyd.

"You and Jonah went from nothing to each other's everything when you were stranded together." She used the same gentle tone when she was talking to her chickens in the morning. "Now you're not together all the time, but you're not really separate. I imagine his thoughts are as consumed with you as yours are with him."

"I doubt that," I said bitterly.

"Which is why some time to yourself might be a good thing. Give him time, Summer. Give yourself the same."

Time to what? Frustration built and more tears rolled down my face with it. I'd called Mama for comfort. I'd wanted her to tell me that I was going to be fine and everything would work out, like she had when I'd first arrived at her house a scared little girl.

"Okay, Mama." I wanted off the phone, to crawl into my bed and cry some more. I wanted to cry for the little girl who was so scared she'd lose all her family. For the older girl who knew she'd given in to the wrong guy. For the young woman who'd ruined a whole family's life standing up for herself. And for the adult who never seemed to find Mr. Right, only a Mr. Right Now.

"I can talk more, hon."

"I'm tired, Mama. Too much crying. Love you."

"Love you too. I'll talk to you tomorrow."

And I would pretend I was fine. I would answer with only a hint of sadness so she wouldn't know that I probably hadn't gotten out of bed to do more than go pee.

"Night, Mama."

I hung up and let my head hang. God, I was pathetic. I swiped at my eyes and hopped out. My phone buzzed.

I thought Mama was trying to call back, but no. My heart did a hopeful leap and then stalled.

Jonah: I just need to know you made it home okay.

There went the tears again. Was I really not okay with our current arrangement?

I shook my head. **I'm home.**

Several minutes went by before I realized I was still standing in the dark garage, looking at my screen, waiting for him to reply. But he never did. He cared enough to check up on me, and that was it.

I went inside, tossing my purse and keys on the counter. Maybe Mama was right. I needed to make sure I hadn't laid out unrealistic standards for Jonah to live up to.

The problem was, *he* was unrealistic. He was sensitive and caring, sexy as sin, and had muscles galore. He was vulnerable around me and only me. He'd made me feel special. He'd been everything I'd ever wanted in a guy. But even that hadn't been enough.

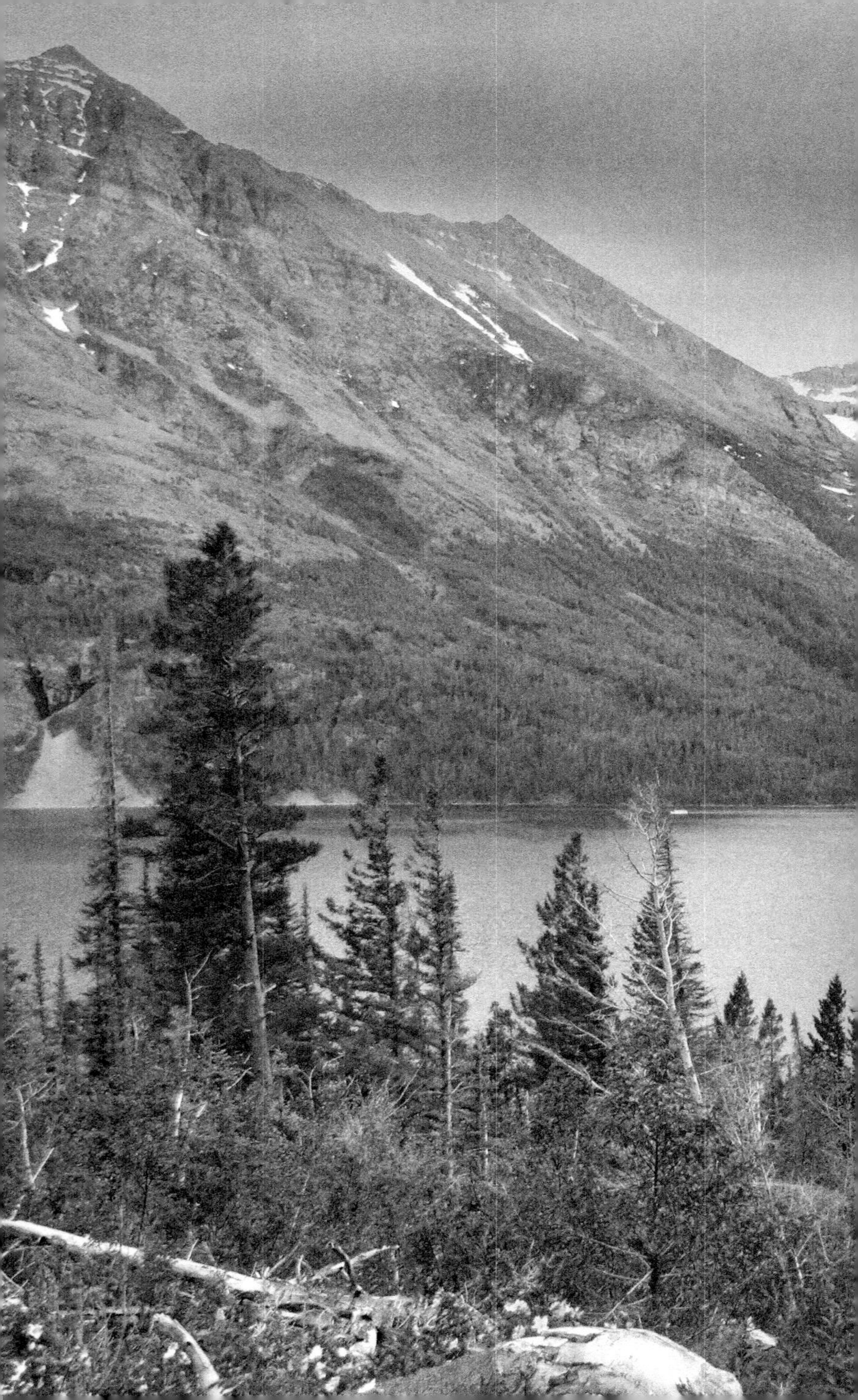

CHAPTER TWENTY-FIVE

Jonah

"I'll be right back, Jonah." Macy scurried off, and I was left waiting in the front of the hardware store. The young guy working the till lifted his chin toward me like this was our usual routine.

Actually, it was.

I pushed a hand through my hair, waiting for the fall of the strands on my forehead, but with regular haircuts, that happened less and less. I had trimmed my beard and my scar showed through the stubble more, but the kid didn't dwell on it.

Actually, no one at Curly's last weekend had either.

I didn't like to think about last weekend. How I'd been an epic dick and lashed out at Summer. How I'd gone to bed alone. How her face had looked when I'd said the shitty things I had.

Wasn't that what I'd done? Pushed her away when she was trying to have an honest conversation?

Fuck. Like usual, my thoughts spun like tractor wheels in mud.

I struggled to concentrate on the task at hand. I had to pick up another order of epoxy, a special-ordered router, and a band-saw blade for another custom project. This time, I made sure the order didn't include heirlooms or collectibles.

But that had been a nice table.

No. I was not making more. The pressure had been absurd.

Yet . . . the detail would take my damn mind off missing Summer every second of the day.

I pinched the bridge of my nose. Loss ripped through my chest, followed by panic that I couldn't turn back time and take back everything I'd said to make Summer leave.

But I had, and I'd meant what I'd said. Summer was better off moving on with someone else and getting what she wanted. I couldn't have her pausing her life to wait on me.

A cart wheel squeaked as Macy returned. "How's this?"

I didn't bother to check the order. Only once in fifteen years had an item been missing, and today, I didn't care if everything was there. I'd come to town to keep from being home and replaying the conversation in my head like I'd done for the last four days.

"It's all been run through your account." Her grin was wider than normal. "You look like the spring air's agreeing with you."

She was digging for information I wasn't willing to give. I felt like hell. Seemed like an insult to what I had with Summer to get compliments on my appearance, as if waking up knowing I wouldn't be seeing her this weekend wasn't hell.

"Thanks." It took all my energy to soften my response. Macy and her husband had been too good to me over the years to bite her head off for thinking I was a stable adult. "Winter's finally done with us for a while."

A piercing hole burned through my chest. Had I said that to remind myself what I'd lost? No more snowstorms until next winter. No Summer getting stranded at my cabin. Just me. Alone. Until next winter.

I gave Macy a tight smile that I hoped didn't look like a grimace and pushed my cart outside.

The wheel squeaked in time with my limp. A breeze blew the smell of burgers across my nose. I glanced toward the bar. Not many cars were in the lot. I didn't care about being a spectacle. The freedom from the fear was short-lived. I also didn't want to be asked about Summer.

What would I tell people?

How did I know anyone would care to ask? They might not have believed the talk if they hadn't been there themselves. And also . . . people might not be fucking talking about me. Why the hell was I newsworthy when others were going about their lives trying to survive and buy groceries?

None of my pondering mattered when my stomach growled. Had I eaten yet?

For the last four days, I'd been eating sandwiches until I was left with nothing but the memory of lunch meat in the fridge. Last night, I'd eaten a cheese sandwich rather than make a meal that might summon memories of Summer puttering around in my kitchen.

With or without Summer, I wasn't going back to being a hermit.

It'd be without Summer. She wasn't with me, and she wasn't planning to go out with me anytime soon. But I'd gone to the dive bar before without her.

Except I'd stopped there and ordered a burger because of her.

A car slowed to pull into the parking spot next to me. I jerked. I was standing right where they wanted to park. How long had I been there, twiddling with myself while I thought about Summer?

I lifted my chin as acknowledgment and shuffled out of the way. I got into my truck and drove to the bar. Then I sat there and stared at the door.

They had good food, and I would've loved to have taken Summer here. We'd eat and then return to the cabin and get lost in each other. The next morning we'd . . . What? I'd go work in the shop. She'd bum around the place and maybe visit her family. Without me. Then we'd go out again. More sex. Rinse and repeat.

I had liked our routine. But going through the motions by myself wasn't the same. Had I been using Summer as my emotional support girlfriend?

Had she been my girlfriend?

Of course she had.

Had I ever called her that?

She'd wanted to know about our future, when I'd been satisfied with the most monogamous semirelationship ever.

Someone pulled up next to me, and I opened my door before I was busted once more staring at nothing. A couple that had to be at least ten years younger than me got out of their car. The guy was vaguely familiar. It took a few moments before I recognized him. His name was Bennett. He'd delivered barrels from Copper Summit a few times.

I grabbed my cane once I got a good look at the pockmarked parking lot. Winter had been hard on the asphalt.

Bennett nodded at me. His wife gave me a friendly smile, then clasped his hand. Together they strode toward the entrance, and I trailed behind them.

After she went inside, Bennett stopped to hold the door. I needed a few seconds to catch up.

"Thanks," I said.

"No problem." After I entered, he followed me in. I stepped back to let him go around me and link back up with his wife. He nodded almost sheepishly. "Our date nights are getting earlier and earlier." His laugh was dry.

When he'd made deliveries, he'd tried chatting before. I'd returned his conversation with little more than grunts. Now, I didn't want to be rude. For once. "Hey, I know the feeling." Did that sound as empty as it felt?

His smile was quick. "Right? When our babysitters aren't much older than the kids, we've gotta be in earlier than them."

I had no fucking idea what he was talking about, but I nodded. Idle chatter like this hadn't happened to me in a long time. Strangers didn't talk to me unless it was about my injuries. If I weren't feeling like a kicked dog, I'd appreciate the man's efforts.

"It's like the best of both worlds," his wife added, tangling her fingers through his. "We get to eat out, but then we get to tuck them into bed."

Normally, I'd want to get away, but the couple's openness made me want to reciprocate. "That sounds nice."

Something twisted behind my sternum. Then longing took its place. Well, fuck me. This was what I got, trying to move on mere days after Summer had left me. Why couldn't I run across a couple that'd talk about cars or the weather or something? Why did I have to run across two parents excited to be on a date in the earliest hours of the evening? I should've stayed in my shop and found some priceless artwork some customer wanted me to pour epoxy on.

"Oh, over here." She tugged Bennett toward a table by the window.

"See ya, Jonah."

"Later, Bennett."

He hadn't thought twice about chatting with me, even after his experiences with me had been less than stellar. Had people's reactions for the last decade or more been in my head?

Had I used them as an excuse not to leave my cabin?

I veered to the bar so I could put my back solidly toward the happy couple who'd be tucking their kids in tonight.

I scrubbed my face when Mike stopped in front of me.

"What'll you have?"

"Patty melt and fries with a Sprite."

"Got it." He knocked on the bar top and walked away.

I planted my gaze firmly on the baseball game on the TV. I wasn't with it enough to register the teams, or even what league they played for.

Did I want kids?

Terror squeezed the sides of my heart together. That was a nope.

So I'd done the right thing. For me. And for Summer.

I kept the mantra on repeat until my food was slid in front of me. People entered and I didn't pay an ounce of attention. I'd eat and get home, and if I was lucky, I wouldn't see happy couples on my way out.

I was about to take a bite when a familiar cloying perfume wafted by my nose.

"Jonah?"

A long breath left me. My burger was almost to my lips, and I was tempted to take a bite so huge I couldn't talk. Then I remembered how she'd treated me the last time we'd run into each other. Either this was a fucked-up coincidence and evidence of my shitty luck, or Jackie was a regular at the bar. I suspected I knew the answer.

"You sure you want to talk to me?" I asked. "We're in public."

She had the grace to appear chagrined. "You're so easy to talk to," she said sarcastically.

Convenient excuse. Summer hadn't been daunted. Well, not for the last couple of months. "Sure." I took that bite. Expecting the food to taste like dust thanks to Jackie, I moaned when flavor burst over my tongue.

Summer would like—

Now the hamburger tasted like dirt. I chewed and caught the way Jackie turned sideways in her stool.

"You look good."

"Thanks," I said around my mouthful and continued eating. Despite my taste buds, now that my stomach had seen solid food, I wasn't leaving without polishing off every bite.

"You busy later?"

That was how our texts usually started.

Me or her: **You busy?**

Followed by **Yes** or **No** and then agreeing to meet at her house if we were both ready and willing.

Never at the bar. Never at a restaurant. No coffeehouse. She was never seen with me.

I took a long pull of my Sprite. I might've fucked up with Summer—been too honest too early until she was so wrapped up in me she'd never leave. Damn. That made me sound like a selfish dick.

I was selfish. And I was a dick. I dug out my wallet.

"I haven't ordered yet. Want to come over?" she asked.

She'd read my actions wrong. I polished off my Sprite. "Nope." When I set the glass down, I grabbed my cane and thumped it on the floor.

Did she wince? "So the rumors are true? You're seeing Summer Kerrigan?"

"No, not anymore. She deserves better than me, but at least she showed me what it's like to be with someone who isn't embarrassed by me." I thunked the cane again.

The corner of Jackie's mouth curled up. "What happened with you and the golden girl? Did she want more and realize that she's nothing more than a fuck?"

"She was more than that," I growled.

"Then why'd you break up?" She must've gotten her answer from my features. "Exactly. You can blame me all you want, but all I did was give you a taste of what it was like to be with you. I don't give a shit about your cane or your scar or your limp. I just didn't want anyone saying, 'There goes poor Jackie. Didn't she learn the first time?' " She shrugged and turned back to the bar. "At least the way we did it, everyone knew we were only fucking, and that I controlled when and where."

Her words settled into my brain like fresh concrete, smothering assumptions I'd made. "We were kids."

"We were old enough to drink. We'd been seeing each other since high school. Yet all you wanted to do was hunt and fish and hang out with Teller. You know, I wondered if you guys had a thing. A bromance that was actually the real thing. But when I met a guy who actually gave me attention, I saw that it didn't matter. I wanted to be important to you and all you gave me were scraps."

I . . . had been exactly how she'd described. I still was. I'd let her down. Not only then, but now. She hadn't been more than a fuck. The arrangement I had wanted. If she'd asked for more at any point since she'd moved back to Bourbon Canyon, would I have cut her off as cleanly as she'd left town when we'd been together the first time?

I would've. Distance would've been crucial, and I wouldn't have returned her texts.

Goddammit, I was an asshole. "I'm sorry."

She whipped her head around to glare at me. Her expression faltered when she saw my face. "You're serious?"

"I am, Jackie. You're . . . you deserved better than me too. Always have and still do."

She drew in a long breath, considering me for a few long moments. I endured her scrutiny, but my nervous energy escaped when I tapped the base of the cane on the top of my boot. She didn't pay it any mind. I'd painted her as a villain when I was the bad guy.

"I get that you and I weren't meant to be, but if

Summer's behind this?" She flicked her hand up and down my body. "And you're not out to find someone else to hook up with? And her history with Eli didn't stop you?" She huffed like she couldn't believe it. "Then maybe you were more committed than you thought."

Maybe I was. And that terrified me.

Sleep had been an elusive bitch. Tomorrow marked two weeks since Summer had left. I was tired and cranky and I had rammed the drill into the side of my hand two days ago. The damn wound still seeped through my bandages, but then I hadn't let up enough for the injury to heal.

I'd had worse and they'd mended. Eventually. In their own way.

I would get better, but I wasn't going to quit working. I'd go nuts if I did. Waiting for the rest of my supplies to arrive made me restless enough.

The barrels were supposed to come today. A delivery driver from Copper Summit would be here soon. Thankfully, I'd just had to email the guy in charge of repurposing the barrels and hadn't had to go through a Bailey. I hadn't seen any of them since Summer had stormed out.

I also hadn't been to town since I'd run into Jackie.

I heard the engine before the doorbell outside my shop rang. I didn't bother looking at the camera footage to see which high school kid they'd sent this time. The boys were usually prompt and wanted to get the hell done with the job so they could clock out. They usually didn't pay enough attention to my leg or try to tell me to quit trying to help them.

Hitting the button on the big overhead door, I waited, my hands propped on my hips. Cool air snaked in along with plenty of sunshine. Spring was here and I could feel it in the warm hints on the breeze.

The back end of a short, white delivery truck came into view. A shadow was visible around the delivery truck. Teller faced me, his face carved from stone.

"What the hell are you doing here?" Fucking Baileys. I didn't need any more people from my present or future telling me how badly I'd fucked up.

"Last week, you snarled at Dougie."

"He almost backed into the garage door."

"He didn't and you know it." He crossed his arms, in no hurry to open the back of the truck and start offloading barrels. "He can back between two semis going eighty side by side on the interstate and not touch either one."

"That doesn't make any fucking sense."

"What a coincidence. Neither do you."

I went to flip the latch on the back of the truck. Teller's big hand slammed over it.

"I can still take you," I said through gritted teeth.

"You couldn't then, and you sure as fuck can't now, but you won't try, because both of us will have to take an ice bath and pop too many ibuprofen. It's not worth feeling our age, man."

I couldn't argue. I didn't want to fight Teller. I had enough on my conscience about him. "Why are you here?"

"I don't know. You're fucking my sister. Can't I stop by and say hi?"

"We're not—"

Teller snapped his fingers. "Right. You broke up." He gave me a fake perplexed look. "Or were you even together?"

"We were together." I'd never said anything with more certainty.

"You sure? You seemed to hide the fact. Only eating with Mama, not seeing the rest of us, going out of town." He let go of the latch and propped his hands on his hips.

"I had a lot of shit to deal with."

"Are you saying Summer was some of that shit?"

"No." He was goading me and I knew it, but I continued defending myself. "She was the reason I did any of that. She's the only reason I wanted to."

"Then why the hell aren't you two together? Why are Tenor and I getting emails from people Summer manages, wondering if she's okay?"

Alarm spiked hot in my blood. "Is she okay?"

"Melancholy as hell. I'd almost rather see her with Boyd—"

A low rumble left my chest.

"I said almost. Summer's not a sad or beaten-down person. The only other time I worried about her was a couple months after Eli died."

Only twice and both times had been my fault. "Has she ever talked to you about that day?"

"Only recently. She told me that she'd broken up with him."

"She tried to tell me that in the hospital, years ago, but I yelled at her and drove her away before she could explain."

He nodded like he'd expected as much. "You had the hots for my sister."

Shock would've floored me if I hadn't had the truck to lean against. "You knew?"

"Anyone who saw you two pass within spitting distance of each other knew. I felt bad for her." At my questioning gaze, he shrugged. "She was with Eli. He had hearts in his eyes when it came to her, and I thought, well, she fucked that up. Not that I thought you'd go for her."

"I was an immature dick back then." And now.

"You were protective of him. I think you two would've gotten together eventually. Years after Eli had moved on."

But he hadn't. He never would. He was gone. "I should've been there."

"To do what? Let him see what was gonna go through your mind when you heard Summer was single?" Teller shook his head. "Eli was the opposite of you. You keep shit deep." He thumped his chest. "In here. Eli turned it outward. It made him one of the most likable guys around, but remember when he'd get in one of his moods?"

Eli had had a hot temper, and he had lashed out when he was hurt or upset. He'd been both that night. "But he'd still be here."

"He would, yet we can't go back and change a thing. No matter how much either of us wants to."

I studied him. Eli had been sort of a younger brother to him too, between being my friend and having Eli at his house, thanks to Summer. Teller had lost Eli too. "I wasn't there for you either. After the accident."

"We were all a little more worried about you surviving."

"I did."

"You had a fuck ton of close calls. Besides, I had my parents. They wouldn't let me weather a thing alone. My siblings were annoying as fuck. I gave you space to heal, and then . . . All you wanted was space."

"I couldn't do what I used to."

"We could've done other stuff. Hell"—he spread his arms out to encompass my shop—"what you're doing here is fascinating."

"I wouldn't have been fun to be around."

"You know damn well I'm not like that. You locked everyone out. When I heard about you and Summer, I thought you were finally coming around. Instead, you hurt her and here you are alone. Again."

"I'm not a family man."

Teller crossed his arms. "Why not?"

I opened my mouth. Slammed it shut. "I'm just not. I never was."

"Bullshit. You'd have grown up and matured."

"Is that what you did?" I'd give anything to get the focus off me. The spotlight was hot and I was getting sweaty and itchy under the collar.

"I haven't found the right person. Who knows if I ever will, but we're not talking about me. Why the hell do you think you're better off up here by yourself?"

"I've always been—"

"Bullshit."

My anger burned hot, compressing my lungs. "No wonder I quit talking to you, asshole."

"I should've kept pushing, but don't worry. I learned my lesson. And you were never alone. You were always with someone. Your dad. Eli. Me. My brothers—"

"And I let them all down!" I roared. I pounded the truck with the side of my hand. The noise scared a bird out of the trees. "Goddammit."

I squeezed my hand and lurched away before I did something epically stupid like break a bone. Then I'd have jack all to do in my shop. I walked in a small circle, and for once since he'd arrived, Teller shut up.

I stopped with my back to him, staring at the house that had been built for a family. My future family. The house that'd had only me for the last fifteen years. Until Summer.

Thinking of her was like taking a hot brand to my heart. I barely noticed the gash in my hand throbbing after hitting the truck. "I let Summer down too. She wanted more from me, and I can't give her more."

"Bullshit."

I spun, and the fire in my hip flared, but I ignored it. "Say that word one more time and I'll roll each and every one of those barrels over you."

"Well, they're empty."

Just like my threat.

"You've been able to lie to yourself for years." He continued his onslaught. I couldn't even walk away. He was at my goddamn house. "Which I reckon is why you prefer to be alone. No one can call you on it."

"You need to leave."

The fucker crossed his arms and leaned against the delivery truck. "No, man. I'm delivering some reality today."

All the energy drained out of me. For two weeks, I'd tortured myself about Summer. Jackie had hit me with some hard truths. And now one of those guys I'd let down was berating me.

He was right on every account. I limped to the shop. My hip was not happy about my circles, but the ache was dull and would fade quickly. I sagged against the side of the shop. I let my head rest against the cool metal siding and soaked up the sun.

I was tired. Weary from it all.

Fuck it all, I was lonely too. "I have to live with not being there for Eli. I ditched you. I'm still not around for my parents, so much so that they're moving and leaving almost everything behind. I can't take that risk with Summer." I squeezed my eyes shut and swallowed hard. "And if we had kids . . ."

"You really think tragedy doesn't strike anyone because they never let anyone down?"

"Teller."

"I didn't say bullshit, so you have to listen."

My lips twitched. How could I find humor in this situation? "You're a jackass."

"I've been told that a time or so, in case we ever revisit the why-I'm-single conversation again. By the way, I failed you worse."

I cracked an eye open. His stricken expression caught me off guard.

"I should've been there. You were like a brother to me, and I didn't know how to deal with you being so angry, and it was easier to let you push me away. Then I didn't have to figure shit out. I was a crappy friend."

Would I have kept chasing him away, or would he have called me on the same stubbornness that made him relentless today? "We were young."

"Not that young. Though Eli was. If nothing had happened that day because we'd packed up our fishing supplies early, then what about later when another girlfriend broke his heart? No one knows if he'd have made the same stupid decision, or if he'd still be with us today. We don't even know if he'd have been out getting groceries only to get T-boned by another dude who got drunk over a girl."

Logically, I knew everything he was saying made sense. Emotionally, I didn't want to listen.

"But, yeah, you feel guilty. Honestly, I would too. I do. No one can tell me different. I talked you into staying out longer. So maybe we should quit telling you what not to feel and tell you that you have to learn to accept it and move on."

I hadn't accepted what had happened. The way I was living wasn't moving on.

"As for your parents, have you talked to them about how you feel like you've been no help?"

I could barely shake my head. "They'd lie to keep from hurting me. They're selling because Dad's been alone for too long. He can't do it by himself anymore."

"Or they'll say something that totally surprises you." He pushed off the truck and paced between the rear end and the open shop door. "You know my dad used to say he liked ranching as a break from all things distilling. Dad fucking loved to ranch. He loved watching his kids learn about the animals and growing seasons and birth rates. He'd go into the hardware store for a box of screws and stay for an hour, shooting the breeze about feed prices."

Darin Bailey had been thrilled about everything he did. Raising kids, ranching cattle, and distilling. He'd had an enthusiasm that was rare. But I didn't know what point Teller was making.

As if he heard my unspoken thought, he stopped his pacing. "I never got that impression from your dad."

"What do you mean?" Dad liked working the animals and land just fine.

"Talk to him. You might find out that the thought of never getting a real retirement was a hell of a downer."

"He never planned to retire." Dad had never mentioned a thing about it.

"Yet he never pushed you into following his footsteps. He encouraged you to get out in nature as often as you wanted."

"Eli was going to take over."

"Because Eli loved the life. Hell, I don't know. Maybe your dad is disappointed to sell, but that's not your problem. My dad was always clear with us—no expectations. If we don't love it, don't do it. Just because we have two family businesses doesn't mean they're our destiny."

Frowning, I contemplated the concrete pad under my boots. What if my dad didn't think the same way?

What if he did?

"I can't just talk to you and my parents and then go tell Summer I'm ready for all of it—kids and a minivan."

"A minivan would suck on this road. Make sure it's all-wheel drive."

I scowled. "I'm serious."

"I am too. Do the emotional work. I doubt Summer's moving on anytime soon from the funk I heard she's in." He smirked. "That's why I'm not there cheering her up. She's dated some doozies. You saw that asshole Boyd? He was the most ambitious of the bunch." Teller shuddered.

The anger was back, but the target wasn't Teller. Nameless, faceless men who weren't good enough for Summer Kerrigan. My blood boiled hot enough to cook them all alive.

"She's doing okay overall though?" She shouldn't have to be as miserable as me. I was the one who'd done this to us.

"I'll make sure of it. How about we unload these barrels and go grab a bite to eat?"

He said it so casually, so easily, it was almost like we'd gone back in time. His question shouldn't be a big deal, but it was. The last time he'd asked, I'd probably had some caustic response like *Do I look like I can just go grab a bite?*

I didn't deserve Teller as a friend, no matter what he said. But I might need him. Just like I needed to talk to my parents. And I'd needed to hear what Jackie had had to say.

I was a long way from giving Summer everything she wanted. I had some work to do on myself, or I'd be just another nameless, faceless dick who didn't treat her right.

And when that work was done, maybe I could inspect that longing every time I thought about how this house was supposed to be for so much more than me.

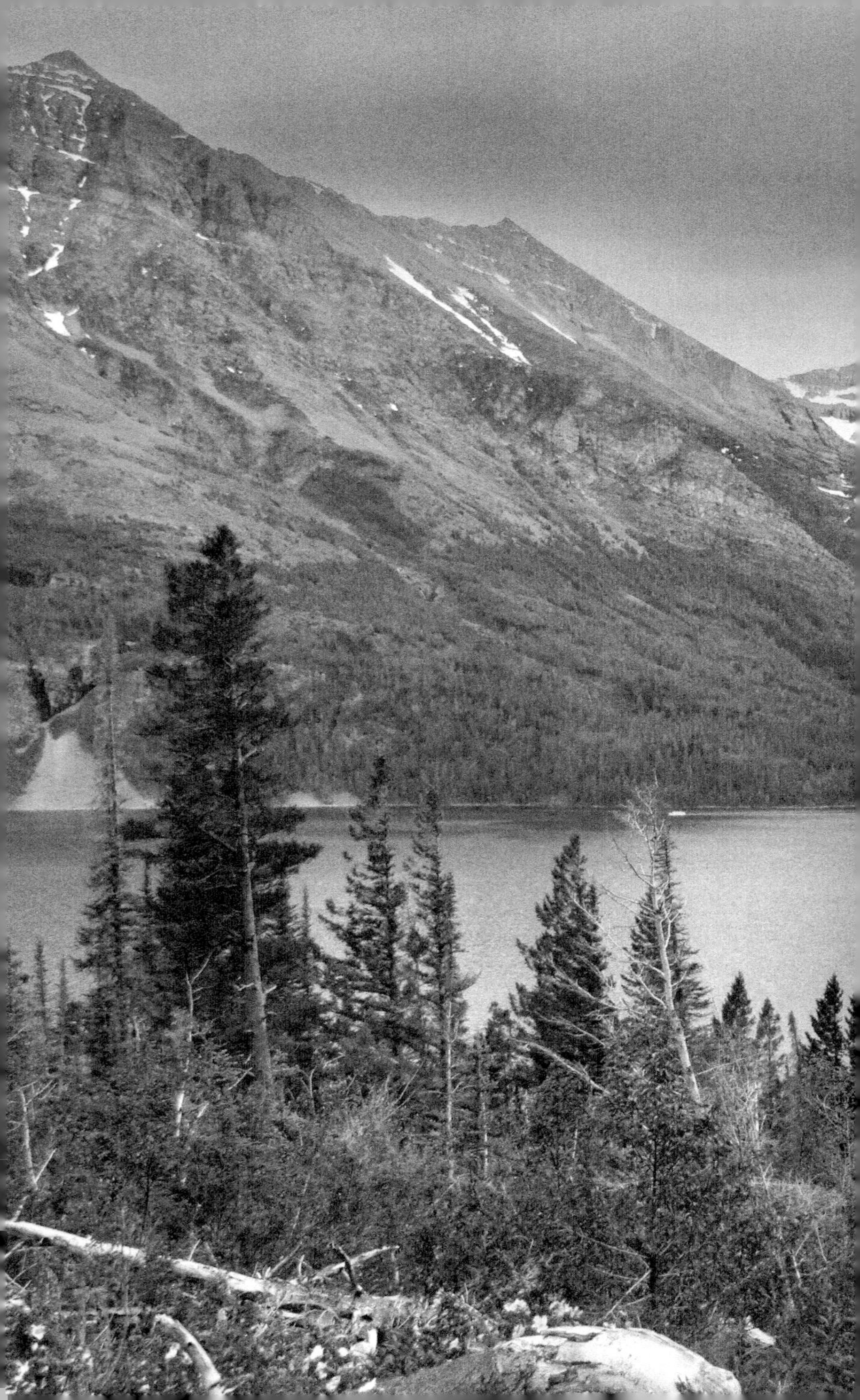

CHAPTER TWENTY-SIX

Summer

My hand was in the grip of little Brinley as she toddled around the yard. I had Darin in a carrier, but he was getting squirmy. They'd both need a snack and a nap soon.

I was at Scarlett and Tate's place. Tate was working somewhere on the ranch, and I was giving Scarlett and Chance time to go to town on their own. Tate was meeting them in town for lunch and then she'd send Chance with him to work and come home to talk.

I was ready to . . . I didn't know. In the weeks since Jonah and I had broken up, I'd been listless. I'd wake up, go to work, work well past when everyone else left, then go home and watch movies. I'd learned to keep my morning alarm on even on the weekends, otherwise I'd fall asleep on the couch and sleep too late.

On the weekends, I went to help Wynter and Myles. Since I was around more, Myles would take his Denver trips over the weekend. Between me, Mama, and Autumn, we made sure Wynter got some sleep. Little Elsa wasn't a fan of sleeping at night.

As for today, I had reached out to Scarlett since we didn't get too much time together and she'd jumped on the chance to have some one-on-one time. I got the impression she wanted to check on me. I also got the impression everyone was worried about me.

I was worried about me, but not in the way everyone thought. Mama had said I might need time to work through what I really wanted, but mostly, I had needed time to reflect.

Darin wiggled his arms and legs. Brinley tripped, but I held her up.

"I go down," she said.

"You almost did," I agreed. "Snack?"

"Da!" Darin said.

I smiled and put my arm around him. My shoulders were aching, and my back was wondering why my cargo was moving so much, but I loved every minute. In the few months I'd been wrapped up in Jonah, I'd missed these kids. I'd missed having time with my sisters and Tate. While I saw Teller and Tenor at work, or at least talked with them on the phone or through email, I didn't get to hang out with them as siblings.

I couldn't put the blame solely on Jonah. I had wanted to spend every spare moment with him. After being with a guy who wasn't invested in me like Boyd, it'd been nice to think someone was as tied up with me.

My heart hurt again. I took the kids inside. Someday, I would get over my heartache. I'd quit wondering what he was doing and if he'd continued getting out of his house. I'd quit obsessing if he'd started dating.

That last part piped caustic fuel into my veins. Only a month had passed. He couldn't have moved on yet. Right?

I was splitting a muffin with Brinley when a car pulled up. Scarlett came into the house through the door to the garage. Her smile faltered as she took us in. "It's definitely close to nap time."

I tried to see the picture we made. Darin was sleepy eyed and he was pushing his muffin crumbs around on his highchair tray. Brinley had her head in one hand and was close to losing the battle with slumber. I was subdued. Fun Aunt Summer had been Mellow Aunt Summer lately.

"I was just going to clean them up and lay them down."

She gestured for me to keep sitting. "I've got him. Brinley was chanting your name all morning, so I'll let you tuck her in."

I wiped the crumbs off both of us. I had no excuse for being a messy eater. Then I let Brinley lead me to her room. She crawled into her little bed, and I curled beside her, my ass hanging off the end.

"Nigh, nigh." She kissed my cheek and left half her muffin behind.

"Sleep tight, sweetheart."

She closed her eyes like the tiny princess she was, and only moments passed before her little lips puffed open. She was fast asleep.

I had a lot of favorites being an aunt, but this topped everything. I got to cuddle and snuggle my nieces and nephews—even Chance would let me crush him in a smothering hug. I didn't have the full range of parent experiences, but did I need them to be happy when I had a guy who made me feel like his world revolved around me?

I'd known going in that Jonah had hang-ups. So did I. Yet I'd pushed him. And when he'd refused to budge, I'd walked. Tears pricked my eyes.

God, I was still a mess.

I carefully rolled off the bed, which wasn't hard. It was barely a foot off the floor.

I found Scarlett in the living room, curled into the corner of the couch with her legs tucked under her. She had a cup of lemonade in her hand, and a second full glass was sitting on the opposite end of the coffee table.

Dropping to sit on the other end of the couch, I grabbed the cherry lemonade and downed it like it was spiked with two shots of Summer's Summit. Wynter and Autumn had actually come up with a mixed drink that included one of our lines of bourbon and Scarlett's lemonade.

"Something on your mind?" she asked softly.

I licked my lips, snatching every last drop of sweetness. I needed the energy to untangle my thoughts. "I think I fucked up."

She set her glass down. "How?"

"I've been so intent on getting married and having a family that I was willing to settle with a guy like Boyd. And when that didn't happen, I gave up a really good man I fell hard for because he wasn't ready and he might never be ready." The admission was cathartic. I had fucked up. But what did I do about it?

She narrowed her eyes as she considered me. "I don't think that's it."

Surprised, I turned to face her, crossing my legs under me. Other than my sisters, Scarlett knew me better than anyone. Sometimes, I was more transparent with her than with my sisters. Scarlett was a friend. I never had to be her role model. "How so?"

"I guess . . . it's not the whole picture. When you told me about Eli, I thought 'that makes sense.' You weren't the Summer I knew with the guys you dated." At my confused look, she gave me a sheepish smile. "You never pressed for what you wanted, and given what happened to Eli after you were honest with him, I can't blame you."

"I led him on."

"How long were you friends with him?"

"Since middle school."

"And how long did you date him?"

I wrinkled my nose. Sometimes the sum of my teen years felt taken over by Eli, but just because he'd been a part of it, didn't mean he'd dominated it. Just that, once, we'd been an item. "Almost a year. He asked me to homecoming and I knew if I said yes, he'd take it as a date. But I liked him and thought maybe there should be more."

"So, a year, maybe, that you gave it a shot? Yet you were with Boyd for how long?"

"Two years."

"And the guy before that?"

"A year and a half, but he'd moved away for the last six months and it was long distance."

"And the relationship before that?"

I had to dig into the vault of my memories. I'd dated guys. Often, they ghosted me. Sometimes, they broke things off, citing my work. Not enough time for them. A complaint Jonah never made. Usually because I wasn't working to keep from having to spend time with someone I was mediocre at best about.

"Let me ask a different way," she said. "When did you know, viscerally *know*, that these guys weren't the one, but you thought 'maybe there should be more'?"

Oh my god. The lemonade soured in my gut. "I led them all on. All of them."

Scarlett held a finger up. "No. You were too afraid to lead them on. You didn't want anyone to get hurt because of you. So when Boyd was the one to hurt you—you could cut things off."

I blinked at her. Was she saying I'd been a scaredy-cat the whole time? Yet wasn't that minimizing everything about Eli? He'd lost his life. Of course I was fucking scared to be honest.

"I tried to tell myself I wasn't to blame." I'd tried to move on. And when Jonah had chased me out of his hospital room, I'd assumed that was my due for being an awful person. A shitty girlfriend to a great guy.

"But deep down, you took all the blame." Her expression was full of compassion. "And maybe you care so much about Jonah, more than any other guy you've been into, that you're terrified that if things go south, neither one of you will come back from it."

We'd already been through a sort of hell. All because of me. "I couldn't do that to him. He's forgiven me for Eli."

She leaned forward, and put a hand on my knee, catching my gaze and refusing to let go. "There was nothing to forgive, but I know you'll never believe that. So you need to forgive yourself."

I bit the inside of my cheek as tears seared the backs of my eyes. I'd thought I had. I'd thought I'd come to terms with my part in Eli's accident and Jonah's injuries and the anguish their parents went through. "I've never told Eli's parents."

"Maybe you should talk to them. What if keeping it to yourself is part of why you really ended things with Jonah?"

A hot tear tracked down my cheek. I didn't want to hurt his parents, but part of me felt they should know the full circumstances behind that day. I couldn't ask Jonah to keep it a secret. He meant too much to me. "I think I'm in love with him."

Compassion rolled off her. "I think you're both head over heels and it terrifies each of you." She gave my knee a pat. "If you need me to, I'll talk to Autumn. The Bourbon Canyon Bachelor Auction is coming up soon, and since Teller and Jonah are friends again, we can recruit Teller to sign him up, and we'll make sure you win the bid."

I chuckled before everything she said sank in. "Teller and Jonah are friends again?"

"They even stopped here so Teller could show him the boat. I think they're going fishing soon."

Happiness for Jonah swept through me. He and Teller would've never thought to use a boat to fish before. If they weren't hauling a canoe to the middle of nowhere, they weren't interested. But Teller was showing Jonah there were ways to adapt the activities they used to love. "That would be so awesome."

She grinned. "Chance is thrilled. That kid tells so many people about his and Tate's secret fishing place that I wonder if he knows what secret means."

I laughed, but my mind ruminated over everything she'd said. Jonah was moving on, maybe not relationship-wise. Or he could be, but I'd made that not my business. Regardless, what Scarlett had said about why I clung to connections that I knew deep down were wrong hit a hard chord in my chest.

Would talking to Eli's parents help?

Every time I saw them, I felt like I should duck and hide. Like they knew what had really happened and hated me. They had no idea, and they could be tearing themselves up inside worse than me. Yet I hadn't wanted to make things worse.

Too much time had passed for that. I hadn't forgiven myself, and having an open discussion with them might help all of us.

Would it help me and Jonah? I didn't know, but if I didn't fix me, I couldn't help us.

Jonah

I parked by my dad's shop. Chickens waddled all over the yard behind the shop. They'd be Rhys's chickens soon. I wandered in. Dad was sorting through tools. He had some laid out on the workshop bench. A small rolling red tool box stood behind him with various drawers open.

I shoved my hands in the pockets of my jeans. I'd worn work clothes for a reason. These were the old clothes I'd worn to work on the ranch. I'd had to go upstairs to the guest room to retrieve them, and I'd had to sit on the bed and remember how my life had changed in that room when I'd gone to bed and woken up with Summer.

Deep down, I knew I wanted that for me for forever. And smothering that fact was the thought of how scared I was. "Can I help?"

Dad glanced up, surprise lining his brow. "Jonah, hey." He glanced at the organized chaos he was making. "I started with a plan, but now I'm just making a mess."

I wandered closer. "What are you doing?"

"I'm taking one tool box with me to the new place. Did your mom tell you we found a house?"

"She did." I'd called her before I'd stopped in to make sure they were both around. She'd gushed about it. Enthusiasm had lit her voice and she'd mentioned at least three times how new the house was and wouldn't it be nice to live in a place that didn't have such a long to-do list. I didn't think their current house, the place I'd grown up in, was bad, but it was old. The plumbing needed constant maintenance and they'd upgraded electrical years ago. Then there were the drafty windows they had slowly been replacing, and the cabinet upgrades and overhauls Mom had done over the years. I had assumed she'd enjoyed all those projects, and maybe she had. Maybe she'd needed to be busy. But now perhaps she wanted to not have to constantly keep up an old house.

"Congrats."

Dad's smile was broad. "I might not need much for tools, but Rhys is going to have his own. I might as well make sure I take what I foresee needing. Need a wrench set?"

"I have two." One had come from this shop.

His chuckle was good-natured. "I've been wondering

how I ended up with so damn many tools over the years, but a lot of these came from my dad." He shoved a set to the side, making them clatter together. "I feel bad leaving so much for Rhys, but I'm also grateful I don't have to offload this heap onto you, and I'm not talking about the tools."

Surprise filtered through me. I'd stopped in to talk to him about just that. "I was afraid I hadn't done enough and that's why you're giving this place up."

He frowned, turning to fully face me. "Why do you think that?"

"I was working for you and then this happened." I indicated my left side. "And then I was useless. Even when I wasn't useless, I didn't reach out to see what you needed."

He chuffed and put his chin down. His brow furrowed and he shifted his stance a few times. "Jonah . . ." Then he took his ball cap off and scratched his head. "I won't lie. I was worried about you. Hell, I still worry about you. You just do with your kids, you know. But . . ." He dragged in a breath. "You know what I wanted to be when I was a teenager?"

"Excuse me?"

"I wanted to be a mechanic." He looked up at the ceiling of the shop, a wistful smile on his face. "Classic cars."

I gaped at Dad. He'd never told me about this. "We've never owned a classic car."

He barked out a laugh. "Exactly. First, we had kids to take care of. Then we had a ranch to keep going. I admire them, but I couldn't spend money on something like that. Then there was the time." He shook his head. "The ranch sucked up every second."

The guilt returned. If I had been working more, he might've had time to indulge.

"I can see what you're thinking," he said, "and you'd be missing the point. That was my dream as a kid, and I couldn't do it. I was expected to take this place over. I was born to be a rancher, and that was all I could ever do. Don't get me wrong, I love it. But it's not my passion. I don't want to turn my back on retirement because this whole place is on my shoulders. I didn't want that for you. Neither did your mother. We could see you were the same as me, and we'd rather see you do what you love."

Being outdoors. Experiencing the land instead of toiling away on it. "What about Eli?"

"Eli was different. There was nothing else he wanted to do." Sadness took over his features. "It took me a long time to admit that I'd have to give up what's been passed down because Eli was gone, but once your mom and I finally talked about it, we realized we were on the same page. We've given up a lot for this place, and we're tired of it."

"So you're okay with the decision?"

He directed his gaze out the open overhead door. "All land changes hands throughout time. We're lucky to be in a spot where we can decide to sell. It's not getting taken away, and I'm not losing it. The Dunns' time with this ranch is over. Rhys gets to raise his family on it and maybe pass it down to his girls. This burden of mine is his dream. And you're free to keep kicking out that damn fine furniture you make."

"I really enjoy it."

"I know you do. It's what's kept your mom from bodily hauling you out of that place for a haircut."

My laughter surprised me, but I sobered. "I thought I was letting you down, just like I let everyone else down."

"As much as you feel like you failed Eli, so do we," he said gruffly. "I'm not going to get into a competition about whose guilt is stronger. In the end, he made his choice and we're all learning to live with it. Some days are easier than others."

"Yeah," I said hoarsely. I had based the last fifteen years of my existence on that guilt. Then I'd piled more on until I was ignoring every important person in my life. "I fucked things up with Summer."

"Ah. I wondered about that." He leaned against the bench. "What happened?"

"I think . . . I *know* I'm scared."

"You've never been scared of a thing in your life. You used to love when you saw bears out on your hikes."

I was more concerned about moose. I had bear spray; nothing for the moose. "She's different. She wants the family life. Kids." The last word came out rough.

"I see." He crossed his arms and frowned at the floor. "Are you scared of losing her or losing those kids?"

"I've lost her, and that sucks pretty bad." I swallowed hard, pushing down the tide of anxiety. "But kids?" My tongue refused to work. "Fucking terrifying."

His chuckle was dry. "Yeah. They are." He pushed off the workbench and paced in front of me like I'd done with Teller. "I was scared spitless when you were born. If your mom wasn't so damn excited, I might've been a goner before you arrived."

I'd never talked to my parents about my birth, or me as a kid. I'd been interested in living life, not dwelling on the past. Seemed like I was trapped by both the past and future.

"It was easier when Eli arrived." His eyes misted over. "Then we lost him." He dragged in a long breath. "And it fucking hurts every day. But everyone's different, Jonah. Your mom and I are stronger, but it took a lot of work to get here. Would I skip having kids to prevent from having that experience?" He shrugged helplessly. "I can't imagine not having had Eli in my life. I can't imagine not having the memories of his little red baby face, or how he laughed at my stupid jokes, or the way he lived for doing the chicken dance at wedding receptions. The pain was excruciating. It still is, but there's a lot of joy in my memories. A ton of laughter. A lot of love. Do I have regrets? Of course." He dropped his chin to his chest. "Of course. But I'd regret not getting Eli for the nineteen years we had him."

My throat grew thick. "I miss him."

"We all do. But it's not fair to him to use him as an excuse to hide from life. He's not here to defend himself."

"Shit," I coughed out. "Don't hold back, Dad."

"Reckon I've held back enough. You look like someone kicked your puppy, son. Get that girl back. Face down the bear."

"I don't think she'd appreciate being called that."

He chuckled. "Keep that between you and me."

"Dad, there's something I want to talk to you about first. It has to do with—" The approach of an engine stopped my words. I hadn't wanted to broach the subject of Summer's breakup with Eli. It felt like it wasn't my story to tell. Yet I couldn't move forward without everything in the open.

But when I wandered to the doorway, shock rooted me in place. Summer was pulling to a stop by the house. Suddenly, the story could wait. I had to catch my runaway bride one more time.

Summer

My stomach was twisted into a hundred knots. I'd had all week to ponder what I had to do. I should've called. I should've asked to meet them somewhere. Instead, I'd tossed and turned all night and then driven down. It was Saturday morning and I hoped that Adam and Vera were around. If I caught only one, what would I do? The last time I'd just shown up on their ranch, I'd been seeing Eli.

When I had turned down their winding drive, memories had cascaded through my head. Eli and I taking the horses out for a ride—and spying on Jonah doing chores. Eli and I watching movies—and me watching Jonah packing his gear for another trip with my brothers.

Most of my Eli memories came paired with Jonah memories.

World's Crappiest Girlfriend, right here.

I got out of my car and smoothed down the skirt of one of the dresses I had bought for my honeymoon. It was meant for a beach, but it could work for a farm-chic photoshoot when paired with cowboy boots like I wore now. The familiar smells of a ranch in early summer greeted me. Fresh air with a mix of cow manure. Rich soil filled with new growth.

When I walked out of my condo, I sometimes caught a whiff of my neighbor's pot smoke from their back porch. More than once, I'd wondered if I'd gotten a secondhand high pulling weeds in my flower bed. The smell always reminded me of burning ditches. I missed home.

But I was tempted to get back in my car, hope Vera hadn't seen me, and drive away.

No. I wasn't running away again. This was for Jonah as much as me. He wouldn't want to keep this from his parents. I reached the front door and my hand was shaking when I knocked.

Vera opened the door. Her brows lifted and surprise filled her face. "Summer." She smiled and shook her head. "Sorry, I'm having flashbacks. You're at the door again." She laughed. "Nice to see you."

"Do you have a few minutes to talk?"

"Absolutely." She pushed the door open farther. "Come on in. Careful of all the boxes. We can go into the kitchen." She looked past me. "Isn't Jonah with you?"

Shocked at her question, I shook my head and silently panicked. Hadn't he told them we were no longer a thing? What if she asked me? I'd come to confess about Eli. I wasn't ready to break down in front of her over Jonah.

She just shrugged and made space for me to enter.

I stepped in. The scent in here was the same too—a little maple syrupy. Vera must still make pancakes on the weekends. "Is Adam here? I'd like to talk to you both."

"Sure. He's around somewhere. I can give him a call."

The front door opened and my heart jumped in my

throat. I'd almost been counting on the time it'd take Vera to find her husband. But when I turned, it was Jonah I locked eyes with. His hair wasn't styled and it was slightly longer than when I'd seen him last. His gaze simmered with an unidentifiable emotion, but whatever it was, he didn't look happy to see me.

"O-oh. I can come back." I would rush out the door, but Jonah was blocking me.

His dad came in behind him. "Hey, Summer. Nice to see you again."

My knees trembled. I was not a scaredy-cat, but it was daunting enough to face telling Adam and Vera. Jonah knew the story, but he wasn't here as my support. I wanted to dry heave a few times.

"Hi. Um." Did I leave? Did I forge ahead?

"Hey, guys," Jonah said. I wanted to close my eyes and sink into that deep timbre. I missed his voice. "Can I talk with Summer for a few minutes?"

Vera opened her mouth to say something, but Adam circled around Jonah to go to his wife. He smiled at me, almost encouragingly. "Vera, should we get some lemonade out for everyone?"

They disappeared into the kitchen.

"Hey," I said quietly.

Jonah crossed to stop in front of me. "What's going on?" he asked just as softly.

"I need to tell them. They should know the whole story."

"I agree. Want me to be with you?"

The tremor in my legs grew. I wanted to lean on him. Could I sit in his lap when I said the words? I might be determined not to run, but I'd siphon his strength. "You don't mind?"

"No." He brushed the backs of his fingers down my cheek. I turned my head into his touch. "It'll be fine."

"How can you be sure?" My whisper was ragged.

"Because out of all of us, they dealt with the grief the best. Dad just schooled me real hard in the shop."

A shaky laugh left me. "I guess it's my turn. You didn't tell them about us breaking up."

"I didn't want to worry them even more. They'd think I'd regress." He twined his fingers with mine and led me into the kitchen. "And because I didn't want it to be true."

"Me either."

He gave my hand a squeeze. "Come on. First them. Then us."

Us.

Despite my small rise of hope, my legs moved like lead poles. The warm, familiar roughness of his skin kept me rooted to the present. His hold calmed my heart rate.

His parents were sitting at the table. Vera was pouring lemonade into each of the four glasses Adam handed her.

Jonah pulled a chair out for me. My stomach waffled as I sat and settled once he was positioned next to me.

I stared at the lemonade in front of me. Adam and Vera sipped theirs and shifted in their seats. They must sense the heaviness from me.

I licked my dry lips. "I'm going to get right to the point. You two were very important to me, and then I just ghosted you after Eli died." I closed my eyes because I couldn't see their expressions. My determination dipped, then a big, warm hand closed over one of mine again. Jonah's fresh-cut-pine scent surrounded me. I could do this. "I was too afraid to tell you that I broke up with Eli right before he got drunk. I'm the reason why he was drinking."

I sucked in a shuddering breath. There. I'd done it. I had to face whatever repercussions came my way. I wouldn't run away anymore.

Jonah squeezed my hand, and I opened my eyes to him. His supportive expression was exactly what I needed to see.

Vera's eyes were wide, disbelieving. "Summer, have you been holding that in all these years?"

I nodded, tears springing into my eyes. "I'm so sorry. I should've told you, but he'd been so upset and it was my fault."

"No." Adam shook his head, his troubled gaze stuck on the table. "No, it's not your fault. Vera and I haven't come this far to start assigning fault to anyone now."

She barked a laugh and scrubbed her face with both hands. "Oh, Summer. If only you knew how much we've already done that."

Jonah's grip was fused with mine. Did he understand their reaction any more than I did?

Vera's sigh was packed with ironic humor. "We blamed ourselves. You. Jonah. Copper Summit. Ourselves some more. Eli. The pickup manufacturer. Copper Summit some more. Each other."

"We've run the gamut," Adam said. "And if Eli was so upset from the breakup, and that's why he did what he did, then I'm sorry you had to deal with that. I'm truly sorry."

"You two were so young," Vera whispered. "We knew it wouldn't last. Just like we knew you and Jonah might have a thing for each other instead."

Shock slammed through me like a thundercloud. "Was it that obvious? I never wanted to hurt Eli. I swear." I'd been into Jonah, but enough to broadcast to the world I was into him?

She smiled. "Only to those of us who knew both Eli and Jonah. You were close with Eli, but we could tell what you felt wasn't . . . epic. It was more age appropriate in our opinion."

"Eli knew," I whispered.

She couldn't hide her pain, and she exchanged a look with Adam. "I was afraid he'd noticed too, but it was like that for him. You know that."

I nodded. I did. He'd looked up to his big brother, but there'd been a healthy dose of jealousy.

"Don't blame yourself," Adam said gruffly. "Don't blame anyone. Eli was going through more change than he cared to deal with."

"How so?" Jonah asked.

Adam lifted his shoulder. "He was lonely. Summer was in college and I think he could sense they were growing apart." He smiled encouragingly at me. "But it wasn't just you. He missed his friends who'd gone off to college. He wanted to ranch, but he also wanted to live life, and we'd been having talks about how he could see and experience the world and also be tied to a hundred head of cattle."

"He was a little lost, but he was right where he wanted to be," Vera added. "I think we've all been there."

We all nodded. Some of us were still going through that.

Vera's smile turned watery. "Since I know the both of you . . . At least, Summer, I think you're still the same, strong girl who wants to solve everyone's problems but your own?"

I dipped my head before I realized what I was agreeing to. Then I let out a humorless laugh. "What gave you that impression? My canceled wedding with a guy I should've dumped two years before I put on a wedding dress?"

"And why you stayed with Eli." She pinned me with an understanding look. "I know you didn't want to hurt him and we appreciate that more than you can know. None of us could've guessed how it'd turn out, but seeing what Jonah went through almost broke us. And here you are again, and it's clear how much you care for him." Her lips took on an ironic twist. "Only it's nice to see that you two aren't repeating old patterns. You weren't afraid to make Jonah face the truth. And Jonah's been to the house more in the last few months than in the last few years."

"I've only been by three times," Jonah said quietly.

His mom's smile had a hint of sadness. "I know."

I exchanged a look with Jonah. His hand was still on mine. He'd lost some weight and I'd tease him about scurvy later . . . if he meant that thing about an *us*.

"She turned me toward the truth," Jonah said roughly, "but Teller made me face it head-on. That asshole won't leave me alone." Jonah's eyes twinkled. "I also don't want him to."

I smiled weakly, but focused on Adam and Vera. "I should've talked to you both sooner."

Vera's mouth tightened and she looked regretful. "I don't know if I could've heard it much earlier. Like Adam said, we blamed everyone, and you know, I think it was easier to have a round robin for targets. We'll never know, and that's not the point. You told us when you were ready, and we just happened to be ready to hear it."

Adam nodded and clasped his wife's hand like Jonah and I were doing.

I could've floated away from the table, I was so light. Eli's parents didn't hate me. Jonah was still moving forward. And I was . . . content.

"So, what about you two?" Vera asked. "Is everything all right?"

Jonah's dad pinned him with an expectant look.

"That's what I have to talk to Summer about," Jonah said, pushing his chair back. He caught my gaze and I wanted to get lost in his dark eyes. He rose and held his hand out.

I took it, my hopes soaring almost as high as my fears.

Jonah

I walked with Summer outside, under the bright blue sky with the puffy white clouds, and we kept going to the fence line of the pasture behind the barn. The path was gravel until we wrapped around the barn, but even then, the grass was level and neatly trimmed. When he moved, he wouldn't have all the extra work.

"I always thought it was so beautiful out here." She pushed her hair out of her face. She hadn't put it up, and I liked the way the sun glinted off her strawberry highlights.

"I miss you."

The peaceful look on her face turned timid. "I miss you too."

"But I needed the time. I can't deny I needed it."

Her slender neck worked with her swallow. "Good."

"Now, what I need is you." I rubbed a lock of her light strands through my fingers.

"Jonah?" She tilted her head up to me.

"When I was alone and figuring out how much I'd intentionally left myself out of life and why, all I wanted was you. Everything was easier with you. You make me feel like my old self, but also like my present self isn't so bad either."

The corner of her mouth tipped up. "He isn't."

"Then Teller pestered me until I got my head out of my ass. I was terrified, Summer."

"Of me?"

"Of loving you and losing you. Of failing you. Add in kids and I was ready to run, which admittedly wouldn't be far."

"So how do you feel now?"

"Like I'm crazy in love with you."

Her pink lips parted and her small inhale was audible. "You are?"

"So damn in love." I brushed a thumb over her cheek. "Please tell me I didn't fuck up too bad and that you'll give me another chance."

She closed her eyes and turned her cheek into my touch. "I don't want to push you too fast either."

"You didn't. It wouldn't have been fair to you to go at a glacial pace when I've held up so much of my life—and yours—for years already."

"Remember what your parents said. Don't feel guilty over my decisions. I lived my life, and you lived yours, and we both faced our repercussions from that day." She gripped my wrist with her small soft hand. "I love you too."

My heart soared. Goddamn. Summer Kerrigan had fallen in love with my grumpy ass?

She held me in her amber gaze. "What exactly do you want? I need to make sure we do this right and that we're on the same page."

"I want it all. I want to give you that summer wedding you want. I want to parade you around town on my arm. I even took another table order with some guy's collectible baseball cards."

Her gasp was louder this time. "You did? Baseball cards?"

"My eye twitches when I think about it, but also . . ." A slow grin spread across my face. "I had him sign several waivers in case I run into issues and things go wrong. But I'm kind of looking forward to the challenge."

"Are you charging a ton?"

"I can take you anywhere for a honeymoon, sunshine." I dropped a kiss on her forehead. She hadn't fully committed to me. She needed more reassurance and I understood. "As long as it's in driving distance, because I know you hate to fly."

"Jonah," she whispered and she stepped into me. "Are you proposing to me?"

"I'm warning you that I'm going to do it properly."

Her amber eyes swam with emotion—all for me. "I'm warning you that I'll say yes."

Hot damn. This was really happening. I hadn't

fucked up beyond all possibility. "I also have enough socked away to start an addition to the house."

Confusion filled those gorgeous eyes. "Why?"

"More bedrooms. We can make the upstairs your office—shit. Do I need to move to Bozeman?" I was back to messing it up. "I'll go wherever you are. I just need space for a shop—"

She pressed a quick kiss to my mouth. "I want to come home," she whispered. "I can work from anywhere. But are you sure?"

"I've never been more certain." This time, I pressed a kiss to the corner of her mouth. "I'm still terrified, but if I could survive fucking up what I had with you, then I can thrive raising kids with you."

She curled her hands into my shirt. "I've really missed you."

"Then you'll take me back?"

"I already have."

I plastered my mouth to hers and lifted her. She didn't question it, hooking her legs around my hips like the first time I'd done this. Her trust meant more to me than she'd ever know. I walked us backward until her back hit the warm barn wall.

"We shouldn't do this here," I murmured as I kissed my way down her neck.

She clawed at my shoulders but didn't drag my shirt off. We weren't in public, but we were outside. I was relatively sure my parents wouldn't seek us out, but I wouldn't strip her down unless I was sure her privacy was secure.

Good thing she was wearing a dress.

I flipped the material up and skimmed my hands

over her hips and thighs. "I dreamed of you every night," I said into the crook of her neck.

"My own hand *does not* rival you."

"Show me." I pulled away enough to give us a few inches of space. Her legs were still wrapped around me. "Show me how you tried."

Her lips were already puffy and her eyes glazed over. I never thought I'd get to see my sunshine like this again. And here she was. All mine.

She sank her teeth into her lower lip and skimmed her hand down. "I have toys at home."

I groaned. "You're going to bring them with you?"

"You don't want me to throw them out?"

"Tools are tools, sunshine. I happen to be very good with tools. Now, touch yourself."

She shoved her skirt out of the way to reveal a small scrap of pink lace. When her finger dipped underneath the thin material, a ragged moan left me. Why wasn't I the one touching her?

Because I wasn't willing to let her go.

A delicate shudder shook her body when she circled her finger over her clit.

"Are you wet?"

She nodded.

"How wet?"

"Soaked," she groaned.

My fingers were digging into the flesh of her thigh. My erection pounded at the fly of my jeans, but I was riveted on the slow circles she was making. "How fast did you get yourself off?"

"I gave up twice," she said breathlessly. "I wanted you too bad."

Ordinarily, that'd be a turn-on, but not this time. My fear had left her empty and unfulfilled.

A bigger tremor ran through her. "It's not going to take long."

Fuck, no, it wasn't. She was with me. I wasn't the one teasing her clit, but this thing between us was too real for it to matter when we were this close. I ground against her, pressing her finger between us and her eyelids fluttered.

"I can't be loud," she panted. "Your parents."

We were far from the house, but I didn't want to give her a thing to worry about. I captured her mouth again, fusing us together in at least one point on our bodies. I'd be inside her soon. First, she would explode.

I pumped against her hand, giving her more friction. She went rigid, her legs so tight around my hips she'd leave a perfect impression of my jeans on my skin. The shock waves came next. I swallowed the mewls and cries that escaped her lips, sweeping my tongue deep inside.

When she removed her hand and rested her wrist on my shoulder, I used the space to flick the button on my pants loose and rip the zipper down.

The heat of our bodies hit my needy flesh before the swirl of fresh air. I was straining to rip her underwear off and plunge into her, but despite what we'd just talked about, I had to give her what she wanted. And she wanted us on the same page.

I broke our kiss. "I don't have a condom." The box hadn't been touched since she'd left. Like her, I could barely reach a finish when I stroked myself off.

Her eyelids fluttered open. There it was. The dreamy look in her eyes. The flushed cheeks. Her kiss-swollen lips. This was the look I would dedicate my life to putting on her face.

Her hips rolled, like she couldn't help it, and her underwear scraped against my cock. I hissed in a breath.

She glanced down between us. The fabric of her dress had fallen to cover us. "I want this," she said. "But I'm afraid you'll think it was too soon. I'm afraid you'll second-guess—"

I gripped her hips and placed the head of my erection at her entrance. "I'm not second-guessing a thing. You're it for me, and I want to make your dreams come true."

"Get inside me, Jonah."

I shoved in. She cried out, rocking and adjusting to my size and burying her face in my neck.

A long moan left me. How had I ever thought I didn't want a future with her and any kids we might have? How had I ever locked myself inside my shop when I had her in the house?

I drew back and pushed back in.

"Oh, god, Jonah. No toy can compare to you."

"No, they fucking can't." My lips were back on hers and I was devouring her as her greedy body gripped and hugged mine.

Lust was clouding all my thoughts. I'd never had sex without protection. Never. I honestly hadn't thought it'd happen.

Ecstasy. She was warm and wet. I could feel every ripple and flex of her pussy in sharp detail. Sensation was clearer and stronger. I was a man in love. I was a man obsessed with his woman.

I kissed my way to her ear. "I fucking love you."

"Come inside me."

I couldn't get one more thrust in after that. I came long and hard, slamming a hand against the barn wall. She kept her legs anchored around me, but I had her crushed between me and the building.

When awareness returned from beyond the absolute fucking bliss of being back inside the love of my life, I realized I had missed a critical moment. "Goddamn it."

She turned her face into mine. "What's wrong?" she murmured.

"I didn't make sure you came a second time."

Her chuckle vibrated right through me and coaxed my mouth into a smile. I should've seen to her pleasure first instead of being taken over by her.

She nibbled along my neck. "How sure are you that your parents won't come looking for us?"

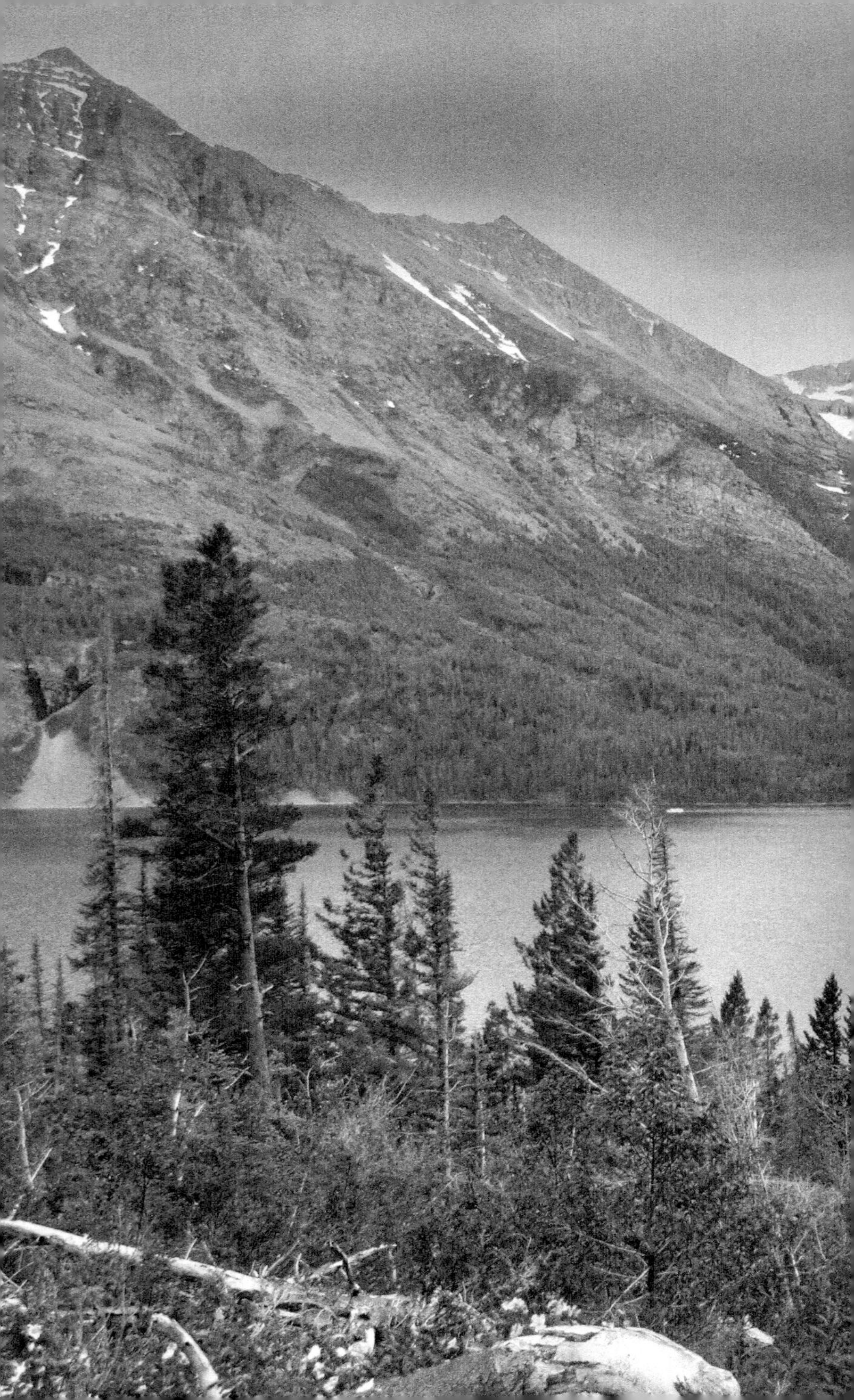

CHAPTER TWENTY-SEVEN

Summer

The grin on Jonah's face could almost make me jealous. He was leaning back against the straining fishing rod. We were on Tate's pontoon. This was the first official time Jonah had gotten out on the water since his accident. I should've left today for the guys, but I couldn't resist seeing Jonah enjoying an activity he used to obsess about.

Autumn and Teller had also joined us. Scarlett was home with the younger kids, while Chance and Tate played tour guides.

We'd dug out a lot of his equipment from the storage room in the garage. Even the tents. I'd even joked about setting one up in the backyard once the construction on the addition started.

Only a month had gone by since we'd reconnected against the back of the barn. I wasn't pregnant yet, but that was fine. I was enjoying my time with Jonah, planning a laid-back wedding at Mama's house, and finishing my move into his cabin—our cabin. Teller and Tenor had given me the office in Copper Summit that I had used when I was supposed to be on my honeymoon. We'd had a talk about hiring another manager for the Bozeman site. I didn't want to have to commute as much as was required, especially during the winter and when we expanded our family.

A small bark sounded from my feet. I picked up our black Lab puppy. He wasn't a service animal, but we were training him to know Jonah and when he might need help. That way, when Jonah and Teller camped outside in someplace that wasn't our backyard, they'd have Stormy for protection. Jonah didn't push me to get over my aversion to camping, and I was grateful he and Teller were discovering all the things Jonah could do. His first choice for an outdoorsy trip was the valley his house overlooked. The land Daddy had gifted me. Our land.

I smooshed the puppy's soft little face and scratched his ears. "You need a nap."

Teller's shadow fell over me as he cheered on Jonah's catch. He reeled in one of the rainbow trout this lake was stocked with, his smile wide and a jubilant cry leaving his mouth.

"Nice catch." Chance was right next to Jonah, ready to help. And Jonah let him. Chance made sure Jonah got a picture with the fish.

Teller turned to me, his gaze falling to the puppy in my arms who refused to miss any fun before he blinked too long and fell fast asleep. "I still say Stormy's a stripper's name."

I rolled my eyes. "Then the dog and the stripper should be honored." The name was more than a thought. Jonah and I had been brought together by winter storms, and we wanted to honor our history. Stormy was a part of our future.

So was this. Being on the lake with family. I'd even heard Tate telling Jonah and Teller about a spot he'd found for fly-fishing that was fairly flat with minimal rocks. The interest on Jonah's face had told me that there'd be a guys' fly-fishing trip soon. Good.

Autumn crossed her legs next to me. She'd already caught her limit of fish, always the lucky duck at hunting and fishing, as my brothers would say. "We're going to be able to feed everyone tonight."

After our barn reconnection, the first place we'd stopped—well, other than at Curly's to eat, since our appetites had roared back after our barn sexfest—was at Mama's. She'd been worried about me and now she was ecstatic. Thrilled in a way she'd never been when I'd told her about Boyd's quick proposal, or with any other guy I'd told her about. Tenor, Lane, and Cruz were getting the yard ready for the ceremony in two weeks, and Mama already had the house spotless.

Autumn propped her elbows behind her and tilted her face to the sun. "Are you getting excited?"

I didn't have to ask what she was talking about: the small, casual summer wedding on my family's land that I had always wanted.

I had a simple white dress that swirled around my legs and fell off my shoulders. A summer dress. My dream dress. My sisters and Scarlett had bought their soft pink dresses—any style they wanted. They could also do their hair how they wanted. My brothers and Adam would stand up with Jonah.

He already had his black jeans and white dress shirt.

We'd both wear cowboy boots and we'd say our vows under the setting sun. Then we'd celebrate with our family into the wee hours of the night. Copper Summit bourbon would be served, but everyone was staying over. None of us were having as much as one sip and driving. Jonah hadn't asked, and neither had I, but Tate had spread the word. Everyone accepted the plan.

A wedding that would turn into a giant sleepover—except for the bride and groom. We had plans to be loud, so we'd drink water and punch and return home to our bed. If we made it that far for the first time together as husband and wife. "I'm so damn excited, Autumn."

She shoulder-bumped me. "Good. You're for-real happy this time."

"Next year, I will legit look forward to Valentine's Day."

"I have a feeling your gift will be wood of some sort."

This time I shouldered her and snickered. "I like his wood gifts."

The guys looked toward us. Jonah was readying his line to cast again, but I only grinned. He gave me a hot look that said he hadn't heard what we were giggling about and he didn't care. He liked seeing and hearing me laugh almost as much as when I came.

"God, what I wouldn't give for a guy to give me that look," Autumn said wistfully.

I gave her an understanding pat. "I'm glad you're not settling for less. Trust me. It's not worth it."

She shrugged. "There is that. Hey, did I tell you what some of us teachers are doing?" When I shook my head, she twisted in her seat to face me. "We're going on a trip to Vegas. A girls' weekend."

"Fun! When?"

"We have a long weekend in October. Scarlett's not coming. She and Tate are taking the kids to Disneyland. But there'll be four of us."

"Promise me you're not going to Gideon James's hotel and casino." The land sale wasn't yet final and Gideon was fighting my brothers and interfering with his dad. What should've been a one-and-done deal was stretching out and growing more contentious.

"I'm not sure where we're going yet." She sat forward and picked at the hem of her shorts. "I doubt he'd want a Bailey in his hotel, and I'm close enough." She wrinkled her nose. "He might think I actually have power in the company."

This wasn't the first time she'd been cryptic about the importance of her role with Copper Summit. "Autumn, have you talked to the guys?"

"The guys," she echoed, and yes, that was part of the conflict. I thought my sisters had accepted that the guys would have more of a role in the distillery and the ranch than us. Mama and Daddy had never treated us like we were lesser Baileys, but we'd naturally stood back and let the brothers take charge.

"They'll listen." They might actually appreciate the help, but one didn't look at Autumn with her arts-and-craft-filled house and think she wanted a manager role.

"I know. I love my job, but I guess it's just the principle. I'm salty about it, that's all."

"That's not all."

She waved her hand like she was erasing the conversation. "I'll be more relaxed after my vacation. It's been a while since I got away."

"Be careful there, yeah?"

She rolled her eyes. "What trouble are a bunch of teachers going to get up to in Vegas?"

Jonah carefully walked toward me. If the water got choppy, he had brought a wide-based cane, but so far he hadn't needed it. He sat next to me.

"She thinks you're getting me wood for Valentine's Day," I said.

He smirked. "Sunshine, I'll get you whatever you want, but I will always have plenty of wood for you."

Seven months later...

Summer

This year, Valentine's Day was much different. I wasn't in an itchy wedding dress and I wasn't dreading a church full of family, friends, and future in-laws I couldn't stand. I was in a living room with a special present for Jonah. I'd gotten home from work an hour ago, but I'd made a stop I hadn't told Jonah about.

I was cuddled on the couch, in the old blanket Vera had made for me when I was a teen. Jonah was busy in the shop, taking fewer but more complex, customized projects like the collectible epoxy tables to free up his time. He could charge top dollar for those, which meant he could schedule long gaps between orders to do what he wanted, like make his parents matching nightstands. He still sold his hobby pieces at the coffee shop, but with Myles's help, he'd started a foundation in Eli's name. People who needed mobility modifications in their homes could get financial aid.

The savory smells of an elk roast Jonah had put in a Crock-Pot before work filled the air. He and my brothers had split the one elk they'd gotten while hunting last fall and then donated another portion of the meat.

I'd made a fresh salad to have with it.

A snowstorm was on the horizon and I'd also brought home my work laptop and a load of groceries. Just in case I got to be stranded with my husband again.

The back door opened. The thumps of Jonah kicking snow off his boots rang through the house. Stormy's claws clattered against the floor and then the sloppy noise of lapping water filled the silence.

"Hey, sunshine," he called.

"Hey, mountain man."

His footsteps and the thump of his cane on the floor grew closer. His leg bothered him more before a weather change. I'd give him a nice long massage tonight. And he'd give me a nice long orgasm or three.

His cool arms wrapped around me. He smelled like fresh-cut pine and impending snowstorm. "Happy Valentine's Day."

"This had been the best one ever." We hadn't done anything different than any other day. With the snow on the way, we hadn't wanted to go out, and it was a weekday. I'd told Jonah that every normal day with him blew away any other day.

He said his greatest gift was when he went to sleep with me and woke up to me, and being inside me, and when he ate with me. He would've kept going if I hadn't shushed him with a kiss.

He reached behind him and produced a short, flat

box wrapped in pink paper with red hearts. "I made this for you."

Grinning, I ripped the paper off. The box was plain with no logos. When I took the lid off, I squealed. A thick pair of pink-and-cream woolly mittens. When we shoveled, I always complained about ruining my cute pairs working outside.

Usually he let me run the skid steer and stay out of the wind.

I put my hands into the cozy mittens. "I love them, and they're so cute." I grabbed a gift bag at my feet that was wrapped in similar wrapping paper. "Here's yours."

His face was full of interest when he came around the couch and sat next to me. He always looked stunned to get a gift. Christmas with him had been interesting. We'd gone to his parents' new place for Christmas Eve. The evening had been cozy and quiet, a way to mellow out before the chaos of Christmas at Mama's.

He opened the bag and a deep laugh rumbled out of him. His grin stayed broad while he withdrew a black pair of Carhartt winter gloves. "I needed a new pair."

"Great minds think alike." I reached behind me where I'd hid the other part of his present. "But that's not all."

"Oh shit, you got me more?"

The panic on his face was endearing. I withdrew the baggie. "It's for both of us."

Shock stole his expression as he took the pregnancy test from my hands. In block letters was PREGNANT. "You're pregnant?"

"Yes." I clapped, my excitement welling over and prompting tears and giggles and more clapping. I didn't know what to do with myself. "Can you believe it?"

He set the test on the cushion on the other side of him and wrapped me in a huge hug. "I can't fucking believe how amazing this life is with you."

A cold nose pushed between us. Laughing, we encompassed a wiggling Stormy in our embrace. He was still a puppy but he was now a big puppy who'd eat the wrapping paper if I didn't pick it up soon.

First a dog, now a baby. "Our family's growing," I murmured.

"Sure is." He pulled me close to him. "We might get stormed in again."

"We might. How are we going to pass the time?" I asked coyly.

He took the remote and flipped to a movie. *Runaway Bride*. He glanced at me, smirking. "It's tradition."

I snuggled in closer. "The only place I'm running is closer to you."

Want to find out happens when Autumn stays at the same casino and hotel that Gideon James works in? Her trip might include bourbon, a wedding chapel, and one very broody CEO. Read more in Bourbon Promises.

You're officially invited to Summer and Jonah's wedding! To read about their happy day, sign up for my newsletter at walkerrosebooks.com/newsletter and you'll get a link to my bonus content and a free copy of Bourbon Bachelor.

ABOUT THE AUTHOR

I live the dream in my own slice of paradise where I get to enjoy colorful sunsets from my rocking chair while I'm working. I have my very own romance hero with Mr. Rose and there's more than a few little rose buds running around. A couple aren't so little anymore! We keep things interesting with cats and a dog and the critters that roam though the yard (fingers crossed the mountain lions stay away).

walkerrosebooks.com

ALSO BY WALKER ROSE

Bourbon Canyon Series

Bourbon Bachelor

Bourbon Lullaby

Bourbon Runaway

Bourbon Promises

Printed in Great Britain
by Amazon